SHINING

LIKE

the

SUN

S T E P H E N   O R R was born in Adelaide in 1967, studied science and education and taught in a range of country and metropolitan schools. One of his early plays, *Attempts to Draw Jesus*, became his first novel, shortlisted for the *Australian*/Vogel's Literary Award.

Since then he has published ten novels (most recently, *Sincerely, Ethel Malley*) and two volumes of short stories (*Datsunland* and *The Boy in Time*). He has been nominated for awards such as the Commonwealth Writers' Prize, the Miles Franklin Award and the International Dublin Literary Award.

SHINING

LIKE

the

SUN

STEPHEN ORR

Wakefield
Press

Wakefield Press
16 Rose Street
Mile End
South Australia 5031
www.wakefieldpress.com.au

First published 2024

Cover designed by Duncan Blachford
Edited by Maddy Sexton, Wakefield Press
Typeset by Jesse Pollard, Wakefield Press

ISBN 978 1 92304 227 8

A catalogue record for this
book is available from the
National Library of Australia

Wakefield Press thanks
Coriole Vineyards for
continued support

The mystery of life is not salved by success, which is an end in itself, but in failure, in perpetual struggle, in becoming.

Patrick White

Posterity is a whim. A shapeless litter of old bones: the midden of a vulgar beast: the most capricious and immense mass public of them all – the dead.

Orson Welles

In Louisville, at the corner of Fourth and Walnut, in the center of the shopping district, I was suddenly overwhelmed with the realization that I loved all those people, that they were mine and I theirs, that we could not be alien to one another even though we were total strangers. It was like waking from a dream of separateness . . . This sense of liberation from an illusory difference was such a relief and such a joy to me that I almost laughed out loud . . .

As if the sorrows and stupidities of the human condition could overwhelm me, now I realize what we all are. And if only everybody could realize this! But it cannot be explained. There is no way of telling people that they are all walking around shining like the sun.

Thomas Merton, *Conjectures of a Guilty Bystander*

PART I

1

Selwyn. Three hundred people coming and going, dying, lost in the cracks. Let me paint a picture, a streetscape really, because the town is just a junction, and the junction a three-way tussle over nothing. You drive in, turn your head a few times, say something like, *Well, at least they've got a pub*, before stopping at the famous signpost, reading some of the fifty suggestions, deciding you'd rather be somewhere else, and leaving (I told our mayor, Patrick, we shouldn't be putting ideas in people's heads). You can do it in under a minute: past the bed and breakfasts, Selwyn Area School, what used to be the deli, although now it's an IGA. You don't even need a minute, really. Monk's Pub to your left (plenty about that later), and the Eat Inn, with its promise of burgers and fries. Quinn's Craft Shop. You get the picture. If you put your foot down you can get in and out in thirty seconds. Past Mrs Quinn's husband, Spencer, who makes biblical tiles with nature scenes, coats them with lacquer and sells them out front of his shop. Not sells. Gives them away. Tourists walking past, wondering what it's all about, *The Lord said unto Paul* . . . All of which makes us seem a little backward. Patrick has asked him to move them, but he says he won't, can't be made to.

Maybe I've started the wrong way. It's not that Selwyn is small, inward-looking, boring, cliquey. That's not the thing. For instance, there's Lillimar Gift Gallery. I'll tell you about Mr and Mrs Lillimar later, but if you look inside you'll find dinosaur teeth set in resin, golf ball-sized meteorites and cards decorated with orchids, as well as Mrs Lillimar's oil paintings of mute swans and voles.

We get some tourists, but most people are on their way somewhere else: the national park, rock paintings, Robinson Caves. Interesting enough, but the money's better spent in Selwyn. The Railway Hotel (though we haven't got one), the Tea Junction at the Y-junction, although the Thomases are looking for someone to take the lease. Tricky spot. No parking. Although you'd think people could walk a few metres from the Shell. Wander down the road to Monk's, open the door, listen to the crackle of wood from the fire in the dining room. And there's Wilf, busy behind the bar, overfilling pints, free tastings for out-of-towners, each of the thirteen types of whisky he keeps behind the bar. 'This is our biggest seller,' he says, sliding the Tullamore down the side of the glass, warming it in his palms, presenting it to a couple from Perth who taste it, smile, wait for more. Although as our story begins, Wilf isn't behind the bar, but upstairs, in his room, writing to his brother, Colin, the one who got away (Wilf tells everyone) to America, to Los Angeles, with its towers and burgers and theme parks (Wilf's never been, but Colin's always sending him photos: 'Come on, brother, all this awaits!'). But Wilf would never leave Selwyn. Which is what this story's about.

Wilf Healy – eldest of three, healer of stones, maker of bones, an eighty year vintage, lover of whiskies (rousing them from a sleep of frosty bees), father of a dead son, husband of a buried wife, walker, driver, deliverer, story-teller, shit-stirrer, toenail-clipper and non-reader – sat at desk running a pen through his fingers. He decided, and began: 'Lucy said she had to stop. Fair enough, but the agreement was that I'd do Monday and Thursday, she'd keep Tuesday and Wednesday, the school would find a teacher, or maybe Noah – who never leaves his office – on Friday. I can't keep this going five days a week, morning and night. The run takes over an hour, and it's just me. Me, brother!' Wilf put down his pen, read what he'd written and decided it was too dramatic. Also, what would his brother make of it? Wilf, and more of his dramas. Is this what he told his neighbours? 'My stupid brother won't leave the place. His problem's that he's never learned to say no.'

Wilf screwed up this attempt, threw it in the bin in the borderlands that separated study from kitchen, from bedroom. This big square of life, with its kitchen lino and dog-smelling carpet, although she was long dead. He'd measured it. Seven strides from bed to desk; eleven from desk to sink. No bathroom or toilet; he shared these with the guests. A scaly bath, old shower and a crapper in the Amenities. Hardly twenty-first century accommodation, but this was Selwyn. He flattened another piece of paper on his desk and wrote: 'What would you do in my position?'

Although he knew, exactly. Colin would pack his bags, throw them in the car and drive off without so much as a goodbye. Because that's exactly what he'd done, years ago. He'd always had that streak. Wilf couldn't fathom people who couldn't love, drive, feed and help others. He and Colin were never blood brothers; just two of three boys from the same mother and father. Wilf even wondered why he bothered writing to him. He underlined the words: <u>What would you do in my position?</u> But more importantly, he thought, what to do next? At eighty, he'd had enough. He wanted to retire from everything: the bus run, the pub, the chemist (the list grew longer by the week, month, year – as Selwyn's young people left, others went broke, the old folk died).

Wilf walked the few steps to his bed, sat down, removed his boots and listened to the insistent thump of fuckery. He moved closer until his ear touched the wall, until the pace quickened, the mattress responded, the couple in the next room (a pair of Frenchies) went about their business. Muffled voices. A minute later the television started blaring and he heard more dramas – scripted, orchestrated, phoney. As for him, he didn't have a television, although if there was something on the telly (for instance, *The Rockford Files*) he'd wander down to the guest room and watch it there, or read a soiled magazine, or make conversation with someone from Broome, or Glasgow.

Wilf removed his socks, his pants, folding them across the back of his chair. His shirt, which would do another day. Then he sat back on his bed and listened to the Frenchies and made out *Oubli langeur travais Silwoon*. He wondered what it meant. *Selwyn*, he wanted to say, through the wall. He wondered what they were talking about. Criticisms, no doubt. Because, mostly, people didn't get Selwyn, didn't understand the place, the people, the music they played, the dishes they cooked. If people understood, they'd stay.

So he was glad it was time for bed. He welcomed it, every night, like a little rehearsal death, a practice for never getting up. Sleep was sweet, and there was never enough of it. Some nights he wanted to lay down, pass out, never wake, never know what the next day might hold (more work, no doubt). But every morning he woke to the alarm, the rubbish truck in the back lane, a crow squawking up and down Sullivan Street. And every day he got up, put on his pants and got to work.

But for now, sleep. He switched off his light and the globe clunked, hummed and swung in the chilled air. Back to bed, two legs under the covers, his small arse, fat belly, sagging tits and old chin, scaly like the bath, liver-specked.

'Shit!'

Remembering, getting up, switching on the light and marching into the kitchen. Filling a glass, finding his heart tablets and taking them. Returning to bed, the moonlight settling across his sheets.

He could always find solace, he thought. A widower's consolation. But although he fiddled a bit, in the end it didn't seem worth the effort. Every year it got harder to imagine the way the tummy sank, the swan circled its little tuft of wilderness. Instead, there was the same photo he studied every night: him, Colin and Brian as twelve, ten and nine-year-olds. The three of them, arms around shoulders, grinning at their dad, his new Leica. The farm on Louth (their childhood years), sheep in the background, and off to the side, their mother calling to their dad to hurry up and fix the water. And beside this photo, Nancy and Steven, aged forty and twelve or thirteen. But more about that later.

Maybe it was ten minutes, maybe fifteen, and Wilf was half asleep when there was a knock on the door. He stirred, waited, and it returned. 'Wilf?'

'Darrin?'

'A job for Mr Daly.'

'Someone else can do it.'

'It's Mr O'Loughlin again. Maybe it could wait until tomorrow?'

'I was asleep.'

Wilf could hear him leaving. 'Wait!' He climbed out of bed, shook the little bit of sleep from his head and stood, hurriedly dressed and appeared in the doorway. 'What time is it?' he said to Darrin.

'Just after twelve.'

'What is it?' Extending his hand.

'Mr Daly reckons it's urgent.'

Wilf twisted his foot to get his shoe on. 'I don't see how people can't . . .' Took the double-pack of pills and slipped them in his pocket. 'Tell George I only agreed to do it during the day. And when's Jack back?'

'I don't know.'

'No one knows anything when it suits them. Middle of the night and I'm eighty years old. You should hurry up and get your licence, do it yourself.'

Twenty minutes later, Wilf and his 1966 Morris J2 were driving up Corkscrew Road, a series of hairpin bends that kept getting higher and higher, tighter and tighter, each stretch narrowing as it moved through the sleety night. There was no point rushing. If Mr O'Loughlin died he died. One wrong turn and it was an early retirement. This slippery road; this undriveable road, even on a good day. The council had been asked to do something about it, but Patrick had just said (words to the effect), 'How else do you make a road go up a hill?' Which was a good point. Eventually he reached the top, noticed his fuel light, muttered, 'Jesus and fuckin' Joseph.' He wondered why he was here in the rain at one in the morning, in his cold van, fogging up, wiping the windscreen, delivering medicine to some old bastard who couldn't plan his own life.

Ten minutes later he stood in a mist on Mr O'Loughlin's doorstep, handed him the medicine and said, 'Bit of a time to remember, James.'

Mr O'Loughlin explained that he would've waited until tomorrow, but when he started getting pains he panicked and thank you, anyway, Wilf, you're a lifesaver – literally.

On the way home, Wilf wondered whether it was time to get a mobile phone. This thought returning, tumbling, jumping around his brain as he watched the petrol gauge, the light brighter and angrier as he drove down the corkscrew, pumping his brakes (they needed fixing, too), wondering whether he should drive off the edge, a few rolls, settling, then poof, a little flame, a bigger one, but what did it matter if you were already dead?

2

Next morning, Wilf was off again. The Morris, a great buy, his father had promised, showing his boys the van on a cold day in 1976. Mr Mooney, the elder of JM Mooney and Sons, had walked past, stopped to say, 'Morrises are known for their poor suspensions, Tom.'

Mr Healy, of Healy and sons, had half-expected this. 'How's that, Jack?'

'They can't handle corrugations, and potholes.'

On like this, because Jack Mooney had owned a Morris and knew all about them, and most cars, really, because he'd completed twelve months of a mechanic's apprenticeship, sometime before the aviation diploma, the economics degree, none of which could be true (Tom had told his sons, lined up in front of their house), seeing how the old liar had only lived in Sydney for twelve months. As Mr Mooney had walked toward town, Tom had said to Wilf, Colin and Brian: 'Mind you don't end up like that old fuck.'

Unusual, because none of the boys could remember their father swearing before.

Now, Wilf fought with the gearbox he'd been cursing for decades. He could fix it, but it worked, so why spend money you didn't have? He pulled out from Monk's Lane, turned right and headed for the school. A few kids (he could name them all, their parents, aunts and uncles) walked along the few inches of path that history had granted them. Pants half down, cuffs dragging, no belt; and the tie they wore loose, like someone was about to garrotte them. And the *way* they walked. Dragging their feet.

Like school didn't matter. The most important years of your life, he'd say to them, helping them weed or fertilise. But they'd always look at him like he was a loaf of out-of-date bread, a lame plover, a mile marker that didn't mean anything to anyone.

Here was the thing: if he did what his brothers had – run, as far as he could, as fast as he could – that would be the future. That sort of fuck-you-silly-old-man glare, the look as they reached for their phones, the deflated bodies as they sat in class watching YouTube on their laptops. The future didn't look after itself. It had to be heated, bent to shape, cooled, the rough edges filed down before they did damage.

Wilf turned into the main drive, tooted for some of the kids to move (they didn't) and followed the service road to the school farm. He parked, got out, and the farmhand, a boy the school employed to feed and water the animals, came out of his shed and said, 'Dave's sick today.'

'It's alright for some.'

'He said it's all ready to go.'

'How's your mother, Jay?'

'She's as thin as a rake, Mr Healy—'

'Wilf.'

'But the doctor said she's past the worst of it.'

Jay Griffin led Wilf into the agriculture shed and the four crates of student-grown vegetables it had become Wilf's job to distribute. 'The carrots are small, but Dave said we shouldn't charge as much.'

'He did, did he?' Lifting the first of the crates and carrying them out to his van. 'Give us a hand, will you, Jay. I'm not getting any younger.'

Jay helped him and a few minutes later they had the van packed. Carrots. Potatoes. A few hothouse tomatoes that had lost their colour. A couple of cucumbers, but they were small and wrinkly and unappealing.

'Tell him I'll drop the money.' Closing the door, and wiping his hands on his pants.

'I saw Connor, Mr Healy.'

'Did you?' But then thinking about it. 'Where?'

'Him and Roman, down near the boat ramp.'

'What were they up to?' Not that he wanted to know his great-nephew's movements.

'Don't know whether I should say.'

'Good or bad?' Getting in and starting the engine.

'They should be in school, shouldn't they?'

'Should be, Jay.' He didn't want to hear more. Then he'd have to tell his niece, and there'd be more drama, and all of that would be down to him to fix, too.

'I'll tell Dave you'll drop the money.'

'Good boy, Jay.' Like a domesticated goat.

As Wilf drove off, Jay said, 'I couldn't tell exactly, but it looked like they were ...'

Wilf put up his window. If you didn't hear, it didn't happen. He could guess anyway. But then, on the way back to the main gate, he saw his great-nephew walking toward the senior block, carrying one of his guitars in a pillowcase. Connor was seventeen, tall, red-faced, a boy in the beginnings of a man's body. He walked head down, into the wind. Wilf slowed, called to him and said, 'How's Mum?'

Connor shrugged.

'Tell her I'll pop around later.'

He almost smiled. 'Righto. She's been up ... cooking.'

'You do it for her, boyo.'

'She won't let me.'

Connor didn't want to stop, so Wilf headed back to town. South, past the pub, tapping the gauge to make the petrol light go off, although it wouldn't. Spencer lining up his tablets along the footpath – Jesus in his boat pulling in his own net, a big Jay-faced fish telling him the turnips had gone mouldy.

Wilf pulled into the Shell, flicked the lid and started filling the Morris. As he did he thought, teachers get paid, Noah gets paid, everyone gets paid except me. Not even a few quid for petrol. Then he worked out how he might say it: *Listen, Noah, I know I offered but that was a few years back and I'm getting older and there are so many jobs ... I'm thinking of retiring.*

Noah saying, *I would, but I'm here till nine every night. With the drop in enrolments, I'm two teachers down.*

That's how it always ended. With him smiling, turning, leaving, and saying, *If you think of anyone.*

Wilf went in and paid. As he continued east, he reached back, found a stick of celery and started eating. It wasn't much; thin and spindly, grown with as much love as the podcasters could muster. Ten minutes later he arrived at Bobby Mullan's farm. It had seen better days. The weeds growing the length of the driveway, scrap iron, piles of bricks and wood and gates that had become a nursery for foxes, the house itself full of cracks. He drove toward the farm sheds, got out and called, 'Bobby?'

'In here.'

Bobby had three dogs, but they didn't look fed, ribs and bony arse, and Wilf avoided patting them because of the froth around their mouths. 'I gotta get started.'

'Just a minute.'

And here too, Wilf thought. This is not a problem of my making. Bobby and his brother had grown vegetables for years, for lifetimes, if you considered their father, and his … Bobby had delivered his crop in his van, now sitting rusting, tyreless and windowless, full of roosting hens. Until he got too old, threw it in and convinced Wilf to continue delivering for him ('You can keep a quarter of everything you get'). But then Bobby had explained, 'I've got thirteen good customers, all of them old, unable to get to town. They rely on me, Wilf.'

'I suppose I could give it a go for a few weeks. But only until you find someone.'

'Of course. I can't let people down, Wilf. It's not my way – *our* way. James, he's housebound, you know that. What'll come of him?'

What'll come of me? Wilf thought, sixteen years later, as he continued into Bobby's shed.

They shook hands. But it wasn't a matter of vegetables so much as Bobby's Air Camper, a small kit plane he'd been building for years. Here, under a pair of old globes, the wing struts held tight by wires, the beginnings of a cockpit with the control column already plumbed in, the engine sitting in its bay. And on a desk, a deep pile of drawings that had turned yellow with the very idea of flying, although Bobby often told Wilf: Before I croak it, even if it's just the wheels off the ground. As Wilf thought: Too old to deliver vegetables, but not fly.

Bobby was knocking one of the spars with a hammer. 'It's ready to go.'

'I've been meaning to have a word about these deliveries.'

'I've got the rudder coming Thursday. You want to come and see?'

'Yes, no … the deliveries? I've got so many commitments, and I've been thinking … Listen, I'm eighty years old, I can't keep this up.'

Bobby put down his hammer, picked up his first box of potatoes and said, 'I better help you then?' He was out the door, across his yard, opening Wilf's van. Wilf picked up the carrots and followed. 'You originally said—'

'Yes, yes, I know. Frank Hogan's boy. Frank says he might be able to help out come November. If you could hold on till then.'

'But you said that last year.'

'Now he's back from England. You could keep more …' Stopping, turning to Wilf. 'Half the money then.'

'The money's not the problem. It's my hips, and back. Look at you, what are you, eighty-three?'

'Five, eighty-five. A lot happens in those coupla years, Wilf.' Returning to the shed, and the next box of vegetables.

'Maybe, but … *Bobby!*'

Bobby stopped, looked surprised, like he hadn't seen any of this coming. 'But you agreed.'

'That was a long time ago.'

'Well …' Picking up the next box and returning to the van. Wilf followed, and they went in and out until the van was loaded. Then Bobby slid the door closed and said, 'It's either this or I give it up.'

'Now I know what you're doing.'

Bobby returned to the shed, and the spar. 'A fella came to see me about a month ago. He said, *Mr Mullan, this is very good soil, rich, lots of iron,* and he's right, Wilf.'

Wilf waited, arms crossed, in the glow of the twin bulbs.

'He said, *Mr Mullan, I work for* . . . I forget, some other fella, *and he's interested in buying a few hundred acres of your land.*'

'Who was this fella?'

'I can't remember. Anyway, I thought of you, I thought of all this land, and the money it could fetch, and the work it could save me, and me being eighty-four . . .'

'Five.'

'Nearly. And I thought, Maybe that's the go? Sell it all, spread the money around. I can't be out ploughing the ground forever.'

Wilf waited.

'I *could* do that, Wilf, but you know, I love the land.'

'I think that's an excellent idea, selling. We've all got to think of the future, Bobby.'

'I could but . . .' Bobby dared to look at Wilf, but he was giving nothing away.

'Some fella, was it?'

'You know, a big company, they buy up fifty farms and plant crops. That's the future. Hold this.' Offering a stringer.

Wilf held it, and Bobby fixed it. 'You can't tell me you wouldn't miss the money, Wilf. Monk doesn't pay you much.'

Wilf knew there was no point. 'So where do you intend flying it?'

'Like I said, I've got a few fields.'

Wilf walked back to his van. As he pulled out, Bobby was watching him. Wilf thought he saw a grin on his face, but maybe it was just the light. He drove further east, to his first customer, Mrs Buckley. She came out and told him which vegetables she needed and he weighed them in a scale hanging inside his Morris. He took her money and gave her the change. She said she wouldn't bother with the school vegetables, and he agreed. 'I'll pass that on, Mrs Buckley.'

'Kids today wouldn't know a vegetable.'

'You're right.'

'But Bobby's carrots are the best I've ever had.'

Wilf wasn't there. None of this was his business. School turnips, Bobby Mullan, Mrs Buckley, the onion skins on the floor of his van, the paint all scratched where his father used to load tools and pallets. He was off, again, in the mist, holding Steven high in the air, realising, for the first time, this is where life began, and possibly ended.

'Tell them there's no use selling tomatoes like that,' Mrs Buckley said.

'I'll pass it on.'

Wilf took three hours to finish his run. On the way back he slowed past the road. *The road.* A right turn from the MacDermott's place (Steven had been making his own deliveries). He pulled over (as he always did) and studied the geography. The way the corner was blind, still; how it had all been a matter of time; and how, after, everyone had told him the council, Patrick, all of them, should be held responsible. Although they never were. Imagine starting all that. The road was clear now. It had been resurfaced. But this was the spot. He could see it, and hear it. The way he slowed toward the two steaming cars, stopped, and ran.

3

Wilf returned to Monk's, threw his celery-smelling clothes into the laundry basket ready for washing (his job, too, every Wednesday and Saturday), went back to his room, finished his letter to his brother and put it in his pocket. He'd hung one of Spencer's plaques on his wall. 'For I know the plans I have for you'. He wondered what. Time was running out. Maybe He'd help him win the lotto. Maybe he was about to meet some thoughtful, caring, good-at-baking lady friend. Is that what God had in store? Or something else? A crash on the way to Milparinka? Spencer had chosen a jungle with panthers and pygmy people. Wilf wondered if he was telling him something. Maybe you had to travel to find fortune. Maybe *that* was his problem.

Wilf went down to the bar and saw the Frenchies sipping cocktails in front of the fire it was his job to stock and stoke. He wondered if he should make conversation, apologise for last night. But he didn't feel up to it. Instead, he went into the kitchen, to the girl they employed three nights a week to make meals. Karen Quinn (daughter of Spencer and Grace, friend of Connor) could cook, sort of. She had a nose ring and black lips, but help was hard to find, and the menu was simple. Now she was mixing some sort of powder in hot water, and Wilf said, 'What's that?'

'Eggs.'

'Haven't we got any?'

'No.' Like that, a why-should-I-care-if-we-don't-have-eggs face.

Wilf checked the fridge. 'You can't serve powdered eggs.'

'It's for emergencies.'

'It's not an emergency. *Wait*, for God's sake.'

Wilf stormed from the kitchen, the pub, checked both ways and crossed the road. He went into the IGA and found a dozen eggs, approached the counter and said to Simon Gould, 'Karen's using powdered stuff. Bloody hopeless (don't tell her mum, we need the help).' Simon scratched his nose and said, 'Mum does what she can, but she's getting on.'

'Don't worry about your mum. Say hello for me.'

'These were laid this morning.' Indicating the shit and feathers.

'Of course.' They continued discussing food, freshness, customers, and kids that just didn't care. Wilf said, 'He pays her well enough . . .'

Like this, for another minute, until Wilf guessed Karen would be cooking the powdered egg, serving it to the Frenchies, who'd send it back, say they'd had enough of the place, pack their bags and write some rotten review on a website. He left, remembered the letter, posted it in the box. Returned to Monk's and cooked the eggs himself. Then he said to Karen, 'Only fresh food,' and she shrugged like, What's your problem, old man?

Not to be put off, Wilf smelled the pot of stew, declared it authentic (and edible; Simon's mother had made it) and spooned some into a sugarcane clamshell. He rang up the cost on the till in the bar and returned to the kitchen, saying, 'I'll be back by eight.'

Wilf liked walking. That was the point of a country town, surely? He'd seen what was happening around Georgetown, even Northhead – farms flattened, roads put in, underground power and dozens, no, hundreds of houses, all the same, lined up where there used to be cows. Each house mainly garage, like the car was the most important member of the family. Cottage gardens, and some people had cacti and succulents, but most people concreted the lot. So in Selwyn you walked, and talked, because you could.

Wilf walked toward his niece's house. It was a cool, crisp evening, the smell of chops and sausages wafting from homes along the main road. The few feet of space provided for walking, close to damp walls, flaking paint on his jumper. There was a drinking fountain near the junction, and further up, JM Mooney and Sons, and beside this, ungrazed acreage. He turned into his niece's driveway and walked the few steps to her door. Bobby Mullan would be proud – the rubbish left around, the half-mown lawn, the garden with a few carnations he'd planted to cheer the place up. Although he guessed, now, it was uncheerable. Orla didn't have the strength or will to do anything. Like Death had settled on the place. Cursed, perhaps. Since Dave had run away from home, life, wife, son. Wilf knew that losing a father could finish a boy. Children said, *Well, that's it*. Certainly Connor had, and the timing had matched his father's disappearance.

He went in and called, 'It's me again. I told Connor . . . are you decent?'

'Coming.'

'*Connor?*'

And Orla: 'He's not home.'

'At this hour?'

Wilf never stopped working. Not that he minded. This is what he couldn't understand about the young ones. Effort kept you young, healthy, horny, and rich. Watching Yianni, or whatever his name was, or DJZee, just sucked the life out of you. He tried to remember his own youth – maybe he'd been just as bad? But all he could recall was digging fence posts, ironing for his mother and, in the island days, watching sheep till all hours. No books or music or downloads. Just sheep, rooting themselves rancid. He went into the kitchen and stopped for breath. The sink full of pots, pans, dishes, all covered with scraps of food, empty bottles and the smell of off milk. 'Jesus.' But this would have to wait. He spooned stew onto a plate and warmed it for his niece. 'Stew's okay?' he called.

'Just a bit, thanks, Uncle. I'm not terribly hungry.'

He came out to the dining room, just as chaotic, met his niece, freshly showered, hair back, in a dressing gown. But he could tell the difference. Every time, her cheeks more prominent, her skin more sallow, her teeth more obvious. This made him feel bad. He thought if he did what he could, and prayed to his pygmies, she'd improve. Goodwill was love, too, and that cured people. She sat down and he put the stew in front of her. 'Same as usual . . . but Mrs Gould says she'll do a chicken curry this week. You liked that last time, eh?'

'Not just for me I hope?' The words soft, raspy, like they'd taken all of her breath.

'No, for the pub, but it's easiest this way.'

Orla Healy started eating her stew. Her hair fell, and she fixed it. 'How are you, Uncle?'

'I'm fine. I'm gonna tell Noah what he can do with his vegetables.'

'You haven't got time.'

'No, I haven't.' Wilf thought, too right. Better things to do. 'And Bobby Mullan. He's a crook, too.'

'Why do you bother?'

'I got to get meaner . . . I promise, I'll tell them. At my age.'

Both of them. Strange. Orla was only forty-five, and half-dead with blood cancer, but she couldn't, never had been able to do the things her uncle could. *Her uncle*. Her father's brother. The three of them, stuck on their boyhood island.

'What you should do,' Orla explained, 'is limit yourself to paid work.'

'I don't need the money.'

She waited with a heavy spoonful. 'You're not having any?'

'I'll have some when I get back. I brought enough for you and Connor. Where'd you say he was?'

'God knows.' She slowly ate, laid the spoon on the table. 'I'm sorry the place is such a mess. I've been in bed all afternoon.'

'He should be helping.'

'He'll be in directly.'

'You shouldn't make excuses for him.'

She tried another mouthful. Wilf stopped himself from giving the same lecture. This boy with his five, six, seven guitars, staying up all night playing music as his mother lay in bed worrying about the future. Orla said, 'Just don't say anything, Uncle. It's not going to help.'

Wilf noticed the pile of pill packets and some sort of medicine she had to drink. A little mountain of hope on the dining room table. 'You got enough money for all that?'

'Yes.'

But he took out his wallet anyway, put down a hundred and said, 'Don't say a word.'

'I'm not short of money.'

'Neither am I. One day you'll find that out. Lots, young lady, so do as you're told and keep it.'

She smiled. 'Lots?'

'*Lots*. I've been selling ice to the kids at school.'

Orla nearly coughed up her stew. 'Don't joke,' she said. 'It's right through the place.'

'As long as Connor stays away from it.'

'He's not that stupid.'

'No, he's not, is he?' Wondering. 'And what else can I get you?'

'Fridge is full.'

It wasn't. He'd checked. And what was there was un-nutritious, packaged, old. 'You need fruit, vegetables. Tomorrow. Half a tonne, I promise. Hidden in the van.'

'Don't get yourself in trouble.'

'I'll pick you up on Friday and we'll go to Northhead, do a proper shop. Right?'

'No.'

'Eleven. Get yourself ready, young lady. A bit of lipstick, your mother's violets. You'll feel better.'

He'd said everything except what needed to be said. He didn't want to ask, because maybe she'd tell the truth, then he'd know. And by the look on her face, the way she walked, slowly, shuffling. The bit of bony ankle and leg. 'Did the doctor ring back?'

'No.' Putting down her spoon for good. 'I'm full.'

'You said he was going to.'

'Well . . . the count was lower.' She tried to smile.

'That's no problem,' he said. 'You're going to have your good days, and bad ones. But at your age, you keep on . . .'

'*Quite* a bit lower.'

Wilf still wasn't sure how you talked your way around such things. He was confused about what to say, or do. Working harder, longer wouldn't help. Only luck, it seemed. He stood, gathered the dishes and went into the kitchen. 'Next time . . . with some of Bobby's carrots. They'll fix anything.'

'You said you were telling him.'

Returning. 'Not just yet. We need his potatoes.' Gathering more dishes and taking them out. Orla told him to stop but he wouldn't, until he had the table cleared and wiped down, the hot water running in the sink.

'Connor can do it,' she said.

'Do what?' the boy said, standing in the doorway.

'Help your uncle with the dishes.' She approached him, tried to touch his face, but he pushed her hand away. Wilf appeared from the kitchen and said, 'I got a stew for you, boyo.'

'Maybe later.' He walked across the room, his guitar swinging in a case, through the kitchen and into his room. Closed the door, but Orla stood outside and said, 'You got to eat.'

Wilf washed the dishes. He knew Connor's moods, and when he should stay quiet. But Orla said, 'Come on, we can heat it up.'

And the muffled reply: 'I'm not hungry.'

Again, silence. Orla returned to the kitchen, picked up a tea towel and said, 'He'll be out in a minute. Nothing as important as his stomach.'

Wilf led her back to the lounge. 'Sing something.'

'Now?'

'Now.' As he rolled up his sleeves, and returned to a week's worth of dishes.

Orla reached across for her own guitar, tuned it and said, 'What do you think?'

'Working music.'

She tried a few chords, played them soft and blended so they wouldn't threaten her own whisper. '*And all about the hills, and all about the sea . . .*'

On cue, Connor emerged wearing shorts, Nirvana T-shirt, leather bracelets. He opened the fridge, drank orange juice from the bottle. 'You're not singing that shit again?' He found a chicken leg and started eating it.

'That's your opinion,' Orla said. 'Compared to all that American rubbish.'

'That's what people listen to now, Mum. *American rubbish.*'

Wilf laid plate upon plate, bowl upon bowl, hoping Connor might offer to pick up a towel and wipe. But he just threw the chicken leg in the bin and said, 'Not going to school tomorrow.'

'Why?'

'Suspended again.'

'*Why?*'

'Blakely. He went off at me, so I told him . . .' He noticed his uncle, knew what he was thinking. 'It wasn't me, Uncle. He was right in my face. I could've reached out and whacked him, but I didn't.'

Although he had before.

'He's a sociopath.'

'Blakely, a sociopath?' Orla asked.

'Yes.'

'And he picks on you?'

'Yes.'

'For doing nothing?'

'*Nothing.* Not a thing. I was doing my work.'

Wilf put the last of the dishes in the rack.

'What?' said Connor.

'I didn't say a word. You'll just have to miss a day of school.'

Connor was watching Orla, but she refused to buy into it. He walked over to her and said, 'Sorry, Mum. I guess I should've backed off. Should I?'

She held his hand. 'It would've made things easier.'

He sat beside her. Wilf came in and said, 'What the hell's Nirvana?'

Connor took his mother's guitar and started playing chords. He screeched something about teen spirit, and Wilf and Orla laughed. He said, 'At least it's better than the . . . *hills*.'

Orla reclaimed the guitar and continued. '*All around the dreams we weave when we leave each other behind . . .*'

'Yuck.' Connor pretended to vomit. 'That's so old and clichéd . . . we're not living in the nineteen hundreds.' He grabbed the guitar and sang another song. Orla liked it, and told him, because it was a way to build a bridge to the son who lived in his room, a million miles away, roaming the wheatbelt like a blinded foal. Wilf said, 'All that about your hoe.'

Connor laughed. 'My *hoe*?'

'Not the gardening type, I suppose.'

Like this, back and forth, old and new. Orla and Wilf knew that Connor was an out-of-tune whistle that just needed a breath of air. Wilf said, 'Hungry yet?'

'I guess.'

For a moment he saw his great-nephew as a six-year-old, full of love and forgiveness. Wilf missed this. He wondered if he could ever get it back. 'Alright, if you're not at school tomorrow you can come and help me with the mail.'

'The *mail*?'

'Or else I'll see if Noah will take you back. And while I'm warming your stew, you can put your clothes away.'

'What?'

'I've seen your room.'

Connor retreated. He knew there was no point staying angry.

4

Leo Quinn had been the postie until (firstly) his hip went, then a slipped disk, at which point he'd asked Wilf to take over for a few weeks, which had become months, and years. Wilf was sent to Sydney and, on a clear April day, walked up George Street, stood in front of the General Post Office in Martin Place, then went in for his day of in-service. He was made to swear this and that, promise the mail would always get through, same day, intact, unread (you had to be a special sort of person to work for Australia Post). Nonetheless, Wilf didn't see himself as a postie. He hadn't asked for the job – he was just helping out. One day Leo might recover, rise from his recliner, declare himself cured and return to work.

'Who else?' Wilf said to Connor, as they drove along Turner Road, with its silage pits and abandoned bluestone cottages.

'Let them worry about it,' Connor said, loading Pearl Jam into the CD player. 'Just tell them.' Choosing a track about scar tissue.

'People want their mail.'

'But how's it *your* problem?'

'It's everyone's problem.'

'Bullshit.'

'*Eh!*'

'Sorry. But that's not the way it works now, Uncle. *They* have to find someone to take over.' Waiting for a response he knew would never come. 'They're making millions, so why do you—'

'I was thinking . . .'

'Here we go.'

So they drove for a while. The long stretches between farms, the yards full of rusted tractors and unshaved sheep. 'That's how it works, Connor. You say you don't like school . . .'

'*Uncle.*'

'I put in a word for you, you get the job. Fresh air, freedom, no one to bother you, and the pay's more than adequate.'

'I don't want to be a postie. Anyway, everything's done by email now.'

'Email? *Email?* How do you deliver a pair of boots by email?'

'I just mean snail mail's dying.'

Wilf accelerated along the open road. '*Snail mail?* You call this snail mail?' He planted his foot and the van took off, ten, twenty clicks above the limit. A rise in the road, airborne, then they thumped down with a little *hmph*. 'You reckon people don't need a postie?'

'I just meant . . .' He turned up the music, but Wilf turned it down.

'I know there are no jobs in Selwyn, but you can have this one. Sick pay, superannuation, the lot.'

'Mum's put you up to it.'

'She has not.'

Wilf loved this bit of country. A big valley that opened up and swallowed them, and they glided down a few hills, past pine trees that carpeted the road with needles, then the landscape opened up and it was like (Wilf often told Connor) they were in Switzerland, that's what it's like, those places like Zurich and Lucerne and . . . and Connor asked if he'd been there, and he said no, but he knew, that's what it'd be like. The shaved sides of hills where they'd harvested trees; the power lines holding it all together; the Angus waiting to become burgers. Old sheds leaning in the breeze; hakea hedges no one had trimmed in years. Pants and footy shirts on lines.

They pulled into Mrs Briton's place, a lone pig, chimney smoking, and she came out to greet them. Wilf handed her a package and she said her son, inside on the computer, had only ordered the mixer on Monday and look, goodness, here already! Wilf turned to his nephew and said, 'See, this is what I was telling Connor. All this buying and selling on the internet, they'll be putting on more postmen soon.'

'They will, Wilf.'

Wilf searched his bag, found a few letters for Mrs Briton and handed them over. Her face lit up. 'Gwenda, at last.' She told them about her sister in Darwin who was busy with photonics, whatever that was, making millions, flying all over the globe. Again Wilf turned to Connor. His that-could-be-you expression. Connor rolled his eyes. 'We better get on, Uncle, the sky's looking grey.'

Although it wasn't. Not at all. Connor was just tired of delivering mail and hearing recycled stories and lessons his mother trusted his uncle to keep telling and re-telling. If life became a tedium of sheep and salvation jane, then what hope was there? So as they drove to their next delivery, Connor said, 'There's no point trying. I know it'd be a good job, but after a few months . . .'

'What?'

'*Boring.*' His body deflating.

'Then you've got to study.'

'Musicians don't need to.'

'Really?' Indicating the radio. 'You'd have to be very lucky. I can't hear any of these fellas with an Aussie accent.'

'*God.*' He shook his head. 'You're all the same. A person wants to have a go . . .'

'I'm just saying, if you want to be a musician you need to study music and understand —'

Connor turned the music to full, glared at his uncle. 'It's rock'n'roll.'

Wilf turned it down. 'Great! You and a million others fighting it out on *Australia's Got* . . . something.'

'*Talent.* Bunch of fakes. Anyway, shouldn't you be encouraging me?'

'I am, I will, but . . . your mother wants—'

'*Screw that.* Going to school, getting an A, how's that help?'

Driving quietly. They stopped at Bobby Mullan's, but he wasn't home, so they left his rivets at the front door. As they set off again, Wilf said, 'Always says he can't leave the place. And me driving up in the rain.'

Connor said, 'I've got sixteen songs, and they're good, Uncle.'

'I have no doubt.'

'If I could just get someone to listen.'

Wilf thought this strange, too. Orla had taught her boy to play guitar. Folk songs, exercises, Beatles, the two of them sitting in the front room for hours at a time, Orla attempting her best Missy Higgins (explaining how they'd once met), waiting until Connor was ready then taking him, on a succession of Thursday nights, to an open mic at Monk's. They'd done alright, sharing harmonies, twelve-strings and high Cs, light applause and the beginnings of greatness. Mother and son, playing for their own sake more than anything.

'Maybe not Nirvana, Uncle, maybe I'll end up writing songs for other people. You got to try plenty of jobs, didn't you?'

'I did. Sold cars once. And encyclopaedias, until people stopped caring. Till your bloody internet fucked it up for everyone.'

'*Eh!* So not everyone wants to be a lawyer.'

'Not everyone *can* be.'

Louder: 'Not everyone *wants* to be, Uncle.'

Another delivery, and by this time Connor seemed to have settled into the landscape, seen something of what his uncle was saying. 'I hate school. Blakely. All them. The bell keeps ringing and we move from room to room and they make us fill in worksheets or answer questions from a book because they can't really teach, just kill time. That's what they're paid to do – keep us in our seats, so we don't look bad on the unemployment statistics, or go round breaking into people's homes.'

'You used to be good with writing. You wanted to be a journalist.'

'They're all getting sacked.'

'So what? Write a book, make a magazine – have a go.'

'I want to.' Turning, glaring. 'But you lot tell me not to.'

'Jesus, Connor.'

'What?'

'*She's sick.*'

'That's not my fault.'

Wilf didn't get it. Even teenagers were meant to care, a bit, weren't they? 'And what about maths? They tested you in school and said you were some sort of genius, and those people get jobs with BP and make millions. Like Mrs Briton's sister, flying all over the place.'

Connor had done the maths, but he repeated it, again. Two more years at school, six at university, then he was twenty-five, then he had to work, learn some job he had no interest in. 'Then I sit around depressed for fifty years 'cos I didn't do what I wanted.'

Wilf was glad. Last time Connor had said this he'd ended with 'like you'. Wilf had said, 'What do you know about what I did or didn't do?' Connor had called him pathetic, because he always gave in to others, and look at you now, Uncle, everyone's bitch. And are you happy? Wilf had said he was, and Connor had argued, and they'd left it there. This time Wilf just said, 'As you get older you'll learn there are other people to think about.'

''Cos I don't know that?'

'And if we all did what we want . . .'

'We'd all be happy.'

'But then your mother would be hungry, and no one would get their mail, and the veggies at the school—'

'Are we done yet?'

'No, we're not. I have a few more deliveries. And anyway, Oz Post would have my balls for lunch.'

They continued through the wheatbelt, their attention taken by a tractor in swampy land; revving, lifting, sinking back into mud. Someone had fetched a bigger tractor to pull it out, but that wasn't helping. Wilf said, 'They should've known better.' Connor thought it funny how there were no trees out here, and how you never missed what you'd never known, and in the end, didn't find necessary.

5

'Jesus.'

The curse of old age, Wilf guessed, waking for the third time that night, shuffling down the hallway for a piss, and when it came, a dribble that splashed on his feet. Strange, because although it was three-forty, there was someone in a cubicle heaving and grunting and groaning. Wilf said, 'Bit of a bad night?' But whoever it was fell quiet. Back to his room, and bed, lying with the window open, the breeze lifting and dropping the blind. A litany of little clunks that offered some reassurance. He was older than his brothers, and the three of them shared a room, all cow-dung, damp mortar, mud floor and wood smoke. Like this, lying awake, learning to call the wind by its name, listening to sheep trying to shit, stray gulls, popping pine. He'd say, 'Brian, did you put those sheep in?' and Brian would say, 'Of course I did.' But not like he was convinced. And then Colin would say, 'Shut your traps and go to sleep,' and Wilf would say, 'I'm awake now, how can I go to sleep?' Like this, until their father called for them to be quiet, and they settled, but Wilf lay awake until the sun arrived. Whispering, 'Colin, how many bombs do you think Russia's got?'

'How would I know?'

'Brian?'

'Shut up!'

And his father: 'If I have to come in there!'

None of that now. Just the stench of old fat from the drums they kept behind the pub (mostly from the Eat Inn, but they shared the cost). An occasional waft of rubbish from the bins; oil, petrol, perhaps, from the carpark. But the same quality of silence. A generator, somewhere; a fridge switching on and off; leaf shadows moving across cracked walls; the cubicle dweller emerging from the bathroom, stumbling along the hallway. And his mother calling, 'Wilf, if you let in the flies . . .' As the screen door slammed and he ran down the hill through the long grass to the creek that never had water.

Wilf lay awake for another half-hour, but he was really lying in bed on Louth, thinking of things he'd like to say to his brothers. Even now, writing to Colin but hardly ever receiving a reply. Eventually he got dressed and went down to make porridge and tea. Then he pissed again, and started setting out plates and bowls for breakfast. There were only eight guests, so he set four tables. Juice that Simon's mum squeezed fresh and bread that Monk told them to take from the freezer. Wilf had warned against it, but Monk had said times were tough. People weren't stopping so much. One, because of Hyland's and its renovations (although Monk's was the real thing, not some American-looking motel); two, because every bugger had opened a bed and breakfast; three, because people were going further afield, eco-cottages stuck out in the middle of the forest. Why, Wilf wasn't sure. What if a kiddy got sick in the night? It could end badly. They (his family) had moved to town for just that reason.

Soon it was six and Karen arrived and asked what he was doing up and he told her about his prostate, and she laughed, and he said it wasn't funny. She told him to drink nettle tea, but he said there was no cure for it. His dad'd had the same problem, rising in the middle of the night, waking them as he stood pissing in his pot. They cooked eggs and bacon and opened for breakfast. No mushrooms, either. Monk said nobody wanted peasant food anymore. *Peasant?* He, Brian and Colin would be sent out collecting every morning, and their father would sit eating a bowl of shaggy ink cap before going to work. Iron. Zinc. Prostate-strengthening. Perhaps that's what I need, Wilf thought. Spinach from the school, all limp and flavourless, probably because the boys had pissed on it.

At seven-fifteen, Wilf walked down the street and waved to Simon, opening his shop. The younger Gould (his sister had fled, too) didn't wave back. Wilf knew he could be moody. Why he'd taken on the shop, he didn't know. Although there weren't that many ways to make money in Selwyn. Which is why he worried about Connor so much. He wasn't practical. This was no place for dreamers, especially if they weren't that talented (the boy's songs were like a million others – and anyway, how many rock stars had Selwyn produced?). He unlocked the school bus and started the engine. Left it running and went in for another piss, then came out, and Noah was arriving. He made for the administration block, but Wilf called, 'Noah, you got a minute?'

Noah waited for him to come over and say, 'I wanted to talk about the bus.'

'It needs something doing?'

'No, driving it. Me.'

'*Ah.*' Shaking his head, looking like he had to get on with things.

'You said you might find someone who . . .?'

'But someone with the proper licence, Wilf.'

'You said Mr McDonald—'

'That hasn't worked out. Give me another week will you, Wilf?' But then he gave up, put down his briefcase and said, 'If it's the money?'

'No.'

'I need someone who's good with the kids, and safe . . . I hear it from the parents. *Wilf keeps them under control. He doesn't take any rubbish.*'

Wilf was beyond flattery. 'It's getting a bit much for me, Noah.'

'For all of us, Wilf.' Smiling his painted-on smile (Wilf thought).

Wilf wanted to say, *Now listen, I'm not on the money you are, and I'm an old man with a leaky prostate, half a job, a sick niece and troubled nephew.* Still, what was the point? People only heard what they wanted. Noah picked up his case and almost ran toward the admin block, and Wilf called, 'Let me know then?'

'I will.'

Ten minutes later, Wilf was headed out of town, east, to the scattered farms clinging to the highway. Sienna Taylor was first. A nice girl, homely (his mother used to say), a bit heavy (although he'd learned to keep his mouth shut). Her parents had a car, and they were always at home, so he couldn't understand why they couldn't take her to school. But that's how it was now: the government brought up your kids for you. A long way from Louth, where they'd be out at the crack of dawn milking, checking animals, collecting eggs, gathering wood. Colin, even then, peering across the ocean and saying, 'I reckon if you look hard enough you could see the South Pole.' Brian telling him he was a fool, Wilf saying, 'It's fifty thousand miles.'

Colin – Wilf often thought, often told Brian, Orla, anyone – had always seen his future elsewhere. The desire (he told his brothers) to make millions so he wasn't picking up cow shit to put on the fire when he was thirty years old. It'd worked out for him. Maybe he was the only sensible one. Maybe Selwyn was a dump, and needed bulldozing (Colin had once said). But in the meantime, someone had to bake the bread and drive the school bus.

Sienna, sitting at the front eating a snack bar. Wilf said, 'Is that your breakfast?'

'Yes.'

'Doesn't your mum cook you something nice?'

'She gives me this.'

Keep your mouth shut, Wilf told himself.

Sienna said, 'Why am I always the first one you pick up?'

'You're the first I get to.'

'The others get to sleep longer.'

'The others live further away.'

Sienna wasn't happy with this. Wilf knew why. The world was against her; everyone hated her, and expected too much. The only way to deal with it, apparently, was to check your phone every two minutes, which Sienna (having finished her bar) did. So, Wilf said, 'What you doing on that?'

'Checking.'

'What?'

'Stuff.'

'What stuff?'

'Messages. Snapchat. Instagram. And here …' Grinning, finding a recording and showing him: a middle-aged man, asleep in an armchair in front of the television, snoring.

'Who's that?'

'Dad.'

The snoring got louder, a few people laughing in the background. Wilf said, 'That's mean.'

'He's like a whale.'

'You should ask if you film someone.'

She didn't care. 'You're meant to have a phone, aren't you?'

'Meant to.'

'What if we had an accident?'

'We'd be dead. Your phone wouldn't help you then. They can sack me if they like. No one else wants to drive you lot around.'

She didn't care. She just fiddled with her phone. 'It's helpful with emergencies.'

'What emergency? You've never had an emergency.'

'Yes, I have. My brother had an asthma attack once.'

'So that means you're going to spend the rest of your life looking at that stupid thing?'

Wilf slowed for a T-junction. He checked both ways, then moved off. Just as he did a car sped around the bend, braked hard and sounded its horn. As they continued, Sienna said, 'That was close.'

'No, it wasn't.'

'It was.'

'*Leave the driving to me!*'

She returned to her phone, but Wilf guessed she'd tell her parents and they'd call the school and complain and Noah would ask about it. So what? He'd say, *You're right, Noah, I'm too old, and dangerous, so I'll stop, shall I?*

Sienna said, 'How old are you?'

'Mind your business.'

'There's no need to be rude.'

'*Me?* Jesus.'

'Mum says you shouldn't use the Lord's name in vain.'

'It's not in vain.'

They stopped at a farm gate for Luke Thomson – seven, fair-haired, always at the back, never a word. Wilf would say to him, 'A big day?' He'd just smile. Wilf would try to get him talking, but he never did. Sienna would say, 'He doesn't have to talk if he doesn't want to.' Wilf would tell her to mind her business. He'd say to Luke, 'What you reading?' and he'd show him some end-of-the-world novel with zombies wandering London. So Wilf left him alone. One day he'd be ready. That's how kids worked. It was just a matter of waiting. Even Connor, perhaps, although his clock was well and truly ticking.

It was almost eight when Trevor Pearse climbed aboard, and Wilf said to him (as he did every time), 'Time to start a revolution?'

Trevor said, 'Yes, Mr Healy.' Like that, like, God, why do you keep saying the same thing? Wilf would tell him about Peter Lalor and the Eureka Stockade, but Trevor wasn't interested in any of that. He'd put in his earbuds and listen to a drumbeat with no singing. Wilf thought this was a shame, but not unusual. Connor was just as much work. None of them could be told. He'd tried to turn his bus into a classroom. 'Hey, Sienna – *wie geht es dir*?'

'What?'

'*Pardon.* I asked how you were feeling.'

'I'm fine.'

'You're meant to say – *Ich bin schön, danke.*'

'You keep saying that. Is it the only German you know?'

'*Nein, aber* . . .' Giving up.

Finally, fourteen-year-old Darcy Davis. Darcy gave Connor a run for his money. All slumped shoulder and what's-your-problem, sitting at the back with his arm out the window, spitting (Wilf had given up warning him). Darcy's people had money. The boy emerged from behind a security gate every morning. Wilf could see the house further up the hill. Big, brash, with acres of window looking out across the sea. Again, why they couldn't drive their own kid to school. Money ruined people. Colin proved it; Darcy, too. This was why his no-bathroom existence pleased him. He called back to Darcy, 'How are you this morning, young man?'

Darcy said, 'Good. What about you, old man?'

Wilf wanted to put his head through the window. 'I'm only eighty.'

'Should you be driving the bus then?'

'That's what I reckon,' Sienna said.

But Wilf said, 'If you want to have a go, you're welcome.'

They both shut up, studied their phones. Wilf couldn't help it. 'Your parents could always drive you.'

'They're still in bed,' Sienna said.

No doubt, Wilf thought.

'You're paid to do it,' Darcy added.

I'm going to kill him. 'When I was your age, Darcy, I had to get up at four to milk the cow – we only had one and—'

'Haven't we heard all this shit before?'

Wilf braked hard, turned and said, 'I'm not gonna . . .'

Darcy grinned. 'Not gonna what?'

'Every morning, your rudeness. Where's it come from?'

'Well, I keep it in a box, and every morning I get it out and polish it.'

The other kids smiled. Darcy said, 'If someone comes along they'll collect us.'

Wilf glared at him. 'I've got a good mind to speak to your parents.'

'Go on then.'

Wilf could feel his heart racing. He knew this sort of thing wasn't good for his health. He didn't want to keel over, here, now, because of this little shit. So he continued toward Selwyn, all the time watching Darcy in the rear-vison. Darcy waved to him, smiled, even blew a kiss.

After they arrived at school, Wilf parked the bus and stormed into the administration block. Straight to Noah's office, but he wasn't there. He asked Sally, the office girl, who had no idea about anything, so he checked the staff room, went up and down the hallways until he found the principal in a classroom. He went in and said, 'Can I talk to you?'

Noah took him to his office. Wilf sat, took a few deep breaths and said, 'I'm finished.' He told him about Darcy, and Noah said he knew all about him and his bad attitude and don't you worry, Wilf, I'll deal with him. But Wilf said, 'I'm done. I don't need this at my age.'

'Don't worry about him. A few days at home . . .'

'He'd love that.'

'I'll talk to his parents.'

'There's too much talk. He needs a kick up the arse.'

No, leave it with me, Noah promised.

Wilf told himself – stick to your guns, old man. Tell him, tomorrow, someone else can take over. But for some reason he said, 'I tell you, Noah, he's a bad one.'

'You wait, tomorrow. Things will be very different, Wilf.'

Wilf felt his heart slowing, his fury flagging. He wasn't sure how to stay angry, and make Noah understand he meant what he said.

Noah said, 'After all, we're the adults, aren't we, Wilf? We're running things.'

6

Wilf stood in the IGA, fending off Spencer Quinn, who'd made his case to the school. 'I don't want any money.'

'They don't want any Jesus,' Simon said.

'Well, that's a shame, but I think we should do something about it.'

'What?'

'A petition, perhaps.'

Simon shook his head. 'Keep it for yourself,' he said to Spencer, maker of tablets, lover of Psalms and Revelations.

'We're under an obligation to spread the Word.'

'No, we're not,' Wilf said, reading the fine print on his phone recharge card.

'It's God's word,' Spencer continued. 'You let it go this way . . . I've seen it, the essay they set my grandson. Blah, blah, describe the ways Islamic women are discriminated against in Australia.'

Simon was stacking chips. Perhaps his biggest seller. He didn't like all the yokels coming in for a conflab, crowding the place. When tourists arrived (the few they had) it made him, the shop, the town look like some documentary about dying, single-silo towns. 'Spencer, that's what they teach them now.'

'*Islamic women*? What about *our* women? Catholic, although there's no talk of that any more. Which is why I think it's important.'

'Noah's got other concerns,' Wilf said. 'Instead of worrying about you coming into classes telling them about St Paul.'

'Someone's got to. Their parents don't.'

'How do you know?'

'I know.'

The crinkle of chips, Spencer's slurp from the milk bottle and Wilf studying his phone card and saying, 'Why do they write it so small? Who could read it?'

'You'll need a computer,' Simon said. 'You'll have to create an account, get a password and then activate it.'

'For a phone call?'

'That's everything now.'

'Used to be able to come in here, hand over my money . . .'

'Used to be able to do a lot of things, but you gotta get with the times.'

'One hour a week,' Spencer said. 'A few slides, a few verses. Dilon told me – they've spent a term going on about Mohammad, and all the problems *we've* made. Mention it to Noah, will you, Wilf?'

A young couple, strangers, came in, and Simon said, 'We might need to create a bit of room, gentlemen.'

Wilf took the hint, left the shop and crossed the road. Smoke hung over the town, backlighting a cloud of midges above a scummy pond from a leaking pipe the council hadn't fixed ('Three months,' Spencer had complained, 'and not a sign of them'). Into the foyer, with its old Selwyn photographs, yellowed from forty years of sun. He'd mentioned this to Monk, too: new decor, carpets, or perhaps the industrial look? *That'd* do the trick. But no, always no. Monk's Pub was jammed between past and present, smelling of old dogs and naphthalene, a signed portrait of Slim Dusty and a 1942 Selwyn Ladies' Hockey League trophy no one knew anything about. So that even if tourists wanted a place to stay, they'd think, Jesus, where else is there? Even if they decided to stay, and went into the bar? Mr Lillimar and Jack Mooney sharing a pint, looking up, whispering something to each other. Cheesy. Charming once, but not in the age of computer passwords and Islamic essays. Things had changed, but Niall 'Monk' Macartan and his half-arsed attempt at an Irish pub hadn't.

Through the foyer into the Men's. Wilf pissing, stopping to change the toilet rolls. See, the thing – clean floors, wiped thrones, hand cleaner, towels, arse wrap, the lot. From the smallest to the biggest things. And where was Monk? Always at Reception, thumbing through his book, with its three or four guests.

Wilf went into the bar and Connor and his friend Roman were setting up for open mic Thursday. The little stage with its microphone stands, stools and cords running back to a small mixing desk the council had bought. Wilf said, 'I wouldn't bother, Connor.' He showed him the sign-on sheet – no names, no one brave enough to pick up a guitar or belt out a *Cheap Wine*. He approached his nephew, presented his pre-paid card and said, 'Simon reckons I need to start an account.'

Connor's laptop was open. He started searching, entering a few numbers, asking for the phone Wilf refused to use, checking the number. 'You've decided to use it?'

'Noah gave me twenty dollars to recharge.' Indicating.

'It's only a phone, you needn't be scared of it.'

'Was a time,' he said, going behind the bar, opening the dishwasher and unpacking glasses, 'when you rang someone to tell them something.'

'There.' Connor handed him the phone.

'Now there's all this Facebook business.'

'It's not new, Uncle.'

'Telling people about what you had for breakfast.' He tried the phone. Rang the bar, and it worked.

Roman didn't say much. In fact, Wilf only ever heard a few grunts. Apparently, he talked to Connor. Connor told him to do something, and Roman replied, but Wilf couldn't understand the words. Not much to look at either, Wilf thought. All peach fuzz and pimples, stale-smelling clothes and a T-shirt with a picture of the Queen with her face crossed out. Old sandshoes, like his parents had put him out with the rubbish and told him to fend for himself. And worse, Connor had mentioned some trouble Roman had got himself into, how they'd put him on some program to get him clean.

Connor opened his case, took out his electric guitar, plugged it in and sat on a stool. Roman followed, removing his bass from a box and tuning it. The hum, crash and fuzz of frequencies, then Connor played a chord and said to his mate, 'Ready.'

They spent a few minutes playing what Wilf had learned was a Kurt Cobain song. This fella who'd killed himself because life was too much. Stupid boy. If he'd grown up on Louth he would've known better. Life was meant to be shit, expectations low, the path (to any sort of) success covered in prickles. But as Wilf listened, he wondered whether this wasn't the best thing for his nephew. '*Come as you are . . .*' A certain sweetness to his voice; a sort of throaty Lee Kernaghan. There was a chorus about guns and people shooting each other. Then Connor sang the last words and Roman covered them in enharmonic notes. Wilf said, 'You got it down. You think anyone will want to hear it?'

'Do you?'

'What about one that your mother taught you?'

'*Uncle.*'

'What do you think, Roman?'

'They're all about forests, and . . . *birds.*'

'I've never heard a song about birds.'

An older couple entered, and Wilf could tell they were Americans. She, in a cheap-looking polyester dress, heels too high for any sort of tourism, he in corduroy slacks and a DARWIN T-shirt. They said they'd just checked in and Monk said you, Wilf is it, might help out with a whisky tasting.

Nerve of them, Wilf thought. Bloody Americans. Walk in and want something for free. I'm not a Walmart, he wanted to say. They serve burgers and fries at the Eat Inn if that's what you want. But what they really wanted was outback hospitality, and he was it, apparently. So he took out his tumblers, started with Glenfiddich and asked where they were from.

'Florida,' the woman, Daisy, told him. 'Tampa Bay.'

'Hot there, I bet?'

'Hotter than July.' As she sipped, and Max, the husband, sniffed the whisky and said, 'Very smooth.'

Wilf didn't know where Tampa Bay was, nor did he care. Max and Daisy told him about their new apartment, and Wilf wondered why they'd come all the way to Selwyn to say this. Max slid a few dollars across the bar and waited for his next whisky. 'My brother visited a few years ago . . . said it was worth a few days.'

Wilf thought that was nice. A few days. Hours. Minutes, perhaps? They could hear a few stories, take some pictures, climb a silo (and fall off, hopefully) and leave. Jameson, Locke's, Midleton, then Wilf said, 'This is my nephew, Connor, and his friend.'

Greetings all round as the Americans surveyed the boys, but seemed somehow disappointed.

'We Healys came from Louth,' Wilf said.

'Louth?'

Like they couldn't give a shit. But Wilf wasn't put off. 'An island off the coast. Deserted now. Our dad brought us to the mainland (me, my brothers) for school. He believed in education. And my brother, Colin, ended up in California . . . LA. But me, I'm holding the fort in Selwyn. Someone's got to, I guess. Everyone's gone. Me and Connor practically run the place, don't we, boy?'

'Practically.'

'Connor plays guitar,' Wilf said. 'And his friend . . .'

Max asked if they could play something. While Wilf poured Greenore Single Grain, the boys repeated their Nirvana. This man, this Max, reminded Wilf of Mr Moore (long dead now). Same moustache, fat face, red eyes. Wilf was lined up in front of Moore's Motor Works with Colin and Brian. The boys were twenty, eighteen and seventeen respectively and Mr Moore wanted an apprentice. Only one. Their dad stood behind them and said, 'Well, Terrance, they're all good workers. Colin knows motors, and Wilf learns as he goes, don't you, son? Brian, he'll turn his hand to anything.'

Mr Moore walked up and down the line, smelling of his own whisky. 'You've got three strong lads, Tom. You did a good job. All that island air, I guess.'

Wilf stepped forward and said, 'I can't go against my brothers, Mr Moore.'

'No?'

'If you gave me the job, but not them . . .' He wasn't sure why he'd done it, or what he wanted to say to Mr Moore, but now he felt it was along the lines of not taking anything from anyone, or being better, or leaving someone behind. All of these things made him feel sad, and somehow more alone, and lonely. Only by plucking a few feathers off your own wings, flesh from your arse, sweat from your skin, were you worthy of a name.

So Colin was given the job and, a year later, the chance to study engineering at university. After that, the job with BP, the transfer to Shell, to America, to the Mansions. So he wasn't jealous of Max at all.

Daisy was getting bored. She asked Connor and Roman to play something else, and Connor said, 'I write some of my own.'

'Go on then.'

They played a ballad. Just a bass line repeating, and a chord over the top.

Turn to the left, turn to the right, all of the stars and the moon and the night,
Look up and down, look all around, to the hills to the sight and the sound of you,
All of the shards that remain,
I'm waiting for the last of the cold, clear rain . . .

Jesus, Wilf thought. What was that? Maybe it was the memory of Brian, or his dad, in his suit, trying to sell his sons to Mr Moore. Or maybe it was just what Connor could do with a guitar, three chords and a few dumb lyrics. 'Where have you been hiding that, Connor?'

Who just looked away, fiddled with his guitar, almost ashamed.

* * *

Wilf was right. No one came to their open mic. As the boys played, the Americans sat in a little nook, close to the fire, and Max kept tipping Wilf, so Wilf kept it for Orla. But Max got quite drunk, his wallet quite open, and as Connor and Roman worked their way through their covers and originals, he kept slipping them five, ten dollars, like money only had a paper value.

It wasn't all bad. Monk came in for an hour and spelled Wilf from the bar. Wilf sat apart, but close, to the action, with Steven. Eighteen years was enough for him to remember, reconstruct him, hear him, smell him, anticipate what he'd say, how he'd respond. So they could just sit and talk. Even the topics, scribed, like a song list ready for singing. Or Nance, sitting beside him telling him to do up his fly, stop wearing the jumper with the holes, the shoes with the loose sole. Wilf said to her, *They still haven't cleared those bushes.*

She said, *It'll all happen again.*

He agreed. It wasn't a safe turn.

Patrick Tear came in and introduced himself to the guests. Wilf didn't know why; it wasn't like they could vote for him. Noah was there with his wife, but Wilf guessed this wasn't the time. Dave Duffy, the agriculture teacher, who told him they were slaughtering the pigs next week if he wanted to order pork, but Wilf told him to see Monk. Eventually people drifted off to bed. In the end it was only Wilf and his nephew. Wilf said, 'That's your mother coming out in you.'

'What?' With a whisky Wilf had allowed him.

'That song. That's her singing.'

Connor thought about this. 'Perhaps.'

'You've played it to her?'

'No.'

'You bloody idiot. Get home, show her.'

Connor looked up at him suspiciously. 'She wouldn't care.'

'No?' Sipping more than was useful. 'Do what you're told, *Nephew.*'

'Yes, *Uncle.*'

'How was she today?'

Connor didn't answer. Wilf knew this was a bad sign. 'I'm taking her shopping.'

'I can.'

'Just play her a few songs, will you?'

7

Wilf hated the place. Exactly the reason everything was going wrong, towns dying, people put out of work. Simon, for instance. How, Wilf asked Orla, could he compete with this? As they continued around the Northhead ALDI, Orla popping this and that into her trolley, replying, 'But Simon's only got a few things.'

'Enough.'

Wilf hated the way the staff had been reduced to their most basic function; moving something; stacking products, adding their value and asking (absently), 'Cash or credit?' Customers becoming an inconvenience, units that had to be moved in the right direction, placed in lines, trusted with a trolley, perhaps, pack, leave, don't talk to the girl, she's too busy. 'If this is what it's all coming to, then what's the point?'

'Of what?'

But he thought better of it. Why should Orla have to deal with the problems of the world? He thought she looked better today. A bit chunkier, perhaps, fuller in the face, colour in her cheeks. But she wasn't the old Orla. The Thursday night marvel punching out a few songs at Monk's, telling jokes, disarming the crustiest locals with her charm.

Cheesecakes in the trolley, and Orla said, 'Connor loves these.'

'Don't worry about Connor. Get what you want.'

She held his arm. 'Don't worry, Uncle, I'm fine.'

'He should . . . why didn't he come?'

'Just you and me, Uncle.'

Wilf hated how she always made excuses for him. He'd told her, it'll all come back to bite you on the arse, but she always found a reason.

A selection of pre-packed meals. Wilf said, 'They're no good for you.'

'But they're easy.'

'We'll stop on the way home, see what Bobby's got.' Fruit and veg; small, pale-looking, the life washed out of it. Some kid was spraying it to make it look edible, but Wilf said, 'Imagine what my dad'd say.'

'What?'

'People getting about like this. We had to grow our own stuff on Louth. Me and Brian would be out on a Saturday morning, thinning, digging in the cow shit.'

Orla was keeping herself upright with the trolley, pushing herself forward, giving herself reason (Wilf guessed) to continue. Since he'd picked her up that morning, been pleased she'd got herself dressed in her old jeans and T-shirt, put on some makeup, said to Connor (on his device in the lounge room), 'Come on then, we'll all make a day of it.'

'I hate shops.'

Wilf thinking, What's it matter what you want? What about your mother? But there was no point; that'd lead to an argument and that would sour an almost perfect day, with sun that was actually warm, the promise of fresh buns and strong coffee.

So they skipped the vegetables. Orla searched a box of compact discs hoping, perhaps, to find something to disrupt the ordinary, the marked down, the low GI and high fibre. Some song, some feeling of lasting happiness, of hope, a cure for the four walls and smell of lasagne that filled her days. 'Men at Work,' she said, holding up the disc.

'God, not more of that,' Wilf said.

'Monk's still playing it?'

'Says that's what the tourists want. Shows how much he understands.'

She popped it in the trolley anyway. A boy, fifteen or sixteen, was mopping the already clean floor and this made Wilf feel even more glum. Like this child had been made in a factory, packaged, described in a brochure, taught what to say and how to say it. At least Connor was authentic. Imperfect, but authentic.

Orla stopped, took a moment, then continued. Wilf asked if she was okay and she said, 'Fine. Don't worry . . . every little thing, Uncle.'

'You were told.'

'What do they know?'

'*Doctors*? Enough to get you better, young lady.'

'God, you still call me that?'

'You are. Young. And . . . maybe we should get a coffee? That latte business.'

She smiled. 'Uncle, you really did crawl from under a rock.'

'No cappuccinos on Louth.'

'And that place, you always go on about it.'

'It was the beginning,' he said. 'Where I came from. That's everything, isn't it?'

'Perhaps.' Placing currywurst, bockwurst and other sausages in her trolley. Wilf knew who they were for, but said nothing.

'People should know where they come from. If you haven't got that you've got *this*.'

She knew he was getting started, but didn't care. He was an old shrew, stuck in his hole, refusing to come out. 'Dave always said that about you.'

'What?'

But she was smelling the air fresheners. Wilf wondered why; Selwyn had a thousand smells, all real, all knowable.

'You haven't heard from him?' Wilf asked.

'He called Connor the other day.'

'Not you?'

'Asking what he was up to. About school.' A wheel of the trolley with a squeak, which would soon be corrected. 'I asked Connor after and he said . . .'

Orla standing in her son's doorway. 'That's it? Nothing else?'

'I don't know, shit, stuff, crap. Whatever.'

'Did you tell him I was on those pills again?'

'No.'

'Why?'

'He didn't ask.'

This had made her furious. Dave had never got anything. Rocketed through life with his pre-made tuna casserole, a bottle of Bundy and a pack of smokes. Never known how to get to work on time, to work, to stick at anything. Never known what anyone else was going through, and if she or anyone said anything it was just, I'll get to it, fix it, make it.

'So I called him,' Wilf said.

They arrived at the checkout and Wilf unloaded their groceries onto a conveyor belt that never stopped moving. 'I thought I better. I recharged my phone and found his number and called him.'

'You didn't?'

'Someone had to.' He worked faster, the cans and boxes tumbling into the next person's groceries. 'I said maybe if he could ... if he had the time?'

'What did he say?'

'*Oh, I better call her, I guess.*'

Wilf didn't get this, either. When his mum got sick, his dad was there, day and night, asking if she wanted this or that, should he cook a stew, iron the clothes, and the boys, what do they need doing? 'I still don't get why you married him.'

'You shouldn't have called him. If he's not going to show interest ...'

The girl whipped through the groceries and Orla tried to pay, but Wilf moved her aside, handed over the cash and took the change. Then they packed their things on the approved bench. No one to do it for you, Wilf thought. Would it kill them to give someone a job packing groceries for people with blood cancer?

Orla sat and rested as Wilf worked. 'Let me,' she said, but she knew she wasn't up to it. 'Don't call him again. If that's how he wants it.'

This annoyed Wilf no end. People had to be taught. He'd been taught that if you wanted to eat you had to put a seed in the ground, or cut a lamb's throat.

'What's he up to?'

Wilf loaded the bags into the trolley. 'I didn't ask. I don't care.' Although

Dave had mentioned June and her job and her two kids he was helping look after. So what? He'd soon dump her, too, and the kids, and find some other woman who asked nothing of him.

They drove into Northhead and parked beside St Columba's. Orla said, 'Just a minute,' and they went into the church. Deserted, a few votive candles burnt down to the sand, taped organ music playing through the rafters. Orla tried to kneel to cross herself but almost overbalanced. Wilf held her, sat her in the back row and said, 'Someone we should pray for?'

But she didn't reply. So he walked the few steps to the side, lit a candle for Steven and Nance, his niece, his great-nephew (who, he guessed, was beyond even this) and stood watching the four flames flickering in the breeze coming in from the street.

At least Steven wasn't Connor, although maybe Connor would come good. Given time, some understanding of what really mattered. Songs mattered, too, but people came first. This is what he needed to teach him. But he wasn't sure how. Time might do it. Might. All he knew was the way his own son stood at the altar in his little sash waiting for the priest to confirm him. His bony legs and long arms, on a morning like this. The boy looking back at him and Nance and smiling and whispering, 'I got to go toilet.' Him and Nance almost laughing, but stopping themselves as the priest came out, introduced himself to the boys, patted their heads, asked what teams they supported. Wilf remembered it like this. Like, at that moment, Steven forgot where he was, or that anything was expected from him. This, he thought, was how it worked. When you realised you were part of something bigger, and saw how you fit in.

Wilf Healy sat beside his niece and said, 'That's where Steven stood. What was it . . . how many years ago?' He felt himself descending, every bit of muscle and willpower deserting him, as he wiped his eyes and said, 'Now I'm going to start blubbering.'

Orla put her arm around him, squeezed him. 'You know you shouldn't come into churches.'

'Yes.' Realising he was giving in to the worst sort of self-pity. 'Not that he believed in God.'

'No?'

'Thought it was a pack of lies. He couldn't believe that someone had made the universe, cows, giraffes, and just sat on his arse all day doing nothing.' Thinking, except giving people cancer, or watching them die from hunger. Wilf knew this was a misunderstanding of God, and the necessities of grace, but what did it matter now? 'He used to say to me – they told us at school the world's five billion years old. So how can there be a god?'

Wilf had said, 'That's not the point.'

'What is?'

'You either believe or you don't.'

'But if the Bible's all wrong?'

'The Bible's not wrong.'

'Yes, it is.'

Wilf had just said, 'There's no point deciding now. One day it will all make sense, then we can have this conversation again.'

Orla said to her uncle, 'Did you put in a word for me?'

'I did.'

'Will it help?'

'Most certainly.'

'When can I expect to hear from Him?'

'Directly, my dear. It's not ALDI. You've got to *trust*.' He put his arm around her. 'You have to put your faith in the doctors.'

'I do.'

Followed by a few moments' silence, in which both arguments were tried and tested.

'If not . . .' she said.

'There's no point thinking that. It's early days.'

This annoyed her, too. If she was happy to deal with facts, then why wasn't he? 'It can't all be down to you.'

'It won't be.'

'And Dave . . .'

'I've already eliminated him from my thinking. Barring a miracle.' He closed then opened his eyes. 'I have a plan.'

'You do?' Turning to him.

'I'm eighty years old. I want to retire. I want to go back to Louth.' He felt proud. It was out. 'And to do so, I need to . . . I worked out I have obligations to thirty-three people, including the kids I drive, you, Connor, Monk, Bobby. And if I'm serious about retiring, I'll need someone to become me.'

'Someone?'

'Exactly. But don't tell him all this. I need to find a way to convince him, without convincing him. He's not one to be told, but he is one to be *persuaded*.'

'You scheming old bastard.'

'I'll take that as a compliment.'

She felt better. She knew Wilf always got his way.

'The main thing is,' Wilf said, 'you can't say a word. That'd ruin everything. He's got to know it's *his* decision.'

'But yours?'

'Exactly.'

They continued into Northhead, past the Fergus and its fish ladder, stones set out to catch unwary fish. The connection was so obvious it needn't be made, but Wilf made it anyway. 'If you take the time to build a trap . . .'

She agreed, but said, 'He's more moody than a fish.'

Down Abbey Street in search of candles that Orla burned in memory of, and hope that, there was some sort of spirit wandering the Selwyn Industrial Estate, leaving footprints in old sump oil. Or maybe the abattoir? The roofless ruin where Ted Clarke had tried to start a porn shop. Certainly not the cemetery. It was too late by then.

Wilf liked wandering through shops. Not that he bought anything. A place that sold cupcakes, a shoe shop where the kids could sit in a castle on a hill to have their feet measured. He asked his niece what she wanted for lunch and she said Chinese (as they laughed about Monk's sweet and sour pork). So they walked down to the New Dynasty on Main Street and settled in beside a small window, the smell of ALDI air freshener, a family of five busy with a banquet. Orla ordered King Prawn Chop Suey. 'It was Dad's favourite.'

'He brought you?'

'Every time we were in town.'

Town being Northhead: civilisation that hadn't bothered becoming a city, sticking to its frock and cardigan roots, floating dangerously close to the Fergus's flood-line, its small streets still trying to cope with cars. Wilf asked for a recommendation and they decided on General Tso's Chicken. As they waited, as Orla watched this small family, she said, 'Dad always said we should travel more.'

'Travel's overestimated.'

'Said he'd take us to Japan.'

'*Japan?* Did he even know where it was?'

She shrugged. 'He probably saw it in a movie.'

'Anyway, there's time for all that. You and Connor and me, after all this business is cleared up.'

Orla laughed as the little boy, three perhaps, disappeared under the table, pulled the cloth, and the meals and drinks shook.

'Not even as far as France,' Orla said.

'I'll take you. The Eiffel Tower and the Louvre would be worth a look.'

The meals came and they ate, and Orla said, 'It's not like how I remember it.'

'How's that?'

'It was the biggest treat ever, Uncle.'

'Unlike your father. Mum couldn't get him to eat anything – he hated vegetables, which was strange, considering it's all we had. Dad would take off his belt and threaten him – *You're sitting there till you eat it.*' He played with the celery and the broccoli and tried the chicken. 'Not bad,' he said. 'But it'll have me on the toilet all night.'

8

'They don't know their arse from their elbow.'

'Who?' Orla asked, clutching a small bear Wilf had bought her.

'Take your pick. That school . . . Noah doesn't have a spine. Monk, and his wife. None of them. Sometimes I think it'd be best if someone came along with a grader and removed Selwyn from the map.'

'You don't believe that.'

'And that fella that started the ice cream shop. My arse. You know what he sells?'

'He does not.'

'Well, where's it coming from?'

They pulled into Orla's drive, and the Morris sat chugging in a late afternoon of hungry gulls, and silage. A newsprint day – grainy images and indistinct headlines. Wilf watched the excitable temperature gauge and said, 'That can't be good.'

The groceries, Wilf weighed down with three big bags, the Coke Orla shouldn't drink, the popcorn, chips and chocolate the doctors had warned her about. Why? Anyway, she'd bought apples, too. Wilf called out, 'Connor!' but there was no response.

At four in the afternoon, most of Selwyn was asleep, paralysed, drifting. They went in and the smell hit them first. Wilf sniffed and said, 'Tobacco?'

'Connor!' Orla called.

Nothing but a distorted grind of chords from his room, his voice testing phrases, soft, loud, then shouting them. The lounge room, two piles of clothes Orla had washed, dried and sorted sitting squashed into the sofa. Three or four plates, some with rewarmed pizza, a bowl of Corn Flakes, milk spilled over the table beside sheet music propped up with empty cans. The television with the sound turned down, stray socks across the carpet. Wilf looked at Orla and said, 'Didn't you ask him?'

'Maybe I left it . . .' She sat among the mess of clothes with a lemon-scented loss of faith, and hope. Wilf went into the kitchen and dropped the groceries on the bench. Dishes, spilled orange juice that he, the obedient uncle, had bought and delivered. 'Connor?'

But the music continued. Chords bleeding into each other, the effects pedals (that Wilf had helped pay for) cutting in and out – distortion, fuzz, feedback, all shaking the timbers of the house. Orla knew what Wilf was thinking. 'Let it go.'

'Why?' He stormed up the hallway, opened Connor's door and said, 'What's going on?'

Connor didn't understand what this old man was doing in his room. 'Hi, Uncle.'

'Get out here and look at this.' Back to the lounge room.

Connor followed, stood in the doorway watching his mum – the lack of eye contact, the slumped shoulders that said everything.

'When we left it was half-decent,' Wilf said, 'but we asked you to clean the place. Vacuum the carpet.'

'Fuck, I forgot.'

'You didn't forget. You couldn't be bothered.'

'I was going to . . . I thought you'd take longer.'

'Look,' Wilf said, lifting the clothes and throwing them across the room. 'This filth.'

'Roman came over.'

'I can smell smoke.'

'He had one.'

'In *your mother's* house?'

Orla refused to join in. It'd been a big day, and now she just wanted to sleep. Her eyes, her body, didn't have the power to make her son clean his room, the lounge, the kitchen, to put the lid on the milk or take the vacuum from the laundry, plug it in, use it.

Connor stood waiting. Wilf hated him for being this lanky, dull-eyed, semi-shaved zombie. He could see him standing in front of *his* father, as he removed his belt (as his pants just about dropped) and flicked it through the air until it sang. *Then* explaining why he was angry. But even now, Connor couldn't commit to words, action, apologies. Couldn't pick up the plates and take them out. 'I was working on a lyric . . . I'll help with all this.'

Wilf knew what came next: he or Brian or Colin would be laid over the end of the lounge and his father would let fly, four, five, six times, full of fury for the way they'd answered their mother or forgotten to shovel some shit.

'Wilf,' Orla said, starting to gather a few dishes.

'No.' He stopped her, turned to the boy and said, 'Get on with it.'

'You're not my father.'

'What's that got to do with being a lazy ass?'

'You can't come in here and order me about.'

'*Wilf,*' Orla said.

Wilf could feel his heart racing. He tried to remember if he'd had his pills. Probably not; most days he forgot. He wondered if it would be best if he dropped dead here, now, and the boy had to live with this, but even that wouldn't matter.

'You said I should practice,' Connor said to him.

Wilf looked at Orla, then the boy, then decided he'd had enough. So he turned, left the house and headed for his van. But Connor came out and said, 'What's the rush? I get things done, ask Mum.'

Wilf got in and started the engine. The needle went straight to red. Connor came up to his window and said, 'Why should I be so bloody perfect? You're not.'

Reverse.

'Or else you wouldn't be in this shithole, serving in that bar, taking all your shit out on other people.'

Orla was at the door. 'Connor, come here.'

'Just because you ...' But the words trailed off. Regardless, Wilf knew. The motor chugged, Connor bit his lip a few times, and Orla said, 'Connor?'

Wilf said, 'Get in.'

'What?'

'Get in the van, we've got jobs to do.'

Connor took a moment, decided. He turned to his mother and she said, 'Go on then.' He got in and Wilf backed down the drive, drove along the road that was mostly potholes, until he was in town. Past Mooney's, the fountain, Greene's and Quinn's and a dozen other places that defined, and limited, his life. All this time, Connor said nothing. Heading out of town, the small roads that could barely fit two cars, that lacked turnoffs, the same shrubs and trees and birds, the same signs, and discounts for three or more tyres, motor repairs that had promised the same deal for twenty years.

Eventually Wilf said, 'I don't remember when I said I was your dad.'

Connor took his time. 'I was halfway through writing this song and I thought I'll get it finished and then clean up, and then you came in.'

'It was his choice.'

'What?'

'Your father.' Turning to him, weaving along the narrow road without looking, because he'd delivered Mrs Rooney's pills so many times. 'What else did he say to you?'

'Nothing.'

'See, you need to learn to communicate.'

'What?'

'That phone, and computer and ... were you smoking?'

'No.'

Wilf couldn't be sure. He'd read reports about ice, small towns full of bored, jobless kids. He felt sorry for them, couldn't blame them, knew he shouldn't always see things through the prism of Louth, 1949. 'So let's just pretend I *am* your bloody father, right? And I get to tell you what to do, and you do it. *Okay?*'

'Why?'

'*Why?* Because your mother's home cleaning your dishes and folding your clothes because you had some great song that's going to change the world.'

'I didn't say it was going to do that.'

'The little things first, old man.'

'I hate when you call me that.'

Wilf pulled into Bobby Mullan's drive and they continued up the hill, got out and found Bobby in his shed bolting the Air Camper's wings to the fuselage. 'Brought my nephew,' Wilf said.

Bobby had heard Wilf complain about him enough times. What he expected: a couple of girly wrist bands, hair down to his collar.

'You said, didn't you,' Wilf continued, 'you had a bunch of cucumbers needed picking?'

'Yes, that's right. And with me back and all. Scoliosis. You heard of it, Connor?'

'No.'

'Well, it makes it hard to bend over, sit in one spot, which is why your uncle delivers my vegetables.'

'For now,' Wilf added.

Connor said, 'So you want me to . . .?'

'If you're offering.'

And Wilf: 'Connor reckons he might take over my run.'

'When did I say that?'

'You could lend him your van, Bobby, and he could do it three times a week, and the arrangement we have, you two could have. And I'd be excused from—'

'When did I say that?' Connor said.

'It's a nice bit of money for a boy with no job.'

'I've got school.'

'We've all got commitments. But you could go on Saturday, and Wednesdays you dismiss early?'

Connor shook his head, but he was outnumbered. 'I guess you're joking, Uncle?'

'I never joke. I don't have a sense of humour, do I, Bobby?'

'None.' Laying his wrench on the floor. 'We're almost there.'

Wilf surveyed the collection of wood and metal held together with pegs and rope and rivets. 'How much longer?'

'I'd be surprised if it was more than . . . three, four years.'

Connor felt like he was in a comedy sketch. In a way, he wanted to play along; in a way, start walking home, pick up his guitar and continue his song. Bobby said, 'I'm eighty-four. Still, if I drop dead you'll finish it for me, won't you, Connor?'

'A plane?'

'Instructions are all there.' Indicating the plans on his workbench. 'Mind you, I haven't used them a lot – just tried to work out what went where. You could get a licence and all that, but you don't need one. Just pull back to go up, down for down.'

Wilf took his nephew out into the failing light and together they picked cucumbers and put them into a waxed box. Two, three boxes, and Wilf said, 'So what's your song about?'

Connor shrugged. 'It's called *Singing for your supper.* Like, you know . . . this.'

'You gonna sing us a bit?'

Connor didn't know whether this was patronising or not, or the sort of crap you did when you spent your day picking cucumbers. '*The art of eating doggy bones, when she gets hungry doggy moans, she's got a dozen bills to pay . . .*' He looked at his uncle. 'What?'

'Go on.'

'*She tries to make the mush go round, the balance going up and down, two jobs a day to make it pay. And there's the boy inside the box, Jesus darning all the socks . . .*'

'Why?'

'What?'

'The socks?'

Connor shook his head. '*Singing for your supper waiting for another chance to make a dollar singing for your supper, you're singing for your supper . . .*'

Wilf said, 'That's fine.'

'You're just saying that.' Standing, looking at the thousands of cucumbers still to be picked.

'I just love working outside, don't you, Nephew?'

'I guess.' Continuing.

Standing, straightening his back. 'I don't know how much of this an eighty-year-old can take.'

Connor knew the script and admired the way Wilf delivered his lines. 'Now's the bit when you tell me the value of hard work and if I don't like school I could be out here with the cucumbers.'

'God no,' Wilf replied. 'I hope you can amount to more than this.'

They continued until dark, then Wilf found another box and said to his nephew, 'If you want to help your mother, pick what she needs.'

Connor took a moment, but accepted the box, and set out into the dark gathering turnips, potatoes, and in the hothouse, tomatoes and lettuces and even herbs, because he knew she was good with curries.

9

'This one here,' Wilf said. 'This is where it nearly ended.'

'Why?' Connor asked, sitting beside his uncle.

'My first day, and it was dark, and I was going along here – see, those hedges, that house on the hill – and then I'm heading down, toward this valley . . .'

Connor was looking, but not looking, interested, but not, and Wilf could tell. This mood, this Connor-somewhere-else, listening to the Red Hot Chili Pepper CD he'd plugged into the bus's stereo.

'Down I go,' Wilf said, and Darcy, at the back of the bus again: '*Doon, doon I go.*' Although none of the other kids laughed. Wilf checked the rear vision and said, 'You haven't improved then?'

'No,' he called.

'After your talking to, and your detention?'

Darcy shrugged.

'Anyway,' Wilf said, 'I'm hurtling down the hill, it's dark, and bang, water! This whole valley, flooded up to that tree. I hit the brakes and ten kids went flying, and there's me stopped five inches from the water.'

Wilf had often wondered what would've happened if he'd braked later, or not at all. Him and ten kids floating down the valley, the bus floundering. 'So I'm telling you,' he said. 'It floods. The council hadn't – *haven't* – even put out a sign, a light, nothing. Go on, add it.' Indicating the 1:50000 topographical on the clipboard in Connor's lap.

Connor noted the valley on the map Wilf had provided. The map he'd use, eventually, when he got his bus licence, when he took over the run.

'A few months you'd get used to it,' Wilf said.

'I would.' Flat. Monotone.

'Do it without thinking.'

Connor didn't reply. He had no intention of driving the bus, of dealing with Darcy and the other kids, making his village idiot life in Selwyn. But the alternative was school, and this way (a fact-finding mission with his uncle) he got the morning off. Which was something.

'Now, slow here,' Wilf said, 'because these trees are close. I've scratched the side several times.' Demonstrating how it should be done.

Sienna, sitting in front of Darcy, said, 'This isn't the proper way.'

'I'm showing him,' Wilf called back.

'We'll be late.'

'So? If you want someone to drive you to school . . .'

'They should pay someone. A *proper* driver.'

Wilf glanced at the little cow, still busy on her phone. 'You'll have to deal with that one.'

'I heard that.'

'It wasn't for your ears.'

Darcy said, 'You're not meant to make personal comments.'

'No? Well, how's this for personal? You need to pull your head in and show some respect.' Turning to Connor, who looked at Darcy and said, 'You're such a goat.'

'Fuck off.'

'Yeah, that's really tough. *Fuck off.*'

Wilf said, 'I'll stop up here and put on the plates.'

'Tomorrow, Uncle.'

'Tomorrow,' Sienna said.

'You need to practice.'

'I will.'

Considering how, after a year of nagging, Wilf had persuaded Connor to take the test, emerging (surprisingly, he thought) with his Learner's permit. Telling him: 'See, now you're all set to go.' Connor had only seen it as a way to leave Selwyn quicker, but Wilf didn't get this. To him, it was his great-nephew showing signs of life.

'Here, this corner, see, it's blind,' Wilf said, indicating a driveway that emerged onto the main road on a bend. 'I've often had someone pull out and not see me. Go on, mark it down.'

So Connor wrote it on the map: BLIND CORNER. He knew what it meant; imagined, too, Wilf's thoughts every time he passed. 'There's not even a sign.'

'Exactly. I've rung them and told them, but no sign. And this bloke in a BMW comes racing out, so watch it.'

'You talk like I've already agreed.'

'I live in hope.' And checking the mirror. 'Darcy, you do that again . . .'

'What?'

'I'm not bloody stupid, I saw you.'

'*What?*' Grinning.

Darcy waiting until a car slowed behind them, turning to the driver and giving her the finger.

'How does that make you feel?' Wilf called back.

'Didn't do anything.'

This time Connor was too busy choosing a new track, sitting back and relaxing in the sun.

'This is an easy stretch,' Wilf said.

'We're late,' Sienna called.

'Stop your fucking complaining,' Connor called back. And whispering to Wilf, 'Spoilt little fat bitch.'

If she heard it, she didn't say. Connor didn't care. Neither did Wilf, really. Then Luke walked to the front of the bus, sat opposite Connor and said, 'I'm writing a novel.'

Connor smiled. 'Yeah? What's it called?'

'*Morpheus and the Midnight Hour.* Do you want to hear some?'

'Of course.'

Luke opened a notebook and smoothed a page. '*It was all about the valley that Morpheus had risen from his sleep and was angry. He'd woken with a headache after ten thousand years, and wanted to eat something. Flesh. Human flesh.*'

'That's fantastic,' Connor said, and Wilf heard something strange in his nephew's voice.

'*So he set off for Selwyn, following the scent of humans.*' He looked up, and Connor said, 'That sounds quite scary, actually.'

'*Quite scary,*' Darcy said.

They ignored him. Connor asked Luke what he was going to do with his novel and he said, 'Get it published,' explaining how JK Rowling had written her thingo in a cafe he'd seen when his mum and dad had taken him to Edinburgh.

'I'll be the first to buy a copy,' Connor said.

Luke continued with his story. Wilf kept driving, slowing to indicate points of importance and make sure Connor marked them on the map. Eventually Darcy gave a woman the finger, licked the back window and used his fingers to indicate what he wanted to do to her. Wilf braked hard and, stooping, went back to him. 'Out!' Indicating the door.

'What?' Sitting innocently.

'Get out and walk, you little shit.'

'You can't call me that. I'll tell Mr Foley.'

'Get out!' Thundering, his hand shaking.

The car behind tooted, but Wilf didn't care. He wanted to slap this boy. He knew how it felt, hard, across your cheek and temple.

'Someone could kidnap me,' Darcy said.

'We can only hope,' Connor said.

Trevor was watching, too, but after a moment, returned to his phone.

'It's miles yet,' Darcy said.

Wilf dropped his hand and took a breath. Connor said to him, 'Leave it, Uncle, it's not worth getting worked up over such an abortion.'

Wilf returned to his seat, put on his belt and sat thinking. Connor didn't need any persuasion. He stood, walked to the back of the bus, pushed Darcy's head against the window and said, 'Next time . . .'

'Get off!' Struggling. Although Connor was too strong, pushing his temple into the glass, knocking it a few times for good measure before releasing.

Darcy said, 'I'll go to the police.'

'Go on, then. We'll take you, yeah? Now. What do you say, Uncle?'

'Fine. We'll even go to Georgetown.'

Quiet. Just the tooting again, before the driver edged past and drove off at speed.

'Just keep your mouth shut,' Connor said.

Luke looked shocked, his mouth wide open, the monster of Selwyn made real. Enough for a few more chapters, at least.

'Do we have an understanding?' Connor said to the fourteen-year-old.

'Yes.'

'Good.' Returning to his seat, adjusting the music, and saying, 'Drive on, Uncle.'

The green earth, dried around the edges, mown low by quadrupeds. Luke explained: '*On the way to Selwyn, Morpheus got hungry and ate all the sheep and cows, so by the time he arrived he was full. But he continued anyway and found the kids in maths and ate them then had a few teachers.*' When he'd finished, he said, 'That's the first. I've written seventeen more, and planned another thirty. But you never know where the story will take you.'

Amen, Connor thought, guessing it would make a good song title. As with Wilf, saying, 'You never know, Luke. If you work hard and behave, it all works out.' Looking back. 'Doesn't it, Darcy?'

Luke returned to his sixth re-reading of Harry Potter number one, Sienna gave up on her phone and Trevor stared out of the window. Of all of them, Wilf thought, he's the one I don't understand. Refusing to show himself, despite the hundreds of hours they'd spent together.

'Anyway, it would be hard,' Connor said, 'if I moved.'

'Moved?'

'Uncle, you can't have a music career in Selwyn. You can't have any sort of career.'

'I thought . . .'

'There's this bloke in Georgetown, Ben's older brother.'

'Who's Ben?'

'Some kid at school, and his brother is twenty-two or three and runs a recording studio.'

'And you'd . . .?' Wilf saw another blind corner but wondered if there was any point telling his nephew. 'But your mother?'

'She'll be okay.'

'*Will she?*' Glaring at him.

'I mean, she'll get better. I wouldn't go if she's still sick or anything.'

'But what if . . .? Jesus, Connor.'

'Okay then, I'll have a go.'

Wilf stopped, put the plates on the bus and settled his nephew into the driver's seat. Darcy said they couldn't do it with kids on board, and Sienna agreed, but Luke said it would be fun, and Trevor said it needs to be done, I guess. Connor set off slowly, hesitantly, on the journey home. Wilf sat close, telling him when to brake, to start turning. After a while, Connor got it, started going faster. Wilf said, 'Slow, stop, watch this one, she won't give way.' And she didn't. After a while, Luke moved closer and gave Connor encouragement. Sienna complained again, because now they were well into first lesson and what sort of trouble will we be in, Mr Healy? But Wilf said, 'I'll tell Noah.'

Eventually Connor drove through the narrow gate into the carpark, the school already silent with work. Luke got out first, saying, 'You're just as good as Wilf,' and Connor replying, 'Imagine what I'd be like with some practice?' But Wilf said, 'Pity you don't reckon it's worthwhile.'

Sienna, still checking her phone, mumbling, 'That was like more than an hour.'

'It wasn't like it, it was more than an hour,' Wilf said. 'You don't live in Oklahoma, you know, girl.'

She shook her head and went in. Then Darcy, stopping on the bottom step and mumbling, 'I hope your niece is okay, *Wilf*.' Waiting a second before continuing.

Wilf stood and said, 'I'm going to kill him.'

'Don't bother,' Connor said. 'There are better ways.' Gathering his school bag, placing the half-marked map inside and saying, 'Thanks for the driving lesson.'

10

Wilf took another swig from the bottle of whisky he'd fetched from the store room (all paid for) and let it settle in his stomach. A drinkable love that roamed his synapses, down through his spine, his toes and finger tips, until he lost stability, closed and opened his eyes, smiled, swigged again. Not that he was drunk. Drunk was common, vulgar, like the winos in Georgetown. He used one finger to type 'Louth'. It read 'Rsrgbail' so he tried again. The letters so small, his finger so big. Eventually he got something closer to the name and the island appeared on his screen. 'Beautiful,' he said, scrolling through the images, the sugar-crystal beach with its abandoned candy-striped lighthouse, the homes that used to be full to overflowing with stubbled farmers and dozens of children, sheep, goats. The rotten stock pens leading down to the race, the beach, the ramps. Or, when they'd given up on this, the now roofless cold store where they'd kept the freshly butchered carcasses. Wilf could remember, him and Brian and Colin sneaking in at night, moonlight in the cataract eyes, fleshless faces, fresh grass between the claws.

He fortified himself again, peered out at the flagging sun, knocked on the wall. This time, someone playing electronic music, whizzes and whoops that passed through six inches of mortar. 'Is it loud enough?' he shouted, but no, just a voice going on about bike races.

Again, the sun, and he remembered Louth. The glow that sat and shat on the horizon, spewing its yellow light across the land. Fat sheep shadows, their legs a hundred metres long, their heads as big as a Morris. Muslin light; the haze, the dust, the smoke. Beautiful, Wilf remembered (taking account of the whisky's effect). Him and his brothers walking home from their small school, dragging their feet, their enthusiasm for learning, their anticipation of the dozens of jobs waiting for them. Brian saying, 'Can't see the point of history.'

Colin agreeing, adding, 'Especially what happened in America. Who cares?'

'You might,' Wilf said.

'Why?'

'You might want to live there one day.'

'Rubbish. As if Dad would ever let us.'

'They won't live forever,' Brian added, although Wilf guessed they would, or at least should.

Down this long road to their house, and another laneway running behind Monk's, full of its own shadows, crates of empties and dry kegs, a row of stinking rubbish bins.

More of the music. 'Could you please . . .!'

Nothing. More grog helped, anyway. He used his finger to stumble between screens. Here, a few shops, a butcher, a bakery he could almost remember. Black-and-white shots with ghost people watching the photographer. Sepia horses and hazy children snatching the bacon. He couldn't recognise anyone. One woman leaned against a post, smiling at someone in a shop. He wondered whether the place had ever had a prostitute.

He read about Louth's last recorded inhabitant, a Mr Ronald Graney, who lived by himself until moving to the mainland in the early fifties. There was a picture of him: old, dove-tail beard, skin a molten landscape. He was wearing pyjamas. He'd gone mad, placed in an asylum in Georgetown, where he'd died in 1974.

Wilf tried to remember through the alcoholic haze. *Graney?* He googled it, and the name came up: 'Graney Engineering'. Of course. Lansdowne Road. There was a map, and it was only a street away from Orla's place. He slipped on his shoes (almost overbalancing), gathered his wallet and keys and left. Walked past room 21, knocked on the door and said, 'Turn that shit down.' Still no effect. 'Do you hear me?' Monk wouldn't be happy, but Monk didn't have to live with the guests. He had his own apartment at the back, nice, warm, with new carpet and curtains, away from the noise of the pub, the smell of the couplings.

Wilf knocked again. 'Oi!'

A man in his underwear came to the door, and Wilf said, 'I got to live next door to you.'

'So?'

Continuing into the bathroom, stopping at the sink, emptying the rest of his whisky into his hip flask and going downstairs. There was a crowd in the bar, and Monk was mingling, singing, trying his best to be everyone's friend. Wilf knew the danger of that; a man could only be spread so thin. The couple from Florida, still, a dozen others. Monk was setting up the Wheel o' Whisky! Perhaps he had a good feeling. Wilf didn't care.

He walked from the pub, onto the deserted street. Selwyn was always deserted. A small population, admittedly, but where was everyone? At home, on their phone, or watching the cooking people or the home renovators? Even Louth had been busier than this, and they'd only had fifty people. Croom's single street was always alive, full of smell and sound and spirit (as he swigged from his flask, felt his legs giving way, but continued up the street anyway). Always people, he remembered. Some sort of molester their mum had warned them about. Him and his brothers had spied on him, watched his house, gone to his window and looked inside. Only Brian had got a peek before they were disturbed.

'Did he have someone in there?' Wilf had asked.

And Colin: 'He did, eh?'

'No, he didn't. He was cooking a sausage.'

Wilf noticed the light in Noah's office and wondered whether he should walk up the hill to see him, confront him, demand action, or resign. Yes, now while he had the spirit. But no, no, he said to himself. *Graney*. Keep going, Wilf.

Up the road, past Simon stacking a shelf with noodles. No lamb shanks cooking over a fire for five hours. *Noodles*. Scoops n' Smiles: milkshakes, bubble gum and chocolate. The new fella was in the kitchen washing dishes. Young, with his hair in a ponytail. Maybe he was a girl? They'd been teaching that at school, and he'd had a word to Noah, said a boy's a boy and a girl's a girl, isn't he, or she? Noah had tended to agree, but explained how the government wanted the kids to know it didn't have to be that way. Spencer wandered across the road, looked into the darkened shop and said, 'You met Grant?'

'No.'

'I can introduce you.'

Wilf wasn't sure how far this web stretched. 'Ice, they reckon,' he said to Spencer.

Spencer studied the man in the kitchen, waved at him, and he waved back. 'Ice?'

'I've heard it, from others. It's all over the place now. They test the waste water.'

'And?'

'One in ten. It's not me. Is it you?'

'No.'

'Well, then . . .' Still watching him wash his dishes.

'He's a nice fella, Wilf.'

'That's what they're good at, and when the kids trust them . . .'

'Rubbish. I don't know where you get such things.'

'An ice cream place, in *Selwyn*?'

'You're always going on about how the town needs new people. And when you get them . . . I swear, Wilf.' Returning to his shop, turning and saying. 'Maybe you should stop drinking?'

Maybe you should stop breathing, Wilf thought, watching Spencer line up his little God tablets against the shop, stop a few people and ask if they knew what the Lord had in store for them. Wilf wished he knew, but sensed it wasn't in God's hands. So, to fix it. He set off with renewed vigour, refusing to stop and chat when Patrick Tear approached, Dave Duffy, in his sheep-shitty boots, even Karen, heading toward the pub, saying, 'Monk reckons there's a big crowd tonight.'

'There is. You go and help, will you, I got an appointment.'

'With whom?'

'It doesn't matter. There are plenty of spring rolls in the freezer.' But not stopping, drifting past the fountain, the bits of acreage, past Orla's street and further, toward where the road split into country or sea. Up Lansdowne Road, to the house he recognised from Google. Not a house, as such. More a dwelling connected to a shed, which was lit up, glowing. He navigated a garden path, knocked on the door and waited. 'Hello, Mr Graney?'

And waited. Knocked again, harder, and called, louder. What was wrong with the world, in its electrical haze, eyes screenwards, ears blocked with buds, nobody listening? No wonder the old stories were dying. He gave up and walked around to the shed, and there, inside, this old man, bent over his own anvil, hammering. 'Ced?'

The man was making some sort of box. He put down his hammer, studied Wilf and said, 'You're the fella works at Monk's?'

'Yes. Wilf.' He went in, offered his hand, and they did the normal Selwyn orientation – names, surnames, family, addresses, relatives. Then Wilf said, 'It was your dad, wasn't it? Ronald? The last person on Louth?'

Ced Graney lit up with the mention of the name. 'He held out until 1953. Said they'd have to take him off in a box, but when his waterworks gave up . . .'

They went into the house, full of piles of papers and clothes and history. It was clear there hadn't been anyone else for years. Perhaps Ced was also holding out against time. He asked Wilf to sit down, offered him more whisky, and Wilf explained he had his own, but Graney insisted. 'Not this one. It'd remove rust from the *Titanic*.'

There was a photo album, and Ced showed Wilf a few old shots from Louth. Not many, there had never been money for a camera. One showed Ced and his dad standing proudly in front of their weatherboard house. Wilf said, 'We lived just up the hill from there.' Indicating. Ced said he remembered a family with three boys, suggested they'd probably played together. More whisky, and another well-worn photo of Ronald in the overgrown main street, sometime in the early fifties. 'That was right toward the end,' he said.

Wilf pointed out each of the shops, or what was left of them. 'Mum would send us there for grain' and 'That's where they used to keep the batteries.' On and on, this small world bubbling back to life. Eventually, Wilf said, 'I want to go back to live there.'

'But there's nothing there.'

'Enough.' Studying the few faded visions of his past, and maybe, future.

'But there's no power, or water, gas . . . and at our age. You'd soon be needing a hospital.'

'Perhaps. But the old people lived there, so why can't I?'

'They had no choice. Plus, they were tough.'

'Aren't we, Ced?'

'You really want to?'

Wilf nodded. His head felt like it might tumble off, roll across the carpet, out the front door. 'If all that mattered was me, I'd do up our old place, start a fire, plant a few things to eat.'

'But it's not just you?'

'No.' Thinking about Orla, wondering why he was sitting here studying impossibilities. What about the bus kids; Mr O'Loughlin waiting for his pills and his pumpkins; Luke, with his version of Selwyn-made-zombie?

'I wish you the best of luck, Wilf. Maybe I could come with you?'

Wilf didn't like the sound of that at all. If he was going, he was going alone. But maybe it would take years, if he still had them. Maybe this was an old man's dream, one that couldn't, or shouldn't, be realised.

'No one's ever gone back?' he said to Ced.

'Not that I know of.'

* * *

An hour later, Wilf walked home. Shops closed, lights off. He'd been up and down this stretch a thousand times. So often he never noticed any changes. Spencer had left out some of his giveaway tablets. *The Lord is our Redeemer.* Bullshit. So he kicked a few over. He went into the bar and Karen was cleaning glasses, listening to the Floridians, stuck to the footpath like lumps of gum. Daisy said something to him but he just smiled. He had no idea what she was on about.

'Monk's gone to bed,' Karen said, across the bar.

'Of course.'

'He told me to keep the beer flowing.'

It was a possibility. There were forty or fifty people, a few regulars, Dave, Jay, and Simon Gould and his mother, nursing her stump. Wilf closed his eyes and the room spun, counter-clockwise, down the sink like the last of the toothpaste. He grabbed the bar to steady himself and said to Karen, 'I just saw that old Ced cunt.'

She smiled. 'I must say, Wilf, you only ever get drunk once a year, but when you do, you do a proper job of it.'

He lifted his flask, smiled, and drank. It was empty. 'Give us another, will you?'

'No, I've gotta do the wheel.'

'I'll do it.'

'*Wilf.*'

Monk had placed three bottles of his cheapest whisky on the prize table. Wilf stood, steadied himself and called out, 'Have your tickets ready, ladies and gentlemen.' He'd done the Wheel o' Whisky! dozens of times, knew that it always stopped on five, thirteen and twenty-six. Everyone knew. Which meant the same few people always won Monk's whisky. Which is why he only ever gave away the cheap stuff.

Wilf waited for silence, then said, 'Nice to get something for nothing these days, isn't it?'

No one was sure if he was joking, or angry. Either way, he was drunk. He spun the wheel and it stopped on seven. Unusual. There was some disappointment. Simon's mum had the ticket, so Wilf delivered the bottle, tripping on the rug, almost falling in her lap.

And again. This time it stopped between two numbers. Wilf studied the crowd and said, 'Who wants to come with me to Louth?'

No reply.

'Win a free trip, ladies and gents. See the old place, eh?'

'What you going on about?' someone said.

'Oh, see here,' Wilf said, indicating the two numbers. 'This one wins a job driving the school bus, and this one, delivering pills for George Daly. Who's a winner then?'

Karen came over from the bar, tried to stop him, but he said, 'No, not yet. Two prizes. I give them away, then I'm home free.' He spun again, and this time it came up fifty-four, but they hadn't sold this many tickets. 'Anyone? Fifty-four? Bobby's vegetables? Somehow I ended up with that job, too. Who wants it? Anyone?'

'Spin again, you silly old bugger.' The same voice.

'We've got a vegetable garden, and someone could win a mail round. Plenty more. Once they're gone they're gone.' Searching the room. Silence. Then he spun the wheel again, and it was thirteen, and the mayor got his bottle of watered whisky. Wilf said, 'Always good when your number comes up, Patrick.'

Karen took him under the arm, and led him upstairs.

After they were gone, Patrick said to Mrs Gould, 'Not sure we can rely on him much longer.'

11

Wilf got out of the shower, dried off, returned to his room. Cursing the world, opening his window and smelling Selwyn – the stench washed away by a squall, a blanket of misfortune suffocating any hope of blue sky. Maybe that's why people left? But like his father had always said, 'It toughens a man. Tempers him, like steel.' Standing, messing his hair as half an ocean dripped from his jumper. Colin had never bought it, telling him, in the early years, 'This is a place to be gotten away from, Wilf.'

'So go.'

'Else you'll regret it, come another fifty years.'

'No one's stopping you.'

And now, standing at his window, smelling the salt and vapours, the fresh bread from the Tea Junction, he wondered if it was too late. Lost years, admittedly, but maybe a man shouldn't give up on happiness. As his face and neck turned Louth-blue, a cold so cold your blood gave up on your skin. He dressed, went downstairs and asked Monk if he needed him. He felt like saying, *I'm not available today. I'm off to California. You can take your inbred dump of a town and shove it up your arse.* But instead, Monk asked if he could be back by eleven.

Wilf walked down the main street, past the junction, reminding him of the distances to Sydney, Melbourne, Hobart. Fifty options, only a few of which he'd tried. He stopped and realised he'd never studied this pole, its green and white signs listing places to make a better life. Maybe they should just take it down? What you don't know. The council had put it up in the sixties, but Mr Moore, before he'd dropped dead with a stroke, had kept making more signs, adding one or two a week for a while, and when he was gone, Mr Mooney took over, before losing interest.

'Hi, Mr Healy.'

Sienna, standing with her mother in the misty rain, both of them wearing see-through plastic jackets.

'Mum's buying me shoes,' the girl said, and the mother (whom he'd never met) smiled. He wondered whether she mightn't have thanked him, considering he wasn't the real bus driver, just took time out of his day to chauffeur her little princess around. But she didn't, of course. Like mother, like daughter. The woman just said, 'Out early today, Mr Healy?'

'No.' Because it was already after nine. But that made sense, considering *she* couldn't get out of bed and drive her own kid to school. Sienna said, 'Is Lucy coming back soon?'

Ungrateful little cow. 'No. I told you all. She's too old . . . she's not up to it anymore.'

Wilf continued toward the old post office. As he went he heard Sienna say, 'Lucy was better,' and wanted to go back, start the whole exchange again. But he didn't, wouldn't, never did. That was his problem, he guessed. But he did say, 'A simple thank you might suffice.' There was no response, but they heard.

He arrived at a shopfront that had been a post office before it closed due to a lack of customers. More like a lack of profitability. That was the world today. You had to turn a quick profit or else you were gone. Being a small town didn't help. In a way, Selwyn, and its dwindling population, was a liability, a pimple on the arse of Oz. Still, it was there, and had to be scratched, so they were sent a bag of mail every second day and Leo was paid to sort it, deliver it. Although he couldn't anymore. Which is where Wilf came into it.

Except for a few signs on the wall, the post office had been stripped bare. Now, just an empty room with the old counter, pigeonholes and equipment piled in the corner. The lino had been taken up, and there were fresh boards. The hot water heater removed from the wall, although they'd left the toilet down the hallway. Along which sat another three rooms. Since Australia Post hadn't sold the building, or even come to look, Monk had started using the place for storage.

Wilf greeted Leo, and they sat reading addresses, putting letters and parcels in order of delivery. Leo said, 'Thanks for agreeing again, Wilf. I'll give you the money.'

'I don't want your money. I got plenty of my own.'

'You haven't. From where?'

'Trust me. Plenty. And I'm going to use it.'

They were almost drowned out by the sound of rain on the roof. Leo placed letters on piles. Wilf noticed one for Scoops n' Smiles, lifted it to the light of the uncleaned window and tried to look inside. He smelled it and said, 'Something's going on in there.'

'Use it on what?' Leo said, straightening his scoliotic back.

'I'm going back to Louth.'

'*Louth?*'

'Do up the old place, plant a few vegetables.'

'To live?'

'Yes.'

'But there's nothing there.'

Wilf shrugged. 'That's the point. I've done my bit for Selwyn, now it's time.'

Leo wasn't happy with this silliness. Wilf was much more sensible. 'By yourself?'

'Yes.'

'And what about food?'

'I'll get a boat and fetch it from the mainland.'

'A boat? At your age?' Leo shook his head, and kept sorting. One from some Bible fellowship for the Quinns. Again, Wilf examined it, tried to read a few lines, but gave up. 'You can get Spencer down here,' he said. 'He's got plenty of time on his hands making his little Jesus pictures.'

'And what about when you get sick?' Leo asked.

'Then I'll go see a doctor.'

'No, *really* sick. Like when you need help. I mean, you help others, Wilf, it's only right you should expect something in return.'

'I don't expect anything from anyone.' Feeling this might sit well on one of Spencer's tablets.

'That age, you might need to go into a nursing home,' Leo said.

'We'll see. You have to deal with matters as they arise.'

Leo seemed to accept this. Poor old Wilf, more than any man, deserved a quiet life, a happy ending. Even on Louth.

Wilf found a parcel addressed 'The Church Selwin' and showed Leo, who examined it and said, 'That's for Mrs Davies.'

'How can you tell?'

'That's her cousin's hand. She was, you know' – tapping his head – 'kicked by a horse.'

There was a parcel from China for Connor Healy. Wilf shook it, but couldn't tell. Asked Leo what he thought, and he said a book, perhaps. Wilf wasn't happy with this. Shaking it again, smelling it, lifting the top to peer in.

'You can't do that,' Leo said, taking it and doing it himself. 'It's a T-shirt, or something soft.'

Wilf was relieved. Not that he thought Connor would go behind his mother's back. Drugs? What else? Magazines? Leo asked after him, and Wilf explained, the lack of attention to detail, to life, to his sick mother. 'But what can you do?' he said. 'He's always busy on his guitar. Doesn't see a thing. By the time he does it might be too late.'

'How do you mean?'

Wilf wasn't sure he wanted to explain. It had started with a package from a doctor in Northhead. He and Leo had tried to work out what it was before Leo (with the aid of a torch) had managed to read: CYTOTOXIC DRUGS.

'What's all that about?' Wilf had asked.

'That's for cancer, I reckon.'

Then Wilf had delivered it to his niece, asked what it was about, and eventually got it out of her. She'd said, 'A postman's meant to respect people's privacy,' and he'd said, 'A niece is meant to tell her uncle what's going on.' Sitting, poker-faced, until she gave him the diagnosis, at which point she cried and he held her and Connor came in and the whole lot went off like D-Day. She'd told him, 'I've only just found out myself,' explaining how she'd been driving to Northhead, Georgetown, for the doctors, the tests. It had all ended with strong coffee and a laugh, but the lingering feeling that things were going to get shittier before they got better. When he'd left to finish his deliveries, he'd said, 'I'll come back tomorrow,' and she'd said, 'Don't worry, Uncle, they reckon they can take care of it.'

'What, you're not talking?' Leo said.

Wilf returned to the bare room, the single globe hanging from the ceiling (they'd taken the shade, too). He put Connor's parcel aside and said, 'You get suspicious in your old age.'

'And sick.' Moving around to ease the pain. 'Which is why I can't imagine . . . Louth? What's left in Croom?'

'Nothing. Nothing's left in Croom. Doesn't mean . . .'

'People are relying on you, Wilf.'

'Well,' he said, determined, 'they'll just have to find someone else.'

Wilf found one from America – studied his brother's stamp: 'Colin Healy, The Mansions, Venice Beach, California'. Just like Colin, he thought. 'Here he is,' he said, showing Leo. 'Making sure I'm still alive, no doubt.' He opened the letter and, of course, it was done on a computer in a fancy font. '"How's the cold treating you, Wilf?" . . . not that he'd care.' A photo fell out: Colin, paunchy, his gullet covered in grey hair and a gold chain, a few bangly things on his wrist. Wilf showed Leo and said, 'Do you think that's a Healy?'

'He's put on some weight.'

Standing on a beach, a sea of mist and city of smog, a few kids running around in the background. '"Another scare with the angina, but the doctor's onto it. Are you getting checked? The quack reckons these things run in the family."' Looking up again. 'Not that he'd care. Wouldn't even come back to bury me.' Continuing: '"So I'm coming home to see you at long last. The old place. What do you think of that?"'

'There you go,' Leo said. 'Eat your words, Wilf.'

Who kept reading, his lips moving without making a sound. Returning to Leo again. 'The thirteenth. When's that?'

'Thursday fortnight.'

'Talk about notice.' Checking the postmark.

'You're just complaining you haven't seen him in, how many years?'

'I'm not complaining.' Although he was. The *idea* of Colin was one thing, his presence, another.

'That'll be quite a treat,' Leo said.

'Yeah, a treat.' Folding the letter and pocketing it.

A letter for Simon's mum, and Leo said it's probably from her sister in New Zealand.

'And that was a pity too,' Wilf said.

Because Mrs Gould had been set to go with her sister for a job in Auckland. But she'd spent the summer helping with her uncle's harvest, and she'd been sheathing, and accidentally got her hand caught in the machine. Six months later she'd returned to Selwyn, minus her right hand, her job, her life in New Zealand. Although her sister had gone ahead, met some man and moved in with him. Wilf examined the stamp, the blue-and-white kiwi, the letter itself, which seemed new and shiny and full of hope.

Plenty of letters, Wilf thought, placing this one on the pile. Another, years ago, from some government department telling him what he had to fill in, pay for, now that Nance (not that they called her that, or gave a shit) was gone. But those were the days before he sorted letters for Leo Quinn. There were questions about her bank accounts, and how much tax had been paid. He'd got Orla to help him reply. Eventually it was sorted. But growing old, and even death, he learned, were functions of a greater bureaucracy. All the more reason to tell them where to shove it, buy his small boat and pack it with a few books.

'Who will I get once you're gone?' Leo asked.

'I have someone in mind,' Wilf said.

There was a letter for Monk from some accountant in Northhead. Wilf tried his best, but couldn't read it. Leo tried every trick he'd learned in his fifty years of sorting and delivering, but it was too well sealed. 'Typical accountants,' Wilf said, giving up. 'I bet he's in debt.'

'Why?'

'So few guests. Most nights we sell three, four meals. Not worth paying Mrs Gould or Karen or me. Come a time it'll all need to be paid for.'

'How's that your problem?'

Wilf hated when people said this. The reason towns died. Selfish, or stupid, people. 'It's *our* problem, Leo. Or didn't you notice – we haven't got any kids left, no young people, no jobs. Just ice, from this bastard.' Picking up and waving the ice cream shop letter.

'*Wilf.* It's not *my* fault . . . or yours.'

'But it is, Leo. We just sat here, and when they closed the post office, we let them.'

'*We?*'

'And the Diving Pig, and the market (that used to get a hundred people on a Friday) and all the rest.'

'And here's you saying you're moving to some shithole.'

Thank God they were finished, because Wilf knew he had a lot more to say, but shouldn't. He loaded the letters in the old canvas bag, and Leo said, 'I'll fetch the money for you.'

'I don't want your money.'

'Keep your pants on.'

'If *you'd* rather . . .' Stopping, sitting on his stool, taking a breath and gazing out of the window. 'I better get going. Monk wants me back for lunch.'

'You take your tablets?' Afraid the old bastard would drop dead, leaving him with a body to get rid of, as well as all of the paperwork.

'Yes, I took my bloody tablets. Don't worry, I'm not dying here, with the weather like this.' Watching the rain. 'When I go, Leo, it's gonna be a blue sky.'

'How do you know?'

'I know. Sitting on a rock, a line in the water, a light breeze smelling of old seaweed.'

But Leo just said, 'I don't think the rain's going to let up.'

Wilf was on his rock, holding his line, and Brian and Colin were asking for a go. Wilf said, 'It's not been ten minutes.'

'You're doing it all wrong,' Brian was saying.

'How? How am I doing it all wrong?'

'You need proper bait. Meat.'

'Fish don't eat meat,' Colin was saying. 'You need bread.'

As they fought over the line, then a fish bit and they tried to pull it in but it got away. Brian had told them they were fools, and walked off toward home. Colin had said to Wilf, 'We'll just try again then.' Both of them sitting for another ten minutes before they got one, took it home and proudly presented it to their mum. Brian had said something like, 'Beginner's luck,' but they'd told him to piss off, and their dad had whacked them on the back of the head.

Wilf headed out into the squall. It was funny how it just kept raining – where all the water came from, how it stayed in the sky. He'd had this thought as a kid, and never worked it out. Past Hyland's, its two palms out front, its trying-to-be-posh driveway leading up to the front door. None of the charm of Monk's. A Miami motel experience with twelve sanitised-for-your-convenience rooms. No self-shagging in the shared showers. No waft of old food from the dumpster in the back lane. He went into Reception, all polished chrome and some sort of Liberace arrangement on the speakers. Handed over a few letters and said to Mary Tonkin's boy, 'Tell your mum hello.'

'Thanks, Mr Healy.'

Along Sullivan Street, more parcels and letters for the medical centre. *And how's my niece keeping?* he wanted to ask, but apparently you had to respect people's privacy. Although Leo hadn't become the encyclopaedia of Selwyn for no reason. Rumours were, in the old days, he'd steam letters. There'd been an accusation, and investigation, but nothing was proven. Still, people knew. Little things that only a postman could know.

And then Wilf was left on the southern edge of town. Looking out toward the limey hills, the worst of the storm still headed their way. But he couldn't help himself – Nance was saying, *You need to go back to the doctor and have your pills changed.*

So he crossed the road and walked through the small gates, overgrown with blueberries and fresh oats. Along Row 45, Section A. Not that they needed such a scheme, but that was the sort of thing councils liked. When he arrived he said: *They're plenty strong enough*, and Nance said, *It's been three years. Your body changes, Wilf.*

Not so much. I'm still standing, aren't I?

NANCY ROSE HEALY
In the arms of a loving God

That's all they had. No birth date, no death, like these things hadn't happened. This was the tradition, his mother and father asleep on Louth in the same arms, minus their chronology. He'd had a lower-case god (considering what had happened to his son), but he'd been persuaded by Orla and Dave to make him capital. He knew Steven would be angry about this. If there was one thing he'd worked out in his eighteen years, it was the fallacy of Jesus. Still, headstones were for the living, not the dead.

Nance said, *What's all this rot about Louth?*

I'm going, he said.

Nonsense, at your age . . . honestly, Wilf.

Steven, asleep beside his mother, agreed. He shook off his own verses to tell his dad he needed to be where people could look after him, in the same way he'd looked after the town.

Wilf cleared away some weeds. It'd been a few days since he'd come. He put down the mail bag and letters spilled out over the wet grass. He put them back in, but some of the ink smudged. Then he knelt, and although the rain was getting heavier, he could smell the earth, and the rough, herby scent of life.

12

Wilf noticed the clock. The wrong time (3.45 am), as it had been four years ago. Teasing itself silly, but stuck in the moment. He'd sat here, watching it, wondering why no one had fixed it. He'd thought, It wouldn't take much effort. But it hadn't been just that. The spotted and fragrant orchids, although they weren't fragrant, because they weren't real. The same worn carpet and magazines and the same girl sitting at the desk saying, 'They say there's more bad weather on the way.' As Nance came out with the same doctor and said, 'Come on, Wilf, before the rain arrives.'

Him taking her by the arm, leading her out. 'So what did he say?'

'He said we'll need to be patient.'

'But he must have given you some idea?'

She hadn't let him come in. She knew how he'd react, demanding answers and explanations, like it was somehow the doctor's fault.

He wanted to offer to change the battery. He'd even bring one next time. The Primary Care Medical Centre, sitting on a landscape of gaff, shop, fountain and Shell, its two doctors, physio and, every second Thursday, paediatrician. They'd tried an osteopath but the locals weren't having any of that.

'You're not telling me everything,' Wilf had said to Nance, as they'd crossed the carpark, got into the Morris and sat waiting as he tried to get it started.

'At our age, Husband, you have to expect a few cogs to stop turning.'

He didn't get this. 'The test results?'

She took them out of her purse, unfolded the piece of paper and said, 'It's the starter motor?'

'No.'

'That's what Leo reckons.'

'What's Leo know?'

'It was good of you to agree to help him.'

Wilf grabbed the results, and started reading.

The same cross with the same Jesus on the wall behind the desk. A lot of good he'd done. Steven asking, when they'd brought him for his asthma, aged nine, 'They actually nailed him up?'

'Apparently.'

'But wouldn't your hands just come off?'

'Apparently not.'

The phone with the same ring. And she answered it the same way, in the same light, the same temperature, and smell, part antiseptic, part alpine forest. Eventually Orla came out of the doctor's room, leaving the door open behind her. She approached her uncle, sat and said, 'He told me to wait.'

'You're not finished?'

'I don't think. He's not terribly communicative.'

'We should find someone else.'

She seemed tired, pale, her head completing little circuits and finishing where it began. Like some doll with its mechanism broken. Mrs Lillimar came out of the second doctor's office and said, 'Wilf, Orla. How are you, dear?'

'She's fine,' Wilf said, but Orla said, 'Just another check-up, Mrs Lillimar. And you?'

'Waterworks.'

Wilf guessed you could read a lot into that, or nothing. It seemed everyone in Selwyn had problems with their waterworks.

'Well, look after yourselves.' Gathering her purse, and leaving.

Wilf said, 'Silly old cow.'

'She's been good to you.'

'How?'

'When Nance got sick.'

'*Good*? Gave me a jumper. How did that help?' Stewing in his own resentment. 'Too much drama. This place is like *Midsomer Murders*.'

'It's nothing like that.' Thinking for a moment. 'Anyway, isn't that what you're always on about? People helping each other?'

Wilf knew she was right. Life should be *Coronation Street*, everyone working together, looking after kids, abortions, the lot. When that was gone, people drifted. Lacked purpose, connection, a reason to set the alarm in the morning.

'When I think back,' Orla said. 'Those Christmases when I was a kid. You and Colin and Dad sitting drunk on the couch, and Mum and Nance . . . and me and Steven (he was a toddler then, remember?) tearing around the place. And the smell of the roast burning.' And now, she didn't say, the remnants of those days drifting through the gates, two minutes' walk away. 'But you make do, Uncle.'

'You do.'

'And if someone gives you a jumper . . .'

Wilf put his arm around her and said, 'Should I consider myself told?'

'You should.' Smiling, but remembering, and checking the door.

The same smell of lasagne cooking in the lunch room. The ding of the bell, and the sound of the oven door.

'I hope Connor's okay,' Orla said.

'He knows what he's doing.'

'Is Roman with him?'

'Yes. They're old enough to run a bar for a few hours. I showed him how to work the register. And Monk's there if need be. They were practising their guitars when I left.'

The doctor – a tall, freckled man with red hair, his own pallid skin, and high cheekbones – stepped out and said, 'Mrs Healy?'

Orla went back in. The woman at the counter watched her go. Maybe she'd seen her results, or just knew, after so many years. When the door shut, this woman said, 'I remember her mum.'

Wilf didn't care, but he thought about Orla's words and said, 'A rough trot.'

'Just as well Brian's not about.'

The window was open and Wilf heard rain dripping from the gutters onto a path; the sound of a shrike, was it, or an ibis dragging itself from the man-made lake, landing on a bin to scavenge a smorgasbord of disappointments. After a while, Orla emerged again, this time smiling, squeezing the doctor's arm. She came over to her uncle and said, 'Come on, let's go home for a coffee.'

The same walk to the car, the same grey sky, the same day. How the engine didn't want to start, how Wilf said, 'So?'

'Down.'

'*Down*? Is that good or bad?'

'It means my body's still fighting, Uncle.'

Wilf didn't like this at all. They counted cells and wrote a number and that predicted the future. 'Still fighting?'

'You said you weren't going to ask.'

'I never did.' Pulling onto the road, shaking his head. 'You always said you'd tell me.'

'I'm telling you.' Smiling, content, as though she'd just emerged from the lake. 'The count's down . . . turn yourself around, you do the hokey-pokey . . .' Tickling him on the ribs.

'Orla!'

She took a deep breath. 'I don't feel like talking about it, Uncle.'

Wilf's phone rang and he took it from his pocket, answered it as he drove. 'Yes?'

'Wilf?'

'Monk?'

'That nephew of yours . . .'

Wilf guessed Orla couldn't hear. From the tone of Monk's voice, she mightn't want to. She said, 'You shouldn't be doing that as you drive.'

'You might want to come and deal with this,' Monk said. 'Someone can pay for the drink.'

Wilf smiled at Orla. 'Right, five minutes.' Ringing off, slipping the phone in his pocket, although it fell to the floor. 'I'll drop you home. We'll have that coffee tomorrow and you can tell me what he said.'

Five minutes later he pulled into the lane behind Monk's. Karen was emptying the rubbish. 'He's not happy.' He went in and Connor and Roman were sitting on the floor against the wall, heads down, slumped. The pub was empty. Monk came out from behind the bar carrying two bottles – whisky and bourbon – slammed them down on a table and said, 'For a start, these will have to be paid for.'

Wilf looked from Monk to Connor, to Roman. He didn't care about him so much. A little bony waif of a kid with dull eyes, a nose that was too big for his face. 'You got something to tell me, Connor?'

Who managed to look up and say, 'Uncle?'

'Yes, *Uncle*. What happened?'

'This is what happened,' Monk said. 'They stood there, for two hours. One for the customer, two for them.'

Connor was sensible enough to say, 'It was just a nip, but then . . .'

'What's your mate got to say?' Wilf asked.

Connor nudged Roman, but he didn't move.

Wilf noticed vomit on his nephew's jeans. He turned to Monk and said, 'I'm sorry – I misjudged. Didn't I, Connor?'

'It doesn't take much before . . .'

'You're bloody useless,' Monk said to the boys, and Wilf. 'I checked every so often, but they hid it.'

Wilf knelt in front of Connor and said, 'And your mother down at the doctor's, getting her results.'

He raised his head. 'Is she okay?'

'Do you care?'

'Of course.'

'Rubbish . . . stealing drink. You're going to have to grow up soon.'

Connor closed and opened his eyes. 'What did the doctor say?'

'You want to drink? You can go all day – maybe that'll solve your problems.' Going behind the bar, as Monk sat, smiling, watching the drama unfold. Finding a bottle of whisky, opening it, returning to his nephew, tilting his head and pouring it down his throat. Connor fell forward, coughed up the alcohol, then stood, stumbled, fell. 'Get off!'

'Plenty of grog if that's what you want. But don't rely on me, *Nephew*.' Repeating the whole exercise, Connor swallowing more, but vomiting on the floorboards. Monk lit a cigarette, and smiled.

Connor sat up and said to Wilf: 'You're meant to . . .'

'What? Look after you? At your age? Come on then, I'll look after you.' He took the boy under the arm and, with Monk following, dragged him out of the room, up the stairs into the shared bathroom. Let him drop to the ground, pulled off his T-shirt. 'This is how I used to do it when you were a boy.' Shoes, socks, pants. He stood, turned on the water and watched him squirm. 'Cold enough?' Threw his clothes under the water. 'Wash these. If your mother finds out . . .'

Connor blubbered. The water ran down his back, and over the few hairs on his chest.

'You want to kill her?' Wilf said.

'No!'

'Well, grow up.' Storming from the bathroom.

It took a minute, but then Connor stood, turned off the water and said to Monk: 'You talk to him for me.'

'No one's doing nothing for you.' Stepping out his cigarette, and walking from the bathroom.

* * *

When Connor woke at three am – in his uncle's bed, his uncle's pyjamas – he saw a figure sitting in a chair staring out of an open window. It was cold. He said, 'It's freezing.'

So the figure closed the window. Connor saw his clothes folded neatly on the table across the room. 'Is that you, Uncle?' As his eyes adjusted.

'Well, at least we've made a start.'

'On what?'

But there was no reply.

When Connor woke an hour later he heard talking from the hallway. He tried to make out words, but just vomited on the towel someone had laid across the bed. Then he heard the voices laughing. At last they came into the room. Two shadows, made taller in the light. One said, 'I called your mother.'

'What did she say?'

'I told her you were staying the night, to help with breakfast.'

'Thanks, Uncle.' He vomited again, and the men laughed again, and he said, 'Not a drop, I promise.'

13

They set out early. Past Roman, in the kitchen, peeling potatoes and pumpkins. 'Have we got time for breakfast?' Connor asked his uncle.

'No,' Wilf said. 'I told your mother I'd take you to school.'

'I'm not going to school.'

But Wilf glared at him. Monk, too, busy with the eight-piece toaster.

'You might want to reconsider,' Wilf said, presenting the bag he'd already fetched from Orla's place, telling his niece about Connor's change of mind. Her asking why; him telling her how he and Monk had explained things more clearly.

'I'm hungry,' Connor said to his uncle.

'Best you don't put anything in your stomach. It's had a big night.'

So they left for school. Just as Simon was crossing the road with a pot of chicken curry his mum had made, one-handed. Wilf said to him, 'I don't know how she does it.'

'She loves it,' Simon said. 'She was cooking for a family of nine when she was eleven, twelve. She had to – her father broke his back. And how are you this morning, Connor?'

'Fine.' Glaring at both men.

'He's been helping out at the bar,' Wilf said.

'Can we go, *Uncle*?'

A short walk to school. The morning was cold, but clearing, the grass icy, but thawing. The sun promised a decent day. Wilf felt most useful at times like this.

'What did Mum say?' Connor asked.

'I didn't tell her.'

'You will.'

'Why's she need to know? She's ill. We can work this out between us, can't we?'

Connor dragged his feet, and Wilf told him to lift them. Upright and slumped; eager and reluctant, but Wilf didn't care. He could smell the wet pallets Simon had stacked at the far end of his car park.

'*Work this out* means what you want me to . . .?'

'I just want a workable situation. You content, earning some money. Or maybe finishing school and going to university. You'd like that, wouldn't you?'

'No.'

'When you were little you wanted to be an architect.'

'I don't now.'

'Why?'

'I want to write music, and perform it.'

'*Ah*, that again.'

'You don't think I can?'

Wilf stopped to check the Rotary noticeboard: Sunday's market cancelled, an old, pissy looking lounge for sale, a few Bible verses from Spencer, fifty litres of drench for $30 (or best offer). Walking on, he said, 'Architecture is good because it combines the technical and creative. And you can design your mother a new house.'

Connor picked up the pace. 'So what did the doctor say?'

'*Now* you ask.'

'Alright, I should've but . . . I wasn't thinking. You shouldn't have hosed me down like a pig.'

'You stunk like one.'

'I was drunk.'

'All the more reason.'

'It was freezing cold.'

Wilf stopped and said, 'You're pissed off with the world, but the world doesn't care. I don't. Your mother doesn't – she's got enough on her plate.

You gotta work your own shit out, *dude*.' He walked on, and Connor followed. He knew why the boy was angry. It wasn't his fault; it wasn't an unreasonable reaction to losing your dad, and maybe your mother. 'And at one point you wanted to be a fisherman.'

'That's when I was seven.'

'So? People will always need fish.'

'And songs.'

'*Jesus.*' Singing: '*There's a track winding back . . .*' Messing the boy's hair. Connor just pulled away and said, 'Get off.'

'When I retire in a few months, Monk's going to need someone, then there's the medicines—'

'Good luck to them. I think I should expect more than . . . carrots.'

'People need potatoes, too, turnips—'

They went in, past the school farm, a couple of shaggy sheep, and Wilf said to Dave Duffy (already late for the bell), 'You'll need to shear them, Dave.'

'Do you want to?'

'Never done it.'

'What about you, Connor?'

Who just shrugged.

'Nice to see you back at school. I'm late for roll call. Sorry I didn't have time to pick the last of the cabbages, Wilf. If you wait I'll send a few kids out.'

'No need for that,' Wilf said. 'Connor can help me. Can't you, Nephew?'

'It's first lesson.'

'I'll tick your name,' Dave said, walking up the path, running for the final bell.

'Come on,' Wilf said to Connor.

'This won't work.'

'What?'

'Making me into you.'

Wilf smiled. 'I wouldn't wish that upon anyone.'

Ten minutes later they were picking. One cabbage at a time, into the waxed box, each put aside for delivery. Connor going as slow as he could, bending, cutting stems, examining, smelling.

'They're not going to bite you,' Wilf said.

Connor shaking his head. Throwing the thing into the box, Wilf telling him to go easy, they bruise.

'Cabbages don't bruise.'

'No, but you will, my boy.' Laughing, as the sun warmed his skin and the breeze rustled the still living and recently picked cabbage leaves. 'Anyway, they pay people to write songs these days.'

'So?'

'Not like the old days, the Beatles, where you wrote your own songs and played them and people . . . now it's all controlled.'

Connor was silent.

'They've taken people out of everything. That's what you've got to understand.'

'Still need people to write songs.'

'True, but what I'm saying is . . .'

Mud, Connor wanted to say. Just because you crawled from the mud, managed to make a living doing this sort of shit: 'Doesn't mean I have to.'

'Sorry?'

'This shit. Picking cabbages. Just 'cos you . . .' Mud people, with your noseless faces and lack of ambition, creativity, wit or talent to do anything apart from picking cabbages.

'If I didn't work my family wouldn't eat,' Wilf said.

'Not your bloody *island* again.' Dropping his cabbage. 'You can't see it. Mum can't. Until I do what *you* want. Pick this shit, and if I get anything wrong . . .' Crushing the cabbage with his foot.

'You're only seventeen, Connor.'

Connor didn't care. Seventeen, twenty, thirty, fifty. What was the point of waiting? So he dropped his knife and walked from the vegetable patch. Back up the roadway, past the school bus, and through the gates.

'What now?' Wilf called after him.

He didn't reply. He knew he was doing the right thing. It was simple. The road to Northhead, and beyond, travelled so many times he knew each turn, each stop sign, each off-ramp and roundabout.

Wilf ran after him. Up the hill, shaking soil from his hands, wiping them on his pants. He was twenty metres behind him when he called, 'Where are you going?'

Connor walked past Gould's, Simon busy out front stacking yesterday's bread. He looked up and said, 'School's out, is it, Connor?' Thirty seconds later, Wilf hobbled past. Simon said, 'No luck then?'

'Do you want the little bastard?'

Scoops n' Smiles, the junction, the fountain dripping the same drops it had for years. And always would, Connor thought, caught up in Sullivan's John, the road you've gone – shit shit shit – the same wind through the willows, the same incessant eternal, pointless blather about Mr Blah-Blah's varicose veins and Mr Daly's fresh pork.

'Connor, you're not to go home to your mother like this,' Wilf called. Nothing.

'Do you hear me?' He had to sit on the side of the fountain to get his breath, but he was determined Connor wouldn't succeed. He tried the water, all lead and lime, spat it out and continued. 'Connor! It's not just you.'

'No, it's you,' he called back.

'Stop – be sensible!'

Turning without stopping. '*Me?*'

Connor went into his house, and there was silence. Wilf stood, waiting. *It's not me, Nance. Is it?* Cloud was coming, threatening more rain. 'Right.' Up the driveway, into the house. He heard Orla in the hallway, Connor in his room, banging about. He went the few metres and saw Connor throwing clothes into a bag, heard Orla saying, 'Why?'

Connor turning back and saying, 'As good a time as any.'

Orla turned to her uncle and said, 'What is it?'

'I took him to school, and he didn't want to help me with the cabbages.'

'Jesus, Uncle. That's it? My fault?'

'Calm down,' Orla said, going into her son's room and trying to take him around the shoulders. But he just pushed her away. 'Georgetown's not that far anyway.'

'You're going to Georgetown?'

'Ben's brother said I could . . .'

'You don't even know him,' Orla said.

'I met him once.'

'What's his name?'

'Patrick.' He looked at her for a moment, thought about it, placed his acoustic guitar in its case and shoved a heap of manuscript, a book, his phone in on top.

'Alright, he had a bad night,' Wilf said, moving closer. 'He got a bit drunk, I put him in the shower and now he's shitty with me.'

'*My fault*?' For the first time, standing upright, clear-voiced, confident.

'It was stupid of me,' Wilf said. 'Just the way my dad woulda done it.'

Connor moved closer to him. 'It had nothing to do with that.' He picked up his bag and guitar and squeezed past his mother and uncle. Out through the house, down the steps and across the yard. As he went, Wilf called, 'You'd do this to your mother?'

Connor turned back. 'Fucking cabbages? Jesus.' Then kept walking.

'I'll go,' Wilf said, as they watched the boy walk toward town and the bus, they supposed, that left from the IGA at ten-thirty every day.

'No,' Orla said, stopping him. 'Not with him like this.'

Connor disappeared from sight.

'He won't go. He'll be back in a minute.'

Wilf wasn't so sure. He guessed Connor had been rehearsing this moment for months, years, perhaps. And what was stopping him? The promise of being an architect in ten years' time? Of delivering James O'Loughlin's pills and driving Sienna and Darcy (and their children) to school for the rest of eternity?

So they went in and Wilf told Orla about the last eighteen hours. She said she'd already given up on her son's schooling, which was a shame, because he was smart. But maybe too smart to want to stay in Selwyn and take what was coming.

Wilf said, 'I'll ring Simon, see if he's out the front?'

Orla told him not to. They just had to wait. And if he ended up in Georgetown, he'd soon learn. 'It's been a long time coming. It's just that it had to be today.'

PART II

14

The Morris followed the curves of the hills and valleys. Wilf kept one wheel on the middle line. Orla studied the hobby farms and big homes with dolomite driveways and knee-high hedges. She was quiet. Four days without her son and she'd retreated into some cave, some cocoon that was getting hairier by the day. Soundproof. The world made opaque, and invisible. Wilf didn't like this at all. He'd seen it before. He knew people only fought for so long before laying down their arms and surrendering. So he said, 'I'd like a dollar for every time I've driven this road.'

'So what brings him?' Orla managed.

Wilf shrugged. 'The only reason he does anything: money.' He wasn't looking forward to the visit. The phone call telling him when Colin was arriving, 'You couldn't fetch me, Brother?'

'Georgetown?'

'I could get a taxi, or hire a car?'

'No, of course I'll get you.'

Wilf said to Orla, 'Now I'll have to drive him everywhere. He's worth millions but . . .'

'Uncle . . . he's come all this way.'

'What's a hire car? Fifty dollars a day?'

She smiled, emerging long enough to tell him to be good. He only had one brother, and it had been a long time. 'You're stuck in your ways.'

'*Me*?' The road lifting and falling with the land, its bitumen rhythms. 'As a boy he worked for Mr O'Neill, who had the shop before Simon's dad took it. He was there every minute, always asking for more shifts, even when there was work at home, which me and Brian ended up doing.'

Orla sat up, sighed.

'What?'

'If it starts like this . . .'

'I'm just saying. He could have hired a car. But not with his decent, helpful, loving brother handy.'

Orla refused to be drawn. The land was too beautiful, the grass too green, mowed flat and striped along the road; the hills too blue and purple, too distant, fresh, like they'd been put there yesterday. Her eyes closing, seeking sleep, her head dropping onto her shoulder. Wilf asking if she was alright, her returning to the landscape, the way some farmer had set out an orchard with the canopy of each tree precisely a metre from the next.

'You shouldn't have come,' Wilf said.

'Perhaps he'll have a cheque for both of us?'

'Ha! All that money he earned, straight into a bank account. None for Mum and Dad. That's what he was like . . . is.'

'Sounds like you were glad to see the back of him.'

'I'm not sure why he's coming.'

'I'm looking forward to seeing him again.'

Wilf smiled at her. 'He liked you. Anyone that didn't argue with him.'

Orla tried Connor again. No answer. Sent him another text. Nothing. 'Little sod.'

'You'd soon hear from him if he was in trouble, or needed money.'

She thought about this. Not necessarily. If Connor's pride was at stake he'd find another way. 'Even for him, it's unusual.'

'Patience. He's probably too scared to contact you. Worried about what you'll say.'

'I've tried that.' The text saying she'd already forgiven him. 'Nothing on yours?'

'No.'

Packsaddle and Paroo, Noona, the road settling into the landscape. Salt off the sea, barking dogs, as Orla closed her eyes. 'I'm not cleaning his room,' she said. 'He can come home and do it himself.'

Wilf didn't reply. The several ways of dealing with a missing child. But he knew it wouldn't work. Connor was all she had, and needed. 'If we had a suburb, a street, we could go look. Or where would musical people hang about?'

She sank into her seat. 'I did what I could.'

'Leave that to me. I'll get it out of him.'

Both of them had sat and waited outside Noah's office, as Wilf demanded to see him, I know he's in there, Sheena. Sheena had told them he wouldn't be able to help, and when Wilf stood and went in, Orla following, he said, 'Connor's gone to Georgetown.'

'Sorry?'

'Connor. Just up and went. On the bus.' Wilf had explained the morning, the cabbages, the argument, and what had followed. Then he'd said, 'It's his mate, Ben, his brother. If you could give us his address, we could ask the parents where he is in Georgetown.'

'I can't give out anything, Wilf.'

'Well, I can't drive a school bus.'

'Don't be ridiculous. I'd love to help you, Orla' – smiling at her – 'but the rules are clear. Still . . . I don't think it would be hard . . . for anyone who's passed the Marten's B and B. You know, just as you're coming past Mooney's?'

So they'd visited Ben and Patrick's mother (the father long gone) and she said, 'You want me to give you my son's address so you can go to Georgetown, knock on his door and demand your boy back?'

'Yes,' Orla had said.

'I'm not sure I want my family dragged into this.'

'They are,' she said. 'Connor's gone off to stay with him.'

'I haven't heard about that.'

'You might want to call him.'

'You might want to mind your own business. But even if he was, *even if*, I wouldn't be giving you his address. Knocking on his door all hours and accusing him of stealing your son.'

Back in the Morris, Orla said, 'We could get the police onto her?'

Wilf wasn't so sure. Their one visit had ended badly. After explaining, only an hour after the bus had left. The constable had said, 'So he's not missing, as such?'

And Orla: 'Sorry?'

'You just told me. He packed his bags, told you where he was going and left. So he's not missing, is he?'

'He won't reply to my calls.'

The young policeman had shrugged. 'I'm not sure what I can do about that. But it's not uncommon, is it? People arguing, not returning calls. Maybe if there was some evidence of him being . . . *cajoled*, kept against his will?'

She'd stormed out, saying what did they want, a dead body? They'd have one soon enough. Wilf following her. Holding it all together, still, as he passed through another shithole town, a row of empty shops, dead dog and stripped-down header. Wilf checked and Orla was nearly asleep. So he said nothing, just drove. Ran low on petrol just before Happy Valley, stopped, filled up, but she didn't wake.

Two hours later, Wilf drove into the airport. 'Orla, we're here.'

She blinked, focused on him. 'I slept . . .'

'Feel better?'

'You should've woken me.'

'Why? Just a load of pigs and petrol stations.'

A newish, non-descript terminal, like Colin himself. All glass and steel, trying to look like every other airport in the world, as 'value neutral' (Noah's words) as it could be. They left the van half-a-mile from the terminal and walked. The breeze washing over them, avgas and something deep-fried. Wilf helped his niece, but she said she felt better, and walked by herself. 'Remember what we talked about.'

'You talked, I listened.'

'He came all this way to see you, right?'

'There'll be something else.'

'No, there won't. Sometimes people just do things for other people, don't they, Uncle?'

'Seldom.'

She shook her head. 'I still don't understand you.'

'There's nothing to understand. A man sleeps, eats, works (for everyone else), discharges gas.' Smiling.

Colin was waiting for them. The plane had got in early and he'd tried to call but your phone wasn't on, Brother. Wilf said it was, and showed him, then they checked numbers and Wilf said you couldn't have called or it'd say. Orla couldn't believe it had already begun. Wilf said, 'You've gotten so fat.'

'*Me?* Look at you.'

'I haven't gained a pound in forty years.'

'That remains to be seen. There's some scales.' Indicating.

'They don't work.'

They stood surveying each other. Shook hands, and Colin squeezed his brother's arm. 'How are you, Wilf?'

'Still breathing.'

'I came all this way to see you. What have you got to say about that?'

Wilf glanced at Orla, and she was grinning, so Colin hugged her for a full minute and said, 'You're looking thin.'

But she didn't explain.

There was a cafe, and Colin said they should sit down, but Wilf reminded him it was a long drive. Colin laughed at this. 'Thirty years, and you sound exactly the same. Have you cracked a smile since I left?'

Orla was enjoying it immensely. She'd never met anyone who could deconstruct Wilf so quickly, and efficiently.

So they drove north, toward Selwyn, toward the wheat country that, according to Colin, 'Stays with you every day.'

Apparently not, Wilf said, but he remembered Orla's words. He glanced at his brother as they cleared the few suburbs around Georgetown, passed the few factories, roadworks, a sprawl of houses that was eating into the land. Colin, two inches shorter, three inches fatter, with his rounder face and redder cheeks, his little nose (Wilf had got his father's conker) and hair that had receded to the top of his skull. Wilf mentioned this and Colin said, 'It's all that sun.'

Well, we've got plenty of that, too, Wilf wanted to tell him. Not today perhaps. Then Colin said, 'It's not too late for you, Brother.'

'What?'

'To emigrate. I'm a citizen, so you can walk straight in.'

'Why would I want to do that?'

Colin guessed his brother was right. There was nowhere more beautiful, more natural, full of the dead and the living, the smells that had always been, the burning pine. Despite all this, he said, 'There's an apartment coming up at The Mansions.'

'How would I afford that?'

'You've got plenty.' Turning back to Orla. 'Don't believe what he says, Orla. Check his account. Millions, I bet.'

'Nonsense.' Looking over. 'I've got jobs here.'

'So what? Find someone else.'

'I've got vegetables to deliver.'

'Of course. Vegetables. A hundred ways to cook potatoes.'

It's alright for you, Wilf thought. Who else was going to look after Mum and Dad, and deal with Brian's daughter? And take Mr O'Loughlin his pills and . . . Stopping, realising Colin was right. He'd always been right. The path to happiness was doing what you wanted.

'How was your flight?' Orla asked.

'Painful,' Colin conceded. 'My arse was sore after two hours. We had this crying baby and no one would say anything. It wouldn't stop.'

That's what they do, Wilf wanted to say, smiling again, thinking that it was the *idea* of Colin he liked, not Colin himself.

'But then I slept for a while, until this Chinese bloke . . . they just fart, the Chinese. Not like you and me, Brother, thinking about the people around us. That's the future, Wilf. China and its colonies. Lucky you're here. I don't think they're interested in Selwyn.'

'Why not?'

'Well . . .' Smiling. 'And what about you, Orla?' Half-turning to the back seat. 'Wilf said you've been ill?'

She gave him a summary, and he feigned interest (Wilf thought) and said, 'Well, that needs to be taken care of.'

How? How's it to be taken care of? Wilf thought. 'We're on our pills, aren't we, Orla?'

'Yes, Uncle.'

'So I've got it all under control, haven't I, Niece?'

'You have, Uncle.'

Wilf smiling at Colin. 'So you needn't worry.'

'She's my niece. I'm allowed to worry. That's half the reason I came.' Turning back again. 'Get you better, won't we?'

'But when are you leaving?' Wilf said.

'Flying to New Zealand next Saturday.'

Well, it won't be better by then, he wanted to say. Still, New Zealand was more interesting than blood cancer, or potatoes, Selwyn, Australia. 'And what are you planning on seeing here?'

'The old places. St Joseph's Road still there?'

'Yes, but it's been let go. Don't know what Dad would say.'

'He's not here to worry.'

'I am.'

'Go back to Monk's,' Colin said. 'Take Connor. How is he, Orla?'

She explained, and Colin said it didn't matter, they'd go see him anyway. He hadn't come all this way not to see his great-nephew. Wilf said, 'He won't even answer our calls,' and Colin said, 'He'll answer mine.'

The journey continued like this. The little bits of everyone's lives taken out, examined, made light of, praised, mourned. Five minutes out of Selwyn, Colin said, 'Nothing's changed.'

'That's how we like it,' Wilf replied.

'LA, people flocking there. Millions now.'

Wilf knew he could count the population of Selwyn. 'Better the devil you know,' he said to his brother. 'The *people* you know.'

Colin said, 'Although you don't want to end up marrying your cousin.' He laughed. Orla laughed, but Wilf just said, 'I got a week to remind you, Brother.'

'Of what?'

But Wilf didn't say.

It was getting dark as they drove down Sullivan Street. Colin sat amazed, recalling who lived where, asking his brother what had happened to them. Mrs Gould was crossing the street, walking back to her son's shop, and Wilf stopped and said, 'Here, you remember my brother?' And she kissed his hand through the window, because she remembered when he'd had chicken pox, propped up in bed like a little angel waiting for God.

Wilf pulled into the lane, parked behind Monk's. Colin said, 'Still puts his bin in the same place.'

Wilf turned off the engine.

'Should I walk down?' Colin said.

'Where?'

'To Hyland's. I've booked a room.'

'Hyland's? Monk's got you a room, next to mine.'

'Is the place still one star?'

15

'Shit,' Colin said, sitting down to breakfast.

'What?' Wilf asked, surveying the eggs and bacon, wild mushrooms and tomatoes he'd cooked. The best the IGA could muster.

'What sort of eggs are they?'

'What do you mean? The normal sort.'

'So it's not powdered?'

'No. Real. Look. Yolk.'

Colin tested the eggs, and seemed happy. 'And how do you sleep? Those walls . . . what was he doing all night?'

'*She*. Karen. She needs the radio on for her insomnia.'

Colin tasted the mushrooms and said, 'Are they safe?'

'Of course they're safe. I know it's not The Mansions.'

Colin glanced at him and said, 'And that rubbish truck in the back lane . . . is that every morning?'

'Mondays and Thursdays. You've got to sleep with your window closed.'

Colin finished loading his fork. 'I don't know why you don't buy a house, Brother.'

'At my age?'

'Or come to California.'

'Monk only charges fifty a week.'

'No wonder.'

'Shh.' Because Monk was standing at the breakfast bar, arranging food for the somnolent guests. He called out, 'Everything alright, Colin?' Then came over and said, 'Sleep well?'

'Not so much. Jetlag.'

'You got to expect that. A couple of days . . . what you up to today?'

'School bus in ten minutes,' Wilf said.

Colin smiled at Monk, who said, 'Catch up with some of the old folks?'

'We'll try. Won't we, Brother?'

'Bet they don't have mushrooms like that in California.'

'No.' Although Colin wasn't sure that eating fungus was any signal achievement. Or getting up in the middle of the night to go to the shared bathroom, the cold toilet, piddling while he was half-asleep, while someone (at three in the morning, mind you, Brother!) said, 'It's going to be a beautiful day.'

Monk returned to his guests, and Colin said, 'Then the showers? Jesus. I cut myself on a tile. If it gets infected . . .'

'I've lived here a decade and never had any problems.'

'In this day and age, Wilf. People expect more.' Smiling across at Monk.

Next, they fetched the bus, drove to the Shell and filled up. Then set off for the first pickup. Colin, sitting beside his brother, studying the roads and houses. 'You must enjoy doing it, Brother.'

'I must.' Thinking. 'So who was Trish?'

'Mooney's, just like it was. Haven't even painted the place.' As Mr Mooney came out and Wilf slowed, put down the window and said, 'This is Colin back, Jack.'

The usual niceties, Colin finishing with how he'll pop down to see him later, although Wilf doubted he would.

Into the country, the corrugated roads, burnt-out shelter-belts, flowering wattle. Colin said, 'How many years since I've smelled that?'

'Trish?' Wilf said.

'That was just a quickie.'

'What's that mean? You said you were engaged.'

'For a time, but she wasn't a happy woman. She'd had a violent husband, and was very nervous. Apprehensive. Very guarded.'

'But you were engaged?' Colin had even sent a photo – this older woman, standing with her three sons in front of the Golden Gate.

'Engaged for a time,' Colin said, 'until I thought better of it.'

'You got rid of her?'

'It was mutual.'

'No, *you* got rid of her?'

They stopped for Sienna, who got on and said, 'Who's this?'

Wilf introduced his brother, told Sienna about the City of Angels, the movie stars, the smog, but none of that mattered to her. She sat down and started playing with her phone. As Wilf set off, Colin said, 'My brother's a good driver, is he?'

'I guess.'

Wilf said, 'She's a woman of few words, aren't you, Sienna?'

'Sorry?'

Wilf said to his brother, 'I was all set to come to America. I assumed I'd be the best man.'

Sienna was filming the landscape for no particular reason. A field that had been let go, covered in mallow, and Colin said, 'It used to be the Duncan's. They had cattle, didn't they?'

'Did. No one bought it after they left.'

Next, Luke, waiting at his front gate with three books and a soccer ball, climbing aboard, shaking Colin's hand and saying, 'Wilf said you were coming from America.'

'To see you,' Colin said.

Luke was too sensible for that. 'I have an aunt in Canada. Mum reckons she'd like to stick a knife between her ribs.' He was eager to introduce the new man to the world of Morpheus and his midnight hour. He sat a seat back, leafing through his novel, explaining the illustrations. Sienna told him the man doesn't want to see all your shit, Luke, but Colin put her in her place.

Wilf said, 'That's a pity, Brother.'

'What?'

'Trish. You could've had a happy . . . *dotage*.' Smiling.

'It's happy enough. Up at six, along the canal, stop for a croissant and a coffee. Back up to read the paper, then down to the gym at eleven.'

'*Gym*?' Navigating a narrow road, and tricky T-junction.

'You should try.'

'Too busy, aren't I, Luke?' Reaching out to touch his head. 'Anyway, it's nice to be needed.'

'It's nice to relax, at our age, Brother.'

'Your age, perhaps.'

The ruins of the Mullan's old place. 'Do you remember?' Wilf said to his brother.

How they'd ridden on the bikes they'd been given for their birthdays, with the cigarettes Brian had shoplifted, and how they'd smoked a few, laughed, talked about Mary Slocombe's titties (what there were of them) and felt like the world was as rare and plastic-fresh as their smokes. Until they got home.

'Do you remember when Mum smelled it?' Wilf said.

'Yes, and Dad said . . . *Smells of what*? She wouldn't say, then he came over and sniffed us.' Watching Luke. 'Don't you never do nothing like that, Luke. Me and Brian and Wilf here all got six of the best. And we never smoked again after that, did we, Brother?'

'No. I'd never seen Dad so mad.'

Quiet, as both men remembered, the way the woodbines glowed, the big, blue barley-green sky absolving them of any blame. 'I can still feel it,' Colin said.

'And me,' Wilf added. 'When he hit, he hit hard, didn't he?'

'He'd be arrested now,' Sienna called, from toward the back.

'That's how we learned back then,' Colin said.

'It's child abuse.'

Next was Trevor, sitting against a wall reading his own book. He grabbed his bag, climbed aboard and shook the stranger's hand. Then he sat in his usual spot between Luke and Sienna and stared out of the window. As they drove, Wilf said to his brother, 'He's a quiet one.'

Trevor heard and looked up.

Luke showed Colin a new chapter and said, 'Would you like me to read you some?'

'Okay,' Colin said.

'*Chapter Three – Morpheus had just arrived in the Dark Land and knew he'd have to find shelter until the night.*'

'That's from Tolkien,' Sienna said.

Luke sneered at her.

Colin was more interested in Trevor. The blank expression, the tight lips, the small, careful eyes studying the landscape.

'*He knew this land was full of flesh-eating Trilobites* . . . but these Trilobites are carnivores, so you can imagine . . .'

Colin thought he was a beautiful boy, but not in a physical sense. More, in a quiet, prayerful way. Like he was guarding each thought and feeling.

'Luke, we've heard that *so* many times,' Sienna called.

'So what?' Wilf called back. 'He's not hurting anyone. Go on, Luke.'

As they drove, as Luke continued, Colin said, 'So you've ended up delivering the mail, the pharmacy orders, the bus . . .' Working his way through the list. Wilf added a few jobs he'd missed then said, 'As well as trying to work.'

'That's ridiculous,' Colin said. 'At our age. You should be relaxing.'

'And out to Bobby's twice a week.'

'*When the night came Morpheus felt hungry, so set off for the closest village.*'

'Luke!'

'Enough!' Wilf called. 'Go on, Luke.'

'Brother,' Colin said. 'You've just got to learn to say no.'

'And Orla, of course. Who's going to look after her?'

'Tell them, Wilf.' He thought about it for a moment. 'You're too nice, you don't want to disappoint people.'

Luke stopped and said, 'Couldn't Connor help you?'

'He's busy,' Wilf said.

'With what?'

'He's just busy.'

'But you said—'

'He's moved to Georgetown.'

'Connor?'

'Yes. He's gone.'

'Good riddance,' Sienna said, and Trevor said nothing, but Colin caught his eye and smiled, although he didn't smile back, just returned to the bush, the ruins of an old cemetery.

'I thought he was learning to drive the bus?' Luke said.

'He was.'

'I thought *he* was going to drive us when you died.'

'When am I dying?'

'Eventually.'

'Well, he won't now,' Wilf said. 'He's going to be a rock star.'

Luke wasn't happy about this. 'He was going to read my book.'

'He will. He'll come back for holidays and he can help me and I'll . . .'

Luke thought about it, then tore a chapter from his book, folded it and handed it to Wilf. Who took it, and said, 'What?'

'Tell him to read my new chapter.'

'I don't know where he is.'

'Isn't he your nephew?'

'He's got the shits on.'

'What's that mean?'

'It means he's an arsehole,' Sienna called.

'It means no such thing,' Wilf called back. 'And I'd ask you to watch your mouth, young lady, and not say things you don't understand.'

'You'll find him,' Luke said. 'Tell him I said he should come back and drive the bus.'

'Okay,' Wilf said. 'I'll find him and give him your chapter and tell him he should come back and drive the bus. How's that sound?'

And finally, Darcy. As he got on he said, 'There's someone different every day.'

Wilf said to his brother, 'This is Darcy.' (They'd already had the conversation.)

'How are you, Darcy?'

'So there's another Wilf?' Grinning, going to the back of the bus.

'No, but I'm much handsomer, aren't I?' Colin said.

'Do you make jokes, too?'

'Sometimes.'

'Funny ones?'

'*Morpheus took the boy and tasted him – a leg first, then an arm . . .*'

'Not that shit,' Darcy said.

'Enough!' Wilf thundered, returning to the road, and a fence he just about collected.

'He's got a point,' Sienna said.

'And you too, *Missy.*'

'What's a missy?' Mostly to Darcy, as they both laughed.

'I see what you mean,' Colin said, remembering the words they'd shared over breakfast. 'All the more reason to retire, Brother. You're not getting any younger. What if you had a heart attack, now, as you're driving?'

The bus shuddered a few times, Wilf changed gears, pumped the accelerator and said, 'It's been doing this.'

'The bus is fucked,' Darcy said. 'No school!'

Then the engine stalled. Darcy applauded, Wilf stood and said, 'I've told you!' Pointing.

Colin said to him, 'It's not really the time, is it, son?'

'No, it's not, *son.*'

Wilf tried to restart the bus, but it wouldn't. Colin said he'd have a go, Wilf said what do you know about engines, Colin invoked his apprenticeship, his years as an engineer, and Wilf said what's that got to do with anything? Darcy said he'd fixed his aunty's hair dryer, did that count? Wilf told him to keep his mouth shut and Darcy said don't get worked up, have you had your pills, *Wilf*, and Wilf told him to get off, all of them, and wait beside the road while he fixed the bus.

As they waited, Luke asked if he could help, Sienna checked her watch and said, 'Twenty minutes and I miss Maths,' and Trevor sat on a big rock reading a book about dancing. Darcy asked him why he was interested, but he wouldn't reply. Sienna said, 'That's what he's into,' and Darcy grinned and said, 'It's okay, Sienna, some boys are like that.' Trevor didn't even look up, so Sienna said, 'Careful, he told me his dad gave him a gun.'

Colin had already learned to hate Darcy. He told him to keep his trap shut, or he'd shut it for him.

Wilf checked the filters, the fan belt, the oil, wiping the residue in the grass. The fuel line, the lot. Colin couldn't see the problem. Luke ran around like a mad dog, stopping beside Trevor and asking if he had any food. Soon they were busy with his lunch. Eventually Wilf stood back and said to his brother, 'Welcome to Australia, Colin.'

'Does it break down often?'

'The country?'

'The bus?'

Wilf tried to start again, but it wouldn't, so he called Lucy, and she said it was probably the transmission. They'd meant to get it replaced, but hadn't. 'So what should I do?' Wilf asked.

'Hold on,' she said.

16

Wilf and his brother walked along Sullivan Street, stopping at Quinn's, Spencer busy inside lacquering more tablets. Wilf knocked, introduced Colin and said, 'Spencer and Grace have a nice little setup.'

'If only we could make money,' Spencer said. Jesus and sheep in a mallee landscape, and Colin thought, When did that happen?

'I thought you had plenty of customers?' Wilf said.

Spencer put his brush in a pot. 'It was a living, then a hobby, now . . .'

'You need tourists,' Colin said. 'You should come to LA.'

'He doesn't want to go to LA,' Wilf said.

'These'd be flying off the shelf.' Admiring God spake unto Matthew, more Messiahs on the streets of Selwyn.

'Hardly,' Wilf said. 'They only believe in one thing over there.'

'What's that?'

Wilf wouldn't say. He was busy with Grace's crocheted rugs, sequinned pillow covers and shell clocks. He could see it – everything dated, old-fashioned, like the shop itself, with its damp walls and sixties decor. And the Quinn's house, working its way into the public sphere – an open door to the kitchen, their lunch bubbling away, a couple of cats playing with tassels on lampshades up for sale.

As they continued, Colin said, 'I don't know how they're still in business.'

'They enjoy it,' Wilf said. 'And it's authentic.'

'What, authentically shit?'

'You can't come back and judge the place.'

'Just saying – if they want to stay in business. Come on, I want to be back by eleven.'

'Why?'

'Move on, Brother!' Pulling him toward the Eat Inn. 'This place is why I was on the bog last night.' He studied the prices, crossed out and re-written four or five times. 'While he was cooking it (simple fish and chips, how can you get that wrong?) he was wiping his nose on the back of his hand.'

They stood watching, and it happened again.

'Thanks for warning me. It's cold in that toilet at three am. About time Monk spent some money, too.'

'If you're not happy . . .'

Colin shook his head. 'You're not getting rid of me that easy. I've got to solve your problems before I leave.'

They continued along Sullivan Street.

Wilf was enjoying having his brother back. Mostly, he was a laugh, quick with a story, to offer his time, ear, stomach to a friend. Like he'd sunk back into the landscape, relinquished his Californian dreams, popped a few buttons, re-learned to express less than thought-out opinions. Wilf said, '*You* could move back.'

'Ha.'

'A man's meant to come home when he gets old. Be with his family.'

Colin wasn't having it. 'Life's like Sullivan Road, Brother. You keep going in one direction, get to the junction, and choose. But you can't turn around and come back. Anyway, you wouldn't last ten minutes on Louth.'

'We'll see. I've got it all planned – the old place, how to get the mortar to rebuild the walls, furniture, a water tank, even gas bottles I can get refilled every six months.'

They passed Green's, Hyland's, Colin peering in and saying, 'That looks more like it.'

'Monk wouldn't be happy. You're a VIP. We made up your bed with the good sheets.'

The Shell, the bus in the garage, Dave Duffy's nephew bent over the engine.

The previous morning, a two-hour wait for a tow, for Noah to fetch the kids. Colin and Wilf sitting on a wall sharing a smoke they'd confiscated from Darcy. Sienna telling him, 'Ben's going to kill you. You haven't paid him for the last lot.'

Wilf asking, 'Ben? Ben Magee?'

A farmer burning off stubble, coming over on his tractor and asking if they needed help. 'No, thanks,' Colin had said to him. 'What a chance to sit in the sun!' This man had driven off, confused. Darcy had said, 'Suits me.' And Sienna: 'Shouldn't you make sure the bus works?' Colin had said, 'It's my big, fat geriatric arse, I suppose.' Trevor and Luke (busy up a tree) had laughed but Sienna had just returned to her phone, saying, 'No chance of any coverage here.'

They went into the Shell and Dave's nephew said it needed a new transmission, but it wouldn't arrive until Thursday. 'What you gonna do about the kids?'

'Not my problem,' Wilf told him. 'Call Noah, will you? Tell him. He can drive them all home.'

'That's more like it,' Colin said to him, as they crossed the street, along St Joseph's Road. 'Don't make things your problem.'

'I don't.'

'Just say fuck it. Go on, try.'

Wilf didn't like the language. 'Bugger it!' Grinning.

'No, Fuck it. Go on.'

'Fuck it.'

'Louder.'

'Fuck it.'

'With some conviction.'

'Fuck it!' Loud enough for the street to hear. One woman, out picking up her children's toys, said, 'Enough of that in public.' Wilf apologised, but after, Colin said, 'Don't say sorry. Mean it. Fuck it. Right? That's the first step.'

St Joseph's Road hadn't changed either. Leeward, two dozen identical homes painted baby-shit beige, each with small, ungenerous windows, patches of grass, low roofs and low roads to a suburbia that infected Selwyn like a dose of gonorrhoea. There was a park in the middle, but not big enough for kids to kick balls. Windward, another row of unremarkable houses, this time painted white. No signs of life apart from someone coiling a hose and someone else moving a blue bin (they were all blue). Someone had a cubby house, someone else a naked cactus blushing with the lack of sun. No death, sex or amputated limbs here. Just Beyoncé and granular insecticide. 'I could never work out why Dad chose this place,' Colin said. 'Coming from Louth, you'd think he would've bought a few acres. Land was cheap. Is.'

'Not anymore.'

'But he comes and lives in like . . . Phoenix, or Broadwater.'

'Maybe he'd had enough of pigs and dirt floors.'

'Still, you'd think it'd get in a man's blood.'

'It didn't get in yours.'

The same single or double chimney pots, a few half-houses, with a wall to show who owned what. Where people could graze sheep, or grow onions. Although there was a by-law against that sort of thing. 'But he wasn't happy,' Wilf said.

'No.'

Wilf could remember him trimming the lawn the same way everyone trimmed their lawn, sitting down, rolling a smoke and saying (something like), 'I didn't think it would be like this.'

'If he'd had time he would've gone back to Louth,' Wilf said. 'Although by then Mum had learned to like the place.'

Agreed, Colin thought, standing in front of their old house, circa 1952. 'So you're doing it for him?' he said to his brother.

'No, for me, you dill.'

The pathway where their father lay, having come out to check the mail, turned to go in, dropped dead. Where they'd found him a few minutes later, the gas bill still clutched in his hand. 'You think I'm joking,' Wilf said.

'No, I don't. I think you're hopeful, but so was Dad.'

'I'm not Dad.'

They walked up the path, knocked and waited, explained who they were to an oldish man with neat sideburns. He told them they could come and look, so they showed him where their television had been, where their dad had cut his toenails, where their mum had sat at the window, in the long hours, knitting. The man asked what year they'd left. They summed up their lives in sixty seconds, and Wilf said, 'I reckon you used to work for Mr Mooney?' This led to another discussion, another ten minutes of remembering. Eventually he showed them the bedrooms, and when they got to theirs Colin told this man, 'Here, my bed, and Brian, Wilf . . . here, weren't you?'

They stood remembering, listening to the banter after the lights had gone out, the farts and burps and curses that were always silenced (for a moment) by their father shouting for them to shut up and get to sleep. Wilf examined his spot, now plugged with a wardrobe. He felt the walls, turned to his brother and said, 'Remember when I scratched my name?' There was no sign of it now. Someone had filled the gaps, painted the walls green, put up sickly-looking curtains. 'All I can remember is Mum telling Dad, and the strap, again.'

Into the backyard, which had been flattened, paved, another square of grass in memory of Louths lost. Wilf thought it funny how people chose to live. Like the very act of breathing was a risk, and had to be managed. 'Dad had a few carrots growing there, remember, Colin?'

The old man out with his farming tools, this overkill of overalls and hobnail boots. The way the carrots were yellow and scrawny because the place had been built on landfill. Colin checked his watch and said, 'Come on, Wilf, we'd better get back.'

As they returned to town, clouds moved in from the west. Already fluffy and threatening, grey around the edges, smelling of rain. 'What's the rush?' Wilf asked, as Colin picked up the pace, checked his watch again and said, 'That was so depressing.'

'Just think of Mum: all those years cooking rabbits in a pot, and going outside to pee.'

'So *small*. Those nasty little rooms, and the smell of it, still. How could anyone stay? And nowhere to go. Where do you go, Wilf? What do you do all day?'

'I work.'

Shaking his head. Quickening. 'Connor's done the right thing. I just hope he goes further. London. America. He's got the spirit.'

'What spirit?'

'*Something better*, Wilf.'

Colin led the way into Monk's, turned to his brother and said, 'Don't be upset.' He opened the door, looked in and said, 'Bugger me.'

'*What?*' Wilf asked.

Colin noticed Karen busy drying glasses. 'It doesn't matter. It's not even surprising.' And smiling. 'We'll catch up tonight.' Turning and going up to his room.

Wilf sat at the bar. He noticed the morning's coffee still bubbling and said, 'Maybe we should change it?'

Karen started fixing it. 'Just what you'd expect.'

'What?'

'The meeting.'

'What meeting?'

'Colin told me this morning. He was going out to tell people. Eleven am, here.'

Wilf didn't get it.

'A meeting to see who'll take your jobs. So you can retire. Didn't he tell you?'

'Colin went out and . . .?'

'Yes. Eleven, and what's it now?' Checking the old clock that couldn't keep time. 'Quarter past, and not a soul. Well, that says it all, doesn't it?'

Wilf was half glad, half angry.

'Monk said he didn't care. We never get many on a Monday.'

Wilf left the bar, stormed up the stairs and knocked on his brother's door. Colin appeared and said, 'Well, that just goes to show, Wilf. No one gives a shit. They're happy to let you do everything. My advice now, is for you to—'

'I don't want your advice, or help.'

'But you want to retire?'

'Not like this. Now what's everyone going to think?'

'See, always worried about other people's opinions.'

'Fuck!'

'That's it.'

'No, fuck!' Storming back down the stairs. Turning back and saying, 'A public meeting? What am I, a lost dog?'

17

Not much was said on the journey to Dogs Bay. The brothers, taking in the land, warmed by a small sun in a big, blue sky. Two fishing rods (courtesy Simon's 'Hire-A-Rod') rattling in the back of the J2. Worms. And talk about fat lambs on the radio. Colin saying something about Wilf holding grudges. 'For days . . . when it suited you.'

'I had to explain to George Daly. I told him you were joking.'

More silence. Old rubber on the road.

'Back on Louth, things were different,' Wilf said. 'People looked out for each other. Ted, remember him? His roof collapses and there's ten men helping him fix it. Imagine that happening today.'

But Colin couldn't help it. 'You were the one saying . . .'

'I'll do it my way.'

'What's that?'

'I had to call Bobby and tell him I'd keep collecting his vegetables. And anyway, you could've told me.'

'I knew what you'd say.'

'Always going behind people's backs.'

'Right.' Letting out a lungful of air. 'Maybe I shouldn't have come?'

They arrived at the beach and followed the path from the carpark. The little trail they'd used as kids. Carrying their rods (as now), their bait, their big feet in small boots, a loaf of bread hollowed out and stuffed with potato chips. Colin said, 'It's not 1949 anymore.'

Wilf selected the rocks (the ones he remembered) and said, 'This was the best spot.'

'It wasn't here,' Colin said.

'It was.'

'No, further along. Don't you remember?'

Wilf knew he was wrong. About everything. He opened the bait and started threading lugworm onto his hook. 'Well?' he said to his brother, who did the same thing.

'It's too shallow,' Colin said.

'We used to get bream, remember? Big ones. Take them home for Mum.'

'That was Seaweed Point.'

Wilf wasn't listening. He cast off and the line snagged in rocks, so he tried again. This time he got it further out, but guessed there was no point trying at low tide. 'Lucy called, just about in tears, asking why I was stopping.'

'And you told her you were retiring?'

'I told her I was looking for someone else, but hadn't had any luck. I said I was patient, and I'd find someone. Maybe Connor.'

'*Connor?*'

'Someone. She was alright after that.'

'Fine,' Colin said, 'but you'll be driving down Corkscrew Road and the lights'll go out and you'll end up in the valley.'

'Worse ways to finish.'

'And better.' Casting off. The right distance, a little plop, the float bobbing just beyond his brother's. 'Me leaving was a big step, but it didn't happen by itself. I had to *make* it happen.'

'Well, not just you.'

'*What?*'

'A lot of sacrifice on other people's part.'

'Well, thank you. Thank. You. If I haven't said it before.'

'You haven't.'

'Ta. *Brother.*'

Standing. Waiting.

'All I meant,' Colin said, 'is that I had to be ruthless. I *wanted* to go.'

'Fine. You wanted to go. You went. You had to leave people. Me and Brian had to stay.'

'You didn't have to do anything. You could've gone anywhere, but you didn't move an inch. You didn't *want* to. So don't blame me now.'

Two boys went past with their own rods. One of them said, 'You'll never catch anything there. You'll have to move.' Indicating, then passing on.

'He's right,' Colin said.

And Wilf: 'Even when Dad died?'

'Okay, I should've come back earlier.'

'It was all down to me and Brian. And then you've got the nerve to waltz in and organise this meeting and make people think that I . . .'

Colin said, 'Is there any point standing here if there are no fish?' He reeled in his line, took his rod and set off along the path. Wilf cursed him, but packed up, followed him to the new spot and said, 'It wasn't here.'

'Yes, it was.' Casting off.

The boys called again: 'You won't catch anything with worms.'

But they waited, playing with their lines, and the boys watched them, laughed, and one called, 'Do you want to use our bait?'

'No, we do bloody not,' Wilf said, and they laughed again.

'You're just stubborn,' Colin said.

'And you're . . .'

'What?' But then laughing. 'I am glad I came. To see how little things have changed.'

'Plenty's changed.'

'What?'

New shops. The school's expanded. But apart from that. Not that he was going to let on.

'Do you remember that day . . . we were here? You and Brian jumped in the water, and went out in a rip. Brian got back, but you started calling, "Someone! Please!"'

'I can't remember that.'

'So I get in and swim out and take you under the arms and you're kicking and screaming and making a big drama, but I slowly head back to these rocks.'

'You're mixing me up with someone else.'

'I only ever came with you two. I saved your life, Brother.'

'You saw that in a film.'

'We went home and I told Dad what had happened and he exploded, said what sort of idiot goes swimming in a rip?'

Then one of the boys was beside them, a lid covered in mackerel. 'Use these. We've got three already.'

Colin thanked him, roughed his hair, and Wilf was left standing alone, on the cliffs of Louth, watching the world from a distance.

Despite the mackerel, they headed back, fishless, along the path, an hour later. Wilf said, 'Just as well. I'm not up to cooking fish tonight.'

'We can go to the Eat Inn, I haven't had diarrhoea since yesterday. Although it's funny. Three decades beside a beach and I haven't once been fishing.'

'Why's that?'

'It's not the same, is it?'

Wilf knew what he meant. The bay so shallow it took the water a hundred metres to turn blue. The beach, or lack of it, all rock and froth. Three old men, fat and white, up to their stomachs in the water and, further back, a teenage girl scared to go in past her hips.

Home to Selwyn. All the ghosts in the graveyard, although Wilf avoided it. The turn off from the McDermott's place. Colin didn't say anything. Perhaps he didn't realise, or remember. Past the school, the kids trailing out of their rooms, across the yard, toward town.

'Isn't that your friend?' Colin said.

Wilf slowed and saw Trevor, on his knees, gathering the contents of his school bag from the ground. He pulled over and the brothers helped him gather his dancing shoes, books, uneaten lunch. Colin strayed onto the road and someone braked hard to avoid him, tooted, and he shouted, 'You should go slow around kids.' Wilf asked Trevor where he was going and he said, 'Mum wants me to meet her in town . . . to drive me home. Have you stopped?'

'No, I haven't.' He noticed the small, blue eyes, the mouth that rarely bothered with words. 'How did all this end up on the ground?' As he packed the bag, jammed the mess of papers to make them fit.

'They just fell out.'

Colin helped, and they returned the bag to him.

'Just fell out? All of that?'

Trevor glanced up, but then away. A tall boy, fifteen or sixteen, standing further along the road, leaning on a fence, stretching back like he was trying to break his body in two. There was a girl close by, getting closer, impressed with whatever this boy had to say.

'Him?' Wilf asked.

'He was just mucking around.'

'What's his name?'

'Ben.'

Wilf thought for a moment, and remembered. 'Ben what?'

'Magee.'

He surveyed the cocky face, the body language, the girl about to jump on him. He stormed along the road, and Trevor called, 'Wilf!' But he didn't hear, or care. Colin was a few steps behind. This is how they'd do it, when they were at school.

'You did that?' Wilf said to Ben, indicating.

'I did not.' Calling. 'You little liar.'

Wilf was going to do it, but his brother saved him the time, taking the teenager by the throat with his unforgiving pincers and turning him around, placing a knee in his back and pinning him against the wall. 'I saw it.'

'Fuck off. I'll have you for assault.'

The brothers laughed. They still said this!

'I saw you empty his bag, and I know what's been going on.'

'I never—'

'Shh. I'll tell you when to speak. Your name is Ben Magee, and you sell cigarettes to children.' Wilf opened his bag, and pulled out two cartons.

'They're not mine.'

'Your mother buys them at the IGA, and gives them to you.'

'Who are you?'

'I'm fucking Morpheus, mate, and I've come to eat your kidneys. Got it?'

The girl backed off then walked away. Wilf checked the boy's pockets, pulled out notes and coins that fell on the ground. 'And what do you do with your pocket money?'

No reply.

'Or your brother? Patrick, isn't it?'

The boy relaxed. 'Let go.'

So Colin released him.

'I need his address.'

'Fuck off.'

Colin tried again, and Wilf moved his face an inch from the boy's. 'Street, and number.'

Colin persuaded him, and he said, 'Church Street. Twenty.'

'Good boy.' Taking a pen and book from his bag and writing it down.

'So, we'll take these smokes,' Wilf said, 'and this money, and we'll lock them away until you're twenty-one. Or until I hear anything else about your behaviour. Your conduct around thirteen-year-old boys.' Looking back at Trevor, standing petrified. 'I guess that makes it clear?'

Nothing.

'Brother? I'm glad you showed such restraint.' And to Ben. 'Nothing broken?'

18

'No, it wouldn't work,' Wilf said to his niece, gently holding her arm, guiding her back inside the house.

'He's my son.'

'All under control,' Colin called from the garden (the orchids lying lifeless in the mud, a spotted rose, struggling).

But Orla wouldn't be told. She put on her cardigan and said, 'I'm not going to say anything. There must be a reason.'

Wilf had her inside the house, into the lounge room, sat her down. 'The minute I know anything I'll call.'

'*Uncle!*'

There were various reasons, but mostly, Wilf didn't like how she looked. Not one particular thing, or day, but when he compared her to the pictures on the wall it became obvious. The skin hanging from her cheeks, dark eyes, bony ridges of shoulder and collarbone. 'We'll sort it out.'

'I know what'll happen.'

Colin was behind his brother. 'It's all taken care of, Orla. We'll buy him a beer.'

'I bet he's contacted his father.'

'We don't know,' Wilf said, switching on the television. 'We just don't know.'

Wilf knew it had to be fixed. Whatever medicine she was taking, however good or bad a job her body was doing, none of this would matter if Connor stayed in Georgetown. It had been six days now. Wilf stopping by and finding his niece in bed, in tears, old food in the fridge, dishes in the sink. He and Colin had taken care of it, and then he'd said, 'Enough.'

Orla seemed to accept the offer. 'Just don't make things worse.'

'We won't,' Colin said. 'Just a chat.'

'Tell him I'm missing him and everything's made up, ready, and he doesn't have to go back to school if he doesn't want to.'

'Under control, Niece,' Wilf said, throwing a rug over her legs, switching on *The Chase*, arranging the pills he'd picked up from George, the freshly-sliced apple, the carrot juice the doctor had recommended. The clean kitchen. The washed sheets that Colin had helped him hang out, saying, 'Brian would be turning in his grave.'

'Brian's not here. We are. We've got to fix this, or else that boy's going to finish her off. All of us.'

Orla, sitting in her spot, had heard all of this. As she called, messaged, WhatsApp, Facebook – none of it working.

As they set off toward town – narrow streets, an old dog lying in the middle of the road – Wilf said to his brother, 'I can imagine what he's up to . . . with this Magee character.'

'You don't know.'

'I can imagine.' A small bedsit on Church Street, three, four, five druggies in each room, all day orgies, pizza, beer and heroin. 'He's smart. I can remember him getting top marks, and Orla being so proud. Not like us.'

'Speak for yourself.'

Wilf's phone rang and he answered it. Noah asked if he had five minutes, and Wilf said not really, we're headed to Georgetown to find my nephew. But the principal insisted: five minutes.

Wilf arriving, telling his brother to wait in Reception, Noah coming out and telling him he'd like to see him, too. So Wilf guessed what it was about. He whispered to his brother, 'Just like in the old days.'

'That was you.'

'What's that?' Noah asked, offering them a seat.

'Called in to see the principal,' Wilf said. 'Only once, when that old bastard Davids gave me the cane. On the arse . . . if it's about the bus?'

'No, it's fixed. I should've got it done earlier. I'm sorry.'

Wilf said, 'My brother's been helping me.'

Noah smiled. 'Los Angeles?'

'You've been?'

'No. Busier than Selwyn, I suppose?' The concert band started playing *Greensleeves* and Noah stood, closed the door and returned. 'What happened with Darcy?' he said to Wilf, leaning forward.

'Well, you know Darcy. Him and Connor (I was trying to teach him the bus) didn't get along, and there were words, and Connor – I tell you, Noah, I warned him, I told him to sit down – but Connor being Connor.'

'His mother said Connor just about put his head through the window.'

'No.'

'Well?'

'He did . . . manhandle him, but I put a stop to it. The boy's a terror, and he needs sorting out.'

'By Connor?'

'Someone. No one's doing it.'

'They are. He's had several detentions this year.'

Wilf laughed. 'What, you sit him down for an hour after school and let him do his homework?'

'What would you suggest?'

'Well, if Darcy's to be sorted . . . I say something but he ignores me, and poor Luke and Trevor have to put up with it. But Connor didn't.'

Colin said, 'You can't let them run things, Noah. *We're* the adults.'

'And Ben?'

Colin said to his brother, 'Who's that?'

Wilf shrugged.

'I haven't heard anything from his mother, but people saw what happened.'

Wilf thought, and decided. 'You won't be having any trouble from him.'

'Why?'

'I tell you, Noah, what he's been up to. What he does to other kids. And you can sort it all.'

Noah thought about this. 'If I get reports.'

'A kid's hardly going to tell you.'

'Colin?'

'There was a scuffle. I had to remove this boy, this turd. Nothing vindictive. Everyone got the message, everything was sorted.'

And Noah: 'I'll be the one in the shit.'

'We're just saving you a lot of paperwork, Noah.' Smiling. 'Although you could be right. In which case you'd need to find someone else to drive your bus.'

But Noah said, 'I've had a talk to Darcy, he won't cause you any more trouble. But if you could have a word to Connor.'

Back on the road to Georgetown, Colin said to his brother, 'I thought we handled that well, Wilf.'

'Agreed.'

It was a good day for driving. The needle stayed in the green. Wilf sped, Colin warned him to slow down, but Wilf said he knew the road so well there was no risk. 'Dad taught us well.'

There'd been a Cortina parked out front of 23 St Joseph's Road. Tom Healy had shown his family, explained how there was only thirty thousand on the clock and how this would mean no more walking, or bus, or asking favours. Faded paint and a lifting duco, but apart from that, a steal. But their mum had said, 'I hate to bring this up, but you don't actually have a licence, Thomas Healy.'

'No, it's easy,' he'd said. 'You put the stick next to D for Drive, and off it goes. Why do I need the government to give me a piece of paper to do that?'

So they'd piled in: the seventeen, eighteen and twenty-year-old brothers in the back, their parents in the front. Tom had driven around town, and his boys had told him to go faster. 'You could walk quicker than this,' Brian had said.

'How much?' their mum had asked, arms crossed.

'Less than you think.'

'How much?'

The price had been mentioned, there'd been more words, Tom had told them how they could go for day trips to Northhead, Georgetown, anywhere.

'Licences are overrated,' Wilf said.

'Tell me you've got one now,' Colin said.

Wilf just smiled.

'You drive a school bus?'

'No one's ever asked to see it. If they do ...' Shrugging. 'Maybe that's my way out?'

'You don't want a way out. You want to keep doing all this, but complaining about it.'

Back into Georgetown, with its own spreading suburbs, a shopping mall Wilf had never dared enter. Colin followed a map. Roads narrowing, cars parked on footpaths, kids on scooters, jumping improvised ramps. Then Church Street. Number twenty. Two-storey, red brick, but crumbling. Wilf parked far enough away to see, but not be seen. He switched off the engine and said, 'What a dump.'

'And it doesn't follow,' Colin said. 'You want to be a pop star you go on *The Voice*. What are your chances of being discovered here?'

So they waited. A young woman opened the front door, looked out then walked down the street. The brothers watched her go. Purple hair and what looked like a nose ring.

'Should we?' Colin said.

'Wait. I want to see what he's up to.'

For an hour, nothing. A rough neighbourhood, a group of young men, bottles in paper bags, wandering. Two mums with their own coloured hair, prams, and a small tribe of kids. A boy, six or seven, fell behind, found a stick and started poking a cat. 'Look at them,' Wilf said. 'They just breed and you and me pay for it.' Counting the kids. 'Where are the fathers?'

'So what are we going to do?' Colin asked.

'Shh.'

The same girl returned with a plastic bag, opened the door and went in.
'Maybe he's got himself a girlfriend?' Colin said.

But Wilf was caught up in the neighbourhood – the way these small villas had been let go. How people had concreted their little bits of yard, left a mess of bins and toys, puddles full of rubbish. Barking dogs. Thumping music. And the homes, peeling and fading, the fascia boards rotting and dropping. 'It's like people have given up.' He only had six square feet, but he looked after them. 'How would Mum be?' he said. Cleaning the toilet every morning, and the boys saying, 'You don't need to do it *every* day.'

'The mess you three make.'

Wilf's phone rang, and he answered it. 'Orla?'

Three or four dogs had set up a conversation. Wilf covered the phone, said, 'They don't stop for breath,' and wound up the window. 'That you, Niece?'

'You there?' she asked.

'Just pulled up. You keeping warm?'

'I'm fine. Have you seen him yet?'

'No. Just about to head in. I'll call you . . . Orla?'

A faint coughing, moving away and then toward the phone. 'Don't get angry with him, Uncle. You know what he'll do.'

'I won't.'

'Like I said – if he doesn't want to come home, tell him to call me.' The voice fading, and disappearing.

She didn't ring off. He could hear her moving, the television in the background. *The Chase*, still, a question about Claudius. Another cough, the phone dropping onto the floor. 'Orla?' He studied the door to number twenty. Not quite closed. A light in the front room. 'Orla?'

'What is it?' Colin asked.

A moment of synchronicity, the barking, music, scooter wheels and voices all moving in and out of phase, and everything making sense.

'Wilf?'

Wilf got out and stormed across the road. Colin was a few steps behind. 'Go easy.'

He'd decided. He knocked, pushed the door open a few inches and called, 'Connor?'

Nothing.

'Connor Healy, it's your uncle.'

Voices from deep inside the house, someone laughing. A faint whiff of smoke, and Wilf recognised the woodbines that Simon sold.

'You're angry,' Colin said. 'Careful.'

Wilf entered, walked down a hallway that finished in a big room, dark, lit by coloured lights. Three figures in bean bags, two of them coupled. Some bloke without a shirt sat up and said, 'Who the fuck are you?'

Wilf approached him and said, 'Patrick?'

No reply.

'I met your mother and brother. That was him, wasn't it, selling smokes?'

'Uncle,' Connor said, from the other bean bag, his guitar across his lap. 'What are you doing?'

Wilf took the three steps it required, and stood in front of him. 'I've just been speaking to your mother.'

'So?'

'*So?* Your mother.'

Pat Magee moved the girl with the purple hair from his lap, stood and said, 'You can't just walk in here.'

Wilf didn't care. He switched on the light and surveyed the piles of clothes, the few guitars, CDs, vinyl and the girl in her panties and bra. And to his brother: 'Help us look, will you?'

'For what?' Patrick said.

The girl picked up the phone and said, 'I'm calling the police,' but Pat said, 'No, no, no.' Taking it off her.

Wilf couldn't find anything, so he returned to his nephew. 'You want to ask how she is? *Your mother.* What's happened to you, boy?'

Connor just shrugged. His FUCK TRUMP T-shirt and his spindly legs trailing across the carpet. 'I told you what I was doing.'

'You don't answer our calls.'

''Cos I know what you're going to say. *Come home to Selwyn.*'

Wilf didn't care. He grabbed Connor by the T-shirt, dragged him out to the kitchen and sat him down. Then he took out his phone and called Orla. He shoved the phone in front of the boy's face. 'Go on, then, tell her what you've been up to.'

Connor ended the call, but Wilf dialled again, then Connor grabbed the phone and threw it across the room. Wilf slapped him hard across the face and Connor said, 'Just because I don't want to drive your bus.' Holding his cheek.

Wilf knew he'd got it wrong. Patrick stood watching, the girl, Colin. Connor said, 'I was gonna call when I was ready.'

'When *you* were ready?' Colin said. 'But your mother . . .'

Connor moved across the room, picked up the phone and returned it to Wilf. 'Go on then.'

Wilf dialled, and returned it. Connor waited, but there was no reply. He said, 'They reckon plenty of people get it . . . and get better.'

'That's it?' Wilf said. ''Cos she'll get better?'

Connor's shoulders dropped, and he stared down at the ground.

'We've got the van out front.'

Connor thought about it. 'We've got an audition in the morning.'

'Who?'

'Me and some blokes.'

'Fucking hopeless.' Wilf stormed out, and Colin said to the boy, 'You need to get yourself home and sort this mess out.'

'Why should he?' the girl asked.

The Healy brothers sat for a few minutes in the van, Wilf tapping his finger on the steering wheel. 'That's exactly what she said'd happen.'

'Wouldn't have mattered,' Colin said.

So Wilf called his niece and told her they'd spoken to him, that he'd settled in and, kids being kids, hadn't thought to ring. But he would. She seemed relieved but, again, a few words and then silence.

19

'This has taken twelve months,' Bobby said, removing the axle from the bag.

They examined it – smooth, turned on each end. 'Chrome and molybdenum,' Bobby said. 'I won't tell you how much.' He inserted the axle in its housing and fixed the pins. Wilf watched how he handled the parts, stroked them, talked to them, like small children he'd had manufactured in Japan. 'So how much longer?'

'No point talking like that,' Bobby said. 'It's ready when it's ready. These things can't be rushed.'

Seventeen years and counting. When he'd started, Bobby had told Wilf it'd take two, three years, perhaps, but then he'd had trouble sourcing the spruce and reverted to plywood; the glue, coming up with his own recipe. Not one part he could buy market-ready.

Light rain on the shed roof. The morning after the mission to Georgetown, the slow journey home. The clouds had moved in, but held off during the night. Now the rain was soaking Bobby's fields, forming puddles and rivulets beside his house and farm buildings. Wilf thought the land, with its own woodbine and fairy thimbles, smelled good. He stood at the door to Bobby's shed and said, 'I'll get them, will I?'

'Wait a minute, I'll help.' Tightening the bolts that would hold it all in place. 'Anyway, I wouldn't have argued with him,' Bobby said.

'It's not that simple. He's a big boy and prone to get . . . physical.'

'So what? If a bolt doesn't fit you have to make it. You shoulda got him by the scruff, dragged him to that van of yours.'

'Maybe I should've.' Studying it, sitting in the yard, dirt washing down the sides.

'Given him a good slap—'

'I did.'

'And told him to grow up. I would've.' Shaking his head at the boy he'd always doubted. 'Made him write an apology to his mother.'

All of this made sense, Wilf thought. But it wouldn't work. 'He's too caught up in himself.'

'All the more reason. My dad had me out on the horse in the dark. I used to curse him, but in the end . . .'

'While he was in here making his Tiger Moth?'

'He didn't have the skills. Someone should've told him.'

Wilf could remember the photos of the wreckage at the bottom of the hill, and how the Tiger Moth had sat mouldering for months before they took it away. Another shot of the ambulance, and two men covering the body with a rug.

'Kids today need a good kick up the arse.' Spinning the wheels. 'Look, they fit beautifully.'

'When you going to test it?'

'All in good time.'

The rain was getting heavier. 'I can pick them myself.'

'Two minutes, Wilf.'

Bobby returned to his work desk, the plans that had guided him for years. 'One thing I worry about's this fairing,' he said, indicating a line running down the side of the fuselage. 'I'm not sure I turned it right.'

'You want to be sure,' Wilf said, gathering rain in the palm of his hand.

Another photo Bobby had shown him – his father, lying in the van, blood on his face, a queer expression. He'd asked why they'd taken it and Bobby had said, 'Mum wanted something to remember him.' And now he explained: 'The bolt anchors on the left wing – they reckon they needed to be three-quarter inch. He used half, said they'd do.'

Bobby straightened his back, came over to his friend and said, 'Did you call her this morning?'

Wilf said he did, and she sounded much the same, so it was important, Bobby, she had some greens. 'She grinds them up in a vitamiser. Reckons they keep her going.'

Bobby took a moment before saying, 'Not much of a day for Mount Shank.'

Colin had got up early, come down for breakfast, greeted his brother and said, 'I booked the bus.'

'What bus?'

'That mountain . . . Shank. Tourist for a day, Wilf.'

Twenty minutes later, the small tour bus out front of Gould's, Colin climbing aboard with another dozen tourists (mostly staying at Hyland's), opening the side window and saying to his brother, 'Give Orla my love.' Wilf could see his brother was already leaving. Tiring of the routines that gave their town weight, and meaning. The process of gathering lettuce leaves from the floor of his van; of making sure George had given the right medicine, and dose.

As they headed out, Bobby said, 'And what happens to the boy if she dies?'

'It'll all come down to me, I suppose.'

'Get him out here. He can stay in my back room and I'll get him working. Those pigs start snorting at four.' He stopped to stroke one on the head.

'No, apparently he's going to be this big star.'

'My arse. That, Wilf, is the path to perdition.' Trudging, slipping in furrows. 'Whereas pigs . . . Sounds like Orla hasn't got long?'

Wilf didn't want to think about it. It was one of a sub-set of unsolvable problems that followed him through life, like the old, mangy dog at his feet. 'He'll be wanting money soon enough. Then we'll hear from him.'

'Don't know. They just go and take it, don't they, these days?'

'Not Connor.' Although he wasn't sure anymore. The boy a village had raised, in his fuck-you T-shirts, always looking down, like it was all too much, like he suffered more than most. 'His dad,' Wilf said, 'was a waste of bloody time. That's what started it all.'

'Rubbish. We had it tough.'

'Connor worshipped him.'

'Well, call the lazy bastard, tell him to get back here and sort his mess out.'

They picked cabbages and dropped them into a hessian sack. Carrots. Potatoes. Bobby, as young as he felt, with his legs spaced, lungs full. Later, Wilf set off for home. The few familiar roads and shafts of light from the clearing sky. The certainty that this day would be much the same as every other, except for the dying, and the grunting and rooting around in the mud. And the birds, still coming. Millions, it seemed. When he arrived back at Orla's he gathered his sack, went in and called, 'You decent?'

No reply.

'Orla?'

He put the vegetables in the kitchen, went to her door and said, 'Can I come in?' Opening it, although it was stopped by a pile of clothes on the ground. 'Orla?'

The small figure, lost in her sheets, her mouth open (this seemed new, and strange), both arms hanging over the side. Wilf thought, Jesus, no, not today, please. With the sky blue, the wind fresh and clean. Not today. Tomorrow, maybe? A month, a year, but not today. He took a few steps and sat beside her. Held her arm, moved it gently, then shook it.

He needed a piss. The first thing he thought of. A piss, a drink, a pill, a reason to step outside of his daily disaster. 'Orla?'

What to do? The course Monk had organised. Placing a person on their side and saying to them, *Can you hear me?* Breathing in their mouth, pushing down on their chest, all nightshirt, still warm.

Warm. 'Orla?' Her eyes moving under her lids. 'Can you hear me?'

She opened her eyes and said, 'Tired.'

'You want to get up? I just been to Bobby's, we picked you some vegetables.'

She smiled, 'Thanks,' but her eyes closed again.

No, not right, Wilf thought. He went out to the lounge, paced a few moments, then took out his phone and dialled 000. A young voice came on and asked if there was a problem. Too bloody right, he thought. 'My niece . . . she's not conscious.'

'The patient's name?'

He told her, and she said it was going to be forty minutes. 'Is she stable?'

'No.'

'Can you take her to the health centre?'

He rang off, went in, woke his niece again and said, 'I reckon we should pop you to the doctor's.'

She only managed to look at him, confused, before closing her eyes again. He found her gown, pulled back her sheets and said, 'You'll have to help me.' Her legs all bone, minus the shedding flesh. He could see her hips, the way her legs tapered and twisted, the pale skin, the bruises, the blue veins and arteries trying their best. 'Can you get up?'

No. So he stepped out again, rang the medical centre and explained. The woman told him they weren't an Emergency and he'd have to call 000, and he said he already had. 'You're going to have to send someone.'

This woman put down the phone, went away for a minute, returned and said, 'He'll be there in a couple of minutes.' She took his address and rang off. Wilf went back in, sat with his niece, stroked the back of her hand and said, 'He played me one of his songs.'

But she didn't respond. He kept checking that blood was moving through the little arteries in her neck. All was good. As good as it had ever been, he tried to tell himself. Pumping. His niece moving to get comfortable. 'He's got a few nice ones. One about Monk's, strangely enough. I think, given time, he'll find an audience. He said he'd been so busy he'd forgotten to ring. But they're idiots, aren't they, kids that age?'

The doctor arrived, let himself in and found the room. Wilf didn't recognise him, and asked if he was new. He didn't reply. He sat beside Orla and said, 'Some people would sleep the whole day if you let them.' Taking her blood pressure, checking her eyes, examining the mostly unopened pills beside the bed. Then he said to Wilf, 'You found her?'

'Yes. I'm her uncle. My brother's daughter. Well, he died but . . .' Wondering why he was blabbering.

The doctor asked him to step out onto the porch, where he lit a cigarette, examined the clearing sky and said, 'She can't stay here any longer.' Explaining that he'd checked her notes, and couldn't see much cause for hope. Like that. A few brutal words. 'We should get her to hospital. You've called, you said?'

'I did but . . .' So he called again.

Then the doctor said, 'They'll take care of her in Northhead.'

And that was it. He put out his smoke, returned to the bedroom and said to Orla, 'Maybe your uncle could pack you a few things?'

Wilf found Orla's bag, went through her drawers, packing what he guessed was necessary. Into the bathroom, a selection of toiletries, all the time, talking. That's what mattered most, he guessed. He placed the bag on the lounge, returned, said, 'Him and this mate, this Pat, they're cooking meals, sort of. Well, you know, the most you could expect from a couple of teenagers. But I pulled him aside and gave him a hundred and said let me know if you need more.'

Wilf greeted the paramedics, shook hands, barely containing his relief. In the sound of cannulas being removed from plastic, the deep-throated chimes, the way they did it all so matter-of-factly. No dramas. The sound of tape fixing the drip to her arm, the way she opened her eyes and smiled at them.

He saw them off, promised to follow, in the morning, cleaned up the worst of his niece's house. He washed her clothes, put everything in its place in the kitchen. Then he went into his nephew's room. She'd made his bed with clean sheets, left an old Paddington on his pillow. He picked it up, smelled it, examined where it had split open. He tried to call his nephew again, but there was no reply. Finally, his brother was at the door. 'Orla?'

Wilf went out to explain and Colin said, 'You should've called me.'

'*I* should've?'

Colin knew his brother's voice, his tone, the fatty deposits on his face, plumped up when he was angry. 'So now you're pissed off with me?'

Wilf turned and went inside.

Colin followed him in. 'What, I knew she'd get sick today?'

'I didn't say a thing.'

'Christ, Wilf. This was meant to be a holiday.'

He glared at his brother. '*A holiday*? That's why you came?'

20

Things didn't get better. When Wilf returned to Monk's an hour later he went upstairs and tried to decide whether to knock on his brother's door. *Why?* Why should he? It was time Colin went back to California, his glass-fronted gym, smoggy canals and movie stars. Karen walked past with an armful of linen and said, 'I wouldn't bother. He packed his things and left an hour ago.'

'For where?'

'Hyland's. Can't say I'm surprised. It's a miracle you two lasted that long.'

Wilf stormed downstairs, along the road to the motel, pan pipes, scent diffuser, the *Financial Times* sitting unopened on a coffee table beside the fire they kept burning all day. He approached Reception and said, 'I'm after Colin Healy.'

The girl checked the book. 'Should I call him?'

'Which room?'

'I can't say.'

'Yes, call him . . . please.'

A minute later, Colin emerged dressed in trackpants, T-shirt, old socks with holes. He approached his brother and said, 'Let's go to my room.'

'Let's not. What are you doing?'

Colin smiled. 'My final night . . . I thought I'd treat myself.'

'Treat yourself? Jesus, Colin. I arranged for you to stay at Monk's.'

'I'll stop by and thank him. Should we get dinner?'

'They've got room service.' Storming off, but stopping and calling across the foyer, 'I'm going to see our niece in the morning, if you've got time.'

Wilf spent the night at the bar, testing his own whiskies. Monk served him, asked why Colin had left, and he said, 'He says he wants a bit of luxury.'

'We've got luxury, haven't we?'

Then to bed, but he tossed and turned all night, caught between Orla, hooked up (no doubt) on a dozen machines, in a clean, white room with a view of the river. Strangers coming and going. Measured serves of pork and potatoes, red jelly. And Colin, sprawling in his underwear, eating oysters and drinking merlot. The last night they might have been together – and this was the choice he'd made. Karen was right – it wasn't surprising, Colin wasn't looking for home, just tea-towel consolations he could hang in his room in The Mansions.

Still, duty called, so he pulled up in front of Hyland's at ten to eight and went in and asked for Mr Colin Healy. He waited between the ceramic logs and cigarette machine. Colin came out, offered his hand and they shook, like he'd just arrived. 'Do you want breakfast? Ten dollars, wild mushrooms, the lot.'

'I've eaten,' Wilf said. He wanted to remind him about Bobby's bacon, Mrs Gould's stew, the freshly baked bread and coffee he brewed at seven every morning. He wanted to say, *It would've been good, wouldn't it? You, me, Brian . . . Mum and Dad . . . sitting down together?* Because that's what his brother meant to him. His last connection with the ghosts of Louth.

As they drove toward Georgetown, Wilf said, 'We didn't do much.'

'We caught up.' Staring out of the window.

Wilf had been listening to Lyric FM, Beethoven's *Emperor*, one of his favourites. The way the piano jiggled with the orchestra. Colin turned it down, but Wilf turned it back up. 'I thought we might go out to Louth.'

'What's there? Some old stones. It's too long ago.'

'Hardly any time.'

'You're serious, about going back to live there?'

'Yes.'

'Well, good luck.'

'What's so strange about that?'

Wilf could remember the way he and Colin had sat outside at night watching the stock, and the sky, littered with stars; the frost of the galaxy; the way the salt came off the ocean. He wanted to say to his brother, *Don't you remember the breakers urging and receding?* All of it. But mostly, how they'd sit together and talk about almost anything. How everyone was going to help the new people, a couple of brothers from Scotland, build a house on the bay. The rocks already gathered, the timber cut and shaped, the bags of concrete ready for the mixer.

But so what? Wilf thought, weaving along the old roads, the miraculous way two cars could pass so closely but never touch.

Colin said, 'I met a woman.'

'Who?'

'From Ohio. She's sixty-three and her husband just died of colon cancer.'

'You met her at Mount Shank?'

'Yes. We spent the whole time together and talked about . . . everything. Bought some lunch. But who knows?'

'From *Ohio*?'

'She gave me her number and said to call when I get home.'

Wilf wasn't surprised. His brother had always had the itch, venturing, most nights, out to the long-drop to study his magazines. He wasn't sure if it was the girl, or the idea of the girl; the person, or the promise of safe passage. 'Romance?'

'You never know. It's been a while, Brother.'

'Yes, but after a certain point . . .'

'It never stops working. The flag just keeps flying, all night, eh?' Grinning.

Wilf wasn't sure he cared. 'So it was all worthwhile?'

'What?'

'Coming all this way, to find what's on your doorstep.'

'My thoughts exactly. Raelene, her name, and she reckons she was thinking of moving to California anyway.'

Colin'd had enough of Beethoven. He said, 'Old fashioned stuff,' and changed the channel to talkback. Wilf said, 'I was listening to that.' And changed it back.

'I never knew you liked classical music.'

There's a lot you don't know, Wilf thought. 'Better than all that prattling. People talk and talk and nothing changes.'

'Yes, it does.'

What are you talking about? Wilf thought. Colin used to make sense, years ago, when they sat on the wall watching the sheep shagging. He used to say, 'If you join that star there' – pointing – 'and that one, they make a woman's titty.'

'How?'

'See.' Connecting the dots for his brother. 'Those Americans gave me a magazine.'

'What sort?'

'Want to see?'

Colin had always been a furious masturbator, making the most of every moment, and opportunity. But people, even brothers, grew apart. There were no titties in the sky, only crabs, and twins, and the man with a sword in his belt.

'This time tomorrow I'll be in Auckland,' Colin said.

'That should be a relief.'

'What do you mean?'

'Get away from this dump.'

'Christ, Wilf. *It's a holiday*. I'm looking forward to it. A few hours' flight. Why not?'

Because our niece might be dead this time tomorrow, Wilf thought.

'Anyway, Raelene said we might catch up before we head home.' Then turning to his brother. 'You can come over for the wedding. The sun might cheer you up.'

'Cheer me up? What, I'm miserable am I?'

The concerto ended and Colin tapped the button and said, 'Thank God for that.'

Wilf braked hard, pulled over and said, 'Do you mind?'

'What?'

Ten seconds became fifteen, twenty, then Colin said, 'Don't bother.' He got out, and slammed the door. 'I'll make my own way back.' Walking off.

Wilf watched his brother growing smaller in the rear-vison, walking, fast and determined, back toward Selwyn. Bugger you, he thought. He put the van into drive and set off toward Georgetown.

Of course, there were no parks in front of the University Hospital. He had to circle three times before finding a spot. Four dollars an hour. Typical blood-sucking councils. He checked his pocket but didn't have change so went into a shop and bought a newspaper he didn't want, returned, and the inspector was hovering. He said, 'It would be nice, wouldn't it, if the council made some parks.'

'You just can't make them.'

'Although you can charge for them.'

Heading in, thinking, this won't do. *Calm* yourself, Wilf. They're just people defined by their job descriptions. 'Always something good,' he mumbled. As his mother used to, setting his father straight, telling him to stop going on about taxes and how this Presley character had killed off music; how stone was preferable to brick, and kidneys to meatloaf.

He asked after his niece, but was told to wait for visiting hours. He said he'd come all the way from Selwyn, but apparently that didn't matter. Rules were rules. So he sat in the foyer while Health Minister Harris (the slide explained), Mid-Western Hospitals Development Trust Chairman Jim Canny and a herd of overfed cattle listened to speeches about the new Leben Building. Then the minister pulled a string and a little curtain opened to reveal a brass plaque. Everyone applauded. Like this man had built it himself.

Stop.

His mother saying to his father, 'What sort of example do you set your boys?'

'A good one.' Spreading sardines on his toast.

'Always so negative. The world wasn't put here for your convenience.'

'Negative? What did I say?'

All three boys grinning.

Plenty to be positive about, Wilf thought. Plenty. As he wondered how far his brother had gotten. Maybe he should've gone back, talked to him.

His mother saying to his father, 'It gets a person down.'

'What, I get you down?'

'Sometimes.'

'Well, maybe I should just jump off a cliff.'

'There's an idea.'

Now the boys were hiding their laughter.

'You can see her now,' the girl said to him.

Orla was sitting up in bed, reading a magazine. Wilf leaned over and kissed her and said, 'You're looking better.'

She straightened herself, put on a smile and said, 'Why'd you drive all that way?'

'It's not so far.'

'Where's Colin?'

Wilf explained and she said, 'You didn't, did you?'

'I tried, but you know what he's like.' Telling her about Raelene and Auckland or wherever it was, and how he was going to marry her and they'd live on the thirtieth floor and hopefully he'd jump from the balcony. 'So, what's the verdict?'

She told him it was nothing; she was run-down, tired. He asked about her count and she said it had improved and he went to check the notes on the end of the bed, but she said, 'You can't do that.'

He did anyway. 'They're down.'

'The same.'

'So what are they going to do?'

'They reckon I can go home in a few days.'

Of course. That would work. 'I've told Monk I'm giving up my room.'

'Why?'

'I'll move into Connor's room, and look after you.'

No, she said, that wasn't necessary. She could look after herself. But he said she couldn't, that was obvious, and she said she couldn't be bothered (thanks, anyway, Uncle) dealing with him fussing about the house all day. He didn't argue, yet. He examined her uneaten lunch and said, 'You don't want it?'

'Not yet.'

'You got to eat.'

'I will when I'm hungry.'

'See, you need someone to look after you. That's what Brian would want.'

No reply.

'And Dave.'

'Ha!'

'You heard from him?'

'No.'

'You should contact him.'

'Not likely.'

'Tell him about Connor.'

And she shot back: 'If he gave a shit about Connor he might call him occasionally.'

Wilf examined the sandwich, felt the thin, lifeless bread, the see-through ham with its bit of mustard. 'This is bloody awful.'

'It's made especially.'

'For a rabbit? How are you meant to get strong eating this? I'll go see them about something hot. A roast, a bit of meat, a bit of veg.'

'I'm not allowed.'

'*Not allowed*? Jesus. Your gran would be in here with a pot of stew.'

Orla said, 'Are you going to talk to Colin?'

'No.'

'You should.'

'You should let me come and cook for you. Or Mrs Gould, she'll make up some extra meals from the pub.'

'Uncle, you've got to go see him. He's all you've got. If he goes back to America . . .'

'Don't worry about that.'

'You're more stubborn than Dad.'

Wilf was scanning the room for more problems. 'He wouldn't listen to anyone. The number of times him and Dad came to blows.' Smiling at her, taking her hand and rubbing it a few times.

'All of the Healy men,' she said.

'Except, Colin. He just got along with everyone. Especially *Raelene*.'

'And what if he did? Nothing's stopping you.'

'Me? Who, Lucy, at ninety-something?'

'There's always hope, Uncle.'

He didn't want to argue. But Colin was beyond hope. 'Look at that.' The windows, grey with grime or dust or whatever it was. 'You think someone would clean them. There's seven of them standing out there in the nurses' bay.'

'They're not paid to clean windows.'

'Someone should. They're out the front fining people for parking.' He studied her small, round face. He'd seen it every day for decades. From this baby, looking up at him from her cot, this teenage girl, biting her lip as she concentrated on a chord. 'As long as you're feeling better.'

'Come on, take me for a walk.'

He helped her into a wheelchair and they went down in the lift and along a path into a small garden full of wood dock, irises and camellias. People were smoking, but Wilf ignored it. In the distance, the inspector was still writing fines.

'I'll be better tomorrow,' Orla said, 'and then I can come home.'

'I'm getting the place ready.'

'Don't.' Glaring at him. 'It's *my* place.'

The smoke was shitting him off. 'It'd be cheaper for me – and an empty room.'

'It's Connor's. He came to see me.'

'He did?'

'This morning.'

'What did he have to say for himself?'

'He said he was an idiot. He was sorry. You'd given him a wake-up.'

'You could call it that.'

'Reckons he'll come home for a few days next week.'

Wilf felt relieved. Of course, Connor had more of the Healy blood, but he wasn't stupid, or nasty.

'*Bellows by the fire and the turf smoke rising higher,*' she sang, and he recognised the tune her dad had taught her.

It was a good day. An honest day, made up of no more than its few, simple parts. The blue sky, the cold breeze, the words carrying across the lawn no one had bothered trimming.

'*The lark that wings and always sings of you.*'

A revving car, a couple of voices from a construction site, crows tearing at the remains of someone's lunch.

'See, there's nothing to complain about,' Orla said.

He took her up, and she went to the toilet. The nurse came in, checked her notes and signed something. She called, 'When you're ready, Orla, your pills.'

Wilf said, 'Did her son stay long?'

'Who?' the nurse replied.

'Her son, Connor?'

'She hasn't had anyone since she arrived.'

It was dark when Wilf drove into Selwyn. He stopped in front of Hyland's, but the girl told him that Colin Healy had checked out. So be it, he thought. He drove down the road, and there he was, in front of Simon's place, waiting for the bus. Wilf stopped and got out and said, 'You weren't even going to say goodbye?'

Colin took a moment. 'I walked an hour before someone picked me up.'

'Well, if you're going to have a tantrum. Have you eaten?'

'No.'

'Come on then. Mrs Gould's making Mexican.'

Wilf was thinking about what his mother would say. That's all she'd asked, at the end. Just look out for each other. 'You wouldn't have got on the bus,' he said.

'I would've.'

'You're just a big baby. You've always been a big baby.'

21

Wilf drove the bus to the Shell, filled up and went inside to pay. Emerging into an unleaded morning with chocolate and cheap coffee. But he didn't care; it kept the heart beating. Anyway, he wasn't in the mood for kids. He'd had to cut his brother's farewell short, waiting at the bus, saying, 'You're welcome back any time.'

'And what about you? Fourteen hours from Sydney.'

'But who'll do all this?'

'Someone will. That's what you don't get, Brother. *Stop saying yes.*'

The bus had come, the bags loaded, and they'd managed a handshake and something resembling a hug. Wilf guessed it would be the last time he saw him. But it was too late to do anything about that now. 'You'll miss Monk's,' he said.

'But not the damp walls, and those plastic toilets from the seventies.' Waving across at Monk, standing in the sun talking to Spencer, who'd come down specially to present Colin with a few words from St Matthew to smooth the journey home.

Wilf checked his clock. Sienna would be waiting. So life went on, regardless. Birth, confirmation, babies and death. The chrism on his and his brothers' foreheads running down their noses into their mouths, tongues tasting this water of life. '*Go forth the holy parakeet . . .*' Although he didn't know where the bird fit in. His brother waving down to him, looking ahead like he'd already forgotten Selwyn.

So much to remember, to discuss, that wasn't even mentioned, Wilf thought. The sash he'd kept under his bed for seventy years. Maybe Connor could have it one day.

Connor. Little shit. He fished his phone from his pocket and pressed the green button. Strange, really, how his nephew had set it up so they could stay in touch. People were made to talk to each other, face to face, word for word. All this shit about the world getting smaller.

Of course, he didn't answer. So Wilf left a message: 'Connor . . . you there? . . . would it hurt you to answer? Just thought I'd say your mother's in hospital. The University Hospital. Ten minutes from your place. I reckon it's about time you pulled your head in, old boy.' Hanging up. What was the point of mincing words? Reason, diplomacy and violence hadn't worked. Orla, of course, would growl at him, but so what?

George Daly came running across the concourse. 'Wilf! It's Lucy, but it has to be this morning.'

'I've got the bus,' Wilf said, indicating.

'It's on your way.' He hobbled north, past the trailers for hire, calling, 'Just a minute.' Wilf didn't care; the kids could wait. He drank the bitter coffee and wondered why he'd bought it. Ced Graney slowed past and said, 'We should catch up, Wilf. Talk about the old days.'

'Perhaps I'll pop by.'

Maybe. Maybe not. Either way, there was George, handing him a clear package containing three boxes of pills. 'Tell her she needs to go back to the doctor. I've been reusing those repeats.'

Wilf set off. Nothing much happened in Selwyn until ten. Dave Duffy even let his old German shepherd wander the block by herself. This is how she'd got a bad leg, struck by Simon, with a van full of drinks. Karen and her mum on the way to church. The wheeze of electrical bellows, the clunking of ivory keys, the wrong notes, for the hundredth time. No. 32: 'All People That On Earth Do Dwell'. He remembered it all. How, after the triple confirmation, his mum and dad had taken them to Monk's for lunch and they'd had fish and chips and his dad had grumbled it was hardly ocean fresh. But they'd been allowed Coke, and mousse. Still wearing their sashes. Proud that God had agreed to take them on.

Sienna, who complained she'd be late again, and why did he always dawdle? Wilf didn't like her tone. 'I wasn't put on this earth to serve you.'

'But you're paid to.'

'Paid? Am I? Really? Do you want to check your facts, young lady?'

This was enough to keep her quiet, retreating to her usual spot, filming herself. Wilf called back to her: 'Do you ever *call* people?'

'Of course. It's a phone, isn't it?'

'I call my nephew, but he never answers.'

'No wonder.'

'What?'

But she just shook her head.

'I was thinking, if phones are for talking . . .'

'They do lots of things now.'

'But not what they're meant to.'

She didn't get it. She didn't answer. That just encouraged him.

'People were meant to get along,' he said.

'I don't know what you're talking about.'

Of course you don't, he thought. 'What I mean is,' looking back in the mirror, 'if people would just *talk*. Look at you four, you don't even know each other's names.'

'We do.' Now she pretended to call someone, he asked who it was, but she said it was none of his business and shouldn't he be concentrating on the road?

Then Luke, who sat next to Wilf, spitting into his handkerchief, explaining his cold, and how, don't you reckon, Wilf, Mum should've let me stay home today?

'If that's what she thinks.'

He'd had her on the phone before. Once bitten.

'It's all green.' Spitting into his handkerchief and showing him. Sienna told him that was disgusting and people could catch his germs. He said, 'You catch a cold by breathing the bugs. You can't get it this way.' Displaying the mess.

'Wilf, tell him to put it away.'

'Have you been to the doctor, Luke?'

'He gave me pills. Mr Daly, see.' Picking up the plastic bag Wilf had left on the dashboard.

'Well, then, it's just a matter of time.'

'I could die.'

'We all could. At least your ticker works.'

'What's a ticker?'

'Heart, stupid,' Sienna called.

'Don't call people stupid,' Wilf said. 'I'll call you stupid.' But then, of course, the mother.

So they settled with Luke and Morpheus, Chapter Twenty-one: '*Morpheus Descends*'. A description of the beast making his way through an underworld of old shops, ruined homes, a nuclear power plant and zombies searching for flesh. Sienna told him he was copying other people, and he told her to shut up, reminding her of his illness, showing her the proof, again, her moaning again, and Wilf having to smooth it all over, again.

'Did Connor like the chapter I gave you?' Luke asked.

'I still haven't given it to him. I told you he's moved to Georgetown?'

'Can you send it?'

'I will.' Roughing his hair, although, technically, there wasn't meant to be any physical contact. 'I'm sure he'll love it, but he's ... you know, because he's going to be a rock star.'

Sienna laughed.

'At least he's got an ambition,' Wilf said to her. This shut her up, but she pretended to call someone again. Probably the dragon mother. 'You've got to have an ambition, don't you, Luke?'

Who kept reading: Morpheus (which means dreams, he said) stewing a few zombies for morning tea. 'Connor can be a rock star, and I'll be JK Rowling.'

'Absolutely.'

'I can write his lyrics.'

'That's just what I was thinking. Here, tell him.' He took out his phone, called Connor, and presented it to Luke. Sienna said he was breaking the law and he said he was sorry but he was old and sometimes forgot things. When the message bank began, Luke said, 'Hi Connor, it's Luke Thomson, from the school bus. I gave Wilf a new chapter and he's going to give it to you to read. I hope you like it. Maybe we'll catch up soon?' He rang off, returned the phone and said, 'He wasn't there.'

'He never is.'

'But you'll give it to him?'

'Yes. I will. I'll give it to him, Luke.'

Wilf pulled up outside Lucy's house, got out and walked up the drive of weeds and loose cobblers. Luke followed him, grabbed the plastic bag and said, 'I'll give it to her.'

Wilf knocked and it took Lucy a minute to emerge, hug them both and ask after the others. She said she hoped Luke was still writing, and he showed her his green spit. She waved to Sienna and she begrudgingly waved back. She said, 'I miss it, sometimes.' Luke said, 'That isn't right.' Reading the script, and the stickers on the boxes. 'This one say Coumadin, but the script says Metformin. Are they the same?'

'I don't think,' Lucy said. 'I have Metformin for my diabetes.'

Wilf said, 'I better return them . . . or ask.'

'No, George will be angry,' Lucy said.

'I could bring them back this afternoon?'

Lucy wasn't happy with this. But as they continued, Luke double-checked. Then Sienna got off to see what the fuss was about, used her phone to google the names and tell them Coumadin was a blood-thinner. 'See, phones can come in handy.'

But Wilf was lost. In the aisles of George's pharmacy. Bad advice, and his own shaking hands. 'I'm sure he just got them mixed up.'

'That could kill someone,' Sienna said.

Wilf said, 'Not a word, right? We don't know. And if we're wrong . . .'

'As if I'd say something.' Shitty. Returning to the bus.

George had done the same to him. Ticker medicine that wasn't ticker medicine. He hadn't noticed until Karen had told him.

Next, Trevor. When Wilf pulled into his drive he was halfway up a tree, reaching for a nest. Wilf tooted and called out the window, 'Careful, if you fall . . .'

Trevor jumped down and Wilf said, 'Watch yourself.' And as he climbed aboard, 'You'll break something.'

But Luke said, 'Our bones are better.'

'No, they break easier. And I'm responsible for you, right?'

'There were chicks in it,' Trevor said.

'Well, you better watch for their mum. She'll be after you.' Looking him over. 'All better?'

He didn't reply. That would assume there was a problem. Although he did say, 'Where's Colin?'

'He's gone to New Zealand.'

'Why?' Settling into his seat.

'To see Raelene.'

'Who's Raelene?'

'Betty's sister.'

'Who's Betty?'

'She's the Queen of New Zealand.'

Trevor seemed confused. Wilf said, 'He wanted to see some other places.'

'You should've gone with him.'

'I've got to drive you lot around.'

'They could've found someone else.'

'Apparently not. And anyway, we disagreed about everything.'

'Like what?'

'What's this, a hundred questions. People disagree. I disagree with Luke. Don't I?'

'Not much.'

'And Sienna.' Calling back. 'Don't I, Sienna?'

But she had her earbuds in. She noticed him, took one out and said, 'What?'

'I was just saying, your uncle, Hitler, he started a war, didn't he?'

But she just went back to her music.

'So you had a fight?' Luke said.

'I never said that. Sometimes, my boy, you're precocious.'

'What's that?'

'Tell him, Trevor.'

Who'd already settled with a book, but looked up. 'Too big for your boots.'

'No, I'm not.'

'Old for your age,' Wilf said. 'Colin wanted to go white water rafting and we don't have it here in Selwyn, do we?'

'Has he got a girlfriend?'

'Yes. Raelene. Eva Braun's sister. They're getting married in a bunker.'

Trevor laughed, and Luke caught on. 'I'm never getting married.'

'Well,' Wilf replied, 'that would be a shame. There are good bits.'

'Weren't you married, Wilf?'

'I was.'

The boys didn't take it further. If he didn't have a wife now then something shit had probably happened, and he probably wouldn't want to talk about it. But Wilf said, 'The next ten years, Luke, Trevor' – looking back – 'a lot of things change. One day you'll be sitting in a pub with some nice girl and you'll remember me and say, He actually did know what he was talking about.'

'Unlikely,' Sienna said.

And finally, Darcy. Stomping aboard, saying, 'Hello, Wilf.'

'Darcy.'

The mood darkening, as it always did. This boy, this rodent, with his peach-fuzz lip. Wilf wanted to tell him to shave it, but that would just start another fight. The way he sat at the back of the bus and glanced up at him, then at his device. Titties, no doubt.

They travelled in silence for a few minutes before Wilf saw him whispering across the aisle to Trevor, smiling, returning to his tablet.

'What's up?' he called back to him.

'Nothing, Mr Healy.' Smiling.

And again, and Wilf said, 'What's he up to, Trevor?'

'Nothing.'

But Luke peered up and whispered, 'He said he's going to get him.'

'Why?'

'Ben.'

Darcy tried again, and Wilf questioned him again, then said, 'You know Ben Magee, do you?'

Trevor was terrified. He buried his head in his book.

'No, sir. No, Wilf . . . Mister Healy.'

'Yes, you do, he's your mate. And you know what happened, don't you?'

Trevor said, 'It doesn't matter.'

'Should we leave it there?' Wilf said to Darcy.

'Don't know what you're talking about.'

Another mile toward Selwyn, and Darcy tried again. Wilf said, 'You know what Ben did to Trevor?'

'And what Colin did,' Darcy said. 'You're meant to be adults.'

'Really? No. Me and Colin, hardly. It's still 1948, and we're still looking out for each other.'

'He could've gone to the police.'

'Wilf, please,' Trevor whispered.

'He should feel free. And we could, too, I suppose?'

Sienna asked what had happened, but neither would tell her, so she returned to her phone.

'Two of you on to him,' Darcy called.

'Him onto Trevor.'

'Wilf!'

'But Trevor's just a faggot, aren't you?' Darcy said.

Later, Wilf couldn't recall what came next. Whether he slammed on his brakes and brought the bus to a stop in the middle of the road, or whether Trevor stood, took the three steps back to Darcy, and started pounding him with a strong, no-nonsense fist. Either way, Darcy didn't fight back. Just shielded his face, and laughed, as Trevor did his best. Wilf managed to pull them apart. 'Sit down!' he said to Trevor, who did as he was told. Then he grabbed Darcy by the collar, took his bag, removed him from the bus, stood in the door-well and said, 'Find your own way back.'

He sat down, put on his belt, and continued along the road. The second time in so many days. The boy growing smaller in the rear-vison, but still laughing, even waving.

As they drove, Luke said, 'Go, Wilf!'

But Trevor wasn't so happy. Sitting with his head in his hands, shaking his head. He said to Wilf, 'How's that help?'

Sienna said, 'You're fucked now.' And to Wilf, too. 'You better go back and get him.'

22

'Can't say I understand,' Wilf said, opening the small gate with the words 'Holy Mary Pray For Us' in blue. Shoulder-high walls leading back to the road. 'I don't care.'

'Stop analysing everything,' Orla said, walking into the grassed area with its four or five pot plants, bright flowers, calendulas and poppies. A conifer had shed needles under the grey sky, the threatening clouds. 'It was just easiest.'

'Why?'

'To keep you quiet, for one.'

Wilf shook his head. He didn't always understand Orla, although these were exceptional circumstances. 'What's that mean?'

'You nag.' Past a plaster Jesus someone had set at the feet of Mary. It had sunk into boggy ground, so she moved it. And Mary herself, in white and the same blue, gazing into an uncertain sky. 'Ave Maria' in the same paint. More plants at her feet, although they were plastic. A row of globes above her head as a sort of halo, although there was no power.

'Who's the daft bugger that built it?' Wilf said.

Alone on the edge of the world, the road, the paddock, waiting for a few sheep. 'Maybe someone was in an accident?' Orla said.

'Maybe,' Wilf conceded, although what was the point, reminding yourself every time you went past?

Orla crossed herself, admired Mary and said, 'Anyway, can't you feel the ghosts?'

'What ghosts?'

'The dead. Or do you reckon they're gone?'

'Not sure what they'd be doing out here.' Surrounded by fields, a few copses of trees, livestock, a shed, nothing else.

They sat on a bench set into the wall. Wilf said, 'Who are you praying for?'

'No one . . . I was just hoping, I guess.'

Wilf shrugged. 'I can go and see him again?'

She thought about it, cupped her hands and cheekily said, '*Now I lay me down to sleep I pray the Lord my soul to keep.* Dad made me say it.'

'What a thing to teach a kid.'

'*And if I die before I wake I pray the Lord my soul to take.*' Smiling. 'At least he believed.'

'Your father was worse than me.'

'He wasn't.'

Wondering if he should tell her how, after they'd been dropped for Sunday school, Brian would say to him and Colin, 'Bugger it. Follow me.' Leading them back into town, an early incarnation of Gould's, liquorice, and the man saying, 'Looks like you three should be somewhere?'

'Waiting for our parents, sir.'

Although he still took the money. 'You're Tom's boys, aren't you?'

Brian leading them down the street, shop by shop. Although later, when the man told Tom, they had their arses tanned by a bamboo reed their father called 'Wilhelm'. Lined up in the kitchen, pants down, the spirit of God deserting them in the same way they'd deserted Him. 'Brian thought it was a load of old . . .'

'That's not what he told me.'

The plaster Jesus had a three-legged sheep, busy with the barley. The mortar had washed from between the bricks and it looked like they might collapse. Still, the place was made with love, Wilf thought. 'I got a wet arse.'

Orla didn't care. Eyes closed, fingers busy with an imaginary rosary.

Cloudy, but a warm morning. Picking his niece up from Reception, loading her bags in the back, telling her she looked a hundred per cent better. Her agreeing, although, Wilf thought, the blood hadn't returned to her face, the meat to her hands, the strength to her arms. She'd said, 'Enough's enough, let's go see him.'

'Connor?'

'Come on.' Asking him to drive, which he did, slowly, trying to talk her out of it. 'You might not like what you see.'

Church Street, a few dogs still barking, and he led her to the front door of Number 20. 'Maybe I'll have a word first?'

But she wouldn't hear of it. Knocking, calling, 'Connor, you there?'

No reply. A neighbour had come out and said, 'I wouldn't bother. They stay out late, come home at all hours and sleep all day.'

Wilf had said, 'See. Come on then.' Orla had insisted on writing a note, leaving it under the door. Wilf hadn't seen what it said, but could guess.

'Brian was the one convinced me,' Wilf said.

'What?'

'God. That's what kept people simple. Religion. And if people wanted to get ahead ...' He could hear bells, although he wasn't sure what church; the cries of children who'd just been released from a purgatory of hymns and phoney homilies. 'But you have to pretend, for your kids. Steven got the same – spilt vinegar all over my stole. *Let the one who is thirsty come.* And our parents made us, with that O'Grady man touching our foreheads.'

'Who?'

'He was arrested.'

'He was not.'

'He was. Dozens of them, in Northhead. He'd been at it for years.' Gazing at Mary, as if she were to blame for it all.

'Well, maybe I've misunderstood my own son,' Orla said. 'I lied because I didn't want you thinking he was ...'

'Boys are stupid. You tell them the water's shallow but they still jump. They have to work it out for themselves.'

Orla's hands came apart. No more prayers, or God, Mary, Jesus and his plaster lamb. 'Should we keep going?'

The Mallee Highway, crumbling on the edges, clinging to hills and valleys, wet and slippery as they drove home. Bare-limbed houses shedding tiles like scales, mortar like skin, cracked roof spines with chimneys hungry for wood, fire, life. Rotten windows hanging from their holes. And gates, open, waiting, although no one had entered for years. *These* were the ghosts, Wilf guessed. They turned into Orla's drive. Someone had mowed the lawn and pulled the weeds along the bit of garden between house and letterbox. She got out and stood inspecting it all. 'Was this you, Uncle?'

'Swear to God, it wasn't.' Taking her bag from the back of his van and heading up the steps. 'Where would I get a lawnmower?'

'You'd find a way.'

Wilf noticed a package on the porch, picked it up and said, 'Connor's writing, isn't it?'

She was quickly up, and examined it. '*See*.' Tearing it open and producing a CD. No letter, no explanation. 'Come on.'

They went inside, and she was struck again. Everything put away, every surface wiped, every book, even, in the shelf, arranged from tallest to shortest. The carpets cleaned and the place smelling of lemon. '*Uncle*,' she said, although she was glad.

'It wasn't just me,' he said. 'I had help.'

He led her into the spotless kitchen, opened the freezer and indicated the Tupperware dishes labelled 'Chicken curry (mild)', 'Lasagne', 'Paella'. A dozen, perhaps, and Wilf explained, 'Mrs Gould. She said every time she cooks for Monk she'll skim a serve, right? He'll never know.'

She removed the CD from its case and returned to the living room. Stereo on, inserted it, and waited. Wilf had his doubts, but the fingerpicking began and Orla said it was his guitar, and she said she knew, you know, don't you, Wilf? '*If I could choose a time to talk to you, I'd choose the longest day . . .*'

'See?' she said to her uncle.

And when this one had finished, more fingerpicking, before Connor's voice, explaining, 'I played this one at the Arms. You might not know it, but I . . . *Singin' for your supper waitin' for your summer days to drift away you're singin' for your supper . . .'*

When it was over, Orla said, 'It's a good start, Uncle?' She found her phone and called her son, but he didn't answer.

Wilf tried to unpack her clothes, but she wouldn't let him. She was fine, she said, sitting on her bed going through papers, notes, reminders. A script that had to be filled. Wilf offered to get it, but wondered if it was wise. He explained, Lucy, the mix-up, and she told him to stop being dramatic. 'Fetch us some milk and bread if you want.'

So he walked to Simon's, told him his niece was home and said to thank his mum for the food. Milk, bread and M&M's, because he remembered she liked them, sitting in front of the *Brady Bunch*, asking how anyone could survive so many brothers and sisters. Simon asked how she was – you know, with the blood problems and all – and Wilf lied. 'Recovering.'

Then to the pharmacy, down the aisle, past eucalypt-smelling balms, the promise of pills and fresh bandages, and George (adjusting the glasses on his nose) saying, 'I got some deliveries to go out, Wilf.'

'Is there someone else?'

'Darrin's hopeless.'

'I've been meaning to mention this but . . . I was thinking of throwing it all in.'

'What?'

'These jobs.'

'But they keep you busy. What else would you be doing?'

'I'm eighty now.'

'I'm not far behind. But we've got to keep the place running, Wilf.'

'No, I mean it,' Wilf said. 'I don't want so many people relying on me.'

George didn't seem to understand. 'But what about the bus and the school and Bobby?' Choosing to ignore him. 'Well, I can get Darrin on this lot but . . .'

There was no point. Wilf fished Lucy's bag of pills from his pocket and said, 'I nearly gave her these.'

George pushed his glasses up his nose, examined the boxes and said,

'I can't think how that happened.' He thought about it, massaging his forehead. 'I took it from there . . . to the desk.' He even retraced his steps, like it might tell him. 'Then I would've stood here and typed . . . ah, that's it! I've typed it off someone else's script. I must ring and apologise. You noticed?'

'One of the kids.'

'Right.' Leaning over the desk, a few nostril hairs flaring.

And after a moment, 'You alright, George?'

'Yes . . . fine. I'll call her. I'll drive it out there myself and explain. If she had have taken them . . .' He threw the pills in the bin, gathered himself and said, 'Something for you, Wilf?'

As he worked, Wilf watched carefully, and when Orla's script was ready, he checked it. 'We're all slowing down, George.'

'Yes.' Focusing everywhere, but nowhere. 'I suppose so.'

Wilf emerged from the pharmacy and stood smelling the bread from the Tea Junction, reading signs that promised Hawaii, Cape Town, San Francisco. But these places weren't real, and hardly worth the effort. Say, for instance, he'd been on the Gold Coast, and Lucy had been given the wrong pills. Rio de Janeiro and New York. A thousand options, but none, and it wasn't like you could visit them all. He turned to see Darcy, grinning. And behind him, his mother (he could remember her, running after the bus with her little darling's forgotten lunch). She said, 'Mr Healy?'

He didn't reply. A face at least as hard as Mary's, although hardly as forgiving.

'I contacted the school, and asked for an explanation.'

'Sorry?'

'Darcy called me and I had to pick him up . . . from where you dumped him.'

'I didn't dump him. He was misbehaving. I've made that clear, Mrs Davis. If they play up . . .'

'I had to drive half an hour.'

And you could, every day, Wilf thought, if you weren't such a lazy bitch.

'Did you tell your mum what you said?' Wilf said to Darcy. 'To Trevor … a younger boy, and very quiet, Mrs Davis, and not one to stand up for himself.'

'He could've been picked up by some sort of predator.'

She was about to blow. Darcy was still grinning. Wilf said, 'See, look, he's enjoying it. Maybe if you didn't believe every bit of shit that came out of his mouth?' He turned and walked toward Orla's place.

She followed him and said, 'Noah convinced me not to go to the police.'

'Feel free. Although we don't have any. Darcy, you going to tell her?'

But she couldn't see, and never would, Wilf realised. So he stopped and said, 'Fine. I'll quit, tomorrow, and you can drive the damn bus.'

She didn't care. 'I settled on an apology.'

'What are you talking about?'

'I said to Noah, you write my son an apology and we'll put this behind us.'

Wilf said, 'If you keep on like this he'll turn on you, too.' Glaring at Darcy, remembering the feel of bamboo on his arse.

23

They'd run out of milk, and Simon had closed his shop because he wanted to win a bottle of Jameson. So Wilf was left with no choice. He walked to the Shell, bought four bottles, loaded them in a box and headed back to Monk's. Past the lacquered verses, promising rest for all men who worked, except, perhaps, Wilf Healy. Jack Mooney offered a hand but Wilf said he'd manage. A light rain settling on the road and footpath, each of the lights a little halo promising grace on Sullivan Street. Mr Lillimar had started playing music from a speaker out front of his shop. All day. All night. Wilf could hear it, distantly, floating in his window of a morning.

He passed Scoops n' Smiles, lit up, noticed Darcy inside, drinking from a plastic cup, playing with something on the bench. The new fella, Grant whatever his name, was explaining this object, or objects. Wilf stopped to look and Darcy noticed, waved and called something. Then he turned to his mate and said something else and they laughed.

The milk was heavy, so Wilf continued, but the shop door opened and Darcy came out and called, 'How are you, *Wilf*?'

He kept walking. He wasn't worth it. But then he was behind him and he said, 'Written my apology yet?'

Wilf stopped, turned and noticed the new fella watching. 'Over my dead body . . . you lying little shit.'

Darcy kept grinning, more confident, checking Roper was still watching before saying, 'You can't just drop a kid in the middle of nowhere. I could've been kidnapped.'

'Who'd want you?'

'Kept in a shed, raped by some pedo, eh?' He came around in front of Wilf and blocked his way. Wilf tried to continue, but Darcy kept moving. 'Either you move . . .'

'Or what?'

'Move!' His heart racing.

But Darcy wouldn't. So Wilf kept walking, pushing against him, and Darcy pretended to fall to the ground, grab his ankle and say, 'Jesus, Wilf, there wasn't any need for that.'

Wilf waited, said, 'Keep away from me, right?' Then continued.

'You better call an ambulance,' Darcy called to Roper.

Wilf kept going, past Sienna, standing in the rain in a parka holding her phone. 'Hi, Wilf.'

'What you doing out at this hour?'

Sienna indicated her parents in the Eat Inn, still glowing, smelling of saturated fat.

Wilf continued to Monk's, went into the kitchen and put the milk in the fridge. Karen was standing in front of the deep fryer, waiting for chips to cook. 'You're all wet.'

'Water doesn't kill you.'

'What does?'

'Children.'

As Wilf went into the bar, opened the dishwasher and started unpacking glasses, Monk said to the crowd, 'Ted was talking about this young fella' – indicating an eighteen or nineteen-year-old boy standing beside him, clutching his guitar – 'and I thought . . .'

Well, *you* didn't, Wilf thought, because he'd heard Ted talking about this kid, the runner up on the *X Factor*, and *he'd* thought, What if? He'd said to Monk, 'We need to do something about Thursday nights.' Then Monk had said something about Jesus curing lepers, and Wilf had said, 'A bit of a name.'

Anyway, it had worked. They'd made a phone call, organised the kid, printed some posters, and here they were with a room full of punters.

Fifteen or so guests, but mainly the stay-at-home-locals who hadn't been to the pub for years. Spencer and Grace done up in their eighties best, anxious to see the kid from the telly; the Lillimars, who'd brought a gift for the Wheel O' Whisky!; Simon and his mum, and Patrick Tear, to make it all official.

Monk approached Sean Lyons and said, 'It's a great honour.' Like he was the prime minister, or Pope. 'Especially someone so young.'

Wilf thought it strange. He wasn't so encouraging of Connor, but then again, Connor hadn't been on the box.

'And what sort of songs do you sing, Sean?'

He told the room about his mother and father (musical inspirations) and his big night. 'Lights everywhere, in your face, and cameras blinking off and on . . . Brian Monaghan was nice enough, but I just concentrated on the music.'

His first song, belted out with a raucous voice, bouffant hair and sugary smile. '*I never should have asked you . . .*'

Okay, Wilf thought, although he preferred Connor, his out-of-tune guitar, his attitude. Real, at least. Still, they loved him, Karen kept the till ringing, the tickets for the three bottles Monk had agreed to give away, meals, chips. Sean told them about his plans for the future, how much he loved Selwyn (and God) and how he'd be sure to come back. He sang another song then said he had to go, he had school in the morning. This made everyone laugh, except Monk, who thought he'd get at least four songs for his money. Not to be put off, he pushed the wheel to the centre of the room and said, 'Has everyone bought a ticket?'

There was some consensus, especially from a Territory couple who were already well gone. Monk brought out the Powers (thirty-four), smooth yet robust, complex for its age (he explained). 'And ancient.' Waiting for quiet. 'In the good old days, when they sacrificed virgins' – and Grace giggled – 'this was much prized.' He invited Patrick up for the first spin and it landed on nineteen, the Quinn's Dreamcatcher. Karen claimed it, hung it behind the bar and said to Wilf, 'What are you meant to do with it?'

He didn't reply. A couple of ghosts, standing at the door. He had to look twice.

'And for our next spin,' Monk said, holding up a bottle of Redbreast. 'Twelve-year-old cast strength edition.'

Wilf stood, went over to the door and said to his brother, 'That was quick.'

Colin said, 'Someone's gotta sort this family out.'

And Connor, freshly-shaved, his small, brown eyes settling on his uncle. 'Still doing the wheel?'

'No one's had a better idea.'

The three of them sat at the back of the room, enclosed in a little spirit-smelling cubby away from the noise. Connor dropped his bag, and guitar. Colin asked what he wanted to drink, and he said water, so he went to fetch it.

'So?' Wilf said. 'You're looking good. You're okay. Are you okay?'

'Fine.'

'Living the high life?'

'Hardly.'

Colin returned with a couple of ales and the water and said, 'At least they've got a crowd this time.'

Wilf studied his nephew, trying to work it all out. But Colin gave Connor a five dollar note and said, 'Number seventeen, go on then.' Connor waited, smiled at him and got up to buy the ticket. Colin said, 'Just like the old days, Brother.'

'What?'

'Saving your arse.'

Before Wilf could reply, Connor sat down, placed the ticket on the table and said, 'It's rigged anyway.'

'It's not,' Wilf said.

'Of course it is,' Colin said. 'No one ever wins whisky.' Draining half a glass and saying, 'It wasn't a bad trip back, was it, Nephew?'

'No, Uncle.'

'I was telling Connor,' Colin said, 'you were the difficult one, growing up. Caught breaking into Mooney's, and the copper at the time, Daniels, was halfway home with you when I said to him . . .'

Monk continued spinning, but the whisky was safe.

'. . . if our parents work out what he's been up to they'll take him out of school and put him down a mine somewhere, and you always wanted to be a draughtsman, didn't you, Wilf?'

Connor said, 'I got to play a few gigs, Uncle.'

'Where?'

'The World's End. A few of us, only six or seven songs, but it kicked off alright.'

Wilf said to his brother, 'What happened to New Zealand?'

'It's still there.' Explaining how he'd decided his nephew needed a firm hand. 'So I decided, didn't I, Connor?'

'*You* decided?' Smiling.

'I hired a car . . . a nice one, isn't it, Nephew?'

'I guess.'

'And drove to Church Street, and Connor and Sam cooked me tea, didn't you, boy?'

'We got pizza.'

'A tandoori pizza. And we talked . . .?'

Monk hadn't got his money's worth, so he led Sean to the centre of the room, sat him on a stool and said, 'One more, before he goes.'

This time, rehashed Frank Sinatra, and Connor listened and said, 'What a fake.'

The old Connor, Wilf thought. He said to him, 'Go on then.'

'What?'

Wilf stood, approached Monk, said a few words and indicated his nephew. Monk didn't seem convinced. After all, they'd built up a head of steam. But Wilf returned to his nephew and explained, 'Come on then . . . a quick one while everyone's listening.'

'No.'

'Come on, your Nirvana, or one of yours?'

Connor thought about it, then started removing his guitar from its case. As Sean's applause subsided, Wilf led his nephew to the microphone, settled him and said, 'Connor's back!'

No one seemed to care. But this didn't stop Connor. He played a few chords, looked up from under the hair he hadn't cut and sang, '*Jesus don't want me for a sunbeam – Sunbeams are never made like me.*'

Wilf said to his brother, 'Well?'

'I wasn't about to get a plane, was I, with you and Orla and . . .' Trying to listen.

'How did you make him listen?'

'I *talked* to him, Wilf. He's not unreasonable, you know.'

They listened. The lyrics were grim, and Monk didn't look happy. All that good work, and money.

'Anyway, I think he was ready,' Colin said.

'For what?'

'You don't get people, Brother. Ready. Himself. To come home.'

'I'll say he was ready. With his mother . . .'

Connor sat down and Wilf said, 'See, they liked that one. What's it about?'

'You didn't get it?'

'Anyway,' Colin said, 'I'm tired. It's been a long day, hasn't it, Nephew?'

Connor didn't say, but Colin didn't care. 'They're making up my old room for me, Wilf.' Finishing his beer, and going up.

There was a long, awkward silence. Wilf said, 'It was good of him to bring you home.'

Connor just watched the wheel spinning.

'So you're settling in, in Georgetown?'

'I'm sleeping on the floor. I can't do that forever.'

'You want to stay here tonight?'

'Why would I do that?'

Monk ran in wearing a wig and his wife's bra, and said, 'I tell you, Susan, there'll be no more of it.'

Connor said, 'What am I going to tell her?' He watched Monk running around the room, hugging Patrick, promising more whisky. 'I don't get how anyone can live here.'

'There's worse.'

Wilf walked his nephew home. When they got to the gate, Wilf said, 'I've got the bus in the morning. Luke wants to see you.'

Connor saw the light in the window and said, 'I better not, eh?'

24

Rogan wasn't a redhead, but his parents had already chosen the name, so Rogan it was. He guided the small boat through the waves, the slow rises and sudden thumps. Wilf could remember his mum, dad and brothers clutching their gear, watching the island disappear for the last time. His dad saying (something like), *Twenty years too late*. His mum explaining how she was looking forward to a bit of lino.

'Couldn't have picked a better day,' Rogan said, surveying Louth, growing bigger, more defined in front of them. Rocks, cliffs, the lighthouse they'd automated after Ron Graney had left. 'Had a fella the other day, chucking over the side the whole time.'

Connor felt the same way. Sitting, clutching his guts, only three days after his return to Selwyn. It had been Wilf's suggestion. To show him the old places, to spend a day with his uncles before Colin left. 'If you don't do it now . . .' he'd said to his brother, both of them sitting in the deserted bar.

'What's the point of going all that way?' Colin had asked.

'You'll never know if you don't go.'

'How much for the boat?'

'Fifty.'

'You've checked?'

'I keep checking. I keep meaning to go, but since you're here . . .'

So Colin had agreed. A day trip to Louth. But now, Connor was sitting with his legs spread, his head low in the boat, his uncles laughing. He said to them, 'It's not funny.'

'No, it's not,' Wilf said.

Rogan didn't care. 'You've got to get your sea legs, boy.'

Wilf explained. 'Every couple of weeks, wasn't it, Colin? We looked forward to it, didn't we, Brother?' Gazing east, a faint whiff of civilisation.

'It's not going to be a trip down memory lane?' Connor said.

'No,' Colin replied. 'Just a quick walk around, eh, Wilf?'

Who wouldn't commit. His agenda was different: a sounding out, a what if? How it might be done, if it were done. 'How do you get things over?' he asked Rogan.

'What things?'

'A table? A chair?'

'Who's taking a table and chair to Louth?'

'My brother might,' Colin said.

'Why?'

Colin left it for Wilf to explain. 'It's just an idea.'

'But there's nothing there anymore. Why?'

Wilf couldn't explain. 'If you have a bigger boat?'

'I do but . . .'

That cleared it up; it could be done. A suitcase, tools for fixing the old place, groceries.

'Not sure they'd even let someone,' Rogan said.

'They couldn't stop me.'

'The government . . .' Losing himself in the swell and the three kilometres between Selwyn Bay and Louth. 'Everyone's left. They all joined your lot, Colin.'

Wilf could see it. The way sea and land joined at the offing, like the whole world was somewhere else and needed to be visited, explored, lived in. The way the clouds dropped to meet the earth. 'No *Baywatch* out here,' he said to his brother. Colin understood, especially as they approached the wharf, the ruin of the boat-keeper's cottage, and beyond that, the profile of Croom, still intact, still hiding from the weather. Wilf fancied he remembered the order of stones, the way they were jammed together, how they supported each other, despite a lack of mortar. A gentle shag of moss, a chain, rusted from its housing, and the steps leading to land.

'What time do you want me?' Rogan asked, capturing the bollard first time.

'Four,' Wilf said.

'Two,' Connor added.

'Split the difference,' Colin said to Rogan.

The steps were slippery. Wilf helped his nephew along the pier, onto solid ground. He said to his brother, 'It's like we never left.'

Colin wasn't so sure. '*Jesus*. It's so grim.'

'How? Look, not a stone moved. Just as I remember it.'

A dirt road snaked its way through a collection of old cottages, a limey sinew joining small homes with even smaller windows, some with a hint of green or red, a few shutters. Most places were roofless. Doors hanging open, or closed against the weather, like their owners might return to a life they'd only ever put on hold.

'Welcome to Croom,' Wilf said to his nephew.

Connor was wondering why Wilf had brought him. It wasn't just to see the ruins, surely? It was to teach him about the old ways, and how they contrasted with the new. How living on an island brought out the best in people, gave them communities with sing-alongs and love as plentiful as the weak-kneed greenshanks. Compared to what he had. That was it. To compare and contrast. Even the bad bits. The times someone got ill and died and how this probably would've ended differently if they'd lived in a town or city, but how these were the choices people made. Yes, that was his uncle's aim, surely. Although he said, 'There's nothing here.'

'You're not looking,' Wilf said. 'See, this place was Mrs Francis's and she sewed for people and cooked bread. Her husband was injured and couldn't fish, so he fixed nets. Come on.'

They opened the door and went in and Wilf said, 'I'm sure they wouldn't mind.' Looking at his brother. 'Do you remember coming here?'

'No.'

'We did. You, me and Brian, to get bread, when Mum was sick.'

The table with a few plates, a couple of knives and forks. A sideboard with its doors missing, full of rat shit and shredded newspaper. Chairs beside the fireplace, with its half-burned dung. Wilf kicked it with his foot and said to Connor, 'That's all we had to keep warm.'

'Great.'

They continued up the hill, in and out of the old places. Jackson's, his yard still full of old bones, scales, rusted tools from where a million fish had been cleaned. Wilf examined them, felt the edges and said, 'A good sharpening and you'd be back in business.' Inside, Mrs Jackson had left a few books. *Stories of the Bay* and *Oliver Twist*. Wilf sat on the remains of a stool and read a few lines, like the stories might summon the ghosts. Connor lifted a few broken plates and said, 'Did they leave in a hurry?'

At last, Wilf thought. A glimmer. 'Perhaps. Although most people had time to plan, pack.'

'Why did they go?'

'Who knows? We were one of the first, weren't we, Colin?'

Colin was standing in the doorway, gazing out. 'How we remember things and how they happened, Wilf.' Turning to Connor. 'One left, then another. The school closed and more left. Some girl was raped, wasn't she?'

'That was never proved.'

'By her uncle, and there was another two families gone, and people saying what's the point of it all? It was grim, it was cold and Mum and Dad couldn't get out quick enough. That's why they left all their old crap, Connor. *Because they were in a rush.*'

Wilf was caught in the smell of the pages, the yellowed images of Oliver and Bill Sikes. 'People wanted to stay.'

'Bullshit. You see what you see.'

Wilf could see the sea, the pull of the small, grey gap between land and water, the opportunities that promised everything but delivered . . . what? A thirtieth-floor view? What was all that? What did it matter?

'Maybe this won't work?' Connor said to Wilf.

'What?'

'My little . . . lesson.' Smiling.

They went in and out, examining, remembering, and Colin said, 'You can smell the damp in the floor, the walls. It's not healthy. No wonder people had bad lungs.'

Wilf ignored him. Smith's. Here you could get papers, tobacco, basic medicines. He examined a few bottles on the shelf, tried to read the labels. 'Long way from George Daly's.'

'Not so far,' Colin said, emptying some powder onto the bench, touching it with his finger, smelling it, tasting it. 'This was the chemist, Connor.'

'It did,' Wilf said. 'Remember when Mum was in bed and Dad sent us down? Waiting in that corner there, remember, Brother? Mr Smith asking what we wanted.'

But again, Colin couldn't remember any of it.

'And he'd always smell of grog,' Wilf said. 'We used to laugh about it.' He could remember Mr Smith talking to customers, the mumbled voices, the boots shifting on the dirt floor, the ad (gone now) for Keenan's Cough Drops. All of it. Like he'd never left. Why couldn't his brother remember? 'You must have come in here a hundred times, Colin.'

Colin took a few photos on his phone and said, 'I'll send them to you.'

And then out of the chunky bit of town, along a road that narrowed as it passed through a patchwork of fields with low walls, forgotten cottages. 'That was Simpson's,' Wilf said to his followers. 'You must remember that, Colin? He had that argument with Dad over money ... what was it?'

Colin shrugged.

'Remember him at our door, threatening Dad?'

'No.'

'It was never settled, but they never spoke again. He had a stroke when he was fifty, fifty-five, something like that, and Dad said, *See, poetic justice*, and Mum growled at him for being so mean.'

'You remember all of this?' Connor said.

'Of course.'

'From seventy years ago?'

'Like it was still happening. It is still happening, isn't it?'

Connor guessed there was a chance these old people knew a few things. He sat down, took off his backpack and got out their lunch. Hardly time, but the fresh air had made him hungry. They ate pastries from a bag and drank coffee from a thermos. Wilf said, 'Smell that.' Taking a lung full of green earth.

'What?' Colin.

'Shit. I can still smell the sheep shit.'

Connor took it for what it was worth. A lesson. That he had left his town of everything important and cast his lot with strangers. Without thinking, he said, 'I just thought, if I came back everything would be the same. So I thought, No, clean break.'

Wilf said, 'No calls? No messages?'

'That was the point.'

'So you could be sure?'

'Yes.'

Wilf filled his mouth with danish, cupped the coffee in his hands, tasted it and said, 'You make awful coffee, Colin.'

'Well, that's all Monk's got. Tell him to buy a proper machine.'

'It didn't help, you laying into me, *Uncle*.' Smiling.

'That was nothing. In the old days, when our dad—'

'Enough about the old days,' Connor said. 'Look, it's all gone. It's *now*, Uncle.'

But if that were the case, Wilf thought, what about your mother? Connor anticipated this question and said, 'I was trying to work out how I might . . .'

'With your mate? What's his name?'

'Pat. I haven't given up.'

'I never said . . . Just seemed strange, with your mother sick.'

'I sent her the parcel.'

'Yes, you did. I guessed you were weakening.'

'I wasn't. I'm not.'

'But your mother's glad to see you. If you could stay a little longer?'

Looking across the valley, Wilf thought it strange how each family had farmed such a small parcel. And gone to such trouble to define it, build it up, protect it. From what? Or maybe it was the detail, knitted together, with the dad-farmers and mum-cooks and kids watching the animals between lessons at the small school where the teacher always spelt accommodation with one c. This interchangeability of people. So that he was his brother, and nephew. He was George and Karen and Luke and Trevor and Darcy, even.

'I bet she was pissed off at me,' Connor said.

'No, *she* wasn't,' Wilf replied.

'You over-analyse,' Colin said.

'What?'

'He was quite happy to come home, weren't you, Connor?'

'Well, luckily *you* were here,' Wilf said.

'You're such a pair of princesses,' Connor said. 'I just worked it out.'

'What?' Wilf said.

He thought, but said, 'It doesn't matter.'

25

'This one's at the end,' Ced Graney said, showing Wilf and Colin the photo (one of many he'd been through). Ced's father, Ron, in a sitting room, wood panelling and barred windows, a single globe, and what might have been plastic flowers. 'He had no idea by that stage.'

Wilf moved uncomfortably on the couch, squeezed in beside his brother. 'An asylum?'

'He was dangerous . . . used to claw people, spit on them.'

Ron Graney was all bone, ghost hands and glowing eyes, pointing at whoever was taking the photo. 'So by then he wouldn't have known anything,' Ced said.

Ced's house was all bone, shag from the sixties, colourised portraits of his family. Each with the same eyes, same expression, wearing their Sunday best. Bookshelves lining most walls, full of manuals, magazines, like the wealth of the world had been deposited, and forgotten. And in one corner, a collection of parts – crankshafts, tappets, filters – piled like they might become a motor, reassembled by small Graney fairies with their own, black-rimmed eyes.

'In the end we stopped visiting him,' Ced explained. 'He didn't know who we were, and it scared the kids, seeing him like that.' Taking back the photograph and slipping it between the pages of the album he'd just been through. Some from the same Selwyn home, a smaller Ced and his sister playing in the shadow of the old shed; a family shot on the back of a Bedford truck. It seemed, Wilf thought, there was little difference between the living and the dead. One passed, the other passing.

Ced squinted and studied Colin's features and said to him, 'Los Angeles, was it?'

'Venice Beach.'

'I was meaning to go and have look, but at a certain age . . .'

'You haven't missed much.' More as a consolation. Looking around the room, Colin decided this is what came from staying, from remembering. Bits of shit your kids would throw in the bin the minute you were gone. What was the point of that?

The brothers Healy continued with the last of their deliveries. Pumpkins from school, although no one wanted them. Bobby's onions and potatoes, his hot-house tomatoes, always the first to go, his coriander and parsley and sage. They stopped at Mr O'Loughlin's and he came out to the van, took six potatoes and a bag of carrots. Colin weighed them and Mr O'Loughlin said, 'Good to see Wilf has got you working.'

'Not for long,' Wilf said. 'He's off home Tuesday.'

Small talk, small change, before Wilf took down the scales and they headed home. It was a cold Sunday evening, just before the shadows began. Wilf said, 'I forgot Mrs Buckley.'

'Can't she live without her vegetables?'

It was dark by the time they approached Selwyn. Slowed, and stopped on the verge opposite MacDermott's place. Wilf explained how Steven had stopped short of the road, inched up to see past that bush there, see, Brother, no one's ever chopped it back – it'll happen again. True. A big wattle, stretching its limbs over a wall. 'You can't see what's coming.' The idea took him, and he got out, stood at the end of MacDermott's drive and tried to see. 'Not more than a few feet,' he called to Colin, still in the Morris. 'I warned them.'

Colin suspected it had nothing to do with the bush. Fixing things hardly ever fixed things – the problem remained, every day, every hour. As they drove back to town, he said, 'It must have been quick then?'

Wilf agreed. It would have been. This kid in this Cortina doing ninety, the skid marks proved it. And what happened to him? 'He got three years and I got . . . that.'

Colin said, 'I should have come for the funeral.'

Wilf said nothing.

'Bloody stupid of me, Brother.'

'It wasn't much,' Wilf said. 'But it's what finished Nance, I reckon.'

Colin wasn't sure what to say. It made sense. 'I was going to come.'

Wilf didn't want to blame him, or excuse him. He'd lost too many people already. What was the point? It was like some board game and you were shit and the other bloke kept taking all your pieces and eventually you were on your own. This is why he felt like asking, again, if his brother would stay. But he realised that was no better than Ced Graney, holding on to a house full of old stuff.

As they headed back to Monk's they passed a figure running – past the junction, the ice cream shop, stopping in front of Simon's place. Wilf pulled up in the middle of the road and said, 'What's the rush?'

And even as he said this he knew, sensed, felt it.

'I tried your phone,' Connor said.

Wilf remembered. On his bed. It was best that way; no one disturbed you. 'What?'

'Mum.'

'Get in.'

Wilf pulled into Monk's laneway, backed out and drove toward Orla's. Wheels lifting at the junction, the Morris swerving but gaining traction as it headed past Mooney's. 'What is it?'

'Maybe I should've called an ambulance?'

'Connor?'

'I just thought . . .'

It didn't matter. Wilf mounted the kerb, handbrake, and inside within a few seconds. It was always going to come to this. The moment he'd thought of a hundred times, a dozen variations, night and day, with this cast or that, the dialogue limited, or extensive. Graphic, like a waking dream, or staged, like *Coronation Street*. Into his niece's room, and she was lying there asleep. He knelt beside her and shook her and said, 'Orla?'

She didn't reply.

At this point, he'd imagined, she'd stir (as she always had) and smile at him and tell him off for fussing. But she didn't. Her breath was laboured. 'Orla? Can you hear me?'

'Uncle?' Connor said, standing with his arms crossed, biting his lip, his legs weakening and twisting and springing back.

'Come on, none of that,' he said to his nephew.

Colin came in, holding his phone. 'The ambulance is on the way.'

'Should I have called?' Connor asked. 'I wasn't sure.'

Wilf had even imagined her dead when he arrived. How he'd deal with the boy, and her body. How he'd take him out and make him a drink and make it seem like it wasn't unusual, unexpected. Another scenario had him pumping her chest, breaking ribs, making a complete mess of it.

Wilf saw a weak pulse, felt Orla's carotid, and told his nephew, 'Probably all a bit much for her.' He didn't think this made sense. But it couldn't be unsaid.

'Right.' He wrapped the rug around his niece, picked her up and carried her out like a sleeping child. 'Connor – get the back door. You can put her head in your lap.'

This only took a few moments. Connor cradling his mum, her head soft and adjustable, Wilf starting the car, Colin asking if he should lock up, but Wilf telling him to get in. Leaving the house open, lights on, the door banging in the breeze. Left, right, and the road to Northhead. 'When did you find her?' Wilf called back.

'She said she wanted a sleep. It'd been a few hours, and I was going to cook . . .'

It had got dark quickly. The van hummed along the road, the rubber warming and responding, the motor growling, the temperature gauge behaving. Connor was thinking about Georgetown. About how all this was happening while he was playing three chords, eating KFC day and night, Pat's girlfriend sneaking into his bed at three am. How all of that grunting and sweating and making and taking pleasure was happening at the same time as *this*.

It wasn't long until they saw the lights of Northhead glowing on the horizon. Connor wasn't sure how to hold his mother's head. Firmly, like it was a box with a snake inside. Or softly, allowing for freedom, but not discomfort. His fingers were on her neck, but the skin was cold, still. 'Uncle?' he said.

PART III

26

Hills rising and falling, pasture for a few sheep, foxes to eat their lambs. Limestone middens, ribbons of fat hen and salvation Jane, a few stock troughs in awkward corners, waiting for the rust. As Wilf guided the Morris along the highway. 'We can stop if you like,' he said to Connor.

'No.' His legs wide, body forward, head low. He'd already thrown up once on the way out. Wilf didn't want to risk what was left of the Morris's carpet. 'Don't know why they bothered ... there's much better land, a few days' walk.'

'Maybe we should stop?' Connor said.

Which wasn't easy. Heading up through, and into the depths of forestry pines. But he found a driveway, pulled in and Connor got out and vomited. Wilf didn't think it needed comment, or consolation. This is what came from stealing a bottle of whisky, a key to an empty room, and sitting all night watching *Afterlife*, *Suck My Pop* and porn on the one channel Monk kept locked. Drinking himself into a stupor, coming down at three am and taking a bottle of gin, drinking it neat.

Connor stood and said, 'Maybe ...?' But then started again.

Wilf quiet, still. What could you say now? Why was this such strange behaviour, so inexcusable – the boy's mother two days' dead? He'd done something similar when his mother had died. Walked from the hospital, spent the night trawling the back streets of Northhead, before returning as the sun rose and phoning his brother. Connor wiped his mouth and got in. Wilf backed onto the road and continued. Connor said, 'I'll pay him.'

'Why?'

'How many bottles did I have?'

'A few. He doesn't want your money.'

Monk and Wilf had found him asleep on the floor of room 17. They'd poked and prodded him. Wilf had explained the last few days, and Monk had said, 'What do you think we should do?' So they'd put him to bed, left him for a few hours, brought coffee and eggs and bacon at lunch time. Connor had stirred, vomited: 'I didn't want to stay home.'

'We know,' Wilf had said. Colin had come in with the bottles. 'That's a pretty decent effort, Nephew.' Connor had almost smiled, but remembered. How empty, how quiet, how shit the house had been; how he'd left it, lights on, again, and walked to the pub; how he'd found them all in bed, and helped himself to the drinks.

As they drove up the hill, Connor said, 'Perhaps I could stay at Monk's again?'

Wilf agreed. That would be better.

'Just for a while.'

'There's no rush. It's not like anyone stays there much anymore.' Continuing. He'd decided there was no point sitting around at Monk's, or returning to the house and cleaning up, avoiding photos or sitting in your own shit remembering more shit that wouldn't quieten any of the voices, dampen the smell from Orla's room. So, to the limestone hills. It had been years since they'd come for a look. At what, Wilf wasn't sure. 'You going to spew?'

Connor studied the way the dirt and small stones had gathered in the floor mat. 'I didn't think she was so sick.'

They'd already been through this – how he'd never meant to be an arsehole; to ignore the calls, the messages for so long. 'I just thought it could all wait, Uncle.'

'You were busy.'

Wilf slowed and moved for another car. 'Arsehole.' And continued. Connor smiled and said, 'Fucking sonofabitch arsehole.' Wilf said, 'She got want she wanted.'

'What?'

'The priest.'

Connor didn't care. What did a priest matter?

'You might not think it's important, but it was to her. That's how we were all brought up.'

'It's a load of shit.'

'It's not. It's something. And when you're . . . it's something.'

Connor could remember – the dimly lit room and the machine casting LED shadows on his mother. The priest had arrived and he'd stepped out, but Wilf had come to look for him, to tell him his mother wanted him. So he'd gone back in, stood holding her hand while the priest went on about Jesus and lambs and our father waits in heaven with gifts and praises and songs. Shit like that.

They stopped and Connor spewed again. When he got back in Wilf said, 'Or would you rather go home?'

'No, all these hills are helping.' Grinning. 'If you could find some windier roads?'

Gliding, the roads leading in and out of blind corners, the surprise of what was over hills. 'We're made that way,' Wilf said to his nephew. 'For example. There's me, eight years of age, just before we left Louth.'

Connor's head slumped.

'What, you don't want to hear another story?'

'Go on.'

'I look at my dad across the table, and his big nose and whiskers and fat cheeks and I . . . you know, *hate* him.'

'Where's this going?' Connor asked.

'I hated him. Like, who are you?' He pointed. 'The old mansion. Should we have a look?'

'If you like.'

'I thought my father was fatter, dumber, meaner than others. I wasn't sure what he had to offer. How to shear a sheep, or dunk it, inseminate a cow. Anyway, this continues, the usual, I get into trouble, out comes the strap and I think, I'll show you, you old bastard.'

'Heady days, Uncle.'

'You were always perceptive.'

Connor shook his head. 'Apparently not.'

'Anyway, here's me thinking, I'll get back at you, Tom Healy. So one night I took his left boot, ran up the road, dumped it into a ditch and covered it with bushes.'

Connor put down his window, extended his head and called, '*Hello, anyone?*'

'The next morning he gets dressed, and can you imagine?'

'*Where's my left boot, sons named Brian, Colin and Wilf. I bet it was you, Wilf? You scallywag. Out with the belt, and punishment will be incurred.* And now the bit where you make the connection, Uncle. The moral of the story.'

'There isn't one.'

'Yes, there is. We're an ungrateful bunch of little fuckers and only later do we realise what we've done.'

Wilf didn't reply.

'But it's not like I'm not aware,' Connor said. 'People dying has that effect on you.' Because an hour after the priest, she started sounding like a vacuum, taking forever to draw breath, her whole body heaving and working and struggling against something Connor knew would kill her. Colin had taken him around the shoulders and led him out. He'd made it to the couch against the wall, before he'd shrunk, collapsed into a cat-sized ball, and lost control of every sense, every thought, every feeling.

'I was only making a point,' Wilf said.

Connor didn't reply. Because he was led downstairs to the cafeteria where Colin fetched him a sandwich made from dry bread and a thin layer of ham that didn't taste like ham and a lettuce leaf that was yellow. None of Bobby Mullan's greenery.

They drove without talking for a while, then Connor said, 'Did he find his boot?'

'I thought about it all that day at school. I felt bad.'

'And?'

'That night I fetched it and left it with the other one, and the next morning he just put them on, you know, without so much as a word. Like he knew.'

Connor didn't care about the lesson; just the boot. 'He never mentioned it?'

'No.'

'So . . . God is great, God forgives. Grace. Parents understand and love their kids and I shouldn't feel bad about going to live in Georgetown while my mother was dying of cancer.'

'God, no,' Wilf said. 'Of course you should feel bad, but I was just saying, you're not the only one to have done it.'

Wilf just drove. 'You'd go mad out here.'

'*You*? You want to live on an island.'

'That's different.'

'Your problem, while we're giving lessons, Uncle, is that you don't like people.'

'*Me*?'

'They waste your time, and you just want to go back to hiding your dad's boot in a hole.'

'I'm the one out and about all day.'

'And complaining about it. Wilf's retirement. What will I do? Sure you wouldn't want my life, Nephew?'

'I never said that.'

'That's why I went.'

'It is, is it?'

'If you're going to your island . . .'

And desert people when they need you, Wilf thought of saying. How will that end? How *did* it end? But he just said, 'People rely on me.'

Connor glared at him.

'What?'

'Nothing.'

Wilf pulled into a muddy park, straightened, turned off the motor. 'You feeling better?'

'Nothing left to spew.'

'You'll find something.'

The long, awkward moment, sitting, at six am, out front of Orla's place. It had been the usual drive from Northhead, but quieter, with less, with nothing at stake. Nothing had been said, because there was nothing to say. Connor hadn't cried. It was the numbness before all of that. Wilf had got out of his van and said, 'We should cook some breakfast.'

Connor had asked why. Was he hungry? Or was he just trying to keep it normal? Okay, Wilf had said, we'll try and get some sleep. Connor had said he didn't want to sleep. 'Why . . . it's my fucking mess, let *me* clean it up.' Storming inside the still open, still lit up house. Wilf and Colin had followed. They'd found him lying on his bed in his room, in the dark, facing the wall, and he'd told them to fuck off, what did they want him to say?

So they'd returned to the lounge room and cleared a few dishes. They'd made a cup of tea. Colin had taken the sheets from Orla's bed and placed them in the washing machine, but Connor had come out, retrieved them and thrown them back on her bed. He'd said, 'It was four hours ago.' Colin hadn't replied. He didn't do death well, either. So he'd returned to Wilf and they'd sat sharing the occasional word, listening to infomercials. Eventually Colin had fallen asleep in Orla's chair. Wilf had written a note saying he was going back to Monk's – clean sheets, food, milk – and he'd be back in an hour.

They walked around the ruin of what had been a big house – five bedrooms, indoor plumbing, a grand ballroom, although now, like the rest, it was a roofless memory. The windows removed for the wood; the floorboards for someone else's floorboards. But the place had good bones, still, and it was clear, someone had done well, and wanted the world to see. But Connor didn't care. 'So fucking what?'

They walked around the old yards. The Selwyn Historical Society (before it'd disbanded) had made some signs saying how Fitzgerald was the first to carry Angus, clear the land, donate money to some university, bring money into the district during some recession. Things like this. Connor wasn't looking. He just said, 'I guess she was pissed off at me?'

'Not at all.'

'You have to say that, now.'

'No, I don't. I agree, you were a selfish little shit, but she knew why you went.'

Connor wasn't happy with this. He kicked an old fence post and someone looked at him like, why would you do that? 'I could just imagine what she thought.'

His mother wondering why he wasn't replying. Finding inadequate explanations, resorting to photographs of her seven-year-old son (they'd found beside her bed). Connor said, 'Anyway, it's too late now.'

'For what?'

'I'm a fucking arsehole. An arse ... hole.' Droning, as he had when Wilf returned from Monk's, come in with a warm curry Karen had put in a plastic container, chocolate that Simon had brought over when he saw Wilf going into the lodge.

Wilf had come in, found his brother snoring, but heard running water. He'd gone to the bathroom and found his nephew standing naked, the razor removed from a shaver, slowly guiding it up his arm. Only a drop of blood, but he'd caught him early. He'd grabbed the razor and thrown it on the ground, taken Connor back to his room and dressed him. Pulling on his pants, windcheater, as he sat staring at the ceiling. After a while Colin had woken, come in and helped settle him. They'd served Mrs Gould's curry, but Connor wouldn't eat it. 'I killed her,' he told them.

Connor still had these marks on his wrist. They'd already formed a scab. He said to his uncle, 'I'm hungry.'

'Well, that's a good sign.'

So they drove back to Selwyn.

As they went, Wilf said, 'Oh, I forgot.' He reached back (almost launching them off a cliff) and found the wad of papers, the chapter, and gave it to Connor. 'I told you he asked after you.'

Connor read: '*Chapter Seventeen: Morpheus Has A Misunderstanding with Zeus*'.

'He keeps asking if you've read it,' Wilf said.

Connor felt bad about this, too. It was funny, because people never asked anything of you, never expected, and weren't disappointed if you didn't come through. They weren't angry or spiteful, or didn't love you any less. They were just patient. He asked Wilf, 'She was waiting?'

'Of course. There was no rush.'

Connor read aloud. '*Morpheus had a body three times the size of a London bus. Although he could crush most people, he walked softly, and talked quietly, and didn't make a fuss about anything.*' He smiled at Wilf. 'He wanted me to read it?'

'Maybe you could call him . . . write him a note?'

Wilf was happy to let him sit quietly, and read, and forget about the room with the cross on the wall, the small sink with lemon-smelling soap, the cannulas and intravenous lines, and the *In Bloom* tempo of the machine.

27

'Listen to it,' Wilf said, lifting a finger and quietening his nephew.

They listened. Connor said, 'What?'

Wilf closed his eyes and seemed inebriated by it, enamoured, perhaps. 'There's never a moment when you're *not* busy,' he said. 'Fixing things, taking them somewhere . . . never a moment.'

This sound, Connor thought, sitting in the lane behind Monk's with his uncle, was made up of a hum of motors, compressors, fans and other machines, of people talking quietly, the rotation of the earth on its axis, perhaps. Deep sounds that accompanied life but were hardly ever recognised, or named. Wilf breathed deeply and said, 'You can smell it, too.'

This, Connor thought, was a bit much. What could you smell? The old oil in the drum beside the fence? The Morris's coolant, oil, vinyl seats?

Wilf said, 'You can choose to believe if you want.'

Connor shook his head and continued polishing his shoes.

'It's not such a stretch.'

Not today, Connor thought. Let's just get it over and done with.

Wilf's attention was broken by someone starting a sports car, revving it a few times, driving off. So he continued, the few photos in his hand, remembering. Sitting on the cold, concrete step of this public house that had become *his* house – the rooms he shared with his nephew and brother. All three, linked by a passageway of worn lino (Wilf had told Monk it would have to be replaced). Roomies. Mates sharing the same pisser and shitter, the same slivers of soap, the same tinea. 'That's why they had wakes.'

Connor started on his next shoe, resting on his knee, the suit Wilf had found for him. Inviting him into his room that morning, showing him the tweeds he'd inherited over a lifetime, saying, 'What about brown?'

'It's old.'

'You can't go in a windcheater.'

'I know but . . . they're musty.'

'Your mother wouldn't have wanted us spending hundreds on a suit. Unless . . .?'

'I don't think I'll be a banker any time soon. I guess this one . . . if it fits.'

So he'd tried it on and it had fit perfectly and Wilf had given him a white shirt and tie that didn't look too old-fashioned. Monk (in his own old suit) had noticed the preparations and offered Connor something more modern. Connor said he didn't care, old was good, and it wasn't like it was a competition. Apparently he'd already won first prize.

Back on the step, Wilf repeated, 'That's why they had wakes.'

'Who?' Connor said, half-angry, woken from the stillness he'd recognised.

'The old people had lead pipes and it made them catatonic, like, in a trance.'

Connor had heard it before, but guessed he had to hear it again.

'So they *seemed* dead, but they weren't, really. So they laid them out in people's houses to keep an eye on them. In case they woke . . . see, a *wake*.'

Connor didn't get how Wilf didn't get it. His mother was dead. Her body was sitting in a coffin in the back of a car on the way to a church. But even now, there had to be a long, pointless, poorly-timed story about some shit that wasn't true and had never happened. 'That's a myth.' Slipping on his uncle's shoes, tightening his laces below the cuff of the suit Wilf had worn to his mother's funeral. 'It wasn't about lead pipes.'

'It might have been.'

Connor waited for the next story – about how the dead person was placed on a table, a window opened so their spirit could leave the house.

You dared not block their path. 'And two hours later the window is closed,' he said to his uncle.

'That's an old wives' tale,' Wilf said.

'*That is*? God. Two hours. So they can't get back in the house. Very nice.'

'Just the way it was . . . is.'

Wilf could remember it this way – the house on St Joseph's Road, people in each room, out into the front yard, the suit tight around his arse and hips, smoked salmon on little biscuits and the corpse on the kitchen table. Brian saying, 'It's grotesque.'

'A few more hours.'

Because it was the way their mother had wanted it: people filing past, placing a spotted orchid on her chest, mumbling a few verses from Daniel and taking one last look as her spirit drifted up past the spot where she'd leave her beef to defrost.

'It's like the stone age,' Brian had said.

'She wanted it.'

'Still . . .' Loosening his tie, because of the three brothers, he was the least formal, or religious, or concerned about offending anyone.

Wilf had got up earlier. He'd set out a big breakfast before the guests had arrived. The three of them, semi-suited, dripping egg from toast, Monk acting as their butler, topping up their coffee and saying, 'This'll be the worst of it.'

Of what, Connor wasn't sure, but he was enjoying the food, the slimy mushrooms and even the soggy tomato. 'How many d'yer reckon?' he'd asked Wilf.

'Plenty. Shops will shut, my boy.'

They had, already, signs going up: 'Open at three, perhaps'.

Eventually Monk had sat with them and said, 'Everyone's got a memory of Orla.'

Connor wasn't sure he wanted to hear. He had his own, and they would suffice. The rest sounded stagey, forced, like it might or might not have happened, or at least had been exaggerated. Monk had said, 'She was my Tristan's age. They went to school together.'

'Where's he now?' Connor had managed.

'London.' Almost apologetically. 'And Orla was just as mischievous as him, wasn't she, Wilf?'

'She had her moments.'

They walked toward church and stopped on the road to take it all in: this small, deep-grey wedding cake of a building with buttresses that served no purpose, sitting like it had been waiting for this day. When Orla, mother of Connor, would arrive to get the nod from God, and the saints, before passing through her own small, stained-glass windows. 'No one much yet,' Colin said.

'It's not a musical,' Wilf said. 'People don't get to these things early.'

The aisle was too narrow for a procession, so when they went in Orla was already sitting at the front in the small gap where people married, baptised their kids, handed over every anniversary to the church. The flowers on her coffin. Three types of orchids, and roses. The decisions they (the three of them) had made, two days after her death. The undertaker at Reception, and they went into the bar and sat down and discussed each point. The pine casket, the gold handles, the familiar hymns, the homily Wilf had agreed to give (as he felt for the sheet in his pocket and wondered if he'd make it through).

Colin said, 'Just as well I didn't go to New Zealand.'

'What about your girlfriend?' Wilf asked.

'She's not my girlfriend.'

'She'll be beside herself.'

Connor laughed. He didn't know why. Perhaps the schtick was for his benefit? Either way. He thought it strange how the church was so close to their house. One block. One minute's walk. He must have gone past it a thousand times, but never thought of it this way. It was just a building, like the gas shop, the bakery, the Tea Junction. Suddenly it all made sense. The musty bible smell, the incense, the undertaker's cologne.

They approached the coffin. Connor thought it best if he faced it, touched it, spoke to it. But not in words, just thoughts. No point apologising, or praising, remembering. It was a box, and his mother was in it. It wouldn't be a box much longer, and his mother wouldn't be Orla. This seemed a pity. In a practical, down-to-earth sense, a pity.

They sat on the front pew and over the next ten minutes a dozen, hundred, several hundred people came in, filled the rows from the back, talked quietly. The church organist (Patrick Tear's brother) fiddled about on the too-perfect-sounding organ and the priest, a fat-cheeked old Brendan who oozed too much confidence for Connor's liking, greeted them, said there was no good day for a funeral (and this sounded like a standard line to Connor), shook their hands and said they'd be getting underway directly. Like it was a flight to Spain, and had you fastened your seatbelt? Eventually the place was full to overflowing. Wilf turned to look and told Connor that was a good sign, surely. 'People liked your mum.'

But this didn't make him feel any better.

Wilf checked again, noticed the Lillimars, Jack Mooney, Dave Duffy, all looking at them, smiling, little waves that wouldn't seem trite. He turned back and said to Connor, 'People have been popping in.'

'What?'

'You know, the bar, Reception, leaving things. Everyone's got a memory.'

'I'll have to write to them.'

'You don't have to do anything.'

'If they've brought stuff.'

'I'll take care of that. You just got to be here . . . and listen. The moment, remember?' And he closed his eyes again, and said wasn't it peaceful?

Connor did the same. It was fine. The little melody and its chords hammered out by fat, unmusical fingers. *Fine*. And even when it kicked off and every word was anxiety and sounded hollow and contrived and annoying, even then, it was nice. *Abide with Me*. Maybe he could write some words for it. Better words. Arrange it, play it, record it? And then he realised he'd missed what the priest was saying.

Father Brendan walked around the coffin sprinkling pizza-smelling holy water and invoking God for the dozenth time. Connor wondered what the fuck God had to do with it and felt angry and annoyed that the Catholics had put Him before Orla. And then the priest returned and read: '*But those with insight shall shine brightly like the splendour of the firmament, and those who lead the many to justice shall be like the stars forever.*' This was sort of neat, but still didn't excuse God who, if he'd wanted, could've saved his mum, or at least not given her cancer. But maybe she would be like the stars forever? Maybe. That was nice, too, as was No. 43: 'His light shineth forevermore'. As were the various smells of old jackets, mothballs, powdered bodies, cheap and expensive colognes, the breath of the hundreds, the hush of their *also with you*, the birds outside, the grind of the earth on its axis, again.

In the end he thought, Okay, God, you can have her.

Whatever fight he'd had, and with whomever, was over. The crying, the shock of her not being alive, the way it was hard to get breath after you'd been howling for twenty minutes, how there was no way of understanding how you could go on living with part of your body nailed into a pine box. But you can have her, God. Take care of her. Make her a star or whatever the fuck you want to do, but no fuss, please.

Wilf got up for the homily. He started off with facts. His brother Brian, his marriage, their child, Orla, where she went to school, what subjects she was good at. Connor thought it lame, but hadn't asked to see what he'd written. Like his uncle was avoiding anything too sentimental or sloppy. Undercooked eggs as language. Just the sound of a rubbish truck, outside, collecting the recycling.

Wilf said, 'It was often up to me and Nance, when Brian was working, to babysit our niece. She enjoyed dressing up in Nance's clothes and putting on her makeup and of course Nance didn't say a thing. I think Nance would like to be here today.' Looking up at them all. 'Although maybe it's best she's not.'

There were refreshments in the church hall. This is what they were called: refreshments. Like they needed to be made fresh, cleansed of all the gloom and shitty bits, fed with fresher, but still ungenerous, sandwiches. Too-thin bread, and cucumber that everyone picked out.

Not enough chicken. Perhaps that was because you couldn't refrigerate it and it'd be tragic if everyone went home with food poisoning. Still, it was strange. Despite his big breakfast, Connor was hungry. Despite his mother being dead, he just wanted to eat as much food as he could. So he stuffed it in – one sandwich after another. One canapé. One croissant. One slice of cake. This is all he wanted: food.

Roman and his mum came up to him and Roman said, 'What a shit, man.'

'Yeah.' Starting on his second coffee, which was too cold.

Roman's mum said, 'She came quite often.'

'Sorry?'

'Your mum. Here. Church.'

'She did?'

'Yes. Not so often on a Sunday, but other times. I locked up. Sometimes we'd talk. She often told me about you and what you were up to. School.'

'Oh.'

'Not like that. She said you had a natural intelligence.'

'Bullshit,' Roman laughed, pushing his friend.

'Well, take care.' And she moved on, because now there was a line of a dozen, more, waiting to say the same sort of shit. But as Spencer and Grace scrambled for words (although Connor guessed they should have had plenty), he just imagined his mum, sitting on the back pew saying a prayer for him, or telling people how he'd had a rough time at school. Then he didn't feel so good. He just wanted to go home and work on this thought. All of the handshakes and sorry-to-hear-it smiles and sandwiches and cold coffee now meant nothing.

Noah was next, and he said sorry, too, and Connor said why, it's not your fault. He said he wondered whose fault it was probably his own – but Noah didn't like where all this was leading. He said, 'You staying home now?'

'Perhaps.'

'We could get you re-enrolled?'

'I'm not sure. Maybe.'

'A few teachers could help you catch up, before exams.'

'I've been away so long.'

'You could redo a year?'

Connor thought this was gracious, so he shook his hand again and said he was sorry for being an arsehole, and Noah gave him a sort of half-hug and said, 'I was the biggest shit in town when I was your age.' Wandering off, returning to the chicken legs, laid out on a bed of Bobby's lettuce. And Connor thought (and heard and smelled and saw and sensed) how everything in this room, in Selwyn and Northhead, and everywhere, was the same – the same people, houses, books, hopes, stories – everything. The same. And how he was just part of it. No more, or less. A small phrase of whatever the priest was singing, his mum was playing (and he could see her now, teaching him bar chords), of whatever story his uncle was making up, whatever bullshit they played on the radio.

The room proved this: Jay Griffin and his mum and dad, Karen, Simon, his mum, Ced, waiting patiently, leaning on his zimmer frame.

For the first time in a long time, Connor felt happy. The cross on the wall. Fuck you God, but thank you, please, be with me, be with me, the chrism on his forehead, the priest's breath, his mother's hand on his shoulder. His two uncles, even, standing slightly behind but either side of him, taking his arm occasionally, squeezing it. George Daly, even Bobby, who just placed his face beside his, held the back of his head and said, 'Another week.' Like he might be ripe by then. But Connor got it. Another week. He said, 'I'll come out with Uncle, and we'll help with your plane. You're not flying yet?'

Smiling, like flying was hardly the point. Face to face again, and Connor smelled him, old and hessiany, his whiskers so tough they scratched his face.

Leo next, and Lucy, Monk, again. Connor asked Colin to get him more sandwiches before they were all gone.

And finally, at the end of the line, a man the same height as him, the same face, nose, eyes, even. Connor took a few moments to remember, then said, 'Dad?'

28

'You've never thought maybe . . . the Colosseum, or Milan or Florence?'

'Doesn't interest me,' Wilf said.

'Or Paris? The Eiffel Tower, a Seine cruise?'

'I'm happy here.' Heading south again, toward Georgetown.

'Or you could meet me in LA, we could go to New York? Or maybe the Grand Canyon?'

Wilf shrugged. 'Never miss what you've never known.'

'But if you've never known . . .' Giving up, returning to the burnt paddocks.

The J2 was growling, flying over the little hills and *hmphing* to earth, almost as though Wilf wanted to get rid of his brother. 'If I want to go to Paris, it's there.'

'All the great works of art, the Louvre, haven't you ever wondered . . . Notre Dame?'

'Why? When we've got St John the Baptist?'

Colin knew that now wasn't the time to say it, but he still didn't understand his brother. What was so great about Selwyn? What a shithole. Hot and baking, or cold and wet, raining when he'd left decades ago, raining today, as they'd loaded his bags into the back of the J2 and set off for the airport. Mr Gould waving across the road, as his father had. The same kids drifting into the same school to learn about Pythagoras despite pre-determined futures selling fertiliser and cooking fried chicken for people visiting from Perth.

Connor sat in the back. They'd been on the road half an hour, but he'd hardly said a word. Just the earbuds, his head resting on his palm, an engagement with but disconnection from the landscape, his uncles. There were six or seven birds heading south. He wondered what type. He asked, and Wilf said cockatiels, but Colin said parrots, and they argued before he said, 'It doesn't matter.' He watched them flying in formation, wondering where they might be going, whether it was worth the energy.

'I said I'd ring Raelene when I arrive,' Colin said. 'But she might be busy.'

And Wilf: 'Not a lot to do in New Zealand.'

'No? Mountains? Glaciers?'

'We've got them.'

'So I should stay in Selwyn?'

'Didn't say that. But you need more than scenery.'

'Right.' Sighing. 'If you want I'll buy you a ticket and we can all spend a few days in Rotorua.' Turning back. 'What do you think, Connor?'

'Sorry?' Catching his uncle's eye in the mirror.

'New Zealand. Rotorua. Mud, you like mud? They've got plenty of mud.'

'We've got mud,' Wilf said. 'And anyway, I've got jobs.'

'Jobs, jobs, jobs, you've always got jobs. It's just a way of avoiding things.'

'What?'

'Things.'

'*What?*'

'Getting on and living, seeing things, meeting new people, spending some of that million dollars you've got in the bank.'

'As if.'

'Right.' Looking at him with his I-know-better expression.

Wilf was content with the land. With the pastures and telephone poles, the hole they were digging for pipes, a farmer out on his tractor spraying weeds. Bobby, just as alone, just as content. That's what Colin didn't get. You didn't need the Louvre, or Roman pizza. Just a thought, a task, a willing ear. 'I'll tell Bobby goodbye.'

'No need. I saw him outside Lillimar's. I said I might not get back in time.'

'For what?'

'*In time*. We shook hands, he smiled, that was it.'

Connor was losing sight of the birds. They were faster than the Morris. So he closed his eyes and settled into the torn seat, the vinyl with its little folds full of old food and soil and bits of lettuce and cauliflower. He could smell all this, feel it with his fingers. It felt good. But as he drifted, he said, 'Rome would be worth seeing.'

'Exactly,' Colin replied. Then he turned to his brother: 'You'll probably be pissed off, but I had a word to Bobby. I said my brother's getting on and if there's someone else you can think of to collect your stuff, sell it.'

'You didn't?' His attention torn between brother and road.

'And I spoke to Noah, too.'

'What?'

'I said I can't see why the school, why you, Noah, can't organise someone else. I said I think people are taking advantage of his, your, good nature.'

'Why'd you do that?'

'It needed saying.'

'If it needed saying, *if*, I'd do it. Jesus, Colin.' Slamming his open palm on the steering wheel.

'It needed saying, before I left.'

'It bloody well did not.'

Connor heard none of this.

'The nerve of you. Now they'll think . . .'

'And I also had a word to George.'

Wilf pushed down on the accelerator and they went too fast, skidding, lifting. Connor opened his eyes and said, 'Go, Uncle!' But Colin just said, 'Don't kill me before I get to the airport.'

'I'd like to.' Slowing.

'People need to know,' Colin explained. 'If you keep agreeing to everything you'll be dead before anything changes. No Paris, no Rome. Stop being so bloody nice.'

'Stop telling me how to . . .' Shaking his head, carefully guiding the car. 'You've always done it.'

No response.

'Even at school. *Miss, Dad made him watch the animals, so he didn't have time, so you can't really expect him to finish his French.*'

'You should be thanking me.'

'I'm not. Who else did you talk to?'

'Come to think of it, I did have a quick word to Leo. I said Oz Post should be dealing with it, not Wilf.'

'But I *enjoy* it.'

They passed Robinson Caves and Colin said, 'Remember us three playing in there?'

'We never did.'

Connor opened his eyes, but the birds had gone. As he sang, '*Hush now baby, baby, don't you cry . . .*'

The brothers listened. Wilf said, 'What's that?'

Connor removed his buds and said, 'Sorry?'

'What's that?'

'Pink Floyd.'

'Who's he?'

'They.'

'*See,*' Colin said to his brother. 'You wouldn't even know.'

Past a BP, and Wilf said, 'All I'm saying is if I didn't have my jobs . . . Now I'll have to talk to them, explain.'

'But you're the one saying you want to be Robinson Crusoe.'

'My own time, my own way.' Checking Connor. Colin noticed and whispered, 'If you think he's going to be the new Wilf.'

No reply.

'I couldn't think of anyone less likely.'

And again, the voice from the back of the van: '*Wrong, do it again! If you don't eat your meat you can't have any pudding.*'

'So, you spoke to Dave?' Colin asked.

'Briefly.'

'And?'

'*Yes, you behind the bike shed, stand still, laddy!*'

The brothers laughed. Connor heard and said, 'What?'

'Who's behind the bike shed?' Colin asked.

'Me, apparently.' Replacing his buds and slipping further into his seat.

But Colin said, 'What did you say to your dad?'

Connor unplugged again. 'Sorry?'

'What did you say to your dad?'

'He's not my dad. My father, perhaps. I didn't say anything.' Descending, again.

Wilf whispered, 'Thirty seconds and it was all over.'

He'd been watching Dave move up the line. He'd nodded to him, but not smiled, not given any sort of approval. When they'd met, Connor had said, 'How did you know?'

'Your uncle told me.'

Connor had just glared at him. Dave had said, 'Don't you reckon I deserve to know?'

'I don't care.'

'She was my wife.'

'If you'd given a fuck.'

Dave had taken a deep breath. 'If I'd known she was sick.'

'Well, she was, and if you'd ever called . . .'

Dave had walked away, taken a few sandwiches from the tray and left the hall. Wilf had watched Connor watching him leave, like he'd put him in the bin years ago. Wilf thought it a pity. Dave offered some hope of a way forward. But thinking about it that night, sitting on his bed next to Connor, he'd said, 'You don't reckon you should talk to him? He's still your father.'

'No, he's not.' Not bothering to mention the absent years.

Wilf had said, 'Some people do improve with age.'

'How?'

'They grow up, mature, learn a bit of responsibility.'

'You think he has?'

'I don't know. Perhaps. He came today. That must have been difficult.'

'*For him*? Jesus, Uncle.'

Connor hadn't mentioned the missed parent-teacher interviews, concerns about school, reports, friendships, bullying, loneliness, other dads watching their kids playing soccer, taking them places, holidays. In the end he'd said, 'Do you want me to list everything?'

'No.'

'Well, that's why. Because he could've, but he didn't. So I don't think he's matured much, do you?'

Wilf had listened to Dave driving off. Revving, planting a skid. Later, he'd gone to Hyland's and asked if he was there. The girl had said yes, should I call him, but he'd said he'd come back later. Any message? she'd asked. But he'd said no.

'*Goodbye, blue sky, goodbye, blue sky . . .*'

'Anyway,' Colin said, surveying the landscape for what he guessed would be the last time, 'most of them were quite receptive to the idea.'

'Who?'

'Noah, for example. He said they could advertise for someone.'

'*Colin.*'

'What, you need the money?'

'I don't mind it. I like the kids.'

'Some you hate. That Darcy sod, he'll give you a heart attack. You had your pills?'

'Yes, I've had my pills. Do you want to wipe my arse? What else would I be doing if I wasn't driving the bus?'

They arrived, and Wilf waited at the boom gate to the car park, reading the rates, refusing to go in. 'Why do they need to charge that?'

'I'll pay it,' Colin said.

'Just because they can.' He drove in anyway, parked, and helped his brother unload his case and bag. It was some sort of designer number, and he said, 'All fancy, aren't you?'

'What? You want me to live in a bog, and work down a mine?'

As they sat in the coffee shop drinking cold cappuccinos, Wilf said, 'This time, get on the bloody plane and stay on it.'

'If I'd done that you wouldn't have had your nephew back.'

Connor drank Coke.

'Stay on it,' Wilf said. 'And find Raelene from Ohio and don't bore her shitless with stories about Selwyn and growing up on Louth.'

'No worries there, Brother.'

'Although thanks are in order, I guess.'

'It don't come easy, does it, Wilfred Healy?'

They sat for a moment, letting everything dissipate, mix with the smell of avgas and Cookie Man.

'I was about to come home anyway,' Connor said.

'You were not,' Colin said, smiling.

'I was!'

'Not how I remember it, boy.'

'What?' Smiling.

'So, Brother, I arrive at this place and knock and there's no answer.'

'This is bullshit,' Connor said.

'I notice the door's open and I go in and walk down the hallway.'

'All made up.'

'No one. So I go up the stairs, open this door and who's lying in bed as bare-arsed and naked as the day he was born, except Connor Francis, and this bird, what was her name?'

'This didn't happen, Uncle.'

'Her, too, not a single thread, both of them, what did Brother Flanagan say – in *delicto flagrante*.'

'No wonder you didn't want to come home,' Wilf said.

Colin pushed his coffee away, took three cigars from his pocket and handed them around. Then he produced a box of matches and lit one, the second, before the girl came over and said, 'The cafe's non-smoking.'

'Fuck it,' Colin said. 'The coffee's shit anyway.'

So he took his brother and nephew outside and they lit up and smoked a cigar together. He said to Connor, 'So, what's the game?'

'Pardon?'

'The next step?'

Connor shrugged. 'I'm not sure.'

'You going back to your mate, to your lady friend?'

'She sort of, you know . . .'

'Or stay in Selwyn and end up like Ced Graney and his enormous flaring nostril hairs?'

Connor said was he was unsure. Early days. He'd have to get used to this orphan thing, decide whether the world needed another twelve songs to add to the billion it already had. He inhaled, and coughed, but realised it didn't take long to get used to cigars. He could go back to school, he said, but not Selwyn Area, with its dipstick teachers and unshorn goats. Maybe Northhead, or Georgetown. 'We could get a place together, Uncle?'

'If need be,' Wilf said.

'Although there's your jobs.'

'They're not my jobs.'

'And your island?'

Not my island either, Wilf thought. Whatever happened, he guessed, would be good.

When they arrived at the gate, boarding had already begun. Colin put down his bag and said, 'Well . . .'

Wilf got it. Now Raelene and the smoggy canals and the bowls club weren't so perfect. Colin said to his brother, 'Like when we were leaving the island.'

'Long time ago,' Wilf said.

But not so long, Colin thought. Sitting with his brother, his mum, his dad, who were everything and everyone and every place, every tree and house and blade of grass, as it was then. 'Nothing to be gained from all this,' he said.

'No,' Wilf replied.

So they shook hands and awkwardly embraced and Colin held his nephew close, and smelled his hair and body and breath, and felt like turning, going back, and making it right. But he couldn't.

29

Most of the bay was shallow, quick to retreat into the ocean at low tide. Wilf could smell it as he put on his shoes, and went downstairs. As he ate breakfast, Karen said, 'How's Connor?'

'Sleeping it off.'

'You should take him somewhere. Cheer him up. Wasn't Colin going to New Zealand? Fly over. Meet him.'

'We said our goodbyes.'

'Honestly, Wilf.'

Wilf tried to work her out. She didn't get much, really. Rugby, *The Voice*, and Bruce Willis, she was always on about him. 'If he gets up . . .'

'He could go with you?'

'Tomorrow, perhaps.'

Wilf walked to school. Skirting the main road, looking across acreage to the bay, the grey sand, the rotting seaweed, two men and a dog scratching for worms. A few boats grounded, waiting for the tide. Ced, perhaps, was it Ced, dragging a rake across the beach? '*How can you have any pudding?*' he asked himself. '*If you don't eat yer meat.*'

On the way home, Connor had explained how each of us, Uncle, is just another brick in the wall (playing him all three parts of the song). Wilf had argued. Hardly. How am I the same as Leo or Bobby, or you, for that matter? Too much of that stuff, he'd said. So Connor had retreated – to the music, and the darkening country toward Northhead. Wilf had wondered if these were really helpful thoughts. 'You've got your whole future ahead of you.'

'Sorry?' De-budding.

'I said you've got your whole future ahead of you.'

But that's where it had ended. The future, Wilf guessed, was too far away. 'Do you want to go home tonight?'

'No.'

'Tomorrow?'

'Sometime.'

Into school and across the damp lawn to the bus. Wilf opened it, found his rag under the seat and wiped the windows. Tuned his radio to talkback and sat listening to the story of a man who'd murdered his wife. He was tired. He hadn't slept well. He closed his eyes and thought of how he'd clean the house this afternoon, change the sheets, remove the old food from the fridge.

'Wilf.'

Noah, standing at the door. 'Got a minute?'

Wilf left the bus running, got out and Noah said, 'You better turn it off.'

'It's got to run a few minutes.'

'You better. I'll take the keys.'

Wilf didn't get it. But he returned to the bus, turned off the engine, removed the keys and gave them to Noah. 'You're happy to go this morning?'

'You can't drive it, Wilf.'

'Why?'

Noah decided. 'You're gonna have to leave the grounds.'

A car drove up, parked, and two men got out. One in a suit, white shirt and tie, the other more casual, corduroy pants, a polo shirt. He was a muscly bastard, Wilf noticed, a small tattoo visible just below his left sleeve. Both men came over and the one in the suit said, 'Wilf, is it?'

Wilf had a bad feeling. Something had been said, and arranged. Phone calls, complaints, perhaps. Perhaps the Department? He noticed the extra aerials on the car, the lights on the dash, and in the back window.

The man in the suit said his name was Derek, without a c. This seemed important, Wilf thought. Detective Sergeant Derek Waters, Georgetown CID. Wilf wondered whether he was related to his old teacher, thought of asking, but decided it probably wasn't the time. The other man was also a detective. Carey. They didn't seem angry, or overly concerned. They shook his hand and asked if he was just setting off and he said, 'Yes, I don't want to be late.'

'Don't worry about that,' Carey said. 'Mr Foley's agreed to take over this morning – alright?'

Noah jingled the keys in his hand. Wilf faced him and said, 'What's wrong?'

Noah checked his watch. 'I better get going.' He got in and started the bus, and they had to make room for him to drive out. Waters said, 'You do it every day?'

'Most. Unless someone . . . Lucy Annald used to do it until she had a double hip operation.' As though this might be enough for them. 'I help out because no one else will. It's hard to get people these days, isn't it? I mean, everyone says they're so busy, but if they weren't on their computer . . .' Slowing, then giving up. He could no longer hear the bus, just someone calling from down on the beach. He could feel his heart racing. He could feel his mouth drying. His hands were shaking. 'What, I'm in trouble?'

'Not sure,' Carey, who wouldn't give his first name, replied.

Wilf tried. 'There was a Carey up Mountebank Road one time. Jimmy? Jack?'

'One of my uncles, I think.'

As they scanned him from top to bottom. Waters said, 'No point standing out in the cold.'

So they went into the staff room and sat on the sofa, the coffee machine already bubbling, the deputy, a woman named Arnold, putting relief slips into teachers' pigeonholes. Wilf asked them to sit, moved a few magazines and hoped his shaky hand wasn't showing. That would make him seem guilty. For whatever he'd done.

'With the bus and everything,' Waters said. 'Until we can get this thing sorted, you know. It's procedure.'

'What is?'

'You can't be around children.'

'Why?'

'It's the law.'

Around children? The voice telling him about meat and pudding, the seagulls searching for their own worms, the rot and coffee and ozone from the photocopier, already glowing in the corner. The flicker of the television with the sound turned down, and breakfast faces telling the world about a bomb blast in Afghanistan.

'There's been an accusation,' Carey said.

Jesus. 'An accusation? About me?' Barely able to get the words out.

The sound of a few early students in the hallway, and the Arnold woman watching him, but then turning away. 'What's it about?'

Waters consulted his notes and said, 'We've had a chat to Noah about this and he seems to think this boy . . . but we have to take it seriously.'

'You've been talking to Noah?'

'We rang him before we came down this morning.'

'From where?'

'Henry Street Police. All of these reports come to us.'

'Who?'

'Criminal Investigation.'

'*Criminal?*'

'Don't worry, Wilf. Like I said, we just have to ask a few questions.'

Wilf didn't feel so good. He was, apparently, a criminal, although he didn't know how. Already, it seemed, people had decided. Arnold glancing at him again, checking the pigeonholes for nothing in particular, before leaving the room.

Carey said, 'You know who, I guess?'

'Darcy?'

'He goes on your bus?'

'He does. He's a real . . .' Although maybe it was best to say nothing. He wondered if he should ask about a lawyer. Is that what happened? Did he have rights? 'He's always the last on. The other kids get on first.'

'Not the bus,' Carey said, consulting his notes. 'Some place called Scoops n' Smiles?'

'I've never been in there.'

'No?'

'Never.'

'Anyway, this complaint comes from the mother.'

'Of course.' Again, he stopped. 'Am I meant to have someone here?'

'You can, but we're not here to charge you. The mother contacted Henry Street, she said the son, this Darcy, told her that you'd had a go at him.'

'A go?'

And reading: '"My son explained that he was in the shop . . ."'

'When's this?'

Carey told him, and he remembered. 'I never went in . . .'

'". . . when Wilf Healy came in, angry, shouting at him. Darcy felt threatened, moved to the back of the shop . . ."' Looking up. 'Familiar?'

'No.'

'Then you followed him and shouted at him about some business on the bus?'

'I've had to discipline him several times.'

'And one time you threw him off the bus?'

'It seemed the only . . . he was giving the other kids . . . he was bullying them.'

'And you left him beside the road and drove off?'

Reluctantly. 'Yes.'

'And because of this his mother complained to the school?'

'She insisted I write an apology. Which I had no intention doing. Knowing him. I mean, the nerve.'

'And because of all this . . .?'

'What's *meant* to have happened?'

Waters read his copy of the notes. '"Mr Healy went behind the bar, threatened my son, lost his temper then pushed him into a bench. Hard. Violently.'

'I didn't even go into the shop,' Wilf said. 'I've never been in. I walked past, saw him inside, grinning, you know, like he does, smugly, and I passed on, but he came out and gave me a mouthful of abuse.'

'Did anyone see this happen?'

'Just me and Darcy and this fella, this man that runs the place. He'd know. He saw it all.'

'Grant Roper?'

'I think so.'

'His statement.' This time they gave Wilf his own copy. He read it and said, 'No, not at all. How did you . . .?'

'Darcy's mother arranged for him to call us.'

'But they've worked it out. He says I went in, I didn't. He says I "threw Darcy against the bar." But it can't be true if it didn't happen.'

Carey handed Wilf a photo. It showed a midriff, right side, the boy holding his jumper up to reveal a long, dark bruise, six inches, already yellowing. 'The mother took this.'

Wilf said, 'He reckons I went in, attacked him, pushed him, did this?'

'He does.'

'But it's a lie. You don't believe him, do you?'

'At this point,' Waters said, 'we're just collecting information, talking to people.'

'But you said I can't drive the bus.'

'No. And once you leave here today you can't return.'

'But even if . . . everyone will think . . .'

'Not necessarily.'

'*But nothing happened.* This Roper fella's made it all up. He's mates with them, these kids, and he sells them . . .'

Carey waited. 'What?'

Wilf knew he was digging a hole. 'I walked past, saw them, walked on with my eggs. Was it eggs? Or bread? I can't remember. We were low and Monk said for me to go out and buy some . . . eggs, I'm sure it was.'

Another teacher came in. Wilf didn't know him. He said hello to them all, glanced at the picture and checked his pigeonhole. Had he seen? Wilf wondered. Did the staff know, because if they did, the whole town would by the end of the day. So he returned the photo and said, 'It's yellow.'

'Sorry?'

He waited for the teacher to fill a glass of water, drink it, leave it in the sink and exit. 'Yellow. It's an old bruise. A week or more, older, perhaps.'

Carey made a note.

Wilf said, 'I dropped him, I shouldn't have, but there's a boy named Luke Thomson and you should hear what Darcy says to him. And Trevor, the way he talks to them and thinks he can get away with it.'

Carey said to Waters, 'Maybe we ought to talk to the mother first?'

They agreed. Wilf took this as a good sign.

So it ended there. With Wilf explaining he'd never hurt a fly, and only tried to help people, and that's why he drove the bus and delivered the vegetables and the mail and helped with the garden and the pills, although sometimes George got them wrong, the pub, too, but that was to pay his bills, hundreds of them, it seemed, and now more since he'd have to support his nephew with his niece, Orla, from around the corner, dying last week. Then Carey said, 'Bit of a shock, hey, Wilf?'

Although Wilf wasn't sure about his tone. 'When I was a kid, with me and my brothers, on Louth, you know, if we did anything wrong . . .'

'What would happen?' Carey asked.

More teachers walked into the room, so Wilf said, 'You'll get back to me?'

'Next day or two. But we'll have to escort you off the place.'

Wilf walked between the detectives. As the rest of the kids arrived and saw him going, and muttered between themselves. More teachers, parents. Noah attempting to back the bus into its spot, failing, trying again, giving up and leaving it at Reception.

Then Darcy was standing in front of him, smiling. 'Bit of a walk, Wilf?'

Wilf didn't reply. He turned, and continued.

Carey and Waters left him at the gates, got in their car and left. Driving past him, saying, 'Might be worth writing down your version of events, Wilf.'

Wilf waved, and they drove off. He surveyed the school, the last of the kids going in, Trevor staring down the hill at him. A small wave, but he dared not wave back.

As Wilf walked back to town he noticed the sea returning. The people, the dogs, Ced Graney, perhaps, had gone. And in the distance, beyond the bay, far out to sea, Louth. Although it wasn't. Just offing, tempting him. Like he'd waited too long, and now it was too late. He walked past Simon's, but he was busy inside with customers. Maybe this meant he already knew. Another hundred metres to Scoops n' Smiles. He stopped and peered in the window and then knocked. The stranger, this man he didn't know, looked up, and then returned to work. Wilf went in and the bell rang. 'I came into your shop, did I?'

'You should go.'

'I came in and threatened that boy, and chased him, did I? And pushed him against where, there, is that the one? And now he's got this bruise. But you know that, don't you? And you probably know how he got it.'

'Should I call the police?'

'No need. They're onto you. And when it comes out . . .'

Roper smiled. 'You just got to keep your hands to yourself.'

There was a display. Seven or eight types of lollies in jars. Wilf pushed them to the floor and they smashed.

The stranger picked up the phone.

'It'll all come out,' Wilf said. 'All of it.' The he turned, let the door slam, and returned to Monk's, telling Karen it had been a big morning and he was going up to sleep it off.

30

Early afternoon, Wilf sat with a tea-stained mug and a bottle of whisky at Monk's bar. He flattened the piece of paper in front of him, picked up a pen and thought what to write first.

The incidents of May? (check) in the main street of Selwyn

Then he filled the cup again ('When in Selwyn do as the locals do' – a small leprechaun toasting the drinker), drank half in one go and continued.

1) The following occurred OUTSIDE Scoops n' Smiles. Inside, Darcy Davis, 14 (check?), and Grant Roper (age? check) . . .

The pen went through the paper. He was writing on a coaster. He moved it and noticed the words someone had scribbled on the reverse side: 'None of us still living is in God's Grace'. Pressed into the wet cardboard, like someone really meant it.

Wiping his mouth, he continued.

2) I passed the shop, noticed Darcy, and stopped to look inside. He waved, smiled, baiting me, in the same way he's always baited the kids on the bus . . .

'What's up?' Karen asked, coming in with a tray of clean glasses.
'I put the money in the till,' Wilf said, indicating the whisky.
'Unlike you.'

He thought to tell her, but didn't. He checked his hand, but it was still, mostly. His mouth dry, but he wet it again, and refilled. Karen said he should watch himself. 'You're working late, aren't you?'

He agreed. The few pills sitting on the bar. Karen asked if he'd had them today, and he said yes, or at least thought he had. She said he needed to be more careful. Two times a day, under the tongue. Yes, he said, I think, this morning. So she started unloading the glasses from the tray onto the bar.

'Writing a poem?' she asked, indicating.

'No, just a letter.' Covering it, folding it, placing it under the coaster.

'Don't mind me.'

'Just to Colin.'

'You missing him already?'

'Hardly.'

'He's all you got, Wilf.' She didn't pursue it. He'd just babble, and get onto Louth, and how things were better back then.

Wilf forgot his letter, sat back and drank. His head was half-wobbly, but he didn't care. 'We never even got along back then.'

'Louth?'

'Yes.'

'But you didn't live there long?'

'No, kids when we left. But you remember the earliest stuff most, don't you?'

'Yes,' she said, regarding him critically, like he might fall from the stool or drop dead with a heart attack. Like he was preoccupied. 'You okay, Wilf?'

'Yes, of course.' But realising. 'I'm fine. I'm just saying, on Louth we didn't . . . we fought, violently, you know. He had his way of seeing things and . . .'

'You did well together then.'

'I guess we did.'

'And he helped you with Connor?'

'He did.'

'So.' Picking up the rack, pushing the pills toward him and saying, 'Don't forget.' Before leaving, and calling from the kitchen: 'You okay to start at six?'

'Of course, why wouldn't I?' No, he told himself, she doesn't know, no one knows.

Then she popped her head back in. 'Are you allowed whisky with the pills?'

'Of course.'

'You sure?'

'Six. Go on. Get about yer business.'

Wilf took the bottle up to his room. He collapsed onto his unmade bed and let his thoughts dissipate. Carey, with his two or three days' growth, the strange way he held his pen. Waters, the sharpest, the meanest of the two, with an expression that gave nothing away. A crooked tooth, a pox scar on his cheek, the way (Wilf could see) he'd carefully filled in his forms, small, precise words all in capitals. The looks from the teachers, and the kids, as he was escorted from the school. Surely, by now, it had got back to the parents?

Shame, he thought, unable to connect the outcome with the event, the way his body had descended into fright, shrunk, helped only (for a while, he guessed) by alcohol. Shame. As he thought of the record, still on the bar, but decided he couldn't be bothered. Let them read it. Let them decide. Let them hate me. Curse me. Remove the sash from my shoulders, the grace from my heart. So he lifted his head enough to drink. A single go, but the whisky splashed on his chin anyway. The same way he'd lifted Nance's head, and helped her with her tea, her food, and later, to the toilet, saying, 'I should come in?'

'No, you shouldn't.'

Waiting as she pissed. Full of grace. No meat, no pudding. Because in the end everything was taken away, people stripped bare, left to suffer the humiliation of a poorly written ending.

A knock on the door. 'Uncle?'

But he didn't reply. He could hear Connor waiting, listening, eventually saying, 'I need a few things.'

He didn't want to go. The window was open and he could hear cars reversing, people loading empties, a delivery. But what would any of this matter if everyone thought he was a criminal?

'Uncle?'

He heard his nephew leaving, his steps on the stairs. Then silence. Never a bird, or one of the old voices, as he sat in bed of a morning listening. 'She won't go, Tom.'

'Wait. Patience.'

'She'll need help. Twins, perhaps.'

'She'll get them out.'

'Or die trying.'

Colin saying, 'We could do it.'

And Wilf: 'You know what you got to do?'

'Yes.'

'Stick your hand up her arse?'

'It's not her arse. It's her womany bits, and they're no different to yours.'

So they'd got dressed and wandered down to see the heavily pregnant ewe. They approached her, lifted her tail, and Brian, who'd come with them, had said, 'Is there anyone up there?'

They'd all laughed.

Colin had held her tummy and tried to squeeze but it had only made her angry, and she'd kicked him. Eventually they'd checked her cloaca and decided there was no way they wanted to deliver dead lambs.

Wilf laid the half-empty bottle aside. He didn't drink much anymore, and this lot had gone to his head. '*None of us still living is in God's grace*,' he said. Did it mean everyone around him was an arsehole? He wasn't sure, so he kept repeating it. '*None of us still living . . .*' Because God was still in his room, like it or not. His verses, his chrism, his hymns and books and crosses above doorways. '*None of us . . .*' Reaching for the whisky again. Even the dead lambs, lying on the wet grass, their soft bodies, suffocating tongues and brown eyes.

The knock on the door again. 'Uncle?'

He sat up, kicked off his shoes and said, 'Not decent.'

Connor waited. 'You there?'

Wilf dropped the bottle and it emptied the rest of its contents. Connor opened the door and peered in. 'Can I . . .?'

Wilf sat up, but rested against the wall.

Connor came in, picked up the bottle, but didn't save any. He placed it on Wilf's table and said, 'You're drunk?' Smiling.

'I'm not.'

'You are bloody too. Your go this time, eh?' He found a tea towel on the sink, placed it over the spill and said, 'It's gonna stink in here.' Sniffing the bottle, and drinking the last few drops.

'You stay away from it,' Wilf said.

Connor sat on the bed, held up Wilf's sheet of paper and said, 'What's this all about?'

So Wilf brought him up to date. Scoops n' Smiles, the look, the encounter. Versions one and two. 'And that's what this Carey fella told me to write,' he said.

Connor said, 'So what's the problem?'

'The problem? They always believe the kid.'

'Not really. Darcy's a shithead. I can tell them that.'

'You stay out of it, after what you've done. That's just what I need, you up in front of a judge.'

'I just had a word to him.'

'So did I. That's enough.'

'No one saw a thing. Why would they believe this Roper bloke?'

Wilf just waited.

'I was out front of Monk's and I saw you coming down the road, but you didn't go into the shop. You stopped, looked, just like you've written.'

Wilf sat on the edge of his bed and said, 'You've got to tell the truth.'

'*Really?*' Grinning. 'The truth? That's how it's done?'

Wilf didn't care. Maybe he was old-fashioned, and maybe he was stupid, but this is how he felt. 'I can sort it out,' he said. 'He hasn't got any evidence.'

'He has a witness.'

'No.'

'As do you.'

'*No.*' He waited, then said, 'It's just . . . when people hear.'

Connor knew he was right. Selwyn was a small town and the exciting bits bounced up and down Sullivan Street, off Green's and Hyland's, Mooney's and Gould's. Once it had begun. He thought this a shame. This is what would hurt the old man. The idea that he wasn't the Wilf people knew, or thought they did.

'I'll finish writing it,' Wilf said, reclaiming the report and slipping it into his pocket.

Connor wiped up the last of the whisky and rinsed the towel in the sink. 'You're whacked,' he said to his uncle.

'The Healy men can hold their liquor, plenty of it. It's in our genes, and yours.' Taking his jaw, and squeezing it.

Connor shook free and said, 'Come on then. Fresh air, and coffee.'

They went downstairs, through the bar, a few locals eating a plate of Mrs Gould's shepherd's pie. Connor propped up his uncle. Karen noticed and said, 'Not the whole bottle, Wilf?'

'He reckons he's okay,' Connor said.

'Should I tell Monk you can't work?'

'No! That's hours away.' And with that he popped the coaster in his pocket, and they left.

Along the road, past Simon, out front unloading old news from its grate. Wilf said to him, 'Quite a ride this morning.'

'Sorry?'

'The bus.'

'What, it broke down again?'

Wilf seemed happy with this. There was no way he knew, yet. Simon wasn't a man to mince words. And anyway, he would've been the first to congratulate him. Darcy had been caught shoplifting at least three times.

Scoops n' Smiles, and they looked in again. Connor went inside, with Wilf saying, 'No, you can't say a word.' He watched Connor talking to Roper. Calm, collected, using his hands to suggest common sense and civility. Connor left the shop, encouraged his uncle to continue and said, 'I just need a few things from home.'

'What did you say to him?'

'Nothing. Couple of guitars, and some music, more clothes.'

'You didn't threaten him?'

'And we should clean up a bit, I guess?'

'Connor?'

'No, I'd never do that. It's not a Healy thing, is it, Uncle?' Smiling.

'You're not going to make it worse, are you?'

'No. Just facts. I reminded him.'

'Of what?'

'And the fridge will be full of old food.'

Wilf just walked. 'So, you're not going to tell me?'

A full minute, with nothing said, before they turned into the drive and stood in front of the house. 'What do you think?' Wilf asked.

Connor wasn't sure. It was only a house, full of old things, cheese graters and rugs, hangers waiting for clothes still hanging on the line. Someone would have to bring them all in, fold them, put them away. 'It's strange,' Connor said.

'What's that?'

He couldn't explain. How things persisted, but people came and went; how they stopped working, like the toaster that shorted the house. Removed to cold rooms, and kept until the undertaker came for them, dressed them, cleaned them and put powder on them. Then drove them around, organised a few hymns and, finally, put them in a big incinerator.

'Come on,' Wilf said, unlocking the door. He went in, checked the lights. Connor followed at a distance. His mum's phone, sitting open, the battery dead. A few bangles she always wore, a magazine with a story about a woman who'd lost half her body weight. Wilf went into the bedroom, stood remembering. Nothing had been moved. Some sort of drink that had mostly evaporated, leaving a brown sludge. Orla's watch, still ticking. 'Should I?' he asked.

Connor helped Wilf strip the sheets from the bed. Then he gathered them, took them out to the laundry and stuffed them into the machine. He called for Wilf, because he'd never done the washing. Together they worked out which knobs to turn. Soon it was going and Wilf said, 'A whole bunch of stuff you'll have to work out.'

Connor just watched the machine, listened to the rhythm, the pulse. 'So, do I stay here?'

'It's up to you. I can move in.'

'But you like Monk's.'

'*I do?* Really? When did I say that?'

'You seem to.'

'No, I don't like that damp, cold, noisy dog box, with its rubbish trucks in the back lane and backpackers rootin' all night. I stay there because it's easiest.'

Connor was unsure. Maybe he was just saying it.

'We live here (your mum told me the mortgage is done), share the jobs, I ... you deliver the letters, drive the van, the bus (they'll need someone soon), the evening shift at Monk's. You learn to love Selwyn, I buy a boat and cast off for Louth.'

'*I learn to love Selwyn?*'

'Why not?'

'It's a shithole.'

'But you hate it *less* than you used to?'

'No.'

'Well, given time.'

The churn of the washer. 'What else?' Wilf said.

Connor took a deep breath, bit his lip and replied, 'I think I'm running out of options.'

They stripped Connor's bed, gathered the tea towels, the clothes from Orla's floor, and spent the next hour hanging out, bringing in, folding, making little piles of Orla's and Connor's clothes on the kitchen table. Wilf asked what Connor wanted to do with these, and he carried them into his mum's room, put them away in the drawer and said, 'For now.'

Then they set to the kitchen. Old ham and bacon, lumpy milk, furry vegetables. They threw it all into a bag and Connor took it out to the bin. They gathered Orla's magazines and threw them away, too. Her prescriptions and medicines, painkillers and, inside her bedside drawer, a big bag of pills neither of them had ever seen. Wilf examined them, but Connor said what was the point? So they threw these, too. Wilf vacuumed and Connor mopped the bathroom. He opened the vanity and examined the powder, the creams, the ointments. Even the vapour rub. He opened it and smelled it, and remembered lying in bed, and his mum coming in, lifting his top and rubbing it on his chest. His legs weakened and he sat on the freshly-mopped floor. The matter-of-fact way she pulled his top back down and told him he'd be better in the morning.

Then Wilf came in, saw him, and said, 'What's that?'

Connor showed him.

So Wilf slid his back down the wall, opened the bag of rubbish he'd been collecting, and said, 'You want to keep it?'

Connor thought about it, put the lid back on, and threw it into the bag.

31

Wilf held. The line played Mozart, a soft voice explaining how enrolments were closing for next year, then Noah saying, 'Everyone's welcome at Selwyn Area School. Ask our office for a personal tour, or better still, drop by and watch our young people at work.'

Bullying each other, Wilf thought. Selling stuff.

Connor came into the bar and said, 'Morning, Uncle.'

Wilf gave him a wave.

'Who you calling?'

'Noah . . . I've already been holding ten minutes. He doesn't want to talk to me.'

Connor noticed the Wheel o' Whisky! and gave it a spin. He waited, helped it stop on thirty-nine. '*One night's free accommodation at Monk's.*' Smiling at Wilf. 'We got lucky again.' Then he sat at the old electric piano in the corner, switched it on, studied some sheet music and played a few bars. Clumsily, two-fingered, but enough to make Wilf smile.

'It's not hard,' Connor said, singing a few lines. Wilf joined in. Between the *Turkish Rondo*, and the same voice telling him the new gym was due for completion next year. 'Bugger you, Noah.'

Connor kept going, working his way through the old chords, refining the melody. The voice on the phone said Selwyn Area School had its own vegetable plot and grew food for the local community, the poor, the homeless. 'My arse,' Wilf said.

'What?'

'When did they start giving food to the homeless?'

Connor played an introduction, verse, chorus, sang: '*Out on the hills the old people sing . . .*' Wilf joined in, an off-key harmony. Then Noah came on and Wilf said, 'You were going to get back to me.'

'I was busy.'

Likely story. 'Can we meet?'

'Today?'

'That'd be best.'

Wilf listened to him going through (what he supposed was) his diary. He was saying, 'It can't be on school grounds.'

'I realise that.'

'Maybe . . . what is it you want to talk about, Wilf?'

'What do you think?'

'I'm not sure that I should be . . .'

Grow a spine, Wilf thought. Although Noah had always been like this. Wilf could remember him as a child, bent on rules. The first at the front on Sunday, the loudest, despite not knowing, even then, what he was singing about. He was a smart man, but that, Wilf thought, didn't extend to wisdom. Or integrity. If the department wanted him to think the Earth was flat, he was more than happy to accommodate.

'Why not?' Wilf asked.

'If it's under investigation.'

'For God's sake, Noah. What about the Tea Junction? I happened to be there, you stopped and had a word. You can't get into trouble for that.'

'Perhaps.'

'How many years did I drive your bloody bus?'

'That's not the point.'

'You didn't want to, no one did. I try to help out and look what happens. So you can give me five minutes of your time.'

'Hold on.' He put the phone down and went away.

Connor paused long enough to say, 'He couldn't give a rat's. He knows about Luke and Trevor, and plenty more.'

'Wilf, you there? What about ten-fifteen, the Tea Junction.'

Wilf thanked him, rang off, turned the wheel a few times, saw what was in store and sat beside his nephew. 'Decent song, isn't it?'

'It's okay.'

'But every time your mum played *If I Could Choose*.'

'Well, that was . . . sentimental.'

Wilf smiled. 'Your granddad and his dad . . . they all sang *The Hills*.' Indicating the yellowing manuscript. '. . . *the old people sing* . . . now it's all what's-his-name, jiggy-jiggy?'

The thought occurred to Connor. 'I could put it into Sibelius.'

'Who's he?'

'It. Music software. Make copies, distribute them.'

Wilf liked this idea. Like, somehow, things *needn't* be forgotten. And there was always a chance the things he thought forgotten, weren't. No different to sitting beside his niece and saying, 'Don't be morbid.'

'*Uncle?*'

Wilf had refused to accept it. He knew it was an option, and what she was saying suggested it was possible, or likely. 'They reckon your blood count . . .'

'Uncle, please?'

He'd finally said, 'Well, what else?'

'He can be difficult.'

'*Really?* Connor can be difficult?'

'You know what I mean.'

'And you know what I mean. Of course. A silly question, Niece. It's well in hand, so don't worry about it.'

'That's the only thing I *do* worry about.'

'Well, you needn't. I had my own, remember?'

She'd waited. 'Just the thought that he'd . . .'

'Who else?' Wilf had said. 'Do you think Colin would come home?'

'No.'

'Exactly. If it came to it, *if*, I'll get him working for Bobby, and Leo.'

Orla had laid back, pulled the sheet up under her chin and said, 'That's something.'

'You, my girl, are melodramatic.'

'What do you mean?'

But that's where it had ended. Wilf had conceded something to death, but that was all. Some small consolation that would act as its own medicine.

'I can print off copies and me and Roman can do it,' Connor said.

'He's still around?'

'If you'd rather I didn't?'

'No, no, go ahead. That'd be appreciated.'

An hour later, Wilf walked down the road, peered through the window of the Tea Junction and saw Noah by himself in the corner. He went in, sat opposite him and said, 'You want a coffee?'

'I've just ordered two.' Short, sharp, clinical.

Wilf waited a moment. 'Connor says hello.'

Noah refused to be drawn. One disaster was enough. Wilf wanted to dissect this too – the story of Connor's detentions, suspension, exclusion. He wanted Noah to justify every decision, tell him why Connor had got in trouble when others hadn't. 'He's slowly coming good.'

'Excellent.' Like the comment had been graded, moderated, submitted. 'So, you wanted to talk?'

Wilf had the feeling this wouldn't get him far. Noah, with his arms crossed, his face set hard. 'Darcy.'

'Go on.'

Wilf noticed two women, one in gym gear, whispering to each other. About him, no doubt. He watched to see if they looked over. He wanted to say to Noah, *See, this is what you've done*. There was an older man, slowly cutting pieces from a cake, lifting them on his fork, dropping them. No doubt he knew, too. And the girl with the coffees saying, 'Haven't seen you for a while, Wilf.'

He forgot who she was. Someone's daughter. 'Too busy driving the school bus, eh, Noah?' He took out his single sheet summary of the day's events, flattened it on the table and moved it toward the principal. 'This is what Carey asked me to do.'

Noah read the details.

'It's all there,' Wilf said, tapping the sheet, raising crumbs from the lace table cloth.

'And this is your side?' Noah said.

'Not my side. It's the way it happened.'

'Your *version* then?'

'How can it be a version if it's the truth?'

'What I mean is, he says A, you say B?'

'But he's lying, isn't he?'

Noah took a deep breath and let it out slowly. 'Between you and me . . .' Scanning the room, whispering: 'You know and I know, but it's up to the police now.'

'Jesus, Noah. Grow a spine. Is this how Connor ended up—'

'That was different.' Quietening. 'What do you want me to do?'

'I want you to *believe me*, Noah. I want you to tell those coppers, there's no way . . . you know *exactly* what Darcy's like.'

Noah didn't reply.

'Years he's been working on Luke. Years. And *you* . . .' Pointing at him, but realising the women were watching. 'What if one of these kids *did* something?'

'What?' Suddenly interested.

'Jumped off a bridge. Then you'd be interested. Because then they'd be asking *you* the questions.'

Noah waited, then said, 'It'll have to run its course.'

'You think I went into that shop, pushed him, and that bruise, have you seen the size of it? Aren't you curious how it *really* got there?'

The old man seemed interested. The coffee machine steaming, talkback quietly in the background.

'You think I pushed him?' Wilf said.

'No, I don't.'

'Well?'

Noah drank half a cup in one go. 'Trust me, it'll sort itself out. I had a call from Carey about an hour ago and he told me Roper's withdrawing his statement.'

Right, Wilf thought. As he saw Connor going into the ice cream shop, speaking a few quiet, thought-out words. 'And why do you reckon that is?'

Noah shrugged.

'Because he doesn't like his chances of getting away with it. The favour.'

'What are you talking about?'

'What he sells to the kids. I'm guessing Darcy's first in line, and when he asked a favour, Roper was more than happy.'

Noah said, 'He just wants to stay out of it. Either way, without a witness . . .'

Wilf tried the coffee, but it was already half cold. The old man gave up on his cake, returned to his tea, studied the menu. 'Thing is, it's about what *you* believe, Noah.'

Wilf walked back to Monk's. Head down, determined. But he stopped, noticing a familiar figure in front of Quinn's, reading the tablets on the footpath. Dave stood with his hands in his pocket, turned, then walked back toward Hyland's.

When Wilf got back to Monk's, Connor was sitting at the bar, drinking Karen's coffee, working on the song on his laptop. He asked his uncle how the meeting went and he explained, then Connor said, 'That sounds about right.' Wilf told him about Roper, and said, 'I wonder what did it?'

Connor said, 'I wonder.'

32

'Not much of a town,' Wilf said, standing outside Selwyn Pioneer Village. Connor with his hands in his pockets, slowly shaking his head. 'I remember Mum bringing me here when I was six. It hasn't changed much.'

Wilf breathed the air. 'Place is full of ghosts.'

'That's the bin.' Full to overflowing, a few used nappies on top.

A sort of themed village, a main street more tumbleweed than wheatbelt, a few old places, chemist, pub, blacksmith, a shop full of kitchen implements and kids' toys, iron-framed beds.

'Where first?' Wilf asked, rubbing his sore hand.

Connor consulted a photocopied map. Purchased with a postcard, although God knows why. Wilf had bought a keyring and small bottle of Jump-Stump whisky. He cracked it, sniffed and swigged. 'God.' Spitting it into the horse trough. He offered it to Connor, who tried and said, 'Not so bad.'

'From what I saw' – smiling, and massaging his knuckles – 'you'd drink anything.'

When they'd gone to Church Street, to Pat's place, and knocked on the door. Two boxes of bottles in what passed as a front yard: whisky, Beam and lots of ale. A mangy-looking cat and *Naked Lesbians* face-down in the mud. Dead lawn, dead plants and a stripped-down car engine. They'd gone in and Pat had given nothing away. Connor had told him about his mum, but he'd only said, 'That's pretty shit.'

'Yeah, shit,' Wilf had said, noticing the piles of clothes, more bottles.

'I've come for my guitar,' Connor had said. 'Is it still in my room?'

'I sold it.'

'Why?'

'You never paid the rent you owed.'

'I paid when I moved in.'

But Pat had just stood, half-naked, half-grinning, rubbing his stomach as he slowly woke. And Wilf: 'You'll have to give him the money.'

'Spent it.'

'You better find it.'

'Can't.' And to Connor. 'You pissed off so quick I couldn't rent the room. You're meant to give two weeks' notice.'

'I couldn't.'

Wilf had tried to stay calm, but it hadn't worked. 'Either you give him his guitar or pay him or we'll take something instead.'

Pat had indicated the door. 'You better leave or I'll call the cops.'

Fuck it, Wilf had thought. There was another guitar, a nice-looking red one, so he'd walked across the room, picked it up and said, 'This'll do.'

Pat had tried to take it from him. Wilf had pushed him away. Pat had stood, come back with a solid hook, but Wilf had replied with a swift right, straight to the jaw. Pat had fallen, got up, decided against it. Connor had just watched. Wilf was good at this sort of thing.

'You decide,' Wilf had said.

So Pat had thought about it, opened a drawer and given Connor the money. Uncle and nephew had left, Wilf rubbing his hand, saying, 'I reckon I broke something.'

First, they followed a sawdust path to a small church – shaded by pines, its thousand awkward-fitting stones losing their mortar. Up the concrete steps, the seventies tube steel handrails, into the void. A few pews, simple altar, baptismal font. Wilf read from the booklet included with the admission price. '. . . *services practised since 1873. In the beginning, Church of England, but later* . . .' He noticed his nephew sitting on the front pew, reading the list from the job centre. 'Anything?'

'All shit.'

He sat beside him. Of course they were going to be shit. Jobs that didn't need any education or experience. They'd arrived at the job centre as it was opening, taken the first ticket, but it was still half an hour wait. Sat, and a man had taken Connor's details, asked about his schooling, his work history, and Wilf had said, 'He's a good worker.'

The clerk, with round glasses and nasal hair, had said, 'Lots of good workers. Not so many jobs.'

Stupid thing to say to a kid, Wilf had thought. 'We were thinking, weren't we, Connor, something like ... music, bookstore, any retail, really.'

The man had smiled. 'Right. You got a car, Connor?'

'Well ... perhaps.'

'Yes, he's got a car,' Wilf had said.

'There's the IGA and a few others ... similar.' Then he'd told them about the pay, and Wilf had wondered how the hell they'd do it. 'That's all?'

'Trust's, chicken processors in Northhead. If you're not too fussy.'

'Anything else?'

'I'll print off a list of this week's jobs.' Standing, scratching his arse, before hobbling over to the printer.

Back in the church, Wilf said, 'I started off spraying under houses. You know, pests. Colin, of course, got the apprenticeship I should have had. Everyone said I was the mechanical one.'

'What about Pop?'

'Straight to the gas board. White shirt, tie and ten sick days a year. But this stupid bastard, on his belly spraying arsenic. It's a miracle I'm still alive.'

Connor sat back, studied the rafters and said, 'They're all shit.'

Wilf thought of Noah. He could be convinced. 'I tell you, Nephew, a few years of study now ... or else you'll end up like me, taking whatever you can get.'

'You like your jobs.'

'I wanted to be an airline pilot. But you know how much the lessons cost. Mum and Dad barely had enough for food.' Turning to him. 'Although there's an idea, if *you* want to be a pilot?'

'Perhaps.'

'Or you could have my jobs.'

'How much do you make each week?'

'Enough.'

'So I stay in Selwyn and make a half-arsed attempt to do *your* stuff . . . yours?'

'Fair enough.' Although it was a reasonable offer. 'Or you go back to school?'

Connor leaned forward and examined the old floorboards, all yellow and cracked.

'You're too bloody smart for chicken boning.'

'It's money.'

'You'd earn five times that much if you went to university. You could be an engineer, a doctor?'

Connor was sick of the talk. 'I just want to do music.' He looked up at his uncle. 'There's a sound engineer's course in Sydney.'

'There you go.'

'Two years. How would I . . .?'

'I promised your mother. We could sell up here, rent something reasonable.'

'You and me?'

'Why not?'

'You want to go to your island.'

'Eventually. I've got another twenty years yet.'

'Twenty?'

'At least.' He stood. There was a lot of village to see yet.

They walked down the main street. A cart full of red and white pansies, an old stable with a table and an amplifier left buzzing, a poster announcing: 'Tony Baloney and Leroy the Talking Dog'. Connor went in, turned off the amp and said, 'That's worth a bit.' Staring at it, like the answers were in front of him. Unlike the small clerk, who returned from the printer, sat down and said, 'One other thing. I have a friend, a plumber, and he's looking for someone reliable.'

'Plumbing?' Connor said.

'Up early, shit pay for the first few years, but later you can start your own company. He's got seven people, vans, the lot – million-dollar turnover.'

Wilf had waited for his nephew to say something. 'What do you think?'

'I guess.'

The clerk wrote a name and number on a piece of paper and handed it to Connor. 'I'll tell him you'll call?'

Connor didn't want to be a plumber, but he took the slip anyway. 'Okay.'

Studying it in the stable, Connor said, 'I could but . . .'

'You get used to almost anything.' Wilf thought his nephew was being precious. The world only needed so many record producers and rock stars. And anyway, if he wanted to do this, sitting in his room writing songs wasn't the best way to get noticed.

From shop to shop, a sort of Monk's-in-a-living room, a bar with beer jugs and enough room for a dozen men, standing. Wilf was on Louth. Cold nights, wind off the sea, the men huddled together like an unshorn flock. He'd come in, looked around, and someone had rubbed his head, spilt beer on him and said, 'What you after?'

'Mum reckons Dad should come home.'

Laughing, calling, 'Hey, Tom, your time's up.'

Tom calling, 'That you, Wilf?'

'Mum reckons—'

'I know what she reckons. Tell her half an hour.'

'She said now.'

Everyone had laughed, Wilf was lifted onto the bar and one man tried to give him his first ale, and another asked for him to dance. 'Go on,' Tom had said, 'give them a jig.' Wilf had danced, the roar had come up from the men and he'd stayed another hour, listening to their stories, his legs dangling over the bar. Until later, his mum was at the door. 'Thomas Healy . . . and you, Wilf!'

From house to house, two-up and down, musty walls with flaking paint. Here, someone with a bit of money, Wilf explained. Nice rugs, curtains and a speckled mirror that reminded him of plovers' eggs. A small desk with books. *A Guide to Modern Dentistry* (1963). A cushioned couch, lamp, family photos, although they looked too recent. Sepia, although one boy was wearing gym boots.

'Always been the way,' Wilf said. 'The workers, and the bosses.' Despite a sign telling them not to sit on the period furniture, Wilf sat down. '*This was Mr Dalgety's living room,*' he read. '*Dalgety worked for the bank for fifty-three years.*' He watched Connor, examining the books. 'There you go, a teller. A bank job?'

'I'd rather slit my wrists now.'

'They make good money.'

'So do prostitutes.'

A similar cottage next door, this time the doctor. An examination table with movable slats for limbs, a pair of leather shackles for the syphilitic. Connor examined the specimens in bottles. A heart, foetal marten, fingers, toes, rabbit. Then he stared out at the deserted street and said, 'Maybe people aren't interested in all this.'

'Of course they are.'

Connor doubted it. It was a bit lame. It was only natural that people would be more interested in the future than the present, the present than the past. Maybe places like this were just for old people? But then why did they have a talking dog, a popcorn machine (with its cover still on), a face-painting stall (packed away beside the magic table)? He read the list and said, 'They want bike couriers.'

'How much do you reckon they get?'

'It's not just about the money.'

'Not yet. But you might meet someone, and breed. Then it will be.'

'What about the house?'

'Leave that to me.'

'When I'm eighteen.'

'*When*. When.'

Connor didn't get it. There was no option. Study, work, shit job, boring job, songs, a Celine and Adele-induced poverty. 'I guess I'll just have to wait and see,' he said.

'I told you, I'll talk to Noah.'

'You're not even allowed on the school grounds.' Grinning.

The doctor had a microscope and a glass case full of surgical instruments. Several sizes of bone saw, prods, syringes. Wilf said, 'I remember that, too.'

'What?'

At eight, running through the rain with Brian to Dr Mellanby's house, knocking, and saying to his wife, 'Mum reckons Colin's really sick.'

She'd told her husband and he'd finished his kidneys, wrapped himself in a coat and followed them. Ten minutes, and sheets of horizontal rain. Finally, they'd presented the doctor to their parents and stood listening as he examined this small, glowing boy who could barely keep his eyes open. The doctor had said something about fifty-fifty, and they'd just have to wait and see. Then he'd left the room, the house, and returned to his offal. He and Brian had sat beside their brother all night, and the next day, and eventually he'd opened his eyes and said, 'I think I peed the bed.'

On the way home, Connor said to his uncle, 'So what did all that achieve?'

Wilf said, 'You got your money.'

Relaxing into the landscape, the hum of the engine, the long shadows. Connor said, 'Plumbing, selling shit, or boning chickens.' Looking over. 'How do you even bone a chicken?'

Wilf just smiled. 'Either that, or the Wheel o' Whisky!'

33

Driving to Bobby's, Wilf realised you couldn't achieve anything if you were anxious. This seemed to be the story of his life – anxious about his father, his mother's health, his brothers, his reputation (as it was slowly being destroyed by Darcy). If you weren't anxious you didn't speed, or feel the need to correct a world that was always on the verge of disaster; to spread yourself thin, avoid offence, *please* people. In the end, he thought, as he slowed, stopped on a bend and got out to look across the wheatbelt, you can only please yourself. Despite the fact that he'd made promises to his parents, Bobby and Leo and Lucy, Monk, Sienna, Luke, Trevor – despite all this, he guessed he didn't owe anyone anything. As the landscape persisted, not responsible for the people that flew above it, the animals that grazed it, the ghosts who'd sacrificed their children to fickle gods.

Closing his eyes, this all made sense.

He drove to Bobby's and delivered the parcel. Rivets, but special ones for the wings. Tempered, strong, accident-proof. He asked him to sign the receipt and Bobby put a cross. He asked Wilf to hold the rudder while he tightened the wires. He said, 'You're famous now.'

Wilf guessed it would happen. The news had bled along the main road, around the corner, past the pump, spreading across the countryside. 'How am I famous?'

'Jack told me you let that Davis kid have it.'

'Who told him?'

'He didn't say.'

'Well, I didn't. Right? So it stops here.'

Bobby grinned. He knew it didn't, wouldn't, couldn't.

'What did he say?'

'The kid had played up and you'd clopped him. At Scoops n' Smiles.'

'Every detail. Who . . .?'

'Jack just said.'

'Well, Jack should keep his mouth shut. I never hit him. I never went into that place.'

'Just saying what I heard.' Tightening clasps to the wires, testing them, continuing.

'Darcy's made the whole lot up to get back at me because I threw him off the bus. And now I've got Noah, the police, the kid's mother to deal with. And you lot, gossiping.'

'I'm not gossiping. I heard. It hasn't gone any further.'

Wilf said goodbye and released the rudder. As he went, Bobby called, 'Five more minutes?'

As Wilf got into his van he imagined his face on television: '*Errant school bus driver beats innocent child*'. And photos of Darcy, and his bandaged body. 'Shit.' Stop caring, he said to himself, as he drove. But the by-line: '*Police gathering evidence for prosecution*'. As he surveyed the options: selling the house, moving to Georgetown or Sydney with Connor (although *The Selwyn Advertiser* would probably find him), or putting a note on Monk's notice board ('*Dear Selwyn I didn't do anything it's all made up but I'm off anyway so do your own dirty work*') and making for Louth.

He parked behind Monk's, opened the back of the J2 and found two parcels he'd missed. So he took them out, read the addresses, and wondered. *Grant Roper, Selwyn*. He checked the laneway. No, he thought, feeling the parcel, shaking it, smelling it. He couldn't help it. He crawled into the back of the van, ripped the brown paper away and surveyed the games: one with aliens, another with zombies, and a mouse.

Shit.

What to do? So he shoved the games under the seat, ripped the package into small pieces and threw them in the bin on top of yesterday's scraps.

Then he used a stick to mix them in. He stopped and thought about what he was doing, but it was too late. And anyway, he thought, I know he lied. *I know*. 'Fuck it.' He locked the van and carried the other parcel down to Quinn's, all the time wondering. He went in and Spencer was sitting at the counter lacquering tablets. He placed the parcel on the counter and Spencer started opening it, asking, 'How you keeping, Wilf?'

'Fine, you?'

'*I'm fine*. Just checking you're okay.'

'Why wouldn't I be?'

Spencer opened a box of glass tiles. For Grace, he explained, and her dreamcatchers.

Good luck with that, Wilf thought, and Spencer said, 'Just remember, if you need any help.'

'With what?'

'It's been a big few weeks, hasn't it?'

'Big?'

'You know?'

No, he didn't. But it was becoming apparent. A husband and wife combination in front of the scented candles, watching him. Turning away when he noticed.

Spencer leaned forward. '*Darcy*.'

Wilf took a deep breath. 'Who did *you* hear it from?'

'Can't say.'

He checked the couple again. He had no idea who they were, but apparently they knew him. Maybe Spencer had been spreading the news. 'Who told you?'

'That doesn't matter. Main thing is, if you need help.'

'It never happened. Nothing happened. The kid's making it all up.'

'*Ah*.' His head rotating. 'As I suspected.'

'So whoever the hell's telling you, and the whole town . . .'

That's it, Wilf thought. Enough's enough. He left the shop, letting the door slam, the bells fall from their hook. He returned to the lane, the bin, and thought, Fuck it. Backing out, he drove west, past the school, an abattoir that loomed ominously on a hill, sheds and barns and other paraphernalia that made Selwyn. Apart from the gossip, which held the place together. His phone rang. It was Colin. He answered as he drove: 'Brother?'

Small talk, news about New Zealand and Raelene and everything going nicely, then, 'I was hoping you and Connor could come over.'

'I've got a lot on.'

'We talked, didn't we? Just get on a plane – let someone else deal with it.'

Should he tell him? 'You and Raelene see the place. We can go any time.'

'But I'm not here anytime. I'm here *now*. What are the chances I'll get back?'

Wilf wanted him gone. 'I'll have to call you back.'

'You won't. What you will do is get on a plane tomorrow. Georgetown to Auckland. I checked – there's a flight at ten, or two-thirty.'

'No, I'll call you tonight.'

'What's the problem?'

'There's always a problem. Your nephew – do you want to have a go?'

A long pause, as Colin realised they were covering well-trodden ground. 'A holiday would be good for him, for you. You've got the money.'

'I've got to go.'

'Wilf?'

'I'll call.' He hung up and his brother was gone. Waited for him to call back. Five, ten minutes, but he didn't. He kept watching the phone. Go off with your girlfriend then. This is what comes from staying, and being decent.

Wilf reached under his seat, found the games and slowed and threw them into a half-cleared forest. Maybe the eagles would eat them. Either way, he didn't care.

His phone again, but it wasn't Colin. PRIVATE. He answered anyway. 'Wilf Healy?'

'Yes.'

'Wonder if you've got a minute to talk about this Darcy Davis case?'

He felt his heart starting, again. 'You're from the police?'

A short pause. 'No, *Georgetown Leader.*'

He went to hang up, but stopped. 'Who gave you my number?'

'I've just spoken to Darcy's mum and she says she's getting a lawyer. Wondering if you had any comment?'

'*How did you get my number?*'

'It was given to me.'

'*By whom?*'

'I thought this might be a good chance for you to put your side of the story. Let people decide.'

Wilf knew how that would end. His side. My arse. He could see the next headline: '*Alleged Child Abuser Claims No Knowledge Despite History*'. And the photo – in his singlet cutting his toenails (Connor had put it on Facebook). But he couldn't help himself. The old Tom Healy temper returning, a lifetime too late. 'You can print that I deny everything.'

At the end of the two-minute tirade, the journalist said, 'So these kids he's bullied . . .?'

'You're the journalist, work it out for yourself.'

And again, the button.

Enough! Wilf drove to the familiar home, the high hedges, the long driveway. He got out and pounded on the door. 'Mrs Davis?' Watching a small pug watching him, gravel in a pair of pots with three cacti in each. Then he saw her at an upstairs window, holding another pug. 'Can I have a word please?'

The first pug barked at him and he told it to fuck off. Stepped toward it, and it ran away. Mrs Davis was on the phone, but opened the window and said, 'You're not allowed to be here.'

'One minute, please.' Calmly, rationally, although he wanted to slap her, too.

She disappeared, the first pug returned. After a moment the door opened and she said, 'So?'

'Wilf Healy.'

'I know.'

'I've been driving your son to school for the last few years.'

'You have.' Conceding the minimum.

'I think we met at a parent-teacher evening.'

'Possibly.' Stroking her pug.

Wilf thought he heard *The Bold and the Beautiful*, or was it *Coronation Street*? 'This Roper fella,' he said, 'has withdrawn his statement because—'

'Because he doesn't want to get involved,' she said. 'But I can understand that.'

'No, because he's decided he could get in a load of shit. I never went into that shop; I never hit your son. Maybe you know where that bruise came from?'

'Is that all you came for?'

'*Is that all*? Everyone in town's talking about this. My reputation, gone. So when this is proved, as it will be, I'll be hiring my own lawyer. So you might want to be very sure of your son's story.'

She glared at him. He guessed she was itching to slam the door, but liked to have the last word. 'I've called the police.'

'Did you make that up, too?'

'I believe my son.'

'You do? Teasing the other kids in the bus. Luke. Trevor. Do you want me to tell you what I've been hearing and seeing for the last few years? You *believe* him?'

'You've obviously got some sort of grudge. Why, I don't know, but if this is the only way to sort it out . . .'

'A grudge? An eighty-year-old man driving a few kids? I've spent my life helping people in this town, including you, although you'd never admit it. Who do you think people'll believe? Me, bashing a kid?'

'I've got a lawyer,' she said, turning to go in.

'Should I wait for the police?'

Wilf drove back to town. As he went, he tried to tell himself, anxiety comes from caring. Don't care. But it didn't work. He slowed beside the logged forest of computer games, stopped, got out and walked into the cool, piney copse. The zombies, his fingerprints all over it, so he put it on a stump and kicked it until it disintegrated. The same with the aliens, and this time Simon drove past, slowed and called out, 'You okay, Wilf?'

He had no idea what to say. 'Just stopped for a piddle. Prostate, you know?'

Simon smiled, and drove on.

Wilf returned to the van, opened the door and picked up the tray from the scales. Then he returned to the forest, and gathered the remains, piece by piece. He took the road to the bay, stopped again, and cast the evidence into the water.

34

Connor was determined to do it. Probably for his mum, although he wasn't about to tell anyone that. He got up, adjusted the microphone, tuned a flat string and said, 'This one's kind of corny, I guess.'

Roman, sitting with his father, nodded agreement, but Connor said, 'I don't think Pearl Jam would work here.' So he started playing. A finger-picked introduction, then full chords as he sang, '*If I could choose a time to talk to you I'd choose the longest day . . .*'

Of course, there was a chance people would think it was about his mum. But it wasn't like he could make a disclaimer. So fuck them, he thought. '*And over the hills I'd shout the news . . .*' He knew he couldn't sing it like his mum. With a sort of dropping-out voice, the wispiness, the colouring that worked with the chords. He was just blocky and to-the-point. Like a bricklayer.

Thursday night again. Monk had been advertising – including a spot on community radio – and this had increased their numbers. A folk group from Northhead who'd come especially, a singer trying to sell her CDs at the door. But enough. Karen was serving meals, Monk busy at the bar. There was a pulse, a murmur, as the two dozen voices listened, critiqued and joined in. All a matter of time, Wilf guessed, sitting in the biggest of the booths with an ale, watching his nephew sing the song he'd heard a thousand times. Not just in concerts, but as his niece hung out washing, cooked pancakes, or busy on the throne.

Connor finished, and there was decent applause. 'This is one I arranged for my uncle, there – Wilf. Everyone knows Wilf, don't they?'

There was general agreement, a few cheers, a few claps. Wilf shook his head and said, 'Get on with it.'

Again, arpeggios, the music crisp through the small speaker Monk had bought especially for tonight. Connor sang about a man watching out his window, wishing his wife would return from America, cursing the fella she'd run off with. Finishing with a broken chord, and a smile. Applause, and he felt warm, minus his various parts and thoughts and fears. But maybe it was the alcohol again? He sat beside his uncle and said, 'You know I'm not the folksy type.'

A figure approached from a back corner, out of the shadows, holding his ale, smiling. He stood a metre from the booth and said, 'That was your mum's favourite.'

Connor surveyed him and said, 'I thought you'd gone home?'

'I've been visiting a few people.'

Dave hadn't shaved for weeks. He wore a food-stained T-shirt with a picture of an elephant in a wheelbarrow. Just how Connor remembered him. Getting around the house at all hours, shouting at Orla to get him this or that, stopping at his door and saying, 'You should be out playing with your friends.'

'I did.'

'Sit in here in the dark . . . it's not normal.'

What's normal? he'd thought. *You?*

He remembered the smell of his father: strong body odour disguised with cheap cologne, methylated breath and a sort of shitty, unresolved fart smell. He remembered hating how he looked, smelled, spoke, his stupidity, his selfishness. Remembered thinking there was nothing to be proud of, or care about. How he just wished he'd go away. But Dave sat down and said, 'How are you, Wilf?'

Wilf nodded.

'You play well,' he said to his son. 'Do you practise?'

Fuck off.

Wilf said, 'You staying long?'

'Well, since you're asking, the original idea, after the funeral, was to hang around and catch up with my son.' Turning to Connor.

'I've been busy,' Connor said. 'I *am* busy.'

'Really? I heard you quit school.'

'They threw me out.'

'Why?'

'Apparently I was trouble. That happens to some kids.'

'What did you do?'

'Refused to cooperate with people I didn't like.'

Dave took a long drink, smiled at his son and said, 'You look different.'

'How?'

'Your face is longer.'

'It's called growing up.'

'You're pissed off, eh?'

'*No.*'

'Don't blame you. And what about you, Wilf? Still working here?'

'You know I do. You've been in.'

'Just trying to make conversation. Jesus, you two are defensive.'

'Well,' Connor said, sitting forward, 'if you want a summary, I went to primary, graduated, scored a hundred per cent for everything, was told I was a clever child with a great future, as long as I worked hard. But I lost interest. I didn't see the point. Went to high school, dealt with puberty, issues, you know, *issues*, girls, bullies, all that shit, went off the rails, beat a few people up, got drunk, thrown out of school, and here I am, minus my mother – the woman you married – happy that you've returned to sort my life out.'

Dave finished his drink. 'I was just talking to Noah. I asked him how you were going, but he didn't . . .' And to Wilf: 'He said you'd had problems. Who was it, Darcy?'

'Jesus,' Wilf said. 'He told you?'

'Said to keep it quiet.'

'I bet he did.'

Connor said, 'I was making an eighty-eight-millimetre gun in my room, you know, by myself, in the dark, no friends. You used to remind me all the time. I think I was halfway through when you left. But I finished it and Mum said it was pretty decent. I've still got it if you'd like to see. I mean, I thought you might visit, or do something with me?'

The woman with the CDs got up, plugged herself in and started playing a folk song. A raspy, slightly flat voice, and she forgot the lyrics and stopped and asked if she could start again. Connor heard Roman saying she was shit, too.

'You should understand why I left.'

'I don't give a shit why you left. Wilf has got ten different jobs but he sticks at them. Because people rely on him. Colin says he should quit, but you won't, will you, Uncle?'

'No.'

'So what don't I understand?'

Dave took a moment. 'Nothing.'

Connor wasn't sure why he was still here. He'd do this sometimes – come into his room, pissed, sit on the end of the bed, staring at him, and he'd ask what's wrong, but his dad would just grin.

Dave said, 'What are you going to do now?'

'I was waiting for your advice.'

'I'm living in Sydney, if you're interested. My girlfriend and my son . . . they'd love to meet you.'

'Your son?' Waiting. 'How old is he?'

'Nine. You two would get along something . . .'

One year more than me, Connor thought.

'You could have our back room, and find a job, or whatever.'

Wilf didn't like the way this was going. Connor might even be persuaded. Now, he wasn't sure this would be a good thing. Connor noticed his uncle and knew what he was thinking, so he said to Dave, 'No, thanks.'

'Offer's there. Hey, what about when I used to take you—'

'No,' Connor said. 'That's a bit predictable, isn't it? Invoke a happy memory, I remember, yes, things were good, they can be again, Dad. *Dad.*'

'You're being unreasonable.'

'*Really?* And what you *didn't* see. Mum borrowing money from Uncle because you, apparently, refused to pay support. So, if we wanted to eat . . .'

'I was short, too.'

'And Mum cleaning rooms at Hyland's until she got too tired. She just wanted to sleep. Maybe a month before she was diagnosed. She had to quit that job, too, but Uncle helped us out, didn't you?'

Wilf just sat, waiting.

'Then there were the trips to Georgetown when she had chemo three times a week. I was at school (and that probably answers your questions about me losing interest and getting suspended), so again, it was Uncle doing all the driving and bringing us food and spending three hours a day sitting with Mum. Between the school bus, groceries, vegetables, the post . . . So, yes, I guess I am being unreasonable.'

Wilf said, 'How did you hear?'

'She called me.'

'She did not,' Connor said. 'She never called you. She hated you. She thought you were a complete fuckwit, so why would she call you?'

'She did.'

'Stop lying.'

'She said I should come back and see you, in case you wanted to . . . but obviously not.'

'Bull-fucking-shit.' He calmed, then said, 'Any more memories? I have some. We can swap stories for hours.'

Dave stared at his son and said, 'I can't do more than apologise.' He wiped his lips, stood and walked out.

'That went well,' Wilf said. 'Although your mum did call him.'

'I don't know why.'

The woman in the gabardine dress finished her second song and told them about her CD, twenty dollars, autographed, and Connor said, 'If that's what I'm up against.'

Wilf recognised Sienna's voice from the next booth. He looked over to a family scene and Sienna greeted them, turned, sat on her knees and said, 'We're missing you, Wilf. Mr Foley's been driving the bus, and he's shit. Did you quit?'

'No.'

'Retired?'

'No.'

'He's having a break,' the father said, from the shadows.

Nice, Wilf thought, unsure if there was anyone who *didn't* know. 'There were some issues, with Darcy.'

'Really? What?'

'Apparently I can't say.'

'I'll ask him.'

'I bet you will.'

'Sienna,' the mother said, 'don't annoy Mr Healy.'

But Sienna ignored her. 'Darcy's an arsehole anyway.'

'Sienna!' The mother.

'You know what he gets up to?'

'No,' Wilf said.

'I better not say.'

'You better not,' the father said.

'He has smokes, and other stuff, I reckon.'

'Sienna.'

'Other stuff?' Wilf asked.

'He sells it to kids. He gets it in town.'

Her mother told her to keep quiet, because talking about what you didn't know was a good way to get in trouble.

'Scoops n' Smiles.'

'Everyone knows that,' Connor said.

'He tried to sell me some.'

And the mother: 'He did?'

'And Luke and Trevor and Jake and Alessio and tonnes of people. I can tell you now, Wilf, because you're not one of them so I can't get in trouble. But he does.'

'He does,' Connor agreed.

'So you coming back?' she said.

'I hope, soon.'

'He's a shocker, I'll show you.' She produced her phone, swiped, pressed and showed them (the parents peering, too) Noah's driving. Trying to tackle the gears, looking up, and a truck coming toward them. Then another clip of Noah going off the road, over-correcting, onto the other side into a wall. The video continued with them looking at the damage to the front bumper, and Noah shouting at her to turn the damn thing off or he'd take it.

'We're not terribly happy,' the mother said, peering over. 'Sienna always reckoned you were a good driver, and the only one who could control Darcy.'

Another clip: this time, Darcy singing, Noah telling him to keep quiet, but the boy continuing, and Noah slamming on the brakes, turning, shouting at him, telling him he had a detention, tonight, got it?

Then Sienna said, 'I took this one, remember, when I was waiting for mum.'

The footage showed Wilf walking along the road, stopping outside Scoops n' Smiles, looking in, but continuing. Then Darcy emerging, saying a few words, laughing, before returning to the shop.

'*Jesus.*'

'What?' Sienna asked.

Connor smiled. Wilf asked the easiest way. Connor asked for Sienna's phone, and she agreed. 'Careful, it's a good one.' Connor took it, fiddled for a moment, checked his uncle's phone for the number and sent the clip. He returned Sienna's phone then said, 'Got it.' Pressing a few more buttons. 'What do you want me to say?'

Wilf thought for a moment, then said, 'This is what really happened. Sienna got it. Should we talk again?'

Connor checked the message, the attachment, and pressed Send.

Later, sitting in an empty bar, Karen vacuuming around them, Connor said, 'I don't believe you didn't know. He's been at it for years.'

'Why didn't you tell me?'

'He's not the only one. There are plenty. Noah wouldn't know. He's an idiot.'

Wilf studied his phone. The message he'd received ten minutes after sending Sienna's footage: I'LL SEND TO CAREY. TALK SOON.

'Arsehole,' Wilf said.

'You're surprised?'

Turning to his nephew. 'And what did you say to him?'

Connor smiled and finished his watery coffee, the remains of the last pot of the day. 'Sometimes, Uncle, I think you crawled out from under a rock.'

35

They'd decided. What was the point of living in two musty rooms above a pub? Of listening to the bass through the floor, trucks through the window, solid waste and recyclables? What was the point of eating whatever Mrs Gould made, or finding a corner of the kitchen to make a Wilf curry or Connor stir fry? So, time to go home. They'd given Monk a few days' notice, and he'd tried to talk them around. Why? When they were in the middle of everything. Okay then, you want free rent?

'I appreciate everything,' Wilf had said.

'With all your jobs, Wilf, and looking after the boy.'

'I don't need looking after,' Connor had said.

'Okay, keeping a house. Costs? Cleaning?'

Which I'm doing for you, free of charge, Wilf had thought. He'd been taken on as a barman, but had become dishwasher, toilet-swabber and scullery maid. But he didn't want to say this. Monk had been good to him, mostly.

So now uncle and nephew sat on the bed in Wilf's room, Wilf going through the kitchen drawer, determined to purge a lifetime of cutlery. But he wasn't ruthless enough. So far he'd thrown some old staples, three pairs of glasses, slide oil, cotton reels, a postcard and a pack of lettuce seeds. 'The shit you accumulate,' he said. Although that wasn't the worst of it. When they'd started, an hour before, a dozen pairs of shoes placed in a box, and Connor had said, 'Screw it,' opened the window and dropped them. Wilf checking, the box split open, his old boots and dress shoes across the back lane. But then Connor had opened his wardrobe and asked, 'This jacket?'

260

'I should keep that.'

'No, you shouldn't.' Smelling it. 'How old is it?'

'It was my dad's.'

Throwing it into another box. Wilf had gone to get it out, but Connor had stopped him. 'Would you wear it again?'

So Wilf had conceded the jacket, more pants and a few pairs of overalls he'd argued would come in handy. Into the box, and when this was full, Connor had dropped it out of the window, too. Then the drawers, and Connor had explored the world of his uncle's underwear. Potato sack undies with a spot where Boris popped out. 'Not something you'd wear?'

'Best that money can buy.'

'They've got holes in them.'

'My dad wore them, my brothers, me, all the men –' And together: '– *on Louth*.'

'Don't be smart.'

So Connor had put these into a third box. Then he'd found a pile of old singlets and asked who wore singlets anymore and Wilf said, 'I do, thank you very much,' and Connor had said, 'Why?'

'You mind your business.' Repossessing them.

Again, Connor had pointed out the holes, the broken elastic, the stains, from what, he couldn't say – but Wilf had insisted, so Connor had insisted they (he) keep three and throw the rest.

Soon there was another box. Out the window.

Next, documents in the drawer: a superannuation statement saying Wilf had a hundred and fifty dollars, and a few words scribbled on a receipt for a cooker: 'Front door never worked properly'. Connor showed Wilf and said, 'Who wrote that?'

'Nance.'

'Your old place?'

'Yes.' Examining dockets, throwing them in the bin.

'Mum said you had it nice.'

'She brought you a few times when you were a baby. Nance used to put you on the rug in front of the television . . . *Teletubbies*, and *Grange Hill*.'

Wilf didn't like this sort of thing. He stood, picked the old lamp off his desk and said, 'This is dangerous.' He checked out the window, then dropped it. He saw Spencer, poking through his clothes, and called down, 'That's all old shit.'

'Nice jacket.'

'It was my dad's. You can have it.'

'Why you throwing it out?'

'Goebbels reckons I should.' He sat down again and said, 'What's next?'

Connor knew there was no point. He approached the kitchenette, opened the drawer and said, 'Is there any point keeping these?' A few knives and forks, cooking implements, all different styles. He pulled out the drawer, approached the bin and said, 'We've got plenty of this sort of stuff.'

Wilf picked out a melamine spoon with a Peter Rabbit. 'Not that one.'

Connor knew, but didn't say. He threw the rest, then repeated the exercise with the plates and bowls, and again, there was children's crockery, more Peter Rabbits, a Bionic Man butter plate. Wilf kept these and allowed Connor to throw the rest. He put them in the box of shitty stuff he wanted to keep. He didn't explain.

'What about this lamp?' Spencer called up.

Wilf didn't reply to him. 'That's pretty much everything.'

He was right. The bed had been stripped to the mattress, which was yellowing, stained. He'd told Monk about this, too – if a hotel inspector ever came. But Monk was too cheap. The pillows, mashed and sweaty, smelling of spit. They'd even removed the curtains and put them in the laundry. Now, it was a small cell. The various boxes that summed up a life. This didn't worry Wilf. Even these things would need to be left behind, eventually. Connor stood, looked around and declared the job finished. 'But we forgot.' He dropped to his knees, checked under the bed. 'I'll get those few things,' Wilf said, standing, offering a box for his nephew to take downstairs. But Connor just removed the small pile of magazines, smiled and said, 'Nice.'

Wilf grabbed them from him and threw them from the window. A few seconds later Spencer called, 'God bless you, Wilf.'

Wilf called down, 'They're not mine.'

Connor noticed more folders, pulled them out, blew the dust and opened one. This time Wilf didn't argue. The first, more receipts, old newspaper clippings – Khrushchev and Nixon, an obituary for Kennedy. And for Nancy Rose Healy. He read a bit then said, 'I never knew she used to live in Sydney.'

Wilf didn't reply.

'. . . *until her return to Selwyn in 1971*.' Looking up. 'What was she doing there?'

'She worked for National Rail for a time.' He could remember writing the obituary, leaving out the bit about the truck driver, the empty house he'd come home to, the phone calls and the trip to Sydney. Waiting in the lamplight until she came past. And then pleading with her, for her son's sake if nothing else.

Next, they carried the boxes downstairs (past Monk saying it wasn't too late to change your mind, Wilf), loaded them in the back of the van and returned for more. Down, again, and Wilf said to Spencer (still busy picking over his old life): 'Help us with them, will you?' Gathering armfuls of clothes, throwing them in the waste bin, returning for more. Eventually Spencer helped, stood deciding about a few stray items, then returned to his pile of second-hand Wilf.

Wilf said, 'Lot of that stuff's fifty years old.'

'Still got wear in it. Why you moving?'

'Look after my nephew.'

Again, Connor came out and said, 'I don't need looking after.'

Fifteen minutes later they pulled up in front of Orla's place. They got out, opened the van and started carrying in the boxes. As they worked, one neighbour walked past and said, 'Haven't seen Orla for a while.'

Going in, Wilf said, 'Was a time you'd know if your neighbour farted.'

'Was a time . . . not now, Uncle. New start, eh?'

Wilf got it. He was okay in small doses; his stories; his memories. 'Right,' he said. 'You take the double bed, I'll take yours.'

'I'm not moving rooms.'

'I insist.'

'*Uncle.*'

Just the two of them, and the boxes.

'If that's how you want it?'

'It's not how I want it – it's practical.' Taking the first of Wilf's boxes and carrying it into his mum's room. Wilf followed with two more. They stood in front of the stripped-down bed, with its own stains. 'We could buy a new mattress,' Connor said.

'What's wrong with this one?' Wilf took the sheets he'd left out and started making up the bed. Connor stood on the other side and helped. 'What should we eat tonight?' Wilf asked.

'Pizza.'

Not a word. Wilf set out his photos: a small portrait of Nance standing with her arm around Steven; him and his new wife, covered in confetti; Orla and Connor, only a hand remaining from where Dave had been excised. 'This will do very nicely,' he said, pulling back the curtain and examining the view.

'I need to go shopping,' Connor said. 'The fridge is empty.'

'We planted that elm.' Indicating. 'Your mum wanted something fast-growing so you'd have something to climb.'

'I'll make a list,' Connor said, leaving the room.

Wilf sat and studied the things he'd never seen before, coming in to help her: cobwebs in the corner, he could've got those; the way paint peeled from the ceiling. He couldn't help it, couldn't explain to Connor. The past was everywhere.

'We can drive to Northhead,' he called.

No reply.

Still, it would have to be better than the pub. Monk at his door at six in the morning asking if he could cover for Karen. No more tinea. No more possums in the roof. 'We can paint,' he called.

'What?'

'Inside. It's all so seventies.'

'If you like.'

'Change the curtains, the carpet. That shag's older than me.'

No reply.

'Connor?'

'I guess.'

'And what about some new furniture? This stuff's flat-pack, I helped your mum put it together years ago . . . Connor?'

'Maybe.'

A sort of who-gives-a-shit maybe. As Wilf made a mental list of what would have to change; not carpet and furniture, but him, dragging life through the grass by the ankles.

'Connor?'

Just the boy, running through the house, slamming the door. Wilf checked outside and saw him walking, quickly, then running toward town. Maybe he'd left something in his room at Monk's. He opened the window and called, 'What's wrong?'

Connor looked back, but continued.

'Shit,' Wilf said to himself. Ten minutes and he'd already fucked it up. So he walked out, past the van with only half of its boxes removed. He went down the street, and turned in time to see Connor going into the church.

Past Ced, walking to town, saying, 'Where you off to, Wilf?'

'I'm your neighbour now.'

Smiling. 'No kidding?'

Wilf went in and sat beside his nephew on the back pew. Connor didn't seem to care. His head low, his eyes studying the floor.

'Didn't take me long,' Wilf said.

No reply.

'I know I gotta make an effort. If I were you I'd get sick of hearing it, too.'

Connor fitted, just a little, to get his breath. Wilf saw he was holding a photo, his own, a twelve-year-old giving the camera the finger, and another, a seven or eight-year-old in bathers, at a pool, beating his chest. Someone had drawn a cross on his face. Connor presented the photos to Wilf and said, 'In the drawer.'

Wilf studied them. And on the reverse of the second: 'Not One Visit'.

'It's Mum's handwriting.' He looked pleadingly at his uncle. 'I didn't want to . . .' He slumped against him, tried to get his breath. Wilf put an arm around him and said, 'It could mean a lot of things.'

Jesus on his cross, but Wilf knew it wouldn't help. He was in it now. Boots and all. 'No point now,' he said. 'She was pissed off, and she had cause to be. But ten minutes later . . . okay? Ten minutes, and she would've been making a coffee.'

36

Connor woke to the smell of frying bacon, the sound of Wilf in the kitchen banging away, cursing no one in particular. 'Uncle?' Nothing except talkback radio. He put in his earbuds and slipped into a Pearl Jam trance, bandsaw guitar and whisky-warmed voice, the same mouldy spot on his ceiling, the dusty fan he'd left on, quietly clomping away all night. And again, his thoughts came back to his mother waking, calling for him, remembering he was in Georgetown. Now, he didn't get it. He hadn't meant anything, he wasn't trying to make a point, he wasn't even particularly pissed off. It was just something he'd done.

Wilf came in with a tray, placed it on his bed, opened the curtains and said, 'I need some help.'

'*What*?'

'The mail.'

'But you said . . .' What was the point? He sat up, de-budded, turned off the music. 'What's the time?'

'Nearly seven.'

'Jesus. Why so early?'

'Clock's ticking. Sun's shining. A lot to get done. You want to help me?'

'I guess.'

'So . . .' He picked up the tray, brought it around and said, 'Eat up.'

Connor surveyed the small feast: three overcooked eggs, slightly-burned bacon, mushrooms, a tomato. 'Is this breakfast?'

'No, it's a car.'

'Who eats *mushrooms* for breakfast?'

'Everyone used to. What do you have?'

'A coffee, perhaps.'

'Well, that's no good. That's why your ribs are showing. We'll have to do something about it. Eat up.'

Connor settled the food in his lap. 'You want to fatten me up?'

'You're too thin.'

'Jesus. *Mum*.'

'Don't start that. I'm not your mum, I'm your uncle, and I cooked you breakfast, so you can eat it.'

Connor didn't know where all of this was heading, but he suspected. 'You fatten pigs for slaughter.'

'It can be arranged.'

He started picking at the bacon as Wilf left the room then returned with a milky coffee. He put it down, and Connor said, 'It's not very strong.'

'I'm not a barrister.'

'*Barista*.'

Wilf watched him eat. 'We can start like this,' he said. 'I get fifty dollars a run for the mail, so you come along and I give you half.'

Connor cut into the egg but it didn't bleed.

'Then when you've learned the route ... got your licence ... it's all yours.'

'Delivering mail?'

'It's a good job. No one to pester you, fresh air, stop for a chat, Bobby'll make you a *proper* coffee.'

'So I'll be Postman Pat?'

'Why not?'

Connor tasted the coffee. 'It's like ...' He put down the cup, played with the mushrooms. 'You eat these?'

'You could be a bit grateful. I got up, went down to Simon's. Between mopping the floor, which was covered in drink.'

'*Ta*.'

'That's okay. It's my job now.'

'Your job?'

'Yes. Something needs doing . . .'

'Like driving a bus, George?'

'Sort of.'

'Things you've *got* to do?'

'Don't start your little games. You know what I mean. My job.'

''Cos you promised Mum?'

'No, 'cos I *want* to. Just eat your mushrooms.'

Connor had a go. They were inedible, and he told Wilf, who told him how much they'd cost and could he at least try? Connor said, 'Maybe we should decide together?'

'I guess we should.'

'That way there'll be no disagreements?'

'Why should there be disagreements?'

'Well, I sleep in 'cos I stay up late, practising. And when Roman comes over . . .'

Well, things will need to change, Wilf thought. 'Boy your age should be in bed by ten.'

'*Ten*? Try three.'

Wilf sighed. Connor heard air through his nostril hairs and said, 'Mum never cared.'

'Well, I'm not your mum.'

'See? If you want to come and live in my house . . .'

'*Your* house?' Again, he backed off. But what was the point of staying up late? Of missing the best part of the day? 'When you've got a bit to do you can't hang about. The mail, then Bobby's got a few crates of—'

'Me? Bobby?'

Wilf waited. Day two, there was no point rushing. He took out his wallet, found a fifty and handed it to Connor. 'I was thinking, how much pocket money did your mum give you?' Holding the note mid-air.

'I've got money.'

'For now. With no income . . . go on.' Waving the note about.

'I don't want your money.'

'Take it, it's not charity. If you want you can pay me back.'

'I can look after myself.'

'I didn't say you couldn't.' Dropping the note on the tray.

'I've got my own. You're not coming in here and . . .' Throwing the fifty back at him.

Half an hour later they stood at the door to the Shell. Wilf had ironed his nephew's slacks, but Connor had said he could've done it; he'd found a nice shirt, laid it out on his bed (made, by him), and then found one of the ties he'd kept. He'd handed him this, too, and said, 'You've got to look the part.'

'*I'm* applying, Uncle.'

'I'm only trying to help.'

'You don't need to.'

'If you want to look professional.'

Back outside the Shell, Wilf said, 'Just make it sound like you want the job. Frank's reasonable but he won't take on a slacker.'

They walked along the confectionery aisle, past the motor oil and tyre gauges, and approached Frank. Seventy-plus, with long, grey sideburns, bloodhound cheeks and no-nonsense eyes.

'How are you, Frank?' Wilf said.

'Good. And you, Wilf?' Then to Connor: 'You're Orla's boy, aren't you?'

'Yes.' He felt four years old. Like he might, any moment, piss himself.

'That's a pity,' Frank Dunney said to him. 'How old are you?'

'Seventeen.'

'Early to be losing your mum. Still, lots had it worse, didn't they, Wilf?'

'They did.'

'After the war. Plenty of kids didn't have a dad. I was lucky, my old man had a reserved occupation.'

Wilf said, 'Connor's looking at getting some work, a few hours here and there, if you need someone?'

Connor turned and glared at his uncle, who backed off. 'I was going to move back to Georgetown, but Wilf said I should get some work here. If you had some.' Shit, he thought. That sounded sloppy, uninspiring. Wilf was thinking the same thing. Frank Dunney clicked his fingernails on the desk. 'Another worker?'

'I'm flexible with hours,' Connor said, 'I only live five minutes up the road, so if you need someone for a late shift.'

That's more like it, Wilf thought.

'And short notice . . . whatever suits. I've got a decent work record, helping Uncle with his deliveries.'

'Why don't you do that?'

'He wants to make a go for himself,' Wilf said.

Uncle!

'That's good, that's the way,' Dunney said, and again, Connor was at the altar with his sash, crossing his legs because he really needed to go.

'I can't blame him,' Wilf said. 'That age, you want to do it for yourself.'

'Uncle,' Connor said.

Dunney smiled. 'You've been told, Wilf.' And to Connor: 'What about school?'

Connor took a moment, checked with Wilf, who said, 'He decided, we decided, I mean, him and his mother.' He waited to see if Frank had heard of Connor, Roman, their nocturnal activities, but he just said, 'School's not for everyone.'

'Exactly. If you got the spirit,' Wilf said.

'Well, Doug's off on holidays in October . . . if you could wait till then?'

Jesus, Connor thought. Four months, for a few hours at a petrol station?

So they thanked him, went out, stood beside the air hose, and Connor said, '*I* was meant to be talking to him.'

'I just thought, if it helped.'

'Well, it obviously didn't, did it?'

'If we go to Greene's, Spencer, even Monk's, that'd still be doing it for yourself, wouldn't it?'

Simon pulled up in his van and called across the concourse: 'How was the move, Wilf?'

'Good.'

'Is he behaving himself, Connor?'

But Wilf waved him off. 'Righto then,' he said, tightening his nephew's tie. 'I'll leave you to it. But Monk, you know, what happened that time with you and the drink? So maybe if I . . .?'

'Uncle. Please?'

The sound of the pumps, traffic on the road and the tempered toughness of this boy who had been through everything, and emerged decent, good. This is what Wilf wanted to say, but had no idea how. *You, my boy, are good.* 'All of that business, with you in Georgetown . . .'

Waiting.

'She understood.'

Connor didn't seem so sure, or how this fit the moment at the Shell, the too-thin tie, the shirt that cut into his neck.

'It's up to you,' Wilf said. 'Whatever you want to do. I don't care.'

Connor extended his hand, and they shook. Wilf held it. Soft, minus muscle.

'Well, I should have a go then,' Connor said.

'Why not? Just tell Monk you're off the bottle. It was a bad day. I think he understood.'

'I bet she was cursing me?' Connor said.

'Never. Not a word. She told me, a few weeks, months, I can wait.'

Connor felt shit again. 'Maybe I can make the beds, clean the toilets?'

'I'll have a word.'

'No, you won't.' Smiling, then punching his shoulder.

Connor walked across the concourse toward Greene's. Wilf felt he was making progress. It'd take time, but they'd get there. Like Bobby, and years of fiddling. The boy went in and Dunney, standing at the door, said, 'He's a good boy, Wilf.'

Wilf smiled, waved and started toward home.

The sky clearing, full of blue, and birds in and out of branches. Like this, repeating, again and again, for no other reason than it always had. Sitting with his dad on a low wall, saying, 'What's in Selwyn?'

'Running water.'

'What else?'

'A good school. Electricity, and they get the television, so you can watch the Queen.'

'But she's a bitch, isn't she?'

'She is, but they got symphonies and plays and quiz shows.'

'What are they?'

'They ask a question and you're meant to know the answer.'

At that age, Wilf suspected his father had all the answers. 'You should go on it.'

'Me? I'm stupid. All the Healy men are thick.'

Wilf remembered watching him as he stared out to sea. He remembered his hand covering his, and him saying, 'No use worrying, Wilf. It all comes out in the wash.'

'What does?'

But he never said.

Connor emerged from Greene's. He gave his uncle the thumbs down, but shrugged, and pulled a who-gives-a-shit face. Wilf smiled, and continued. When he got home he settled in front of the television, sipped bad coffee and watched *Midsomer Murders*. Within minutes he'd lost track of who'd murdered whom, but it didn't matter, because soon he was asleep.

At two or so he woke and heard Connor in his room. He went in and found him, tie off, shirt open to the belly, pyjama pants and bare feet. 'What did they say?'

'Monk said maybe later in the year. Simon reckoned he was barely making a wage himself.'

'Well, hate to tell you I said so.'

'I'm not going to root around with Bobby's cows.'

Wilf smiled. 'Given time.'

37

Connor sat on the passenger side of the J2, checking his watch, hoping he'd beat the bell. He turned up the volume on the crackling, monophonic radio and wondered why his uncle put up with it. The ice cream van he'd been hearing forever, up and down every street of Selwyn every afternoon, three or four times on the weekend. The same electronic *Greensleeves*. 'Come on, Uncle!' He checked his watch. Five minutes until the bell. He even sounded the horn a few times. Mr Whippy came closer, loitering around the school gates as he did, every day, at dismissal. Parents had complained, but the bloke who did it, who lived a few minutes out of town, wasn't about to be told where he could sell his Twisters. The same melody: *Have you ever wondered as years go by that one day my dear you're sure to die?*

'Shut the fuck up!' Hammering the cracked dash. He turned up his music, his guitar, his gay-sounding voice (he'd told Wilf) and listened. A present for his uncle. Wilf had been delighted his nephew had been interested enough to finally record *The Hills*. 'It seemed important,' Connor had said.

'Well, now we'll have a record,' Wilf had replied. 'Make copies, we could sell them?'

Although Connor had thought it'd be nice if Wilf was as interested in *his* songs.

Mr Whippy sat trumpeting, and Connor paused the music. He imagined getting out, going up to this man and saying, *Shut that fucking shit up*. But he knew he'd never do this. He was too much his mother's son, his uncle's grand-nephew. So he sat, with his own stuff on pause, as the bell sounded and kids drifted out of the main building. Some of the Receptions first, parents in hand, holding pictures of dinosaurs and castles, telling their mums and dads about their big day. Then the older kids, shirts out, dragging their bags along the ground, checking their phones. Roman came down the path, saw him and said, 'What's happening?' Offering him a palm, although he didn't respond. 'I'm waiting for Wilf.'

'The pedo?'

'What?'

'Didn't he? Darcy?'

'Didn't he what?' The song in his ear.

'Him and Darcy?' Smiling.

'What's meant to have happened?'

'You know . . .?'

'No, I don't.'

'He touched him up.'

'Bullshit! Darcy said he pushed him, but he didn't. And now there's a clip on Sienna's phone, so Darcy's in the shit. So who's saying that?'

'Everyone.'

'Well, that's crap. Got it?'

'Just saying.'

Fuck, he hated school. Always had, always would. If he were to get any sort of education, it wouldn't be here. 'That had nothing to do with it.'

'Just saying.'

'Tell people. Right?'

The electro-pulse seemed to be getting louder. Roman said, 'Should we have another jam?'

'No.'

'Why?'

'Who's listening? A bunch of pig farmers?' He watched the door, the dozens still streaming out, but no Wilf. He hit the horn again, called out of the window, 'Enough fucking *Greensleeves*.'

Roman walked away and not long after Wilf got in, started the van and said, 'We ready?'

Connor hit play and the music returned, but Wilf just said, 'No apologies, of course.'

'What?'

Backing out, just missing some kids with their mums, apologising and saying, '*Well, Wilf, Detective Carey went out there and showed him and he admitted it. So* . . . And he just sat there, like he couldn't see the problem.'

'That was it?'

'Then he said, *Unpleasant for all, I guess, but you never know with young people.*'

'Sue the cunts.'

'Eh.'

'Sorry, but that can't be it.'

Wilf drove through the school gates, turned left and set off for his first delivery.

'He's made this shit up and now everyone thinks . . .' But he decided no good would come from it. 'They think you hit him.'

'I've got two options. Take it further, keep it in the news, keep everyone talking, or forget about it. People in this place have got short memories. Twelve months it'll be like it never happened.'

They drove up and down rollercoaster roads. 'Get a lawyer and let him do it,' Connor said. 'You shouldn't let him get away with it.'

'Then Noah rang the mother and she said, Oh, Darcy would never make up such a thing.'

'Even with the video?'

'She said, *Any school that would try and do this to a young person* . . . we'd all sat down, dreamed this up, done it to her little cunt of a son.'

'Eh.'

'He is. A little cunt.' He turned down a gravel road toward a distant hill. 'Either way, she said she's pulling him out of the school, effective immediately. She's sending him to Northhead.'

'Nice work, Wilf!' Offering his own high-five. This time, Wilf took it. He touched his foot to the accelerator and the van glided down the hill.

'Then Noah says, *Oh, well, of course, the moment I saw the footage I suspended him.* But I doubt he even did that.'

They stopped outside the Hunters' farmhouse, and Wilf said, 'Off you go then.'

Connor opened the van, searched for the parcel and double-checked it against the list. Then he knocked on the door, made his delivery and got a signature. When he got back in, Wilf said, 'Growth area.'

'What?'

'Oz Post. Millions of people buying shoes from China. Leo's out of action, I'm a danger on the roads, it seems logical. I don't need the money. I'll be dead soon anyway.'

'Would you stop saying that.'

'Just offering. Better than the Shell.'

Next, what looked like a basketball, and ten minutes later, a box of something for the Smiths. 'You'll learn all the names,' Wilf said, heading back to town. 'A few more lessons . . . the school bus?'

'Isn't Noah doing it?'

'No. I said to him, *I got the feeling you were erring on the side of caution, Noah.* He said it was process, but I said that's bullshit. Either you believed me or you didn't.' Sitting back, one hand on the wheel, taking in the scenery. 'I don't think I'll bother with that man anymore. I told him he was spineless. Then he said, *If you're interested in coming back and doing the bus . . .*'

'You're not going to?'

'Well, I was thinking of you. I said, *Okay, but only as long as it takes Connor to learn the job, get his licence, then it's his job, right?*'

'*Uncle.*'

'Don't get yer knickers . . . just in case you decide.'

'*I* decide?'

'Or maybe Shell, a few hours?'

'Or maybe Sydney, tomorrow?' He sat watching the same hills. 'So what did he say?'

'He agreed. I start back tomorrow.'

'And you'll teach me?'

'If you like. I'm not fussed. You can be a rock star if you like.'

Connor turned up the music and Wilf said, again, how sweet the chords, soothing the voice, sentimental the words.

'I know what you're doing, Uncle.'

'What?'

They pulled into Raglan's place and Wilf showed Connor how he'd have to avoid the grates, the narrow gate, the dog that barked at the van (don't worry, she won't bite you). He told him Mr Raglan would talk forever, and time was money, so just smile and tell him you're busy. They stopped and got out, Connor pushed the dog away with his foot and Wilf found another parcel addressed to Roper. Different handwriting, he remembered. He shook it and said, 'I've got a secret.'

'What?'

He explained what he'd done behind Monk's, the return to the forest, the visit to the beach. Connor said, 'So what, anyone could've told you.'

This made Wilf even more interested. He shook the parcel and listened. 'Don't tell anyone. It's three years' prison for fiddling about . . . know what I mean?'

Connor made an improvised tear, stuck his finger in and said, 'Fuck.'

Mr Raglan came to his door and called, 'Anything?'

'Just a moment,' Wilf said.

Connor fiddled about, smiled, held the parcel in the air and a few pills fell out. He examined them, their little 'P', looked at his uncle and said, 'See?'

'Rotten bastard.'

'What do you reckon?'

'Wilf?' Mr Raglan called.

Wilf tossed Roper's parcel into the back of the van and said, 'Not a word.'

'Should we show the police?'

Raglan was coming over, so Wilf gave Connor his parcel and said, 'Give him his oats.'

As they drove back down Martin Raglan's long drive, Connor said, 'We should go to the cops.'

'What do they do? Take a statement, fill in forms, talk to people . . . and nothing happens. Back on Louth . . .'

'Uncle.'

'For example, Graney's dad had been on with someone's wife. This was a big issue, you know, on a small island. So he gets this note to come to the pub, and when he gets there it's dark, and he goes in and the next thing there's a hand on his shoulder and then . . . you know, the place was full of men. They found him the next morning with broken ribs. They had to take him to the mainland to get fixed up.'

'What's that got to do with anything?'

'I remember lying in bed and Dad coming home and Mum asking where he'd been and him saying there'd been a meeting and they'd sorted something out.' He grimaced. Just a bit. Bit his lip and took a deep breath.

'You alright, Uncle?'

'But when he got back, everything was sorted.' He bit his lip again, sat up and tried to take a breath.

'Uncle?'

Wilf slumped, his head on his shoulder, and managed a few breaths as Connor took the wheel and tried to guide the van along the road. Connor shook him and said, 'Uncle!'

Wilf raised his head, clutched his chest, slumped again. Connor slipped off his seatbelt, reached down and used the flat of his hand to press the brake. As he did, he felt the van connecting with the wall, then stopping. He sat up. 'Uncle?'

Wilf straightened himself, kept holding his chest and saying, 'That can't be right.'

'Have you got your pills? Have you had them?'

Connor undid Wilf's seatbelt, got out, went around and manhandled him to the other side. Then he got behind the wheel, tried to straighten up, and the vehicle jumped, sought road, started along it. He steered, slowed along the main street, sounded the horn when it looked like Mrs Gould was about to cross. The T-junction, with its hundred possibilities, but only one, now. To the medical centre. Handbrake. Running in and saying, 'I think my uncle's had a heart attack.'

A moment later, the GP tearing at Wilf's shirt, applying his stethoscope and listening as the nurse said to Connor, 'You drove him?'

Connor indicated the mashed-up front bumper and side panel.

The doctor looked at them and said, 'What's he on?'

Connor tried to think, and the nurse asked Connor, 'Has he had his angina pills?'

'I don't think so.'

And Wilf said, 'The one bloody morning I forget.'

38

A few days later they took the Rover and headed west. Low cloud dispersing, revealing nimbus piggybacking uncooperative rain. These two men, silent in their own thoughts, Connor lost in the land that kept tripping over itself, rolling into the ocean. Wilf more concerned about the erratic temperature gauge. A probationary father and son seeking lost childhoods, ice creams and sand buckets neither of them wanted.

They stopped in a deserted carpark, took off their shoes and socks and Wilf rolled up his pants. An overflowing bin – KFC and three carefully tied bags of dog shit. And walking down to the sea, over the soft sand, the hard sand, a morning of discharged dreams Wilf remembered from Louth. Mr Flynn combing the beach for driftwood. The men standing about predicting what sort of weather they'd have today.

Wilf knelt on the shore, felt the marram and said to Connor, 'I remember on Louth . . .'

'*Louth?*'

'Okay, I won't mention it.'

'You can say what you want.' He knelt and ran the grass through his fingers.

Wilf didn't get how he didn't get it. The small barnacles on a rock, sandpapered palm, sea-salt tape from the IV solution, the hours on the bed before they'd released him (with a warning). The doctor saying, 'That could've gone very differently.'

Wilf had agreed. He was lucky. He'd been stupid, he'd forgotten his pills. He'd felt the pains earlier (he'd admitted) but ignored them.

Connor said, 'I could've been at your funeral about now.'

'Rubbish. They're dramatic.'

Connor stood, shook the weed from his hand and said, 'Hardly.'

'I've got another twenty years.'

Low tide, the sand spreading, following the bay, leading them toward the caves. They were alone, considering the small, persistent whisper of waves, the water's apron, the milky froth that sat for a moment, before succumbing. Wilf rolled his pants up another cuff, pushed his foot into the soft sand, wriggled his toes and said, 'It's the same smell, isn't it?'

'As what?'

This time Wilf didn't say. He pointed to the cave and said, 'Should we see what's inside?'

So they headed along the shore, Connor in his shorts and T-shirt, Wilf in business shirt and cords. 'I wouldn't mind being left with *someone*,' Connor said, dipping his toes in and out of the water.

'You've got your dad.'

The hush of the sea answered each question, propagated the conversation, filled the blanks. Words as little sparks filling the morning air. Wilf sensed this and said, 'It just goes on, doesn't it?' Gazing out again. Indicating and saying, 'Louth must be that way.'

But Connor was walking ahead. 'I'll buy you one of those pill boxes,' he said, 'and I'll make sure you take them.'

'I don't need you checking up on me.'

Again, the ocean. The way the machine lost its light, its sound, its life, when the doctor turned it off and said, 'You can go home, but maybe, next time?'

'I've told him,' Connor said.

'The boy's got more sense than you, old man.'

Old *what*?

Connor reminded his uncle of this, but he just said, 'None of his business.'

'Keeping you alive?'

It was a stupid conversation, so Wilf picked up a worm cast and said, 'They're down there somewhere.'

'Who?'

'Worms. Me and Brian and Colin used to go down to the beach on a Saturday morning and dig for them.' Staring at the rippled sand, the possibility of bait for their rods.

Connor knelt again and said, 'Are they big?'

'Can be.' And he indicated.

'Did you catch anything?' Digging the hole with a finger, flicking away the sand.

'Of course we did. Big bream, like this.' Again, the same size. 'Dad would clean them and that was Sunday lunch.' Staring into the hole, like his childhood might be there. 'With the taste of all that.' Indicating the ocean. 'That rubbish at the Eat Inn, I don't know where he gets it. Doesn't even taste like fish.'

'What else did you do on Louth?'

Wilf seemed surprised – that he was allowed, invited, to talk about it.

'You could push bulls.'

'How?'

'Wait till midnight, when they were asleep.'

'Do bulls sleep?'

'I imagine. Approach them quietly.'

Because he was there beside his brothers, slowly creeping across the field, whispering and laughing, 'Shh, shut the fuck up.'

Closer, and Brian charged and pushed the tonne-and-a-half bull. Although he didn't fall over; just turned, snorted, bellowed. So they ran, back to the fence, with the animal close behind. Jumped, and sat on the other side laughing, Colin getting out a smoke he'd stolen.

Connor thought this sounded great. He was curious why Wilf had never told him before. It sounded made up, like most of what he said. But he guessed that didn't matter. A story had its own life, always running away from the truth. 'So you never pushed one over?'

'Of course. Several. One broke its ribs and Dad had to pay Mr Klein.' Grinning.

'Bullshit.'

'Don't swear, my boy.'

'I'm not a boy.'

'That's yet to be seen.'

Further along, Connor poked his foot into wrack, cast over stones, themselves full of pools and eddies, water warming in the sun. 'What's this?'

'How would I know?' Wilf said.

'You were the one out exploring, on *Louth*.'

Then a starfish: twelve inches across, a purple sparkle. Connor carefully picked it up by the arm and said, 'Cool.' He handed it to Wilf, who inspected it and said, 'It's ill.' He tapped it on a rock, and one arm fell off. 'One thing goes with another. The wrack, the starfish . . . the marram, all of it.'

They moved into the shadow of the cave, stopped, and Wilf surveyed the grand opening. 'There was one of these on Louth, too.' Turning to his nephew. 'A big cave. It was wonderful for hiding if you were in trouble.'

'What goes with what?' Connor asked.

Wilf headed inside, the jagged limestone closing in behind him, the shadows and shards of sunlight, more rock pools full of barnacles, limpets. He knelt again, examined some of the swimming organisms. 'This with that,' he said. 'It's all connected. The barnacle eats the weed, the fish eats the barnacle.' Then looking at him. 'They *need* each other.'

Connor wasn't sure. 'Who?'

And standing: 'Me, Brian, Colin . . . we should've stuck together. That's why I mentioned your dad.' He went further into the dark and the cavern opened up into a cathedral-sized space. 'Colin shouldn't have gone to America.'

'Why?'

'That's what I mean.' Like it was dawning on him. 'Once people disconnect. Once they're no longer part of something bigger.'

Connor studied his starfish and realised it belonged in its tepid pool on the edge of the Southern Ocean.

'But once Colin had made up his mind,' Wilf said. 'Then it was down to me and Brian to help Mum and Dad.' Calling: '*None of us still living . . .*' Again and again, and then Connor joined in, and they had a chorus of echoes. Wilf turned to Connor and said, 'You keep asking why I don't retire.' He pointed to the starfish in Connor's hand. 'It's because of that.'

Wilf went further into the cave, sticking to the smooth, worn stones. A million years apiece, although that, he guessed, was nothing. He kept examining the contents of the pools, the periwinkles and sea grass, the faded chip packets and water bottles. All of it, coming and going with the tide. 'When Dad was fuming,' he said, 'we'd run to the end of the island and hide in the cave.' The three of them, sitting on a rock shelf, holding their knees in close to their bodies, shivering, Brian saying, 'We've got to go home sometime.'

And Wilf, 'What were you thinking, stealing it from the shop?'

'It was just there. They weren't looking.'

Mrs Hanlon standing in their doorway, explaining to their parents. Three boys last seen dashing from her shop.

When they re-emerged from the cave, cloud had greyed the day. Wilf didn't mind. Most of the days of the world had been grey, wet, cold. He stared out to sea and noticed the tide returning. 'The Kemps have got decent fish,' he said to his nephew.

As they drove home, Connor handed Wilf a chip, and he ate it, put out his hand for another, blew on it, dropped it, tried to retrieve it from under his seat, drifted off the road again. Connor corrected him. Wilf said, 'So what did that achieve?'

Connor ripped off a piece of cod, held it by the tips of his fingers, blew on it and said, 'What was it meant to achieve?'

'You going to eat all of the fish?'

Connor handed him a piece.

'And what's all this about sound engineering?'

'One year full-time, two years' part-time.'

'And?'

'I might.' He reached into his pocket, found a business card and showed Wilf. The name of the tutor, the college and, on the bottom, costs. Wilf noticed something drop from his nephew's pocket. A small pink pill with a 'P'. He reached over, picked it up and said, 'Where's this from?'

Connor had no reaction, no explanation.

'It's from the parcel?' Wilf said. He pulled over, got out and went to the back of the van. A few items yet to be delivered, and Roper's, with the hole showing, a few more pills on the floor. He picked some up, examined them then came around to his nephew's side. 'Get out!'

Connor obeyed. He stood, the motor running, a few cars flying past.

'Your pockets?' Wilf said.

'What?'

Wilf stepped forward, stuck his hand in Connor's pocket and Connor pushed back. 'What?'

'Go on.'

'When we were looking, that's all. When you had your . . .'

Wilf could feel his heart again. But it didn't matter. If it were true, if Connor would do this behind his back, then what did anything matter? He could feel his dry mouth, his unsteady gait. So he tried again. One hand in a pocket, a short struggle, and again, retreat. 'You haven't . . .?'

'You think I'm taking them? Does it look like I'm taking ecstasy?'

Wilf had to know. He tried his nephew's pocket and this time Connor didn't resist. The starfish, bits of the glitter, the sand, a few more pills. He held them up to Connor and said, 'You took them?'

'No.'

'How did they get into your pocket?'

'I don't know.'

Wilf wanted to slap him. That's how it was done. You came in, your father presented the evidence, you were all slapped, and belted.

The two of them stood there, but the choke feathered and the engine cut out. So it was silent. Until a van flew past. 'Is that what you reckon?' Connor said. He took a moment, then turned and walked east, toward Selwyn.

'And what about the other pocket?' Wilf called.

No reply.

'At least talk to me.'

And without turning. 'Blah blah . . .' But then he stopped, turned and started back. 'Hold out your hands.' He emptied his other pocket, and there were more pills. Fifteen, twenty, so small it was hard for Wilf to tell. 'I took a few,' he said.

'Why?'

'Why not? They're free, and fun. For a few hours . . . Not hurting anyone.'

Wilf slapped him across the face, but Connor didn't react. 'What else is there to do? Sit and watch the cows? Talk about your pathetic little island? Drive your lettuces around?'

Wilf felt a breeze across his temple. He reached for his nephew's cheek, touching it, soothing it with his thumb, especially where it was turning red.

On the way home, Wilf said, 'You're gonna hate me now.'

'I don't hate you.'

'It's just your mother . . . I promised.'

'You're not Mum.'

'What would she think?'

'She'd understand.'

Wilf knew, somehow, that all of this was part of the promise. Part of the sense that all things were one thing and, given time, would fix themselves. There were no ghosts. Out of the dead and the living, only the living mattered. For the rest of the way home, he wondered what to do next. A brick through the bastard's window? The police? He even had Carey's number. He asked Connor, and he said, 'He sells them to the older kids, and they take them to school.'

So Wilf decided. When they arrived in town, he went into the ice cream shop, placed the parcel in front of Roper and said, 'Australia Post delivery.'

Roper was sitting with a magazine, smoking. The place smelled of it. He looked at his parcel and Wilf tipped it up and a few dozen pills came out. He said, 'I reckon you could have this place packed up by tomorrow night?'

Roper just waited.

'And by Friday you'd be gone?'

Roper said, 'Never seen the stuff,' and tried to take it, but Wilf grabbed it first and said, 'I'll hold onto it.'

'You're not allowed to open shit.'

But Wilf said, 'By Monday perhaps?'

39

Wilf guessed he'd have to do something about his heart. The occasional pill, low-fat milk (if he thought of it) and a bit of lettuce from Monk's salad bar weren't going to get him to triple figures. He had responsibilities now – he had to eat his greens. So he decided. A daily walk of thirty minutes. Fast, vigorous, sweat on the brow. And today was the perfect opportunity: a big, blue sky and unapologetic sun. He started along Sullivan Street, past Scoops n' Smiles, half-empty. On, and Simon tried to start a conversation, but he said, 'Can't stop, gotta make the old girl work.'

Continuing, slowing, closing his eyes and letting the breeze wash over him. Thinking, *The best of everything.* Somehow, this moment, he thought, could cancel out every stinking turd: days, months, years of them. A post-pill ecstasy that only lasted a few seconds, but forever. But more than this, his heart ticking away, establishing a rhythm. As he passed Karen, standing in front of Monk's having a smoke, he said, 'Missing me yet?'

'He's painting your room.'

'Of course. When I'm gone.'

'You working today?'

'Tomorrow.' But fading as he approached Spencer's. 'If the mood takes me.'

'How's Connor?'

'Progressing.'

All the way home, across the yard, jumping up the few steps, blessing the smell of fresh citrus blowing across from next door. Coming in and calling, 'You up yet?'

No reply.

So he went into Connor's room, stood in the doorway and said, 'It's nearly eleven.'

'So?'

'Get up. I'll cook some breakfast.'

'I don't want any.'

Wilf went into the kitchen anyway, put on the kettle to make coffee, but said to himself, 'No, get with it!' So he drank a glass of water, winced, called, 'You gonna help with the vegetables?'

And muffled: 'Fuck the vegetables.'

Wilf tried another glass but only half-finished, then decided one coffee wouldn't kill him, and put the kettle on again. He went back to Connor's room and said, 'It's a beautiful day. Come on, we'll go for a walk. You'll feel better.'

Over the weeks since moving, the room had transformed. Connor had hung another sheet over his curtain and now it was daytime-dark. Half-eaten chips, old bottles of drink, more coffee and lolly wrappers. Most of the floor was covered with clothes, so Wilf picked some up, sniffed them and said, 'I can't wash everything every day.'

'Well, don't.'

'Someone has to.'

'Later.' Although it might have been a different word.

'You can't keep saying that.'

Connor stretched out, yawned and said, 'Jesus, Uncle!'

'I'm trying to help.'

'I'm trying to sleep.'

It occurred to Wilf that this was more than sleep. If you wanted the day, you got up, and grabbed it. If you didn't, you slept. He didn't know where all this was headed – whether Connor was getting worse, better, disengaged. As he turned to go, Connor said, 'Why should I get up?'

'That's what people do.'

'So I can go with you to Bobby's?'

'Christ, Connor. What *do* you want to do then?'

Connor threw off his sheets and sat half-naked, trying to work out his uncle. 'Remember that time you told me your plan? That I'd take over all your shit so you could piss off to Louth.'

'I'm not pissing off anywhere, *Nephew*. I'm staying here, I'm washing your shit and cooking your food and finding out what the hell you want to do, and helping you do it.'

''Cos you promised Mum?'

'Exactly.'

'Not because I want to—'

'Where's this get you? Want some more pills? I've still got them. Four, five, how many? Sit there and shit on about how hard your life is because you lost your mother.'

Connor sat, waiting.

'I lost my son.'

'That was different.'

'How?'

Wilf opened the blind, ripped down the sheet, and Connor protected his eyes. He started picking up the clothes and throwing them out into the hallway. When he was finished, he started clearing the food from the table. Connor said, 'Leave it!'

'No.' Continuing.

'I said I'll do it.'

Wilf glared at him, went out, returned with Roper's package and tipped the pills onto Connor's sheets. 'Go on, get into them.' Picking a few up and throwing them at his nephew. Connor cowered, grabbed his legs, made a cocoon. Wilf returned to the kitchen, spooning coffee into his cup as Connor, covering himself in a rug, came out and said, 'You're determined.'

'Just get dressed.' Emptying the not-quite boiled water into his cup.

'When have I ever said . . .?'

'When?' Turning, going into the lounge room, searching a pile of papers and producing the application form. 'I got it, we filled it in. *I* got it. Me. For you.' Presenting the form ('APPLICATION FOR ADMISSION TO DIPLOMA'). 'So?'

But even then Connor said, 'It doesn't mean . . .'

'Christ.' Returning to his coffee, adding milk and stirring it.

Again, Connor followed. 'How the hell am I going to live in Sydney?'

'I told you.'

'You'll never leave Selwyn.'

'I don't give a shit about this town, this country, any bloody thing.' Stopping, his hand shaking, but drinking the coffee anyway. 'This is shit.'

'You can't sell Mum's house.'

'Why not? We rent it out. Next problem?'

'You'd never quit your jobs.'

'No?'

Wilf grabbed his nephew's fleshy arm and led him back to his room. He picked a pair of pants and a T-shirt from the mess and threw them at him. 'Go on, put them on.'

Connor did as he was told. Dropped his rug, and Wilf saw his bony legs and said, 'It wouldn't hurt if you ate something occasionally.'

'I do.'

'What? Frozen meals. There's a fridge full of vegetables.'

'No one likes vegetables.'

'Correction: everyone but *you* likes vegetables.'

Connor pulled on his pants, socks, sandshoes. He managed to get the T-shirt over his head, and Wilf said, 'No point working for George, or Leo. The money's crap, the jobs are boring, monotonous, repetitive. Get out of this shithole. I should've years ago, when Colin left. I could've, I should've went with him. I don't know what I was thinking.'

Connor smiled. He liked the way his uncle rolled. He was a good man.

'Come on.'

Firstly, they drove to the pharmacy and Wilf asked to see George. He came out of the back room carrying a dish full of re-warmed pasta and said, 'All taken care of today, Wilf.'

Wilf said, 'I've decided to retire.'

'What?' Holding a forkful mid-air.

'I know I've been talking about it for years. I know I've been putting it off. You know, I was trying to find someone to . . . it doesn't matter. Turns out, no one's interested and I'm sick of waiting, so there it is.' He turned to Connor and said, 'What do you think?'

Connor shrugged.

'So, George, any money owing?'

'Of course.' Finally eating the stray mouthful.

Then to school, where they went into Reception, asked for Noah and were told to wait. But Wilf said, 'Can't do.'

Into Noah's office and Wilf told him he was retiring, effective immediately. He'd have to find another bus driver after all. Another idiot willing to flog his febrile, flavourless vegetables to the world. Noah said, 'I thought you were going to teach Connor?'

'No, I don't want him staying here. What's here for the young ones, Noah? For anyone? Best someone bulldozes the place.' He turned to his nephew, smiling. 'What do you think, Connor?'

'Drop a bomb on it, I reckon.'

'So?' Wilf said. 'Do I have to sign anything?'

'What?'

'My resignation. I want to make it official.'

'You were only employed casually, Wilf.'

'So, that fixes that. I think, maybe, you collected superannuation on my behalf?'

'I'll have a word to the department.' Cocking his head, still unsure what all of this was about. 'Is this because of Darcy?'

Wilf thought about it. 'Entirely. Absolutely. You can't take people for granted, can you, Connor?'

'No, Uncle.'

And Noah: 'But he's gone.'

'But not because *you* threw him out.'

'I'm limited in what I can do.'

'So am I,' Wilf said. 'That's why I'm going to live in Sydney.'

Noah didn't get it. 'Weren't you going to live on your island?'

'I lied.' And with that he turned, took a lollipop off Noah's desk and said, 'I think I can feel it, Noah.'

'What?'

Wilf stretched his back, felt his old muscles and said, 'A spine.'

Next, they found Monk in his office. Wilf told him the story and the publican said, 'Maybe you could just cut your hours?'

'No. That'd make it too easy . . . or hard.'

'I don't mean to be rude, but you are eighty.'

'All the more reason to get going. What do you say, Connor?'

'I guess.'

'See, that's the young ones,' Wilf said. 'They can't make up their minds, so we old folk have to do it for them, eh, Connor?'

'Yes, Uncle.'

Driving west, Connor said to his uncle, 'You don't have to do this for me.'

'It's not for you, you bloody idiot. I've only got one more shot at it, Nephew.'

Connor felt bad. His uncle's last shot was his first. 'Mum would be happy,' he managed.

Wilf said, 'It was all a pity . . . but plenty of things are a pity. Anyway, it's just a few old rocks on Louth. Ghosts. They don't need me, and I don't need them . . . *Nephew*.' Smiling at him.

They arrived at Bobby's and Wilf got out and shook the old man's hand, and he said, 'You had enough?'

'What?'

'My brother's boy can help out. He doesn't mind.'

'You've heard?' Wilf said.

'Jesus, Wilf, haven't you learned anything about this place? Come on.'

They walked past the house, down beside the pigs, the few goats Bobby kept for milk. As they went, he said, 'Why Sydney though? Toilet big enough for a country to shit in.'

'Connor's signed up for a course. Recording musicians, you know, sound engineer?'

Bobby squeezed Connor's shoulder and said, 'You'll have to look after your uncle.' And roaring with laughter. 'Can you imagine, you, Wilf, catching the wrong train? Up at Katoomba before you realise.'

'I can handle myself.'

'No, you can't. You'll have to mother him, Connor, he's hopeless. If it wasn't for Nance. She was always saying . . .'

'Don't start that.'

Down another valley, and up another hill, and there was the Air Camper.

'All ready to go,' Bobby said.

Connor and Wilf examined it, and Wilf said, 'How the hell did you get it here?'

'Tractor.'

They checked the fuselage, the ribs, the wings with their prominent spars. Wilf said, 'You're not going to . . .?'

'I was waiting for you.'

Connor wasn't sure. The plane was at the top of a decent-sized hill. But Bobby opened his arms to the sky and said, 'What if? Always what if? But if you never try, my boy.' So he climbed in, buckled up and said, 'The wind's from the west.'

Connor and Wilf waited as he started the engine, worked it up to full power, waved at them, then released the brakes.

Connor said to Wilf, 'You can't just take off from your farm.'

'Why not?'

Bobby released his brake and the plane started its take off. Built up speed, tested the breeze, lifted, dropped and Wilf said, 'It works.'

Another few metres, then a draft pushed it down and they heard the sound of cracking and saw a wheel hanging loose. Bobby set the plane down, the other wheel went, and the whole lot skidded on its belly before coming to a stop.

Connor cracked up. Doubled over, laughing. As did Wilf. They looked up long enough to see Bobby waving back to them, climbing out, examining the failed wheels.

40

Connor checked the docket. The sale of a hotdog and Coke had to be recorded. Everything did: day, time, served by whom, EFTPOS tender, and a message on the bottom: 'Vote for your favourite online retailer and you could win a $10,000 shopping spree'.

This seemed strange. That the real world was made up of the sheep they passed, an old man out in his yard welding metal, someone spraying a field. The docket explained that there were five bonus entry points per person, full Ts & Cs and privacy statement on the docket. But that was all. No how are you? How are you coping? Nothing real passing between two people sitting in an old van heading back to Selwyn. So maybe Wilf was right telling the old stories, remembering the old people, spending his days trying to mend the tears of what things had become. As he screwed up the docket, and slipped it out of the window. 'So what do you reckon?'

'Dalmar Street, perhaps?'

'How much a month?'

Connor checked the list he'd made: six houses they'd managed to visit on their day in Sydney, and now they'd eaten fried chicken and were heading home. It was dark, cold, and Wilf had the breeze on his face to stay awake.

'Nine hundred a month.'

'That's not too bad. What do you reckon?' Smiling over to him.

'Wasn't the best neighbourhood.'

Wilf agreed. Grimy little homes with narrow frontages, overflowing bins left out on the street and a few stray dogs pulling apart bags of people's old shit.

'If that's what we can afford?' Connor said.

'We can afford more.'

'But if we sell the place?'

'No, not yet. Sometime in the future.'

Connor didn't respond. Who knew about the future? He studied the leaflet for Dalmar Street; a version of life that would allow him to get up early, hop on a bus for college, spend his days plugging in cables, setting up microphones. As the thought occurred to him: how much do I really want this? The house in a row of twenty, more. No Selwyn. No Monk's or Mr Gould or his mum carrying a pot of stew across the road.

'So we should agree on it?' Wilf said.

'I guess.'

'What's that mean?'

'We should. It was the best of the lot.' Remembering the shag carpet no one had bothered replacing in forty years, the seventies shades, the beige walls, too, churning every thought and feeling into a blancmange of *MasterChef* and *The Block*. The depressing kitchen facing onto a shed; the tiles someone had tried to repair with electrical tape.

'Just think,' Wilf said, guiding the van with one hand, 'of all the things we've been meaning to do. The Harbour Bridge . . . if you get a band going, you can play every night.'

Yes, Connor thought. That was a plus.

'Or if you change your mind, Sydney Uni.'

'You sound like a tourist brochure.'

'I've never spent much time in Sydney. It'll be great, won't it, Nephew?' Squeezing his knee.

Connor wanted to say, *I'm not seven anymore, Uncle*, but didn't. Because he guessed he'd always be seven.

'Yes, come to think of it . . . this will be good,' Wilf said.

Connor consulted his list for affirmation. 'This one won't be too much?' Indicating the picture of Hamilton Street, Bondi Junction. 'Nineteen ninety-five?'

'That's value for money.'

What he'd kept saying as they'd looked through. Sea salt on the breeze, a patch of garden for him to grow a few vegetables. And Connor had said, 'Really?'

'Why not? We can save. I'll grab some seed from Bobby.'

Wilf had claimed the bedroom overlooking a side lane. He'd had years of this, he explained. He'd be too homesick without a rubbish truck every morning. A nice kitchen/lounge, although no dining room. Still, it would do for a couple of bachelors.

Back in the van, Connor asked, 'Where are you going to get the money?'

'Don't worry about that. When I sold the old place the money went straight into the bank and it's been sitting there ever since, compounding. I always thought I'd leave it to your mum but now . . . what am I going to spend it on?'

'A visit to see your brother?'

'Couldn't think of anything worse.'

Connor studied the picture of Hamilton Street and thought it would do. The old gum out front. He could see himself sitting under it, reading a book. 'But then we've got to find someone to rent our place.'

'Easy.'

'Who?'

'Plenty of people.'

Connor wasn't so sure. The board out front of Greene's showed dozens of homes for sale or rent, the prices dropped again and again, but never any takers. Selwyn was a place you aspired to leave. But Wilf said, 'I know a few people.'

'Who?'

'Leo.'

'Leo? He's in the nursing home.'

'And he hates it. He told me he wants to leave. He wants a place in town, small garden.'

Connor was never sure about his uncle. 'You'll miss everyone?'

'Perhaps . . . for a while. But I'll soon have a few of the old girls at, where was it?'

'Hamilton Street.'

'I'll have them in for a cup of tea and a bit of romance.'

'Jesus.'

'That's the way people are designed. Like this old girl. I've punished her for half a century, but she just keeps going.' Rubbing the dashboard.

'But you don't know Sydney.'

'What's to know? You look up a bus. You get on it.'

Connor still wasn't convinced. 'Hamilton Street has a nice supermarket.'

'It has.'

'So that'll be my job, Uncle. Cook tea. You just take it easy. Go to your bowls. I can do it all now.'

'Course you can. I have every faith, Nephew. I'm just there to keep you in line. Pay the bills. Fetch the milk. Get you out of bed.'

They slowed into Selwyn, passing the school. Long shadows from a lazy, waning moon. Lamp posts and phone poles stretching miles. A small group gathered outside the ice cream shop. The light was on inside, the door open, movement and music. Wilf slowed to see what was happening. He said to Connor, 'He won't be told.' He stopped and saw Trevor, and a girl, ten or eleven, both wearing dancing clothes, velvets, sewn with gold and green piping. Darcy, and a few other boys he didn't recognise, stood in front of them. He put on the handbrake, got out, and Connor said, 'Uncle . . .'

'What's going on?' Wilf called along the road.

'Hi, Wilf!' Darcy called back.

Trevor and the girl were holding hands now. Small doll-figures shrinking in the sodium light. Wilf walked toward them, checked Scoops n' Smiles and said, 'This place is closed.'

Darcy approached Trevor. 'He's got a girlfriend.'

Wilf said, 'Where's you mum, Trevor?'

'She said to wait for her.'

'Uncle,' Connor warned.

Darcy and the other boys laughed. 'He's got a girlfriend and they've been fucking, haven't you, Trevor?'

Connor said, 'You might want to get home, Darcy.'

'Why?' He messed Trevor's oiled-in-place hair and said, 'Didn't win a ribbon this time?'

Wilf closed the gap, placed his hand on Darcy's shoulder and Darcy turned, pushed him away and said, 'Don't touch me, you old cunt.' Loud, the length of Sullivan Street, although no one appeared. Just curtains moving.

So Darcy returned to Trevor, squatted, so they were face-to-face, and said, 'How's the bus? You still sucking that old cunt's cock?'

Connor watched the way Wilf's hand shook. He took a few steps toward Darcy, who said, 'Want to hit me?'

Then Trevor reached into his jacket pocket and produced a gun. A small pistol. Iron, grey, reflecting the little bit of light in the street.

Everyone held their ground.

Trevor said, 'If you come near me . . .'

Wilf knew his father shot – clay targets, rabbits, foxes, anything. That he was president of the local club. That he bought and sold illegally. Everyone knew this.

Trevor stood, deciding, and the girl tried to push his hand down. 'Trevor, don't.'

But Trevor was determined. His hand shaking, his lips clenched, holding the pistol like his father had taught him. Wrapping a finger around the trigger, starting to squeeze it.

'You gonna shoot me?' Darcy asked.

The other boys ran away.

'Trevor,' Connor said. 'The police'll take care of it.' Taking slow, small steps toward the boy.

Wilf had no such patience. He moved quickly, took the pistol from Trevor's hand and said, 'It's okay, son.'

Darcy said, 'You guys are so fucked,' and ran off after his friends.

Wilf watched as Grant Roper came out of the ice cream shop, asking what had happened. A strange, ghost-like figure. He felt the vice again, and whispered, 'Not now.' Then he dropped to his knees, his arse, placed the gun on the ground. He said to Connor, 'It's the ticker again,' holding his chest, then lying on the road.

Everything and everyone stopped. Darcy and the other boys, looking back down the road, Roper, Trevor, the girl.

Connor approached his uncle, knelt beside him and said, 'Get you in the van?'

But Wilf didn't hear him. Just moved his hand, placed it on the road as though he was trying to push himself up.

Connor shook him gently. 'Uncle?'

Wilf wasn't moving. Connor shouted to each of them, 'Someone get some help. Go, now. Trevor.'

So Trevor and the girl ran down the road toward the medical centre, the one that had replaced the hospital the government didn't have enough money to run.

Connor was shaking, too. He realised he had the list, the leaflets, in his hand. He let go, and the breeze took them, across the road, past Monk's, down toward the greasy chicken place and Quinn's and the junction that showed how many possibilities life was made up of. He shook his uncle and repeated, 'Can you hear me?' He took his uncle's pills (in the plastic container he'd bought) from his pocket and looked. 'Angina?' he said to his uncle.

But he didn't respond. So Connor turned him over, listened for breath, moved his head so he might hear something. Something. But he couldn't.

Roper said, 'Is he dead?'

'No, he's not fucking dead.' Remembering, pulling his uncle's head back, trying to pinch his fat nose, covering his mouth with his own, the four-day-growth and scratchy lips.

A small car came down the street, stopped, the doctor got out, ran up to them and said, 'Let's see if we can fix this.' He used a stethoscope, and quickly decided. Starting a rough resuscitation as Connor sat back, watching his uncle, casting a long shadow. Soon there was another car, and the nurse, and the pair worked together.

Connor started gathering the leaflets. Later, he'd think this strange, but at the time it seemed the most logical thing to do. Blowing from one house to another. He noticed the boys gathered watching down the road. Then Trevor, and the girl, who'd returned. Connor went over, put his arm around the boy's shoulder and said, 'This happens.' Smiling.

But Trevor sat, stared into his lap and said, 'It was me.'

Connor sat beside him. 'He'll be okay.'

As the doctor and nurse worked, and the night got colder, and they heard a siren in the distance.

* * *

Two Years Later

Connor paused, checked the use-by date and said, 'Fuck it.' Threw the chocolate milk container the two metres to the bin and, miraculously, it went in. 'Hurry up, Luke,' he called, and Luke, busy pissing into bushes, said, 'It won't come out.'

'Make it.'

The other four kids in the bus put down their windows and called the same thing. Connor didn't care. The bus, the one he'd inherited from Wilf, stunk. Terry, this new fourteen-year-old, getting on with his body odour every afternoon. And Sienna, she'd gone to seed, too – this mostly-overweight, pork-faced fillet who sat at the front telling him about her cousins and uncles all the way home.

A stray dog emerged from the scrub. Connor guessed it wasn't dangerous – half-limp, shoddy back leg, patches of bare skin that it tried to scratch. It made him think of his old dog, Jewel, with her weak bladder, up three times a night for a piss.

'Ready.'

They got back in and there was applause and Luke, more confident now, took a bow and said, 'I had a whole Coke.'

'Well, don't,' Sienna said, and Trevor, a seat back on the right, said, 'I'm meant to be home by four.'

Connor started the bus, checked behind, pulled out and set off along the highway. He still had his old map, but these days he seldom felt the need to check where he was going. Eighteen months of the same route had taught him, the same advice from the kids, the same wrong turns, and corrections. Because that was what it was all about. Making mistakes, and corrections. Maybe there were people in the world who thought things through, came up with the most efficient, the most viable, the most sensible solutions. But he wasn't one of them. He was a muddler. Just like Wilf, and his mum, and pretty much everyone he knew – a muddler.

Luke, sitting beside him (thirteen now, with peach-fuzz on his lip), opened his book and started again. 'Did I finish Chapter Four?'

'Yes, you did,' Sienna said, explaining to Connor how Gert, the girl in her Home Economics class, was sleeping with Tim, who was a year older. She said she'd tell him all about it, but he had to promise not to tell anyone, especially Noah, who was just a very angry man, don't you think, Connor?

'Not particularly.'

'Didn't he throw you out of school?'

'No, I threw myself out.'

'Still.' And she began, although Luke read over the top of her. Connor tuned out, onto the road, as it lifted and dropped, followed the land up gradual hills, into sudden valleys. Wilf saying, 'If you let your speed get away you won't have enough time at the bottom, see, here, to correct.'

And he'd written this down, too. 'Slow here!'

As the voices droned, he remembered how his uncle held the wheel, at the bottom, with a light touch, and how he'd said to him, 'Isn't that dangerous?'

'Not when you've been doing it as long as I have.'

'What if a car pulled out?'

He remembered Wilf taking a minute to respond, and saying, 'I guess you're right,' and slowing. He remembered this moment because even at that age he'd worked how everything people did was down to experience, and how school wasn't really much help. Humans were wired to learn the hard way. Books were pointless, really.

'*When DC Regan arrived, the body was already half-decayed.*'

Because Luke had given up on fantasy. Getting in the bus, six months earlier, and saying, 'I've changed my mind.' Telling Connor how the monster market was saturated and how people wanted bodies, strong plots and troubled detectives with drinking problems. He'd said, 'A bit like our lives,' and Connor had replied, 'How?'

'Look at you.'

'What?'

'Living by yourself. No girlfriend. Eating takeaway.'

'Listen, boyo, I don't eat takeaway, I cook. And how do you know I don't have a girlfriend?'

'You would've told me.'

'No, I wouldn't have. You'd be the last person. I'd end up in one of your stories. No thanks.'

Although Luke was right. He was good at getting to the truth. But Connor did cook once or twice a week, and he had met a girl, Karen's niece, whom Monk had taken on a few weeks after Wilf's death. Not that they were full on, or at it, or that they ever went anywhere much (where the hell could you go in Selwyn?). But Connor had picked her up once, and they'd driven to Northhead for the afternoon. So maybe that counted?

Anyway, it was little lunch. You played, and forgot about school. You swore at people and jumped on their back when they weren't ready and they said you'd hurt them and you said so what, then you argued and there was a fuck-off then you were all sitting in a circle sharing a smoke and it was like the world of geography and mixed fractions didn't exist. And for that moment (Connor had worked out, now) you had the possibility of being happy. It was your choice, of course, but in theory, no one could intrude on the world you'd manufactured, agreed upon, shared with these people. But then the bell would sound and you'd have to drag your arse into this less-than-perfect world and succumb to life, the future, a series of rules that seemed to have no purpose except making you less happy.

'School's shit anyway,' he said to his bus full of kids.

And Trevor: 'Why's it shit?'

'Because, you know' – as he turned a tight corner – 'they lie to you. They tell you, study this and that and you'll get a good job. But even if you do . . .'

Luke was looking up from his hand-written manuscript, waiting for advice, the same stuff Wilf handed out every morning.

'So you get an A and go to university, you go well, leave, there are no jobs, or you get one and you hate what you're doing and then you're stuck in it for fifty years, bored, depressed, cursing yourself for believing what all your teachers and your parents told you.'

Terry, the new boy, said, 'Does that mean we don't have to go?'

'Well, that's for you to work out,' Connor said.

And Dylan, who lived on a farm with his dad. 'What else are we meant to do all day?'

'Like I said,' Connor replied, 'your problem. I'm just saying – if you believe everything you're told you'll end up . . .'

Sienna liked this. Generally, most days, Connor had a nugget of wisdom. Generally, it was something she remembered Wilf saying, but that was okay. Connor was good-looking and had broad shoulders and a strong neck, and she often sat at the back of the bus imagining him undressing her, kissing her all over, and whatever else he wanted. Before they arrived at her gate, and she had to take a deep breath.

When Connor had started, after he'd got back from Sydney, they'd had words. She'd be rattling on and he'd say if you don't have anything nice to say keep your mouth shut. Once, she'd told him to fuck off, and he'd threatened her, like Wilf used to. But after a few weeks they'd settled. She'd learned to listen. He was funny, too. He didn't care who he upset.

'But a junior constable from Georgetown pointed out that the wound was deeply infected, and that this could mean she'd been in the barn for weeks.'

'Why hadn't anyone found her?' Connor asked.

'They'd been away on holidays.'

'That sounds convenient.'

'What?'

'Going away. You've got to make it believable.'

Luke sighed. What did Connor know about plotting a novel? This was his third. He'd had plenty of practice.

'So the home owners go away, this Charles brings the girl to the barn, rapes and murders her and leaves her body there?'

'Violent,' Trevor said. 'How old are you now?'

'Thirteen.'

'Bit demented,' Sienna said.

'What?' Because Luke always fought back now.

'A kid your age writing about people getting raped and murdered and their bodies left to rot.'

'It's a crime novel.'

Connor had discovered that after driving six months, you didn't get sick of a thing, you got used to it. These were different. You could fill it with variation, and new conversation. That's what he'd learned from his kids (he called them now). The thing Wilf never had, or could, make clear. It was all in the words, the tone, the way kids got angry and happy and silly and sad and told you why their parents were pissing them off.

The funny thing about Wilf was that now, two years after the funeral, he persisted. His strange little lessons, eventually making sense. As Connor watched television in his house, walked down to the Shell at three am for a Mother. Popped in to see Dave Duffy and help him pack vegetables into the back of the J2 for his weekly delivery. Or go in to see the new pharmacist, and ask after George. Or help Leo sort the letters, and pack his van. Slowly, bit by bit, making sense. Holding up the starfish and saying to his bus full of kids, 'This is what it's all about.'

No reply.

'It can't survive in the rock pools unless there are millions of little organisms. And they can't survive unless there's plant life. And that can't survive unless . . .' On and on, like this, as they did him the courtesy of listening, with Trevor saying. 'So, we're starfish?'

'We are.'

Because this was Trevor now. Apparently, while Connor had been in Sydney, Trevor had been at the back of the bus, head down, withdrawn. He'd used his hoodie, and never looked at anyone. He'd given up speaking or listening. No one knew, but everyone guessed it was the incident on the main street. The guilt – for popping the lock on his dad's gun cabinet, finding the pistol, loading it, slipping it into the pocket of his dancing pants. And the rest. The interview with the police, the week he'd spent in a hospital, the 'talk' with the doctors, the reports, the release, the newspaper articles and, when he'd eventually returned to school, the looks across the yard. But more than this, the thought that he'd killed Wilf. Until, one day, a week after Connor had been offered the bus job (by a tired and relieved Noah), he'd parked, gone to clean out the rubbish and seen Trevor sitting alone at the back. He'd said, 'You better go in now – classes have started.'

Trevor had said, 'I didn't know you two were going to . . .'

Connor had sat across from him and explained. How the coronary artery was completely blocked and how Wilf, because he was so stubborn, had never got the scan the doctor had requested. 'So it might've been another few weeks, or months, but not much longer.'

Of course, Trevor hadn't accepted this. He was determined he'd killed him, and he'd told Connor this, and he'd said, 'I would've done the same.'

Trevor had told him that it had been going on for years, and he'd thought, truly, really, that if he threatened him he'd back off, and that'd be the end of it. But it didn't end that way, did it, Connor?

'Well, that was one idea,' Connor had said.

'It's not like I would've shot him or anything.'

'I know. The police knew. It dealt with Darcy, anyway, eh?'

Things had improved after this. The hoodie had come off and Trevor had moved, day by day, a seat closer to the front. Until he was sitting with the old guard, close to Connor, which was close to Wilf, and close to his map and his starfish and Mother and chocolate and the smokes he kept getting off to smoke (although he wasn't meant to, although Connor said, *Fuck them, what are they going to do, sack me?*). Although, some days Trevor returned to the back of the bus and stared out at the road. But Connor knew, now, these things took time and there was no rushing it. People were muddlers, and had to muddle. The ones who had it all planned were fuckheads.

So Connor dropped them at school, and as they got out he said, 'Give those teachers hell,' and they smiled, and gave him skin. He told Luke to finish the chapter before tonight. He wanted to know who else might have killed her. And as he watched this boy go he felt, perhaps, he had some sort of ownership, some sort of fathership. This made him feel good. He guessed, as Luke got older, he'd be able to tell him about life, and the attachments, and the shit that stuck to your shoe.

He walked home past Monk's, and Monk was out front with one of the cigars he'd started smoking. 'Can you come in earlier?' he called across the road.

'What time?'

'Four?'

'No worries.'

Monk called out that they had a big Thursday night, and could he do the Wheel O' Whisky! again. He didn't mind. It was fun. Followed by a few of his own songs. Him and Roman and a bass player, a sixteenish girl who'd moved to town with her parents, her father, a Graney, returning to do up Ced's old house (his bones asleep not far from Wilf's – the two of them, Connor fancied, shitting on about Louth all day).

Past Gould's, stopping for bread and milk and a five-minute chat that contained no fewer than six references to Wilf. But that's how it was. Like Wilf said, out of the living and the dead, only the living mattered. And in Selwyn, no one ever died. Past Scoops n' Smiles, boarded up, a lease sign splashed across the window, the T-junction, with its endless promises, although he never stopped to read them anymore. Past the fountain, the empty field with no sheep, the same things he'd been walking past for nineteen years. He didn't mind. They just were, and he just was, and he was happy. To be home.

The funeral – people spilling out of the church, everyone telling him how they'd help. The food they'd cook, the company they'd provide. The money. Anything. A shit day, and although he couldn't bring himself to make a eulogy, he and Roman got up and sang *The Hills*. Given, about death, but at least it was themed.

He'd spent the following days packing, planning, emptying and turning off the fridge, locking up the house and going out to Monk's Chrysler, ready for the drive to Sydney. Hardly a word spoken on the way. Arriving, occupying his Airbnb, unpacking his clothes in his small room and watching television for the rest of that night. The weeks coming and going, returning to his cell with his lemon chicken or his madras, eating it, disposing of the mess, showering and jerking off, the same way, the same time, every night. The lectures about Ohm's Law and acoustics and how reverberation worked. Until one day someone asked their tutor, 'How many jobs are out there?' And he'd half-laughed and said, 'Jobs? God. I'm afraid you're going to have to make your own job. We're not learning to be dentists, are we?'

This helped make up his mind. If that were the case, why bother studying? This, and the stereo thumping next door till two most nights. With the way his shit looked after eating takeaway for six months. The way the room got smaller, and meaner, and somehow, turned against him.

Monk was happy to come and pick him up. And on the way, he'd said, 'I'm surprised you lasted that long.'

'How's that?'

'Just didn't seem . . . you.'

'What's me?'

'I can offer you four nights – as long as you're happy to lock up.'

He'd taken a moment. He didn't want to seem too enthusiastic, too desperate, too willing to follow the path Wilf had laid out. Then Monk had said (something like), 'We all miss the old bastard.'

He hadn't replied. He tried not to think about Wilf, but the old man kept returning at the strangest times to offer advice. Mostly, he listened. He had no choice. And mostly what he heard made sense. He regretted arguing with him, taking him for granted. But that was all done. And anyway, you had to expect angst from kids. They were slightly fucked in the head. Trevor, Luke, Sienna, and another new boy, Rodney, all slightly strange, in need of help.

Connor went home, showered, returned to bed and slept for two hours. When he woke he surveyed the compost of clothes on the floor, the plates and cups and chip packets and Mothers, dozens of them, sitting around. He heard his uncle coming in, and saying, *This is a bloody disgrace.*

I'll clean up later.

If I waited for you . . . Starting to gather the worst of the clothes.

Leave it.

I don't know how you live with the smell of yourself.

Uncle!

The silence, the peace he'd been given, wasn't something he wanted, or liked, after all. He said, 'I'll help.'

Sometimes he couldn't believe how unlucky he'd been. Only nineteen, and everyone had gone. He'd never understood – when he was on the oval, avoiding going in after the bell – that you had no choice. Things were decided for you. Down to the gas bill that arrived every three months, the tax the government took from your pay, the sound of the clunking organ keys at a funeral. Nothing. The way the bloke next door revved his car at six every morning, and how you couldn't have people back.

Connor Healy got dressed, drove to the post office shopfront and loaded his van for the day's deliveries. Leo said, 'It can all wait till tomorrow if you like.'

Connor found this funny. Everything could wait, really. Strange. A world addicted to doing things faster. He couldn't think why. He drove out of town, past the small graveyard. For all this time, he'd avoided going in. All he'd see was an old stone, a fresher stone, and Wilf. Just blocks of granite (he'd had to deal with the quotes). Maybe some grass had grown around them. Maybe he should cut it back. But he liked the old way, the wild way, the sepia-tinted view of the world that separated the living and the dead. So let them rest. Let them lie there, together, for eternity. Maybe the old bastard was already back on Louth with Brian, trying to push bulls.

He pulled in to Bobby's, got out and unloaded the awkward-sized parcel. 'Bobby!'

No reply.

He walked down the side of the house, avoiding the chickens, a loose pig. Then he went into the shed, placed the parcel on the bench and examined the plane. The wheels had been repaired, but Bobby had stripped the fuselage, started again with stronger paper. Connor guessed it would never be finished. He went out, down the road, and searched the fields. There was Bobby, bent over, picking something from his cabbages. He walked across the rows, the land, sinking into the deep, brown soil. When he arrived he said, 'I got a few hours spare.'

'Righto, then. Let's get to it.' Indicating.

Bobby was straight back to work, and Connor followed. There wouldn't be any pay, probably not even a thank you, but that didn't matter. They just worked together, the sun overhead, the birds circling in search of worms. Bobby said, 'Cold.' Connor took this as a statement, not a question. He was still learning about Bobby, Spencer and Grace, Monk, all of them. They took some understanding, but he liked the process. People were more interesting than synthesisers.

When Connor drove home, the shadows were extending, again. Another day done. He had some cabbages, and planned on making chop suey. Monk had given him the usual spare meals: seven of them, packed in takeaway containers, sitting ready in his freezer. But he felt like making his own. It was better that way. Wilf had taught him about the art of bachelorhood. You had to make an effort.

And it would be quite an effort. Another seventy years, perhaps, applying the lessons he'd had to learn so quickly. Still, he was grateful. Wilf had taught him that people stayed with you, helped you, offered (silently, in strange ways) advice. Some days, and some nights, this didn't seem enough to keep him going. The bell had gone, and everyone was going into class, but he refused to yield. This oval, this freshly-mowed grass, the smell of citrus and fires and shit in his soles – perfect. If they wanted him, they could come and get him.

He turned into his drive and noticed a Ford, newish, but caked in mud. Someone had driven a long way. He parked and got out and this figure, sitting on his porch, stood, stepped out a cigarette and said, 'Guessed you might have a spare bed?'

Connor took a moment. It was so quiet, still, even the birds had turned in. Although the grass was knee-high, the weeds spread through the garden, he didn't mind, didn't notice, didn't care. 'Hey, Dad.'

'Hey . . . no one told me about the old bastard.'

Connor just shrugged. He opened the door, turned on the light and they went in.

Songs mentioned

Along the Road to Gundagai (1922), Jack O'Hagan

If I Could Choose (1967), Michael Coffey and Wesley Burrowes

Jesus Doesn't Want Me for a Sunbeam (Nirvana, 1993), originally recorded by the Vaselines as *Jesus Wants Me for a Sunbeam* (1987), Eugene Kelly and Francis McKee

Mother (1979), Roger Waters

The Hills (1871), Owen Carol

www.ingramcontent.com/pod-product-compliance
Lightning Source LLC
Chambersburg PA
CBHW060542030726
47498CB00004B/1290